❖   ❖

CROSSING
AT
IVALO

Also by Rod MacLeish

CROSSING AT IVALO

A NOVEL

BY

ROD MACLEISH

LITTLE, BROWN AND COMPANY

BOSTON   TORONTO   LONDON

FIRST EDITION

The characters and events in this book are fictitious.
Any similarity to real persons, living or dead,
is coincidental and not intended by the author.

Library of Congress Cataloging-in-Publication Data

MacLeish, Roderick, 1926–
    Crossing at Ivalo : a novel / by Rod MacLeish. — 1st ed.
        p.   cm.
    ISBN 0-316-54256-3
    I. Title.
    PS3563.A3183C77   1990
    813'.54 — dc20   89-77590
                                                         CIP

10 9 8 7 6 5 4 3 2 1

MV-PA
*Published simultaneously in Canada
by Little, Brown & Company (Canada) Limited*

PRINTED IN THE UNITED STATES OF AMERICA

For Yanie — With All Love

Russia ought not only to stop, but to begin anew. Is such an effort possible? Can so vast an edifice be taken to pieces and reconstructed?

— The Marquis de Custine, *Empire of The Czar: A Journey Through Eternal Russia* (1839)

These friends and colleagues were more than generous with their advice, support, and enthusiasm during the writing of this story:

Pat Anderson, Flip Brophy, Alex Brummer, Joe Goulden, John Greenya, Simon Hoggart, Lester Hyman, François Lampietti, Cynthia Sumner MacLeish, Eric MacLeish, John Newhouse, Austin Olney, Arnold Sagalyn, Martin Walker, and Leslie Whitten.

Spasibo.

CROSSING
AT
IVALO

❖ O N E ❖

ON THE COLD, STARLESS NIGHT of April 3, a KGB major named Maxim Petrovich Kornilov escaped from the Soviet Union by crossing the frontier into northeastern Finland.

Defections by lower-level KGB personnel exasperate Moscow but usually aren't major traumas. Kornilov's flight west, however, sent shock waves through the military, scientific, and security establishments of the Soviet Union. President Gorbachev took the Kornilov matter out of the hands of the KGB's chairman, Sergei M. Spassky, and threatened him with expulsion from the Politburo. A worldwide manhunt for Kornilov became the supreme priority of the KGB. The organization's first deputy chairman, Valerian Aleksandrovich Galkin, was put in command and told he could have whatever human, technological, and financial resources he required. Gorbachev ordered Galkin to keep him informed of every development.

The first break in the Kornilov case came on April 5. Late that afternoon a military helicopter landed at the barracks of the KGB Border Guards Eighth Regiment, near the Soviet-Finnish frontier. The commanding colonel of the regiment was waiting with a staff car. First Deputy Chairman Galkin, carrying his small dog, got out of the helicopter and into the colonel's car and was driven to a coarse meadow that was divided by the border. A sergeant was waiting for them. A private stood at the top of the meadow near a growth of scrubby trees.

Still numb and disoriented from being beaten, burning with a shame that was more painful than his bloody thumbs, battered face, and bruised ribs, Private I. S. Tsvarsky of the Eighth Regiment watched his colonel, his sergeant, and Galkin talking together a hundred meters down the slope. The grass came up to the thighs of the men. The dog, now on the ground, was invisible.

The spring twilight was deepening over the landscape of birches with their hazy growth of new leaves, undersized evergreens, tall grasses, brambles, stumps, and arctic flowers just coming into bloom. No bird song or breeze whisper broke the profound silence. The faint perfume of mountain avens and diapensia permeated the dry aroma of the forest.

That morning a lieutenant of the Eighth Regiment had found seventy American dollars beneath Tsvarsky's mattress during barracks inspection. The young private refused to say where he'd gotten the money. Aware of the turmoil over the Kornilov defection, the lieutenant tried to find his commanding officer. The colonel was in Murmansk, the bleak Soviet port city on the Tuloma estuary 250 kilometers to the northeast. The lieutenant telephoned the border guards regional headquarters and told the inspector general's office about Tsvarsky's American dollars. This small but possibly significant discovery was immediately passed on to Moscow. Kornilov had last been seen heading for the Tuloma estuary.

Tsvarsky's sergeant, meanwhile, had thrown the young private down the stairs to the barracks basement. He knocked Tsvarsky off his feet, straddled him, and pulled out both his thumbnails with pliers. Tsvarsky fainted. He revived when a bucket of dirty, cold water was thrown into his face. The sergeant tied him to a beam and slugged him with both fists until Tsvarsky told where he got the money. Then the sergeant began hitting Tsvarsky with a club and would have killed him if the lieutenant, hearing the border guard's screams, hadn't come down to the basement and ordered the sergeant to stop.

Tsvarsky knew that his offense, taking a bribe, was unforgivable. But he couldn't see why it would inspire a high KGB official to come all the way from the capital to this remote part of the frontier above the Arctic Circle. He gaped at the visitor. Tsvarsky was puzzled. He had always vaguely imagined that important people were tall, muscular, and dressed in elaborate uniforms.

Valerian A. Galkin was a short, heavy man in his early seventies. He was totally bald and wore expensive suits tailored for him in London. Galkin had sensitive eyes, slightly dilated nostrils, and a small, severe mouth. His jawline was obscured by his fleshy jowls.

"You're certain this was the man?" he asked quietly.

"Yes, he has confessed it, Comrade First Deputy Chairman," the colonel answered. His name was Georgi T. Vezhnesky. He was tall and gray-haired. His facial skin was pitted with acne.

"He's been beaten," Galkin said. He looked up at the officer. "I don't want a scapegoat, Colonel. I did not come all the way from Moscow to investigate payoffs. I need to find the man who took the money from this smuggler you call Old Paavo and to know what that man saw, who Paavo took across here."

They were looking west in the dying light, at a grove of birch trees three hundred meters away. Beyond the grove a sloping meadow and the forest at its upper edge were tinted gray-lavender in the dusk. Off in that indistinct distance, lights sparkled from a farmhouse and log barn. To the north the evening sky was lit by a white glow from the border installations on a highway that ran from the Finnish town of Ivalo to Murmansk.

Finnish citizens are allowed to live along the frontier. Soviet citizens aren't.

On the Soviet side of that border, there is a wilderness of fields, swamps, stunted forest, low hills, and rivers. This vast area is implanted with ground sensors, land mines, and tripwires from the frontier northeast to Murmansk. KGB Border Guards in towers watch everything that moves through the sparse forests, brush, rough meadows, and thicket-bordered lakes. KGB helicopters fly low, crossing and recrossing the air space, while KGB power boats patrol the waterways and propeller craft move through the marshes.

Galkin shifted a pair of gloves and a dog chain from his left hand to his right. "This private — what is his name?"

"Tsvarsky, Comrade First Dep —"

Galkin waved the gloves and leash impatiently. "Stop repeating my title, for God's sake. Just tell me what happened."

"Tsvarsky was on duty in Tower 118 Wednesday night," Colonel Vezhnesky replied. "At about eleven thirty, he says, he went down to the brush —"

"To piss."

"Yes, sir," the colonel said. "He was unarmed, the bloody fool. Some men came out of the forest. Tsvarsky's lucky he wasn't killed — Old Paavo's a mean bastard, sir. We've been chasing him for years. His full name is Paavo Waltari. Too bad Moscow won't let us cross the border — that's his farm over there — and take care of him for good."

Galkin sighed softly and half closed his eyes. He was trying to be patient. He disliked using his authority unless it was absolutely necessary.

"Eight or ten times a year Old Paavo makes an overland run to Murmansk. They use dogs to search all the cargo that comes in there by ship. They don't let foreign crews off the docks anymore. It's almost impossible to smuggle by ship nowadays. That's good for Old Paavo. He brings all the drugs he can carry into the Soviet Union. Sometimes, if he's paid enough, he'll guide people who want to get to Finland. Most of them are criminals."

"Tell me what went on between the smuggler and Private Tsvarsky on the night of April third," Galkin said.

The sergeant turned and gave a high, shrill whistle.

Tsvarsky came down through the grass at a military trot, fists clenched at his sides. He stopped ten feet from his superiors and saluted.

The young man's head had been shaved as a routine springtime precaution against ticks and mosquitos that deposited their larvae in human hair. His right eye was purple and swollen and its opening little more than a slit. His nose had been smashed. His mouth hung open slightly, giving him the appearance of an imbecile.

Galkin felt sorry for him. "Do you know who I am?" he asked.

Tsvarsky shook his head. "No."

"I am from Dzerzhinsky Square in Moscow. That is the headquarters of our organization. I have come to ask you some questions."

Tsvarsky stared. Then he hid his thumbs in the palms of his hands.

"What happened when you ran into the smuggler Wednesday night?" Galkin asked.

"I stopped pissing, *Gospodin*."

"Very good," Galkin said. "What then?"

Tsvarsky cleared his throat. "Paavo had some men with him."

"How many?"

Tsvarsky hesitated. "Old Paavo gave me the money so that I wouldn't watch."

Galkin nodded approvingly. "And, like a good soldier, you kept your word. But you couldn't avoid a little glance, one moment . . ."

Tsvarsky trusted the bald, heavy man. He was like the kindly old worker who counsels young people in Soviet feature films. "There were two men with Old Paavo," he said.

Galkin took an envelope from his coat pocket and pulled out several photographs. He held one out to Tsvarsky. "Was this one of them?"

The bruised private peered closely at the picture. "I can't see," he said.

"Help him," Galkin ordered the colonel.

Colonel Vezhnesky searched his pockets, took out a lighter, and snapped it into flame.

Tsvarsky studied the photograph in the flickering light. Finally he nodded. "That was one of the men with Old Paavo," he said.

Galkin thrust the second photograph into the perimeter of the tiny flame's glow.

His mouth open, head cocked, Tsvarsky gazed at the picture with his left eye. He looked at Galkin and nodded.

"Could you recognize both of these men if you saw them again?"

"Yes, *Gospodin.*"

The dog rose up on its hind legs and braced its front feet on Tsvarsky's thigh. Tsvarsky hesitated and then petted it. He squinted at Galkin again. "Does that make it worse — what I did?"

"You have been very helpful," Galkin said. "If we find these men we will ask you to identify them. Would you do it?"

Tsvarsky didn't answer. The question made him uneasy. The colonel and sergeant were watching him.

There was a roaring in the twilight and an explosion of lights as the helicopter appeared over the tops of the trees, came down slowly, and settled on the meadow. The grasses bent until the engine was switched off and the blade slowed to lethargic rotation. Tsvarsky turned away to watch the immense machine.

Galkin snapped a chain leash on his dog's collar. "Show me your lighter," he said to the colonel.

Vezhnesky took the lighter from his pocket and handed it to Galkin. The KGB official pried the lid up with his thumb, lit the flame, blew it out, and turned the lighter over. He closed the lid and handed the lighter back. "It is a Ronson," Galkin said. "They are not for sale in the Soviet Union."

"Yes," the colonel replied calmly.

Irritated by the man's insolent self-confidence, Valerian A. Galkin turned and walked across the meadow.

Five minutes later the first deputy chairman of the KGB and his dog were lifted by the helicopter into the evening sky. Galkin looked down. He caught a last glimpse of the three military figures in the meadow below. Then they blended into the dusk.

The helicopter made a wide curve and headed northeast toward Severomorsk airport, which serves Murmansk, Kola, and the two immense Soviet naval bases on the Tuloma estuary.

Galkin settled back into his seat. His right hand felt for the dog nestled on the floor by his leg. President Gorbachev had seemed his brisk, confident self when Galkin was summoned to his office to take charge of the Kornilov case. Galkin wondered at the man. Mikhail Sergeivich Gorbachev gave no hint of his vulnerability. The public had become first sullen and then bitter over the shortages caused by *perestroika;* there had been food riots. A half-dozen non-Russian republics were demanding autonomy. In some of them, street mobs and armed guerrillas had fought skirmishes with Soviet troops. Gorbachev and his allies were still struggling to expel thousands of turgid, holdover bureaucrats from the Brezhnev era. They had retired most of the harsh ideologues who cared more about doctrinal purity than the well-being of the Soviet Union. But these entrenched or deposed enemies weren't defeated. They were as dormant as insect larvae in the long, underground sleep. One major blunder, one crisis of the sort that Kornilov's defection threatened, and they would surface, shrilling accusations at Gorbachev like locusts in the trees of summer.

Galkin looked at the stars through the helicopter's plastic bubble. On the meadow he had felt the balm of spring in the evening air. Though the area was above the Arctic Circle, a thousand miles north of Moscow, it was tempered by a warm current flowing down the Murman coast. Time was like that current, indefatigable and self-renewing. The first deputy chairman felt weary and incapable of endeavor. But he forced himself to consider the next problem — to find out where the two men went after they crossed the Finnish border with the smuggler called Old Paavo on the night of April 3.

On the frontier meadow, Colonel Vezhnesky walked back to his car and returned to the barracks. He was unperturbed by the Ronson incident.

The sergeant took Tsvarsky up to the woods, handed him a spade, and told him to start digging. When the private had made a trench two feet deep in the moist, fibrous soil, the sergeant told him to put down the shovel.

Tsvarsky stuck the shovel into the mound of earth.

"Get out of the hole," the sergeant said.

The private didn't move. He knew that when he got out of the trench the sergeant's next order would be to stand at the end of it. Then, once he was positioned so that his body would fall backward, the sergeant would shoot him.

As he was digging it had dawned on Tvarsky why they wanted to kill him. It was not because he'd taken the money from Old Paavo, but because of what he'd seen.

"Get out of the hole!" the sergeant barked again.

The light was fading. Tsvarsky was suddenly filled with wonder. He thought he saw a slender woman of no more substance than a shadow standing in the open field just beyond a brushy creek bed that marked the frontier. Tsvarsky thought he saw stars in the west.

Each star exploded into a million stars that lasted for a millionth of a second. Tsvarsky's head opened like a flower to receive the shower of ice splinters that fell out of the evening sky.

The roar of the pistol shot volleyed out of the Soviet wildlands and across the Finnish meadows and forests. The woman in the meadow started like a snow hare and dashed for the fringe of trees. There she paused, tense with apprehension, and looked up at the Russian grove.

The Forest Lapps who still believed in the old legends knew the identity of the figure on the edge of the meadow. It was Vizi-leany, the water sprite. From a time before time was counted, she had assumed many identities in the spring twilight — an arctic fox, a bear, marten, gigantic man, wolverine, owl, or, sometimes, as she had at present, she turned herself into a girl-woman of unearthly beauty.

She never allowed anyone to get close enough to speak to her. She watched with eyes the color of smoke. The Lapps who still consulted shamans were told that the water sprite's appearance was an omen of terrible events to come.

The sound of the gunshot brought Paavo Waltari to the door of his log barn. He was seventy-three and hard as the dead trees in the forests. He had a permanent squint and his face was red from years of winter cold. It was a bony, flat face with only three upper teeth showing in his mouth. Old Paavo wore a wool cap, greasy trousers, and rubber boots. His shirtsleeves were rolled up to the elbow, exposing strands of muscle like vine wrapped around his bloody forearms. In his right hand Paavo gripped the corpse of a hare, its skin dangling from the waist of its half-naked body. In his left he held a long, slender knife. Its thin, honed blade was slippery with gore.

He looked down his meadow and over a line of brush. The twilight blurred almost everything on the Russian side. Old Paavo saw Tower 118 of the KGB Border Guards standing against the night sky. The pistol shot had come from up there. It couldn't have been the guards blasting at somebody trying to get across. They never fired just once. They let off round after round at fleeing figures. They kept on shooting even after they'd gunned down people trying to make it to Finland.

Old Paavo had long since accepted that someday he'd die that way. The Russian sons of bitches would riddle his corpse with bullets just for the fun of hearing the bones crack and watching him jerk reflexively. He preferred such a death. When they got him it would be because he was too old to outrun them or out- smart them. Paavo didn't want to die in bed or live beyond his time. The Russian bastards would see to it that he didn't.

He stood, looking into the last of the twilight and listening. He saw or heard nothing that would explain the single gunshot. Maybe, he thought, one of the KGB Border Guards shot himself by accident. Old Paavo hoped so.

He was about to turn away when he saw the lithe figure standing at the edge of the meadow. It, too, was looking across, into the western edge of Soviet territory.

Paavo Waltari crouched. The woman had been in the area for two or three weeks. Old Paavo had seen her drinking from a stream in the red light of sunrise. He had caught a glimpse of her flitting through a forest of saplings. The Lapps thought she was one of their spooks. Old Paavo had started leaving food in a wire cage on a plank at the edge of the birch grove. In the mornings he found the cage unlatched and the food gone. He thought she was living in a cave halfway up a nearby hill. He had seen smoke hanging among the trees over there and sometimes in ghostly drift across the moon.

Paavo squatted, watching her. He didn't know what he was going to do with her yet. Maybe he would sell her. Or maybe he'd have her for himself. He wasn't too old. He could still outrun and outthink the Russians.

Below the Russian grove, below the growth of conifers, the sergeant of the KGB Border Guards kicked Tsvarsky's body into the trench. He grunted and swore as he yanked the dead private's shoulders so that he would lie flat. The sergeant picked up the shovel and covered Tsvarsky with moist forest earth.

Old Paavo was still in the doorway of his barn, listening. But the woman at the edge of the meadow had vanished.

❖ TWO ❖

B Y SATURDAY, April 6, the KGB defector was somewhere in Denmark. That morning Maxim Petrovich Kornilov telephoned the American embassy's CIA station chief, Henry Muffin, at his home in a suburb of Copenhagen. In heavily accented English he identified himself as a major in the Soviet *Komitet Gosudarstvennoy Bezopasnosti*. Kornilov said that he wished to apply for political asylum in the United States. If accepted he would hand over valuable information from Soviet military research.

When Muffin heard what information Kornilov was talking about he offered to have a preliminary meeting with the KGB officer immediately. Kornilov refused. He said he wished to speak to someone who could make him a firm offer of asylum in return for the research he had brought west. He said he would telephone the CIA station chief every twelve hours. Then he hung up.

Henry Muffin, a black veteran of twenty-seven years with the agency, dressed and drove into Copenhagen. On a secure line in the U.S. embassy he called Washington, where it was three thirty in the morning.

By 4:45 A.M. on the American East Coast, the combined files of U.S. intelligence had produced a great deal of information about Major Kornilov.

He had been a law student when recruited by the KGB and spent sixteen years in the First Chief Directorate — foreign espionage — Third Department, which operates in Britain, Australia, New Zealand, and Scandinavia. From 1966 to 1968 he was an intelligence officer in Denmark. In 1969 Kornilov was posted to the Soviet embassy in London with the diplomatic cover of a deputy commercial attaché. When the British deported ninety KGB agents in October 1971, Maxim P. Kornilov was among them.

Back in Moscow, the KGB expellees from Britain were all transferred out of the First Chief Directorate. Kornilov was assigned to the Fifth Chief Directorate's Yevsekzia division. The Fifth is looked upon with scorn by the rest of the KGB. It is responsible for suppressing domestic political, religious, and ethnic dissent. Its Yevsekzia section deals with what the Soviet Union calls "the Jewish question." Yevsekzia agents keep files on — and spy on — prominent Soviet Jews, harass and infiltrate Jewish dissident groups, and search for the Jewish conspiracies that, as neurotic fantasies, have haunted the Russian imagination for centuries.

On April 6, the morning his file was being studied in Washington, Kornilov was three months short of his sixtieth birthday. His wife, thirty-four years his junior, had left him the previous November. He had not had an increase in rank and pay for a decade. His only known hobbies were fishing and collecting pornographic pictures. As the files of American intelligence portrayed him, Maxim Petrovich Kornilov had no friends.

The Soviet Union, like the United States, had spent years trying to develop space defenses against nuclear attack, a program known in the United States as the Strategic Defense Initiative. Particle beam physics was a science critical to the so-called Star Wars programs — if, indeed, they could be made to work at all. Professor Gregor Abramovich Mandelbaum, a Nobel laureate in physics, was the director of particle beam research for the Soviet Union's antimissile defense project.

Mandelbaum was a Russian Jew. Major Kornilov, who wished to defect to the United States, was assistant to Mandelbaum's Yevsekzia case officer. In Denmark he had told Henry Muffin that he would hand over the latest data from Professor Mandelbaum's research institute if the United States would grant him asylum.

In addition to the facts on Major Kornilov's life and work, the combined American intelligence files contained more than two dozen photographs of him supplied by Israeli intelligence and Soviet Jewish activists. They showed a frail, gray-haired man of medium height who wore steel-rimmed glasses.

By 5:05 A.M. the CIA had transmitted a transcript of Henry Muffin's telephone conversation with the agency to the basement offices of the National Security Council in the White House. The archive data on Major Kornilov followed. The overnight duty officer read a summary of both files and telephoned General

Wallace Cresteau, national security adviser to President James Forrest Burke.

Shortly after sunup, General Cresteau and Edgar Pollack, the director of Central Intelligence, met in the National Security Council's situation room. At sixty-three, Pollack was a compact, trim man whose sand-colored hair was just beginning to turn gray. He had pale blue eyes. General Cresteau was fifty-eight.

"Have you told the president?" Pollack asked after he had read Muffin's report.

Cresteau shook his head. "Not yet."

"Good," Pollack said cryptically.

General Cresteau was silent for a moment. "Well . . ." He paused. "If Burke's difficult — *when* he's difficult — it's because he's afraid."

"I know," Pollack replied.

Cresteau cleared his throat, signaling that their discussion of the president's much-discussed character was over. "Obviously, what's happened in Copenhagen may amount to something bigger than a routine defection."

"If we decide to take the man," Pollack said, "and if he has the documents he claims he has."

"Exactly," Cresteau answered. "That's why I thought it would be useful to have Jake Yarrow's opinion on how the Soviets are likely to react if they find out we have classified material from the Mandelbaum Institute."

"Good idea," Pollack replied. "Want me to call him?"

"I already have."

As the sun rose higher, a small gray Honda stopped at the inter-section of Cathedral and Connecticut avenues, waited for the light to change, then turned right and headed south across the ornate William Howard Taft Bridge.

The driver, Jake Yarrow, raised his eyes for a moment. At the end of the bridge an Italianate cluster of apartment buildings, one with a cupola and fluted tile roofs, stood against the brightening sky.

Yarrow slowed the Honda as he left the bridge and swung into a curve on Connecticut Avenue. The immense red flag outside the embassy of the People's Republic of China undulated in the morning breeze.

Jake Yarrow was a sixty-four-year-old senior analyst in the CIA's Directorate of Intelligence. He was childless and separated from his wife. He was due to retire in eight months and had not decided how he would spend the rest of his life.

The senior analysts — especially those in the Office of Soviet Affairs — are the Central Intelligence Agency's aristocracy. They carry in their heads secrets that few people know. The conclusions they reach frequently become the basis for policy recommendations to the president and cabinet.

At 6:54 A.M., the Honda turned in at the Southwest Gate of the White House and stopped at the guard post. Yarrow was cleared; he drove up West Executive Avenue and parked. He eased his large frame out of the car, closed the door, put his right hand in his jacket pocket, and went into the White House through its basement entrance.

General Cresteau, the national security adviser, was standing at the guard desk. He was a slender, bald man in a sport shirt, tan slacks, and running shoes. He held out his hand. "This is much appreciated, Jake," he said.

Yarrow shook hands. "My pleasure, Wally. What's up?"

"I have something for you to read," Cresteau said as they walked down the corridor. "Then Ed Pollack and I want to know what you think."

Wallace Cresteau was a soldier-scholar in the American military tradition of Generals Alfred Gruenther, James Gavin, and Matthew Ridgway. Cresteau had commanded combat troops in Vietnam. He had also been military attaché at the U.S. embassy in Peking and the Pentagon's man at the Arms Control and Disarmament Agency. Cresteau and Yarrow had been friends for twenty-five years.

"I take it I've been called in this beautiful morning because you've got a Soviet rumpus going on," Yarrow said.

"Something like that. You'll see."

They went through two more checkpoints, down corridors flanked by empty offices, past a fluorescent-lit room where two dozen Teletype machines — of commercial news agencies and scrambler-doctored government circuits — pattered, hummed, and rang faint bells for attention.

Yarrow and Cresteau walked into the situation room. The large, technology-cluttered chamber was windowless. It conveyed the atmosphere of eternal evening. Edgar Pollack, the director of Central Intelligence, was standing at a table talking to the overnight duty officer who had awakened General Cresteau. Beyond the table, on the room's shadowy perimeter, a woman sat at a computer, reading single-spaced copy. The luminous yellow type was headed "KORNILOV, M.P., URSKGB5, 6April,exCope, exfile229." Beyond the twilight area, in bright corridors and offices, men and women of the National Security Council's newly arrived day shift drank coffee and made telephone calls. A half dozen of them had gathered around the computer in the situation room, reading the file as the woman scrolled it up the screen. Kornilov's contact with the CIA in Copenhagen was the major event of the new day thus far.

Edgar Pollack turned as Yarrow and Cresteau crossed the room. "Good morning, Jake."

"Hello, Edgar," Yarrow said. "If Wally's roused you out early, this must be a national emergency."

Pollack smiled. "Not quite. But I think it'll interest you. Come on back to the conference room."

The three men walked down a fluorescent-bright corridor, leaving the murmur of the situation room behind them.

Nestled in its labyrinth beneath the West Wing of the White House and spilling over into the baroque Executive Office Building, the National Security Council staff is the world's most sophisticated assemblage of clerks. The council itself, established by Harry S. Truman in 1947, is composed of the president, vice president, the secretaries of state and defense, and the director of Central Intelligence. Its function is to coordinate national security and foreign policy.

To that end, the council's staff, headed by the national security adviser, was originally conceived as a group of trained diplomats and intelligence specialists who would read and evaluate an endless flow of information, most of it classified, and decide what should be sent upstairs to the president.

After Henry Kissinger became Richard Nixon's national security adviser in 1969, the NSC turned into a mini State Department that wielded more influence over foreign policy than the real one. The low point of the National Security Council staff's history was achieved during the Reagan presidency. The harebrained armsfor-hostages deal with Iran and illegal contra-funding schemes gave the unsettling impression that the Marx brothers were alive, well, and capering around the White House basement.

General Cresteau opened the door of a room at the end of the corridor. Pollack and Yarrow went in. A blue folder had been placed on a long conference table. "Sit down and have a look," Cresteau said as he closed the door.

"What is it?" Yarrow asked.

"The transcript of a telephone conversation between the overnight duty officer in agency Operations and your friend Henry Muffin at the Copenhagen embassy early this morning," General Cresteau answered. "Then some relevant file data."

Yarrow pulled back the chair from the head of the table, sat down, and took a leather case from the breast pocket of his jacket. He drew out a pair of glasses, put them on, and opened the folder. Cresteau and Pollack took chairs on either side of him.

Frown lines appeared above Yarrow's brows as he began to read. He was a tall, heavy man whose graying hair was combed straight back from his forehead. There were slight pouches beneath his blue eyes. Creases curved down from either side of his nose and framed his mouth. His lower lip was thrust out as he concentrated. His chin was round and cushioned on a fold of excess flesh.

Yarrow had committed himself to tweed jackets and bow ties as other men make commitments to military uniforms or priestly black. That morning he was wearing a blue button-down shirt; the bow tie was patterned yellow, his jacket a russet tweed. He wore gray slacks and highly polished loafers.

He sat, absorbed, for ten minutes, turning each computer-typed page facedown. After finishing he closed the folder. "You're right," he said to Pollack. "It is interesting."

"Ever hear of this Kornilov fellow?" Cresteau asked.

Yarrow shook his head.

"What do you think, Jake?" Pollack asked.

Yarrow was silent for a moment, looking down at the blue folder. "If our file data's right, Kornilov has sufficient personal motives for pulling something like this," he finally answered. "His personal life is empty and his career is ending badly. He's trying to give himself one more chance."

"Before we tell the president, we'd like an educated guess about how the Soviets will react if they know we have current data from the Mandelbaum Institute," Cresteau said.

"That may not be the first thing we should focus on, Wally," Yarrow replied. "Edgar, there's an incongruity in here. Mind if I think about it for a few hours?"

"I'll be in my office all afternoon," Pollack said. He turned to Cresteau. "Can we hold off until evening?"

"Not from briefing the president," Cresteau answered. "I'll tell him we've got somebody checking Kornilov's story."

"Will that satisfy him?"

"God knows."

A quarter of the way around the world, in Denmark, the early afternoon SAS flight from Helsinki landed at Copenhagen's Kastrup airport. It was a bright, breezy day.

A tall man with jet-black hair presented his Finnish passport at customs and took a taxi into City Hall Square. He carried only a small canvas bag. He did not speak. He had a notebook whose title page explained in Danish that he was a deaf-mute. Each subsequent page requested the reader to help the handicapped man with whatever task or function he was trying to perform. He bought a bus ticket for Liseleje, a town on the north coast.

An hour and fifteen minutes later he disembarked at Liseleje and consulted the back pages of his notebook, where his instructions were written. He walked down an avenue called Stranden toward a parking lot and the beach. Dunes, white sand, and the cold, blue waters of the Kattegat strait lay before him. The aromas of salt and kelp were on the spring breeze. Gulls wheeled and cried over the tidal flats. At the last house on the left the black-haired man opened the driveway gates, stepped inside, and re-latched the gates behind him.

A Saab hatchback and a Series 110 Land Rover were parked in front of the garage. Cream-colored paint had been spilled on the Land Rover's roof and the left side of its rear hatch.

The black-haired man took a key from his trouser pocket and unlocked the back door of the house. He saw a neat kitchen that looked as if it hadn't been used for a long time. He hesitated before going in. He was terrified of empty houses, empty barns, even apartments, at any hour of the day or night. He lived in dread of ghosts. He had no qualms about killing people. He had done it many times and was proud of his prowess at various techniques of murder. His mind was dull, yet he remembered the face of everyone he had shot, stabbed, or bludgeoned to death — whether inspired by his own mood or in the performance of his official duties. The faces haunted him.

When he was twelve he had killed his brother with a shovel. His grandmother, a woman thought of in the village as a witch, had warned him that the murdered reappear unexpectedly before their murderers, sodden if they were drowned, smeared with blood if their throats were cut, even as phantom children with their skulls sliced by a shovel blade. These specters grin at the people who killed them, she said.

There was a noise from the interior of the house. Someone was walking. A young man wearing a parka pushed aside a swinging door and stopped in the middle of the kitchen. He looked at his wristwatch. "You are precisely on schedule," he said in Russian. "I wondered if you'd be able to manage by yourself. They say you are an idiot."

The black-haired man closed the back door behind him. He didn't answer, though Russian was his native tongue. He stared with eyes like orbs of glass. His tall, powerful body threatened by its very presence.

"I am Anastas Hagopian," the young man said. "The weapon is on the dining room table. You have seen the vehicle outside."

Hagopian knew what this creature had been hired to do. He was suddenly alarmed. He turned and disappeared through the dining room door. A few moments later the black-haired man heard the front door slam, the driveway gates creak open, and the Saab engine start with a roar. Within forty-five seconds Hagopian was gone.

The silent Russian crossed the kitchen. He was trembling slightly with the fear that he might walk into the dining room and see a phantom smirking at him. He pushed open the door.

A Warsaw Pact–issue Dragunov SVD sniper rifle lay on the dining room table. A telescopic sight had been mounted on it. Six boxes of steel-jacketed ammunition were stacked beside it on the polished table. The Russian reached up and pulled off his black wig. He stuffed it in his jacket pocket. His real hair was brown stubble. He examined the rifle with an expert's eyes and hands, sighting, checking the barrel for cleanliness, working the trigger mechanism and slamming in the ten-shot clip several times.

He put three bullets in his pocket, then took the rifle outdoors and slid it in behind the front seat of the Land Rover. He backed the vehicle onto the beach road, locked the gates, and drove through the town and out into open country.

Ten kilometers south of Liseleje he saw what he wanted. He slowed the Land Rover and turned onto a dirt road that led up a hill between two fenced meadows to a farm. The Russian rifleman parked beneath a large tree and got out. There were no cars or trucks around the farmyard or visible in the garage. He went to the door and banged on it. No one responded. He was afraid to peer into the house through the glass door panel and the gauzy curtain that covered it.

The rifleman looked down the sloping field. Two young golden retrievers were romping in the afternoon sunlight, one rushing the other, which reared and pranced to one side. The dogs crouched, leaped, fell, rolled over, barked, and chased each other in wide circles.

The Russian went back to the Land Rover and took out the Dragunov. He slipped the three bullets into a clip, slammed the clip home, and cocked the first shot up into the firing chamber. He walked to the edge of the farmyard.

Three hundred feet away the two golden retrievers were still playing aggression games. The larger pawed at its friend, which lunged in response. The big dog danced sideways, the smaller dashing after it.

The Russian raised the rifle and looked through the sights. He adjusted the range. He squinted, moving the Dragunov slightly, until the cross-hairs were on the large dog's neck, just behind its right ear.

The golden retriever's hindquarters were in the air, its front legs flat on the stubble grass. Its tail was lashing back and forth, expressing the joy of competition. The smaller dog circled. In less than five seconds it would pounce and the canine tableau would turn into another frenzied romp.

The rifleman fired.

The large dog was thrown sideways by the impact of the bullet. It crashed flat onto the ground, its legs tangled. Its head, freed by the severing of the spinal column, was twisted under its shoulder.

The smaller dog stopped circling and stood, tail wagging, looking at its friend as if the distorted posture of death were a clever new tactic in games of canine pretend-fighting.

The rifleman fired again.

The second golden retriever gave a screaming yelp as its left rear thigh was shattered. It lurched sideways and fell to the ground, dragging itself forward with three thrashing legs as if it could leave the pain behind.

The rifleman fired a third time.

The last shot blew the dog's muzzle off. The frantic struggling stopped.

The Russian put the rifle back in the Land Rover and walked down to the two furry corpses. He grabbed each by a leg and dragged them over to the fence. He threw them onto the road.

Driving down to the highway, he ran over one dog. He backed up, turned the Land Rover to the right, and crushed the body of the second golden retriever with its wheels.

Then he returned to Liseleje, satisfied with his new weapon. He sat on the beach, where, he was sure, he would see no ghosts.

Full morning began in Washington. From the White House, Jake Yarrow drove into Georgetown, up Wisconsin Avenue, and out Reservoir Road. The sun was approaching its midmorning site on the arc of day as he accelerated his gray Honda up the steep incline of Forty-seventh Place and turned into the narrow driveway of his wife's little frame house. Birds trilled in the cool air.

Louise Cassidy Yarrow's fey, wise character had never ceased to enthrall Jake and inspire the guardian instinct in him. She was extravagantly — if unconventionally — beautiful. Yarrow adored her. Their separation had caused him more anguish than even his closest friends realized.

There was much about her Jake did not understand. His wife had loved the pretty little Georgetown house they shared for twenty-three years. When they parted, Yarrow gave it to her. Six months later Louise sold the house and insisted on splitting the proceeds with him. Then she moved to Forty-seventh Place on the outer fringes of metropolitan Washington. It was a short street of plain residences.

Yarrow mounted the steps of the front porch, picked up that morning's copy of the *Washington Post,* and unlocked the door. As she left on a trip to Mexico two days before, she had asked him to keep an eye on her house.

Letters and bills were scattered across the floor of the small entrance hallway. He put them on a table and went into the living room, which Louise used as her studio. He turned on the ceiling track lights.

The walls were pale gray. Books and magazines were piled everywhere. The surface of an old kitchen table that stood beside her enormous easel was cluttered with a sheet of translucent glass that she used as a palette, tubes of paint, sticks of charcoal, tied bundles of rags, and gallon-size tin cans filled with paintbrushes.

On either side of the fireplace floor-to-ceiling racks held dozens of her canvases. A few pencil drawings were taped to the wall and mantelpiece — fragments of imagined cupolas, church steeples and domes, ornate doors, nude figures, characters from *commedia dell'arte,* men with the heads and plumage of griffins, women wearing exotic costumes.

They were studies for a phantasmagorical painting that stood on the easel. The sketches had melted into deliriums of shape and color — a Byzantine church, houses, markets, people at prayer or wandering among ruined columns and the embers of night fires, the corniche above a dun-colored river — all glowing in the first intrusions of dawn.

Yarrow stood in the middle of the room, entranced by the picture and pained as he had been by all of her work in recent years. The Renaissance cityscape reproached him for delaying its existence. Louise had been a conventional, journeyman painter during the years they lived together. Her hallucinatory brilliance blossomed after she left him. She had become immensely successful, commercially as well as artistically.

Four years earlier, Yarrow came home on a stormy January afternoon and found her alone in the studio of the Georgetown house, sitting on a stool before her tilted drawing board. Three brushes were clutched in her left hand. Her chin was propped on her right fist. A large floral painting in acrylics was taped to the board. "Still giving you trouble, is it?" he asked, pulling off his gloves.

Louise shook her head. "No." She stood and walked over to the sink. "It's dead. I was trying to turn it into something alive, but —"

"You're being too hard on yourself," he said, going to the drawing board. "I like it."

"Oh, Jake. For God's sake, say what you *really* think about something —" She turned around. "Just once?"

Flakes of snow were melting on Yarrow's face and the tweed shoulders of his overcoat. A faint alarm sounded within him. Her silences and preoccupation since late autumn were, he sensed, symptoms of a trouble that she had not been able to share with him. "I do like this picture," he replied.

She leaned against the sink. "I can explain one of two things," she said. "I can either give you a critique of the painting or tell you why *we're* as dead as it is."

His solar plexus tightening, Yarrow sat down in a Victorian armchair in the middle of the room. "That's news to me."

"I know," she said. "Try to remember that every word is as painful for me to speak as it is for you to hear."

He nodded.

Louise turned around and began washing the brushes. Muddy rivulets of overmixed paint ran across the backs of her hands and her knuckles. "Jake, I have to start taking some risks," she said, "— as a painter and as a woman."

He didn't answer. The emotional bolt in his upper abdomen wrenched one twist tighter.

She turned off the faucet and gave the brushes five vigorous shakes. "You're — a — very — dear — man," she said. She slid them into a glass jar. She pulled a wad of paper towels off a roll, wiped her hands, and turned around to him. "You've been very —" She closed her eyes for a moment, groped for words, and then reopened them. "What? Protective? Solicitous?"

He waited.

"Most of all, above everything else, very loving." She took a deep breath. "You've been so loving, so protective — all the rest of it — and I've accepted so completely that I've become your emotional ward."

She looked at him sitting with both of his arms on the arms of the chair, his fingers gripping the carved whorls under each hand. His face was expressionless as he listened to her.

She had been preparing herself for this moment since November. She had invented words, sentences, and phrases to convey her feelings — love overpowered by suffocation. Now she felt an urgent need to say it all and make him understand. "I'm fifty years old," she said, "and I'm afraid."

"I didn't know —"

"It isn't your fault," she said. "Let me try to explain. I'm not afraid that something terrible will happen. I'm afraid that *nothing at all* will ever happen to either of us again. I'm afraid you'll go on being your courtly self for the rest of our lives, not telling me about your work or your real feelings, staying way out there ahead of me." She was speaking rapidly, as if, at any moment, he might stop listening. "I'm afraid I'll smother, that I'll never be able to catch up to you, that all I'll ever be able to paint is" — she turned to the technically excellent but vapid picture of flowers in a vase, leaves and petals littering a wooden table — "that! I —"

"Louise," he said suddenly, "what in hell is this all about?"

"Jake," she answered, "wait. It isn't just that I'm a lousy

painter, or that secrecy, which I know you have to practice in your work, has become the metaphor for the rest of your life, it's not just —"

"Damn it, Louise —"

"Splitting," she said. "I'm talking about . . . separation. Divorce? I suppose I could forget I'm a Roman Catholic — lapsed, but still Catholic — if divorce would be best for you . . ."

Yarrow didn't want to surrender to the rage gathering inside him. It would make him glacial, formal, and cruelly polite. He didn't want to inflict that on this woman he loved, now, as the January light was dying, more than he had ever loved her in his life. But he was too afraid not to be angry.

"Before we start talking about the solution," he said, "I think you'd better try to give me a more adequate explanation of the problem."

Louise hated the chill in his voice. She wanted him to understand the complexity of what she had decided and all the reasons for it. She wanted to hear him say that he had grasped her logic even if he despised her for it.

"I know I sound like a pop culture narcissist, but I need to become myself again — whatever that is. I —" She closed her eyes. She opened them again. "I can't afford to be your ward anymore, Jake. I've thought about this — alone — for a long time. I know how much pain I'd be in if you were saying this to me. For that, more than anything else, I'm sorry."

He was sitting erect in the chair. She could sense his withdrawal from her.

Desperately, she tried to keep the circuit between them open until she could say the rest — that she was suffering too, because she couldn't stop loving him, that, more and more, he was cutting her off as if she were an enemy agent bent on stealing his soul. She made a final, desperate try.

"Haven't *you* ever felt —"

"Is there someone else, Louise?"

"No."

"You're saying you want to live alone."

The iceman's hands were upon him. The circuit had snapped.

She nodded. "Yes."

He let an eternity of silence pass. Then he said, "I wish you every happiness."

During the half year that followed, Yarrow had regretted those words more than any others he had ever uttered. He went on with his life, wearing his calm, confident personality like a bandage on his humiliation and self-disgust. He reproached himself for not listening to everything else she had wanted to tell him.

There are moments in life as final as death, terrible and rapturous moments, which cannot be relived. Yarrow and Louise never referred again to what they said to each other in that winter twilight.

Six months after their separation, on the day they met to sign documents for the sale of the Georgetown house, he invited her out to lunch. She seemed composed and cheerful. When she had settled herself in the little house on Forty-seventh Place she asked Yarrow to come for dinner. The themes and style of her painting were undergoing radical transformations. Her new pictures were astonishing dreamscapes wreathed in smoke, mystery, and silence.

Thereafter, as they moved cautiously back into each other's orbits, Yarrow discovered that, having experienced life alone, he needed Louise nearby even if she had resigned from their marriage. She seemed to feel the same. They never mentioned divorce again. They reestablished their mutual sense of humor. She touched him only to kiss his cheek in greeting. The friends of their married years were relieved that they were together albeit in a different arrangement. Yarrow, still deeply shaken over his surrender to fear and rage on the night they separated, could not muster his old confidence in the new relationship. Louise's breakthrough to her full creative capacity had given her a cheerful certainty. She had moved beyond him.

Then, as one apprehends the coming of summer rain before the first sigh of wind and whisper of distant thunder, Yarrow began to sense that yet another change was imminent.

The day after he drove Louise to Dulles airport to catch her flight to Mexico City, a letter addressed to him in her handwriting was delivered with his morning mail.

Until he was summoned to the White House twenty hours later, the letter had been his mind's major preoccupation.

The painting on her easel was resurrecting her in Yarrow's mind. The mosaic of her speech patterns, her sudden smile, her inquisitive mind and capacity for sudden rapture over things seen — the most endearing components of his wife's character — were getting in the way of what he urgently needed to think about before the morning was over.

He telephoned his research assistant, Margery Ferrall. He turned off the track lights in Louise's studio, locked the front door, and went down the porch steps in the cool, bright morning. He got in his car and drove to MacArthur Boulevard. He stopped to let two cars pass, turned left, and went back to Georgetown.

He crossed Key Bridge to the Virginia side of the Potomac River, turned onto the George Washington Parkway, and followed it to the CIA's overcrowded headquarters building surrounded by forest and parking lots. By nine-thirty Yarrow was in his small third-floor office.

The analytic and scientific directorates of the Central Intelligence Agency like to cultivate the aura of academia. Pipes are smoked, tweeds worn, it is fashionable to know and quote classic American poetry. Emily Dickinson and Walt Whitman were favored among Yarrow's contemporaries. There is also a fondness for British terminology. Thus, Yarrow's office was his "room."

Three of its walls were lined with bookcases holding volumes in English, Russian, and French. On a fourth wall was an incongruous photograph of Lenin — showing the father of the Russian Revolution with a tennis racket in his hand. Beside it hung a savage cartoon from the Soviet satire magazine *Krokidil* depicting a CIA analyst who resembled Jake Yarrow sifting through the contents of a Soviet garbage can. Yarrow's desk was a scholarly mess, stacked with folders, copies of *Pravda* and *Kommunist*, the monthly journal of the Communist party of the Soviet Union, letters, reports, memoranda, and books.

He spent the rest of the morning reading files on Gregor Abramovich Mandelbaum and Kornilov, the KGB defector. He had a long talk with a physicist from the CIA's Directorate of Science and Technology. Margery Ferrall brought him the latest CIA and Defense Intelligence Agency analyses of relations between the KGB and the Soviet military intelligence organization, GRU.

Just before 12:30 P.M. Yarrow called Edgar Pollack. "If you'll give me lunch, I'll raise a difficult question for you," he said.

"Fine," said the director of Central Intelligence. "I'll ask Wally to come out and join us if he can."

An hour later Yarrow took the elevator up to the large seventh-floor office of the director of Central Intelligence. Its windows, facing east toward the city, framed the surrounding woodlands and flawless blue sky.

Edgar Pollack's office resembled the office of a university president. There were five sections of floor-to-ceiling bookcases, an 1866 bust of William Ewart Gladstone — Pollack was a member of the Reform Club in London — and two black wooden captain's chairs emblazoned with the crest of Yale's Trumbull College in gold. The CIA's old boys have a fondness for slightly bizarre humor. A large eighteenth-century oil portrait of an American Revolutionary officer hung on one wall of Pollack's office; the subject was alleged to be Benedict Arnold.

General Cresteau had already arrived when Yarrow walked in. The national security adviser to the president had changed into a serge suit and dark tie.

At one end of the large office a luncheon table had been laid for three. Pollack, Cresteau, and Yarrow seated themselves and talked about the new baseball season while a steward served clear soup.

Edgar Pollack was one of Yarrow's oldest friends. They had entered the agency in the same year and served in several bureaus together; Yarrow was godfather to Pollack's son. Edgar Pollack had been dismayed at Jake and Louise's separation and relieved when they formed a new liaison.

The steward finished serving the soup course and withdrew, closing the office door behind him.

"Has the president been told?" Yarrow asked.

Cresteau nodded.

"And?"

"He's upset," Cresteau replied. "It's hardly news that his first priority is setting the agenda for the SDI test ban talks this fall." Cresteau returned his spoon to the plate beneath his soup bowl. "He's afraid that if the Soviets find out we have copies of Mandelbaum's top secret research they'll cancel the negotiations." Cresteau looked at Yarrow. "The president wants to know if there's any way we can tell Kornilov that we don't want him *or* — if I may quote — 'his goddamned Mandelbaum documents.' "

"What'd you say to that?" Yarrow asked.

"I said we could reject Kornilov's offer," Cresteau answered. "But I pointed out to him that a lot of people around Washington already know what's happened. My office included Kornilov's conversation with Henry Muffin in the morning intelligence summary."

"And you told Burke that the likes of Phil Teague will scream bloody murder if we don't grab anything we can get from the Mandelbaum Institute," Pollack said.

Cresteau nodded. "The president doesn't need me to tell him that. His opinion of Teague can't be discussed in mixed company."

The steward reappeared to clear away the soup plates and serve mushroom omelettes. Yarrow, a Boston Red Sox fan, expressed polite skepticism about General Cresteau's enthusiasm for the Baltimore Orioles. The steward left the room.

"All right, Jake," Pollack said, "let's hear this difficult question of yours."

Yarrow looked through the windows. Over the surrounding treetops and gentle hills he could see the yellowish brown Potomac meandering through its valley below. "Mandelbaum's doing military research," he said. "That means he and his institute are policed and protected by the GRU, Soviet military intelligence. The KGB's Yevsekzia — where our friend Kornilov works — keeps a file and a couple of case officers on Mandelbaum because he's a Jew. But their involvement with him is minor compared to the GRU's." Yarrow looked at Pollack. "Relations between the KGB and GRU are just as bad as they've always been. Kornilov says he'll hand over the latest work documents from the Mandelbaum Institute if we'll grant him political asylum. So — the difficult question: How do you suppose a little fellow from the Yevsekzia ever got his hands on classified military research data kept under lock and key by the GRU?"

For a moment Cresteau and Pollack were silent. Then Cresteau said, "Possibly he stole it?"

Yarrow shook his head. "Too difficult for one man."

"He could be a ringer sent over by the KGB with a batch of scientific disinformation," Pollack said.

"Possibly," Yarrow said, "but I doubt it. I was told this morning that phony particle beam research material — if it's to be persuasive — is as difficult to create as the real thing. Also, when the KGB sends us bogus defectors they're always from the First Chief Directorate. The First got rid of Kornilov more than twenty years ago."

Edgar Pollack took a deep breath. "One more guess. Mandelbaum smuggled the data out of his own institute and gave it to Kornilov."

"That," replied Yarrow, "is possible. But it raises another difficult question. Why? Mandelbaum seems to be apolitical. He's never had anything to do with the Jewish dissident or refusenik groups. He seems to be a totally loyal Soviet citizen."

"Does he have any reason for wanting to come west himself?"

"One," Yarrow said. "His daughter, Dvorah Mandelbaum, was sent to live with her aunt in Tel Aviv during the détente period in the early seventies. She apparently had emotional problems and the family wanted her treated in Israel. She's still living there and in France. Mandelbaum may want to come west to be with her. The Soviets obviously won't let him emigrate." Yarrow shrugged. "I haven't found any connection between Dvorah Mandelbaum and this offer Kornilov's made to us."

Pollack looked at the windows. A solitary hawk, wings motionless, was riding the air currents above the forest and the river. "In other words, you don't believe what Kornilov told Henry this morning." The director of Central Intelligence turned back to Yarrow. "At least as it stands."

"I think it's a pack of lies," Yarrow said. "Or, at best, a part of a truth being held out to us as bait."

"What do you want to do, Jake?"

Yarrow pulled back his sleeve and looked at his wristwatch. "There's an SAS flight from New York to Copenhagen at nine tonight," he said. He raised his head. "I think I'd better go have a talk with Major Kornilov and find out what this is all about."

After lunch Yarrow drove home to Cleveland Park. He checked his mail, then went upstairs to his bedroom. There was a bound manuscript lying open on a chaise lounge.

The manuscript had been composed by Yarrow's father, Conrad, between 1919 and his death in 1944. For a moment Jake stood in the middle of the room, rereading a passage whose exact phraseology he'd tried to remember as he was shaving that morning.

"Without the help of Russian Czars, German and Austrian emperors," Conrad Yarrow had written in his minuscule script, now faded to brown, "Marx's and Lenin's books would have been read by nobody; they would have made their speeches in empty meeting halls."

The manuscript, 634 pages long, was in both Czech and English. It was a jumble of autobiography, discourses on central European history, nineteenth- and twentieth-century political theory, and flights of bad poetry.

Jake Yarrow's father, Conrad Jaroslav, had been born in Prague, orphaned at fifteen, and shipped off to America to live with relatives whom he never located. He spent two nightmarish years in the streets of New York, fought for his new country in World War I, and settled in Tulsa, Oklahoma. He changed his name to Yarrow, married, sired a son, and established a printing company that made him wealthy. He had written about his life and thoughts in an unsuccessful attempt to exorcise the traumas of his youth. He died a bitter, taciturn man, bequeathing his manuscript and a comfortable income to his son.

Yarrow put the manuscript on a desk stand he'd had built for it and took a suitcase from his closet. He had just finished packing when the bedroom telephone rang.

"A car will pick you up in fifteen minutes," his assistant, Margery Ferrall, told him. "Your flight to New York leaves at six thirty. You've got plenty of time to connect with the SAS nine o'clock for Copenhagen."

"Fine," Yarrow said. "Any more word —"

"Henry's Russian friend called him again. He knows you'll be there in the morning."

"He sounds anxious," Yarrow said.

"You would be too if the KGB was on your tail," she said.

When the last scattered lights of the Canadian land mass had been obliterated by the darkness at thirty-six thousand feet, Yarrow closed his notebook and pressed the button that released the back of his economy-class seat. He banished Kornilov from his mind.

He took Louise's letter from his inside jacket pocket, slipped it from the envelope, and unfolded it. He didn't really need to read the brief note to puzzle over it. He had already memorized it from dozens of previous readings.

As was her custom, it began without salutation.

> *I think we've both changed a lot. I love you. I'd like to really be your wife again but don't know how you feel about that. So I've gone to Mexico for a while to give you time to think about it.*
> *I don't know what else to say —*
> *L.*

Yarrow looked up. A movie, its colors washed pale by the reading lights in the dusky cabin, was playing silently on the forward bulkhead screen.

He wondered if Louise had written to him on impulse. He wondered if she knew what she really wanted.

He wondered what he really wanted.

❖ THREE ❖

IN HIS RECURRING DREAM Yarrow always knew what he wanted.

He was seated at the supper table with his mother and father. The gray pall of dusk filled the kitchen.

Yarrow identified his parents not by their faces but by his boyhood sense of them. He felt the temperature of his mother's fear as she awkwardly ate her dinner; she was like a vassal at the table of a tyrant, afraid of doing something wrong, uncertain about what was right.

In the dream Conrad Yarrow sat at the end of the table. He was partially obscured by deeper shadow and by his own brooding silence. He never reprimanded or punished. When he spoke about history, political ideas, or his own past, it was with bitterness. Half consciously, Jake came to believe that he was born to make up for his father's tormented life.

He wanted the shadow around Conrad Yarrow to go away. He wanted his family to be like the families of his friends, to have the ceiling light on, to laugh at the supper table and talk about what they had done that day.

In his dream Yarrow never got what he wanted.

At 7:05 in the morning, fifty-five minutes out of Copenhagen, Yarrow opened his eyes. It was one of the blessings of his life that he could sleep soundly on airplanes. He turned his head and looked out the window. The DC-10 was flying through a metallic gray cloud that was faintly tinted with the flame of sunrise breaking across the clear sky far above.

He sat up and pushed aside the blanket that had covered him in the night. He took his worn leather toilet kit from the seat pocket, went back to a lavatory, locked himself in, and brushed his teeth. He shaved and washed, then combed his hair. When he returned to his seat, his breakfast tray was waiting for him. He buckled himself in and looked out the window.

The airliner was descending out of a layer of cloud that covered northern Europe. The sea was frothed with whitecaps. As Yarrow finished his coffee, the lumbering jet banked. He saw Kastrup airport ahead on the Danish landscape.

Minutes later the cabin filled with the hydraulic screech of the wheels coming down. Trees and low buildings whizzed by the window. The tires met the runway with an almost imperceptible touch.

Henry Muffin was waiting for Yarrow in the customs hall. He was a tall, dark-skinned man in his early fifties. He had also served in Finland and Norway. Muffin's blackness had made him so conspicuous among the fair peoples of Scandinavia that the Soviet opposition refused, for years, to believe that he was really an American intelligence officer. His visibility had been his cover. He had been CIA station chief in Copenhagen for three years.

Muffin's powerful shoulders and arms looked as if they might burst the seams of his business suit. His crisp black hair was graying at the temples. His face had been hit a few times. The lumpy knuckles of the large hand he held out implied that he had hit back.

Yarrow and Muffin exchanged greetings with the contrived indifference affected by men who are deeply fond of each other.

"Welcome," Muffin said.

Yarrow grasped his hand. "Henry."

"How do you feel?"

"Fine. Slept like a log," Yarrow answered. "What's up?"

"Kornilov wants a meeting today. At noon."

"Good," Yarrow said. "The sooner the better."

"You can change at my place," Muffin said. "We thought you'd like to stay with us instead of in a hotel."

"You guessed right," Yarrow answered. "I've been hoping I'd see Dorothy while I was here."

"She's been over in Odense for an English teachers' conference," Muffin said. "She'll be back this evening."

Followed by a young woman porter, they left the customs hall and got on an escalator. "Kornilov been in regular contact?" Yarrow asked.

"No. His call last night was late," Muffin said. "He didn't get in touch until after ten. Turns out he was busy."

"Doing what?"

"Catching up with his old buddies," Muffin said. "The Danes tell us that some heavy KGB talent's been in town."

"How heavy?" Yarrow asked.

Muffin led the way as they stepped off the escalator onto the terminal's main floor. "Valerian Galkin and two bodyguards."

"Galkin?" Yarrow said in surprise.

Muffin nodded. "When Kornilov finally did call last night I told him we had a heavy of our own coming in from Washington. That's when he said he wanted to cut a deal with somebody today."

They walked toward the main entrance. Gongs were sounding and a pleasant female voice was announcing flights in Danish, Swedish, and Norwegian.

Outside, the overcast was a vast, dull ceiling on the world. Denmark was having a cold April. The porter put Yarrow's suitcase into Henry Muffin's blue Volvo station wagon.

A light rain began to fall. Muffin switched on the front and rear windshield wipers as he drove out of the airport. "Danish counterintelligence followed Galkin and his guys to Roskilde, about fifty kilometers west of here," he said. "The Danes saw Kornilov and Galkin sitting together in the cathedral. Identified Kornilov from the pictures we gave them. Afterward Galkin and his baby-sitters drove to Helsingør and took the ferry across to Sweden."

Yarrow was silent a moment. "But why did *Galkin* come to see Kornilov? You'd think they'd just send someone to kill him if they knew where he was."

They were on a wet coastal boulevard. Muffin decelerated the station wagon. "Maybe you'll find out this morning."

"Let's hope so," Yarrow replied. "Where am I meeting him?"

"On the beach at a village called Liseleje," Muffin said. "It's west of Helsingør. About an hour and a half, two hours' drive from here. Did you bring warm clothes?"

"Yes," Yarrow said. "Does Kornilov know who he'll be talking to?"

Muffin shook his head as he turned the Volvo into his driveway, then passed a hedgerow, a wide lawn, and perennial beds. "He just knows somebody's coming from Washington."

"So," Yarrow said distractedly as Muffin braked the Volvo to a stop. "He's willing to hold a meeting on a beach in broad daylight. What does that suggest to you, Henry?"

Muffin switched off the ignition. "Same thing it suggests to you, pal. Kornilov isn't operating alone."

Yarrow nodded. "I can hardly wait to find out what he's really up to."

The rain stopped shortly after nine o'clock. The day was still overcast.

They left Muffin's house at ten fifteen. Mist rose from canals and rivers as they drove northwest across the brown landscape.

"How's Louise?" Muffin asked.

To anyone else, Yarrow would have replied that Louise was fine. With Henry Muffin he could be more candid. The two men's friendship had begun at a 1973 Washington conference on Soviet intelligence operations in northern Europe.

"Oh, as she always is," Yarrow said, "well, busy, successful—" He looked through the windshield at the wet earth, sagging fence posts, rusted barbed wire, and rain-darkened barns. "She's talking about trying again, Henry, about resuming where we left off four years ago."

"You've always wanted that," Muffin said. "Or, so I've read you."

Yarrow nodded. "But now . . ." He looked at Muffin. "I suppose it's not unusual to have second thoughts when the wish becomes a possibility."

Muffin braked at a country crossroads and looked both ways on the highway. "Totally normal," he answered. "Who was the saint who said that if God really wants to zap you He'll answer your prayers?"

"Teresa of Avila, I think," Yarrow answered. "I'll have to ask Louise." He smiled. "She's better at saints than I am. And, I expect, more saintly."

Muffin shifted into first and crossed the highway. Light rain had begun again, coming in from the west. "You've lived alone for a long time," Muffin said.

"Yes. And I'm due for retirement in November," Yarrow answered. He looked through the side window. A herd of cold, wet holstein cattle stood morosely in a field. "I don't even know what I'm going to do with myself, much less what I'd do living with a busy, famous painter."

"You could become one of those — what do the pop magazines call them — househusbands?"

Yarrow smiled. "There's that."

The Yarrows had visited the Muffins in Norway the summer after Jake and Henry met. Louise Cassidy Yarrow painted Dorothy Muffin's portrait. The Muffins stayed with the Yarrows whenever they were passing through Washington on home leave or back for consultation. The two couples, both childless, had taken vacations together on and off for years.

"What are you going to do?" Muffin asked.

"I don't know," Yarrow answered. "I think Louise and I have to find out who we are now." Again, he looked at Muffin. "I have an awkward question for you," he said. "I ask it only because I'm groping for insights. Has Louise written to Dorothy about any of this?"

"If she has, Dorothy wouldn't tell me," Muffin answered. "How about a cup of coffee?"

"I'm all for it," Yarrow said. "Have we time?"

They were entering a town named Helsinge. "Enough," Muffin said. "We should be a little late and make Kornilov sweat."

After stopping for coffee they drove on, up the coast to the vacation village of Liseleje on the extreme northern coast of Denmark's main island. It was only half occupied during the off-season. They drove past rows of shuttered houses. Bored teenagers leaned on their bicycles in front of a closed cinema.

The rain had stopped again. Muffin turned down an avenue that ended in a wide parking lot, dunes, the beach, and the Kattegat strait under a sullen sky. The only other vehicle in the parking lot was a Land Rover with a paint spill on its rear roof and back hatch. A cold wind was rushing across the coastal landscape, bending the dead grasses on the sand dunes and lashing the strait's dark waters into breakers.

Muffin and Yarrow got out of the station wagon and climbed onto the sand dunes overlooking the coastal landscape stretching away to the east. Muffin was dressed in a tan windbreaker and jeans. He took a pair of binoculars out of a leather case and scrutinized the beach.

"There," he said, focusing. "There he is." He handed the glasses to Yarrow.

In the binoculars' powerful magnification, Maxim Petrovich Kornilov looked like a figure in a surrealist movie. Two straight-backed wooden chairs had been set side by side on the beach. Kornilov sat in one of them, staring across the stormy waters at the horizon. His thin body was bundled in a black-and-white houndstooth overcoat. His hands were shoved into the pockets. He wore a gray fedora. There was a basket on the sand beside him.

Yarrow refocused the binoculars on the face of the seated man. It conformed precisely to the CIA file photographs that he had memorized. Kornilov's nose and ears were pink with the cold. Yarrow couldn't see his eyes behind the steel-rimmed glasses. The KGB major's mouth curved downward at both ends, giving his face an expression of solemnity.

Muffin took back the binoculars and looked at Kornilov again. "Is he deaf?" he asked.

"Not that I know," Yarrow answered.

"Then that gadget in his ear means he's in radio contact with somebody," Muffin said.

He turned the glasses to the dunes and a scrubby growth of conifers and wind-bent shrubbery inland. "Well," he said softly, as if he were speaking to himself, "I see two guys back there. I'm supposed to see them. One has binoculars and he's looking at me."

Yarrow shrugged deeper into his Italian paratrooper's jacket. "What are they about?" he asked.

"They're Kornilov's bodyguards. One with binoculars is just an ordinary-looking guy," Muffin answered, still peering through his own glasses. "The other . . . tall . . . black hair . . . armed with — yep."

"What is it?"

"Sniper's rifle," Muffin said, adjusting the focus. "Warsaw Pact issue. Dragunov, I think. Fires ten rounds, accurate at eight hundred feet if the shooter's any good."

He put his glasses back in their case. "This isn't your usual scene so listen to me. Walk normally out to Kornilov. I'll go along parallel to you on the dunes. I'm going to be carrying a rifle —"

"Is that really necessary?" Yarrow asked.

Muffin nodded. "Just do it my way, Jake."

"If you say so," Yarrow answered.

He took a pair of gloves from the pocket of his jacket and slipped them on. He tugged a tweed cap down on his head and walked sideways down the dune and out onto the wide beach. He started toward the place where Kornilov was waiting for him.

It was difficult going. The sand was loose and chilly as it slipped into his shoes. He was walking in a crosswind. His facial skin shriveled in the cold and his eyes watered.

The sky was pewter-colored. Except for three sea gulls riding the air currents, nothing moved on the long coast as far as Yarrow could see. The tide had receded almost to its lowest point. Waves thundered onto the beach, hissing up the gleaming sand. Yarrow looked to his right. Henry Muffin was walking on the dunes above him holding a U.S. Army rifle in the crook of his arm.

As Yarrow approached, Kornilov turned his head and stared like a man slowly coming awake. Yarrow was less than thirty feet from him before the KGB officer stood up and took his hands from his overcoat pockets.

Yarrow pulled off his right glove. "Good afternoon, Major," he said in Russian.

Kornilov hesitated, then held out his hand. "Good afternoon, *Gospodin* —"

"My name is Yarrow. I represent the Central Intelligence Agency's Directorate of Intelligence, Office of Soviet Affairs."

The wind blew strands of Kornilov's gray hair around the left side of his face. "Jacob Yarrow?"

"Yes."

"I am honored," Kornilov said. He gestured toward the chairs. "Please."

Yarrow shook his head. "I'll do no business with you until you disconnect your microphone," he said. "What I have to say will be for your ears only — not for your friends in the dunes behind us."

Kornilov looked at him without expression for a long moment. Then he unbuttoned the top of his overcoat, took off a clip microphone, and snapped its thin cord. He dropped the microphone in the sand at his feet.

"That was very intelligent of you," Yarrow said.

He crossed the sand and sat down in the chair nearest him. Kornilov went around behind him and resumed his seat in the other chair. He reached down to the straw basket beside his chair. Kornilov took a thermos and a metal cup from it. "Some coffee, perhaps?"

"*Pazhalsta,*" Yarrow replied. The waves crashed onto the sand, flinging spray into the air, where it was caught by the wind and flung sideways in flecks of foam. No ship or boat was visible on the vast expanse of tempestuous water.

"A drop of brandy?"

Yarrow looked back to Kornilov. He was holding an open pint bottle of Georgian brandy over the metal cup three-quarters filled with steaming black coffee.

"For the cold, yes," Yarrow said. "Thank you."

Kornilov poured brandy into the coffee, handed the cup to Yarrow, and repeated the operation for himself. He raised his head. His eyes were also watering in the wind. "How am I to make you believe what I have to tell you, Mr. Yarrow?"

"How did you persuade Galkin?" Yarrow asked.

Kornilov did not seem surprised. "Galkin knows that what I told him is true," he replied. "You are in a different position. I must convince you."

"Tell me the truth that Galkin already knows."

For twenty seconds Kornilov was silent. "As you wish," he

finally said. "I will tell you what happened. Everything." He looked at Yarrow. "If you are willing to listen to a long story."

"That's what I came here for," Yarrow replied. He handed back the metal cup.

As Kornilov refilled it he said, "You know, of course, in which directorate and division of the Committee for State Security I was employed."

Yarrow nodded. "Your immediate superior was Colonel Ivan Rodilovsky, who reported to General Druznak, director of the Yevsekzia?"

Kornilov refilled his own cup, then replaced the cork on the thermos and returned it to the basket.

"Yes. The events which brought us to this place today, Mr. Yarrow, began on the morning of January eleventh. Almost three months ago. That morning General Druznak called a conference on the Mandelbaum problem at eight o'clock."

Yarrow resettled himself in the chair. The wind had dropped. Kornilov's thin voice was easier to hear.

Kornilov looked at the beach and sea. He sipped from his metal cup as he recalled the physical textures of Moscow as well as the events of the eleventh of January.

It had not snowed for two weeks, he said. The avenues had been cleared of slush, which was heaped against the curbs in mounds of ocher-colored ice. "In November, Colonel Rodilovsky was injured in an automobile accident," he said. "I became the acting case officer of Professor Gregor Abramovich Mandelbaum."

Yarrow hadn't known about the auto accident. "Go on," he said.

"And you are aware that, on the second of January, Professor Mandelbaum made his fifth application to emigrate to Israel?" Kornilov asked.

"Yes."

Kornilov sniffed. "This fifth application to leave the country was accompanied by a campaign of inaction," he said. "Since the day he filed his papers, Mandelbaum had not reported for work at his institute."

Again, Kornilov raised his coffee cup and drank from it. "The situation was a delicate one for the authorities. The work of the Mandelbaum Institute is critical to Soviet national security. But all research there had stopped, so dependent was it on the presence of its director. Yet it is not possible to use force on such a man of genius to make him resume his work."

Kornilov finished his coffee and set the cup on the sand beside his chair. He folded his hands, pressed his two index fingers against his lips, and closed his eyes.

Yarrow waited.

The surf thundered onto the beach. The wind rushed past them.

Kornilov opened his eyes, lowered his hands to his lap, and began to tell Yarrow the facts of what he had done, but not about the dreams that had driven him.

The morning of January 11 was black and bitterly cold. As Major Maxim Petrovich Kornilov entered Dzerzhinsky Square, his shoes crunched on a granular layer of new frost that coated the street and pavement. The 6:30 A.M. weather bulletin on the radio had predicted snow.

Clutching his plastic briefcase to his chest, Kornilov passed the statue of Feliks Dzerzhinsky in the middle of the square. By midmorning the bird droppings that covered the head and shoulders of the Polish nobleman who founded the Bolshevik secret police would be replaced by a cap and epaulets of new snow if the radio's forecast was correct.

As Kornilov turned left on the sidewalk toward the east end of the block-long KGB headquarters building at seven forty-five that freezing morning, he walked with mincing steps to avoid slipping. The conditions in which the day was beginning, he reflected bitterly, were metaphors for the bleakness in which his professional life was ending.

His rage over the departure of his wife, Ailya Ivanovna, alternated in his mind with nostalgic lust for her. Kornilov was periodically assaulted by erotic memories of the dozens of positions for the conjugal act she had taught him. In his desperation he had total recall of her pale, fleshy body, blond pubic hair, and the smell of her cheap perfume.

Such recollections would invariably be overcome in his mind

by new bouts of fury at his wife for running off with an Armenian Aeroflot steward named Anastas Hagopian — although, in his heart, Kornilov knew that her desertion was logical. She had married him only because of his KGB privileges and salary. Now his career was fading. Hagopian had money, a good apartment, and brought her presents from abroad.

Kornilov's other fantasies were scenarios of revenge or murder against his wife and her paramour. He loved making up intricate plots as much as he relished his sexual nostalgia. He often told himself he could be a brilliant author of detective stories and dirty books if only he had a gift for writing. But he didn't.

On that desolate morning in January he had nothing. He needed hope, something to anticipate.

A uniformed guard at the side entrance to the KGB headquarters building recognized him and opened the glass-paneled doors.

A television camera peered at Kornilov in the shadows of the entryway. A buzzer sounded and the second door was opened by another uniformed KGB enlisted man. The sudden heat in the crowded, noisy hallway fogged Kornilov's spectacles. He handed his pass folder to a soldier, who looked at the picture while Kornilov wiped the lenses of his glasses with the end of his scarf.

"Thank you, Comrade Major," the guard said, handing back the pass.

Kornilov put on his glasses and went down the corridor to the lifts. The building was old. Its walls were a dull green and cracked in several places. The floor was wet from the stamping of many icy boots.

General Druznak's conference room was on the fifth floor. Kornilov opened the door and slipped into his chair at precisely eight o'clock.

Druznak was already speaking. Professor Gregor Abramovich Mandelbaum, said the chief of the Yevsekzia, had become an embarrassment. The secretariat of the Central Committee had turned this embarrassment over to the section of the KGB assigned to deal with difficult or defiant Jews.

Ivan Pavelovich Druznak was a short, overweight man with pale skin. He always wore his uniform. He had tiny eyes and spoke so softly that the eleven senior aides seated around the table had difficulty hearing him. "There is no question of granting him a permit to emigrate," he said in his semiwhisper. "The Americans alone would give anything to know how far his research has progressed up to now."

Kornilov's notebook lay open upon the table before him. He wrote that the Americans would give anything to know how far Professor Mandelbaum's particle beam research . . . The words suddenly triggered in his mind a fragment of a scheme so bold and exciting that, for a moment, Kornilov had difficulty suppressing it.

"And what was the result of the meeting?" Yarrow asked.

Kornilov took a handkerchief from a pocket somewhere beneath his overcoat and blew his cold-reddened nose. "I was ordered to go talk to Mandelbaum," he replied, "to convince him, if possible, to withdraw the application. Every other form of persuasion had been tried on this man — even, once, a private dinner with President Gorbachev. Mandelbaum was so valuable that there had never been an attempt to intimidate him with a visit by the KGB. General Druznak wanted to begin the intimidation with me. I had never met Mandelbaum. I am not very frightening."

Yarrow nodded. "Continue," he said.

When Kornilov returned to his office after the meeting, the blizzard had begun. The snow drifted slowly onto the roof of the former prison Lubyanka, behind the KGB headquarters building, and into the slushy courtyards and alleys below.

Kornilov summoned his secretary, a plump young corporal from Perm, and ordered her to call Professor Mandelbaum at his apartment in Mayakovsky Square and tell him that Major Kornilov of the KGB would be coming to talk to him before the morning was over. The call was meant to frighten the physicist, perhaps to inspire apprehensive conjectures in his mind.

When the corporal left, Maxim P. Kornilov opened his notebook and looked at what he had written, inspired by a single sentence General Druznak had uttered almost as an aside. Kornilov had conceived an idea that filled his life with hope, even the hope that Ailya Ivanovna might return to him.

For nearly a half hour he sat motionless, thinking, hands on the desk, the snow falling past the windows behind him. Kornilov became more and more excited as each new detail of his plot fit with an almost miraculous symmetry into the overall design.

His secretary came back at ten fifteen and said that a car and driver from the central motor pool were waiting in the garage.

Kornilov put on his galoshes, overcoat, muffler, and fur hat. For the first time in months — perhaps it was years — there was within him hope so great that he felt it as a lump of joy. He instructed himself to be prudent.

It was still snowing heavily when a uniformed KGB chauffeur drove up the basement ramp and into Dzerzhinsky Square. Although the sun had risen several hours before, blue-white lamps were burning like beacons along the avenues and the Garden Ring that circles inner Moscow.

Gregor Abramovich Mandelbaum's apartment occupied the entire fifth floor of a prerevolutionary building. By some miracle the carved wooden doors with dull brass handles were still intact. Kornilov pressed a white button set in the stone entryway.

The door lock buzzed. Kornilov twisted the handle and pushed. He entered a cold, gloomy hall. He tucked his plastic briefcase under his arm and climbed the curved staircase.

When he reached the fifth-floor landing he saw that Mandelbaum's apartment door was partly open. Small, dirty fingers were curled around the frame. An eye was peering at him.

Kornilov crossed the landing and pushed gently. As the door swung open, a woman who was almost short enough to be a dwarf backed down a hallway. She was wearing a gray smock, and a white cloth was tied over her head. Her face was smudged. She was holding a broom.

Maxim Petrovich Kornilov reached inside his coat and took his KGB identification folder from his breast pocket. He held it out for the tiny woman to see. "I am from the Committee for State Security," he said. "I have come to talk to Professor Mandelbaum."

The woman peered at the identification folder. Her eyes suddenly widened. She turned, scuttled up the corridor dragging the broom behind her, ducked into a room, and slammed the door.

"What's the matter with you?" Kornilov demanded loudly.

"Please come in, Major," said a quiet voice.

Kornilov saw that a man was standing at the head of the passage.

"Good morning, Professor Mandelbaum."

"You are welcome, Major Kornilov."

Gregor Abramovich Mandelbaum stood at the end of the hall, a book held in his left hand, his index finger inserted between its pages. He was tall and slender. His hair was dark and combed back from his forehead. His eyebrows and mustache were also dark and heavy. There was an expression of melancholy mixed with curiosity in his eyes. He appeared unusually fit for a man of sixty-three. That would be the result of the cross-country skiing that, along with fishing and camping, was his only avocation according to his Yevsekzia dossier. He was wearing a suit of greenish brown tweed. His shoes had been polished to a high shine. In his clothes and bearing, Gregor Abramovich Mandelbaum looked like an Edwardian English gentleman.

"What is that woman afraid of?" Kornilov asked.

"God in His mercy made her simple," Mandelbaum replied. "She understands the meaning of only a few things, such as red lights at street crossings." Mandelbaum's voice was soft but cultivated and distinct. "She can read only a few letters. *K, G,* and *B* are among them."

Kornilov nodded.

Mandelbaum gestured toward the door. "The salon . . . perhaps you would be more comfortable . . ."

Kornilov followed him into a long, low-ceilinged room with curtained windows across the far end. A leather-covered sofa stood against one wall with a low table before it. A large desk covered with papers faced the windows. There was a Japanese computer on a stand beside the desk.

Mandelbaum switched on lamps. Kornilov saw a menorah for Hanukkah candles on the mantel and paintings and prints covering the walls. Many were avant-garde.

"I trust Colonel Rodilovsky is better," Mandelbaum said.

Kornilov didn't answer.

"Please give him my best wishes."

Mandelbaum's concern for his Yevsekzia case officer made Kornilov feel diminished. He took off his overcoat and hat, laid them on the sofa, and settled himself beside them. "You will be seated, Professor," he said.

Mandelbaum drew a chair up to the coffee table and sat down.

Kornilov took some papers from the briefcase and pretended to study them. He allowed almost a full minute to pass. Somewhere in the room a small cabinet clock ticked. Wherever the tiny woman had gone in the apartment, she made no sound.

Kornilov raised his head.

Gregor A. Mandelbaum sat with his long hands folded in his lap, the fingers interlaced. The expression of melancholy was still in his eyes. Kornilov began to feel irritation. The physicist was obviously not afraid. "How difficult for you it must be," he said, "this task of yours."

"It is a task that someone must perform, comrade."

Mandelbaum nodded. "So we are told. Have you a family?"

"I am married. On January second —"

"Children?"

"No. Comrade Professor, I have come to discuss —"

Gregor Mandelbaum reached down the table to a cluster of framed photographs. He picked up the largest and handed it to Kornilov. "It is my daughter, Dvorah."

For a moment Kornilov was astonished at the sepia-toned photograph. The Yevsekzia's file pictures were years out of date. Dvorah Mandelbaum's beauty was unique. Even though she was a Jewess she was far lovelier than any woman Kornilov might dream of for himself.

Kornilov knew from her father's dossier that Dvorah Mandelbaum was thirty-four years old, that she had had an illness of some sort in her adolescence. Her long, black hair was streaked with gray, which, in contrast with her youthful complexion, gave her features the glow of polished wood. She had large eyes, a slender nose, and an upper lip curved like the lip of a flutist. In the photograph the young woman's expression also conveyed an emotional fragility.

Kornilov handed the framed picture back across the table. His plot required him to carefully consider every word he said, every attitude he assumed. He decided not to make compliments.

Mandelbaum replaced his daughter's picture among the other photographs. "She is, as you know, living abroad," he said.

"Yes," Kornilov replied. "Professor Mandelbaum, on January second you made your fifth —"

"Dvorah is the reason for my application to emigrate," Mandelbaum replied. "For my last four applications to emigrate." Again, he looked directly into Kornilov's eyes. "As you doubtless also know, Major, my daughter and I are the only members of our family left alive."

"Many people suffer misfortunes," Kornilov replied. "The interests of the party and state must, however . . ."

Mandelbaum turned his head toward the windows of the drawing room. "During the détente period, twenty years ago, many Jews were permitted to leave the Soviet Union," he said, as if he hadn't heard Kornilov's interjection. "Dvorah was fourteen. We sent her to live with my sister in Israel." He looked back at Kornilov. "She needed medical attention for a condition that is better understood there than in this country."

Kornilov bristled at the implied criticism of Soviet medicine. "What was her illness, please?"

"She has been diagnosed as a schizophrenic."

Kornilov stared at the calm man who faced him across the coffee table. "Your daughter is in an institution, then?"

Mandelbaum shook his head. "No. Medication was prescribed for her condition. Her life is a normal one. She is a successful model in Israel and France."

"But the pressures of such work on such a person —"

"As long as the pressures are impersonal, as long as she takes her medication, she is able to function as well as anyone else," Mandelbaum said. He took a deep breath. "Major Kornilov, when Dvorah went to Israel for treatment in 1973, I promised her that we — the rest of the family — would follow soon." Mandelbaum turned back to Kornilov. "But we didn't. The authorities rejected my first application to emigrate."

For a protracted moment he was silent. In the silence Kornilov could not resist yet another mental glimpse at his plan and the rewards he fantasized. *When it was over he would buy Ailya Ivanovna expensive presents. They would live on an island in a tropical sea, go naked, and have orgies on the beach with other women . . .*

Mandelbaum's gaze was still on Kornilov's eyes. "You have doubtless read in official files about what happened to my family since then," he said. "I will tell you the same facts to give you my perspective on these events."

Kornilov dragged his attention back to the present, the prelude to his marvelous scheme.

"My son was at the university, Major Kornilov. He was a homosexual. He had a lover, a student younger than himself. They quarreled. The young man went to the authorities and complained that Ivan had molested him. Our various police organizations are not always efficient. Before the KGB could intervene because Ivan was my son, the MVD beat him. They knocked out eight of his teeth and then said they were letting him off with the beating as a warning."

Mandelbaum took a long breath. He exhaled slowly. "There was gossip. My son became notorious as a Jewish child molester and pederast. He was shunned at the university. Occasionally he would come home with new bruises on his face because some Soviet patriot had punched the perverted Jew." Mandelbaum looked down at his hands. "Ivan endured the situation for more than a year. Then one morning he killed himself. Here, in this apartment, in the bathroom. He cut his wrists and bled to death in the tub. My wife found his body. She never recovered from the shock.

"Perhaps, Major, you are still wondering what all of this has to do with my applications to emigrate?"

"Go on," Kornilov said.

"There isn't much more," Mandelbaum replied. "My wife, as I mentioned, never recovered from what was done to Ivan and what he did to himself. She was a very brave woman — that is her picture on the left, beside the photograph of Dvorah. I knew that something inside of her had been broken and could never be repaired. When she died in the fire on the metro it was as if God wished to release her from her suffering."

The apartment was still. All the sounds of the outside world seemed to be muffled beneath the snow or suspended in the profound cold.

"After my wife's death, I had no reason to remain in Moscow, in the Soviet Union," Mandelbaum said.

"This is your country," Kornilov replied. "That should be reason enough for you to stay and continue with your work."

Gregor Abramovich Mandelbaum smiled. "A Soviet Jew's relationship to his country is, for him, an unrequited love affair, Major Kornilov," he said. "Like imperial Russia before it, the Soviet Union finds us suspect, accuses us of cosmopolitanism, creates a special secret police to watch us. It doubts our patriotism. Yet most Soviet Jews — and I am one of them — love this country, perhaps because we are Russians as well as Jews, perhaps because we know no other place." Mandelbaum raised his hands in a gesture of resignation. "To be Jewish and Soviet is to be afraid of the thing you love. Can you comprehend that, Major Kornilov?"

"It is not the —"

"We Jews are told that Israel is our real country," Mandelbaum said. "Maybe it is — if for no other reason than Israel is the only place in the world where Jews are in the majority. But that is not why I want to go to Israel. My reason is to keep my promise to Dvorah."

"Your promise to join her," Kornilov said.

"Yes. Keeping that promise means, to me, keeping my family alive."

The moment had come for Kornilov to make a gesture of sympathy. He told himself not to overdo it. "It is possible that mistakes were made in the case of Ivan Gregorovich Mandelbaum," he said. "Between us, Professor, I can tell you that it wouldn't be the first time. And the Moscow transit authorities have conceded a share of the responsibility for the fire in which your wife died. I believe you have been paid compensation?"

"I was sent a sum of money," Mandelbaum replied.

Now! Kornilov shouted to himself. *Test his disaffection. Everything depends on it.*

"I must warn you, Professor," he said aloud. "If you persist in these applications to emigrate, you will lose your privileges — this apartment, the dacha in the country, your car and driver —"

Mandelbaum held up his hand. Kornilov, in his eagerness, abruptly stopped speaking. "I will tell you what I said to President Gorbachev when he tried to dissuade me from filing my fourth application," Mandelbaum replied. "I explained to him that if I cannot be with my daughter, then it makes no difference to me whether I continue to live in this fine apartment and my country house. It is not even important that I go on living at all. This is my deepest sentiment, Major Kornilov. You — the state and party — cannot change it by bribery or coercion. I cannot change it and remain faithful to myself."

That was what Kornilov hoped he would hear. He was inwardly elated. The interview had reached its critical moment. "Professor Mandelbaum," he said, "I must give you my candid opinion — and I think you know what I am going to say. You will never be allowed to go to Israel . . . for reasons of state security."

Again, Mandelbaum looked at the long window. "Because of my work." He turned his head and looked at Kornilov. "Because of what I know."

"Yes."

Mandelbaum took a deep breath. "So . . . there is no legal way to leave the country . . ."

Kornilov understood such incomplete sentences. They were ways of saying the unutterable. He struggled to hide his excitement.

He slid his documents back into his plastic briefcase, stood up, and took his overcoat from the sofa. He put it on, then took a small notebook and pen from his inside breast pocket and scribbled, "Perhaps we could meet again — unofficially." As he wrote, Kornilov said aloud, "Withdraw your application, Professor. It will be denied. Return to your work."

He handed the slip of paper to Mandelbaum. The physicist read it in silence, as if he were making a decision. Then he nodded slightly.

Kornilov put on his hat. "Your telephone is tapped," he wrote on his pad. "Someone is always listening. I will let you know by other means when I am coming."

The wind had dropped. To the west a light smear in the overcast showed that the sun was trying to break through.

"The Jews of Moscow have spies everywhere," Kornilov said to Yarrow. "They pry out the secrets of everybody's life, even people inside the KGB. I knew that if Mandelbaum asked questions, some Jew could tell him about the conditions of *my* life — that my wife had left me for another man, that I was the oldest major in the Yevsekzia. I wanted Mandelbaum to find out these things about me. I wanted him to believe in our mutual desperation."

Yarrow's dislike of this drab, deceitful policeman had come upon him almost without his awareness. "What happened after your visit to Mandelbaum?" he asked.

"I wrote my report that afternoon," Kornilov answered. "It was on General Druznak's desk by four o'clock. In it, I suggested a way out of the situation. If Gregor Abramovich Mandelbaum could not be allowed to go to his daughter" — Kornilov shrugged slightly — "then, perhaps, I told Druznak, we could persuade Dvorah Mandelbaum to return to the Soviet Union, live with her father, and inspire him to resume his important work."

"And what did Druznak think of the idea?"

"It pleased him," Kornilov said. "It pleased everyone, including the president, because no one wished to harm Mandelbaum. A week later I was on an aircraft, flying to meet Dvorah Mandelbaum."

Yarrow looked puzzled. "*You* — a member of the Yevsekzia — went to Israel?"

Kornilov raised his head. "No. As well as her apartment in Tel Aviv, Dvorah Mandelbaum has a little house in France, on the Pas de Calais. I met her there on the eighteenth of January."

"And?"

Kornilov unbuttoned his overcoat, thrust his hand into his trouser pocket, and brought out a handkerchief. He blew his nose.

"I made her the offer outlined in my report to General Druznak." He shoved the handkerchief back into his pocket. "I told her she would be guaranteed a brilliant modeling career in the Soviet Union." He sniffed. "She is, as her father said, an unbalanced young woman. She had hysterics and accused me of putting her in an impossible position."

Kornilov turned his head and looked at Yarrow. "I will not try to present the rest of the facts in a good light. I pretended sympathy for Dvorah Mandelbaum. I urged her to keep an open mind. I told her that, in so important a decision, she should have the benefit of Professor Mandelbaum's advice and wisdom. I promised I would set up a postal conduit which would enable Dvorah and her father to write letters freely, without scrutiny by the KGB." He sniffed. "I needed letters in her handwriting as part of my plan," he said. "This part. Here. Now. Mr. Yarrow —"

He bent over and took a package from the straw basket. It was wrapped in stiff, gray paper held together by rubber bands. He handed it to Yarrow. "These are the letters Dvorah Mandelbaum wrote to her father between January twenty-fourth and the first week in March. I do not, obviously, have his replies to her."

Yarrow sat in silence, holding the packet and looking out at the stormy waters of the Kattegat. He could guess the rest of the story but he wanted to hear it in Kornilov's words. "I'm surprised that he trusted you."

A smile of self-satisfaction appeared briefly on Kornilov's face. "I made my motives appear mercenary," he said. "When I saw him next — on a walk around the Garden Ring taken with General Druznak's approval — I told Mandelbaum I would help him escape in return for one hundred thousand dollars, U.S." Kornilov's expression was solemn again. "We discussed the matter during three further meetings. Mandelbaum agreed to my proposal. We both knew that the Israeli government would give such a sum for him. I demanded a written promise that the money would be paid to me. He gave it. I pretended to be satisfied." The renegade KGB major looked out over the stormy waters. There was a note of disdain in his voice when he resumed speaking. "Mandelbaum talks about God and honor. He believes that everyone is as up-right as himself.''

"When did he finally make the decision to try leaving the Soviet Union illegally with your help, Major Kornilov?" Yarrow asked, trying to control his contempt.

"On March tenth," Kornilov replied. "I had Mandelbaum return to his institute and begin reviewing the work that had been done in his absence. He told his staff that he had been under severe strain in making the decision to withdraw his application to emigrate. He said he was going fishing on the Tuloma estuary before returning to work full-time."

"Did General Druznak give you permission to go with him?"

"Yes," Kornilov answered. "In the Yevsekzia I was, by then, considered the only officer who could handle Mandelbaum."

"On what date did you and your associates arrive with Professor Mandelbaum in —"

"Finland? April third, just before midnight."

"And you took these from him" — Yarrow gestured with the packet of papers — "to prove that you have him."

Kornilov nodded. "The Soviets were given photocopies of Dvorah Mandelbaum's letters. You have the originals, Mr. Yarrow."

"I'm flattered," Yarrow said drily. "There are no other Mandelbaum papers, are there, Major?"

Kornilov shook his head. "I told the Soviet and American embassies in Copenhagen that I had documents from the Mandelbaum Institute in order to get your attention. Such documents do not exist."

He took out a crumpled cigarette pack from his overcoat pocket and inserted a forefinger into it. "But Mandelbaum exists. In a place where you will never find him."

Kornilov raised his head and looked at the pale afternoon light on the stormy waters before them. The tide was coming in. The waves were breaking onto the beach twenty meters from where the two men sat. "Professor Mandelbaum is for sale, Mr. Yarrow. Bids will be accepted from the Soviet Union and the United States. The auction will be held the day after tomorrow."

"That is too soon, Major," Yarrow replied.

Kornilov turned his head. He pursed his thin lips. "Galkin said the same thing." He sighed. "It was my hope that the United States would be more flexible, that I could state the terms of the auction and you would —"

"Too soon," Yarrow repeated, barely able to contain his outrage. "There are many implications for the United States government to consider, many official viewpoints to reconcile."

"You are both creating an inconvenience," Kornilov said. He looked back at the waves crashing on the smooth, wet sand. He shrugged. "Very well. Bids for Professor Mandelbaum will be submitted on April thirteenth. The auction results will be announced on the fourteenth — one week from today. You will be informed of the time and place."

FOUR

ON APRIL 8 the rising sun burned like the memories of mystics and tyrants that lie deep in Mother Russia's soul. Its light fell upon Soviet Central Asia, touching the minarets of Alma-Ata with silver and sparkling on the dew of the Kirghiz Steppe, where half a million Turkic resistance fighters fell as martyrs to the Bolshevik Revolution. The new morning erupted in a soundless, blinding explosion over the Ural Mountains, driving the last shades of night westward across European Russia. The dawn was caught by the striped gold and siena domes of the cathedral of St. Basil the Blessed in Moscow. That great edifice, built by Ivan the Terrible and dedicated to the holiest of sixteenth-century Russia's Holy Fools, stands at the western end of Red Square.

The words for "red" and "beautiful" are the same in old Russian. The nine-hundred-yard-long square spread before the parapets and spires of the Kremlin was called Red for centuries before the coming of the commissars in 1917. Once it was filled with stalls, slaughterhouses, shops, whores' cribs, little wooden churches, and scaffolds for public executions. It swarmed with Russian merchants, artisans, priests, and madmen, Tartar horse traders, Jewish money changers, Uzbek hide-renderers, Caucasians, soldiers, and decapitators — all in the proximity of the divine and semi-divine. Behind the Kremlin's tunneled walls the churches and cathedrals of the Orthodox God soar in stunning splendor.

Now Red Square has been cleared of everything except two monuments symbolizing the Russian past and the Soviet present — the great cathedral of St. Basil and the dull red, two-story mausoleum that holds the remains of Vladimir Ilyich Lenin.

At sunup on April 8 Red Square was deserted except for the honor guard at Lenin's tomb and the sentries at the entrances to the Kremlin.

Shortly after 6:30 A.M., a long black limousine emerged from a street by the GUM shopping arcade, crossed the square at seventy kilometers per hour, and disappeared into the Kremlin through the ornate Spassky Gate. The new sun glowed on the gold domes of the Cathedral of the Assumption. Below, the light was a chill blue-gray in the Kremlin's streets and courtyards. As the Zil limousine slowed, it passed a sergeant of the day guard who was walking back to the duty office. He tried to see the passenger in the back seat, but the window glass was tinted and he could not.

The limousine turned a corner and stopped in a small alley behind the Palace of Congresses. The chauffeur, a KGB corporal, leaped out and opened the rear door.

The first deputy chairman of the Committee for State Security, Valerian Aleksandrovich Galkin, emerged slowly from the back seat with an aging man's early-morning stiffness. He stopped for a moment to button his gray raincoat. His little dog hopped out of the limousine and urinated on the curbstone.

Galkin was exhausted. During the previous thirty-six hours he had flown to Denmark on a Soviet courier aircraft, met Kornilov, been driven to Helsingør, taken the ferry to Sweden, gone by air to Stockholm, filed a report from the Soviet embassy directly to President Gorbachev, and then flown back to Moscow, arriving at 1:00 A.M. He had had only a few hours of fitful sleep. He was overwhelmed with disgust by his meeting with Maxim P. Kornilov in the cathedral city of Roskilde. From the top of his hairless head to the jowls that overflowed his collar, Galkin's skin was pallid. His eyes were dull, and his small, disapproving mouth drooped at its corners.

He snapped a leash on the dog's collar, handed its free end to the chauffeur, walked toward a rear entrance to the Palace of Congresses, and went inside. A uniformed sentry of the KGB's Ninth Directorate — which is responsible for the security of Soviet party and government leaders — pressed a button for the elevator.

There was a brief buzzing sound. The small foyer was flooded with green light for five seconds. The elevator doors slid apart. Galkin entered. The doors closed. Almost imperceptibly, the elevator began to rise.

The Mandelbaum-Kornilov affair was unfolding in a series of events that were like seismic shocks. Each created its own havoc. Gorbachev and his aides had absorbed the impact of Mandelbaum's disappearance and its implications for national security. Now Kornilov's proposed auction of the great physicist was a new trauma to test the equanimity of the Soviet president.

The elevator stopped with a slight jolt. The doors opened. Galkin stepped into a narrow, brightly lit corridor. He passed four uniformed sentries as he proceeded toward a closed door at the end. Gorbachev's personal bodyguards were all commissioned KGB officers. Only Russians, Belorussians, and Ukrainians were eligible for this exalted duty.

Galkin stopped at the door. A white-gloved captain inclined his head slightly. "Good morning, Comrade First Deputy Chairman." He held out an oblong device. "Please, say a few words."

"I am here to see President Mikhail Sergeivich Gorbachev," Galkin replied.

They waited for the voice that had just spoken to be matched with V. A. Galkin's voice print by a computer somewhere in the maze of security devices that surrounded the general secretary of the Communist party of the Soviet Union, who was also president of the Soviet state.

A penthouse on top of the Palace of Congresses was a private office complex for Gorbachev and his principal aides. With spacious views of the Kremlin, Moscow, and, on clear mornings, the Lenin Hills, they worked here in the early hours of the day. Gorbachev received visitors, held meetings, and conducted interviews in his official office at Communist party headquarters in Old Square.

The oblong device in the guard's hand chirped a clearance signal.

"Thank you, Comrade," the captain said. He opened the door. Instantly, Galkin was blinded by a burst of morning sunlight.

He stepped into the room, turned his head away from the windows, and closed his eyes for a moment. During that moment he was almost afraid.

It is not true that Peter the Great ordered the beheading of the messenger who brought him the news of his armies' defeat at the battle of Narva in 1700. But the legend underscores the Russian — and later, Soviet — conception of tyranny. It is both dogmatic and occult. Tyrants bestow order and provide an unreachable object for Russian piety to venerate.

When the tyrant falters or when autocracy collapses altogether, as it did between the abdication of Nicholas II and Lenin's seizure of power, fearful conditions ensue. The apocalyptic horsemen of the Russian nightmare — chaos, xenophobia, and want — thunder into reality. When the tyrant returns there is order again. It may be imposed by terror, but it is welcomed with relief.

Russia is goaded by its history. It has no tradition of, can barely conceive of, civil liberties coexisting with civic peace and harmony.

Thus, to intellectuals, to a new bourgeoisie created by *perestroika,* to hip or educated young people, to pleaders of special causes, to champions of democracy, rock music, and God, the freedom of expression that was prudently doled out under Mikhail S. Gorbachev's *glasnost* was a blessing. Gorbachev became their hero.

Millions of other Soviet citizens watched with apprehension as the revolutionary past was denounced, as restraint seemed to collapse, as western pop music and barbaric styles corrupted children, as anti-Soviet subversives bawled their anarchic garbage in the Congress of People's Deputies, as rebellion flared in the non-Russian republics and the promised rewards of economic reform failed to appear. Ancient fears of chaos and want were revived.

In his Soviet incarnation, the tyrant is also the great proprietor. The Communist party controls everything from the center, and the tyrant controls the party. Most Soviet citizens define their rights materially: cheap housing, guaranteed jobs and bonuses, free medical care, and state-subsidized price stability. If the tyrant were not strong he could not provide these things; if he strangles dissent and practices wholesale murder, it is because he is strong.

Mikhail S. Gorbachev was trying to decentralize power. He was warning that there might be unemployment, that the bonus might have to be earned, that manufacturing enterprises might set prices for their goods and wages for their workers. These possibilities were seen by his political enemies and large numbers of ordinary, disgruntled people as the heresies of a weak man whose so-called reforms threatened basic Soviet rights.

Pamyat — memory — stirred in millions of Soviet souls. There was nostalgia for the worshipful monster Stalin.

Galkin opened his eyes. The sun's scorching imprint remained for a moment. Through it he saw the president rise from a desk and approach him.

The pristine morning light lay on sofas, a smoked-glass coffee table, luxurious chairs, an intricate arrangement of icons on one wall, and a breakfast table set for two. As his vision returned to normal, Galkin could see the domes and roofs of the Kremlin. Just outside the windows of Gorbachev's suite, armed Ninth Directorate sentries strolled back and forth on wooden catwalks. Against the glare of the sun, the buildings of Moscow looked as if they were constructed of blue smoke.

"Galkin."

"Comrade President," Galkin replied, shaking the hand that was offered him.

The two men seated themselves at the breakfast table.

A servant came with glasses of fruit juice and poured steaming Turkish coffee. Gorbachev broke a roll and buttered one of its pieces. "I have read your report from Stockholm," he said. "Have the Americans had their discussion with Kornilov yet?" The president spoke rapidly but precisely, expressing neither surprise nor indignation. He was obviously a man who accepted the inevitability of unexpected events.

"We have learned that a senior CIA analyst of Soviet affairs named Yarrow — he is a man I know, Comrade President — arrived in Copenhagen yesterday," Galkin answered. "I believe he went there to see Kornilov on behalf of his government."

Gorbachev started to put the piece of buttered roll in his mouth, then stopped. "The ransom demand for Mandelbaum is unusual," he said. "No less than eight million dollars, U.S., no more than fifteen million. Why do you think Kornilov placed an upper limit on the sum of money he will consider?"

"He knows that we and the Americans will both bid fifteen

million dollars," Galkin answered. "I think that he has put a ceiling on the ransom in order to encourage the United States to offer him political asylum. Such an inducement could be the deciding factor in the auction."

Gorbachev put the piece of roll in his mouth, chewed and swallowed it. He sipped at his coffee and then touched his lips with a napkin. "What extra inducements, either rewards or threats, do we have?"

Galkin's memory for detail was vast. He could summon at will names, dates, statistics, descriptions, and technical data from files of cases he had been engaged in twenty years before. "Kornilov's father is living in a pensioner's hostel at Novokuznetsk," he replied. "Kornilov's wife left him for an Aeroflot steward last autumn. Kornilov tried many times to get her to return. He even offered her money. She is still in Moscow."

Galkin hesitated. He was a fastidious man. "Her name is Ailya Ivanovna Kornilova," he said. "She is a former chambermaid at the National Hotel. An uncultured woman. She was arrested twice before Kornilov married her — for selling herself to foreigners at the hotel."

"I presume you will have the father and this woman picked up," Gorbachev said.

"Yes, Comrade President. The wife in particular might have information that will help us in the search for Kornilov and Mandelbaum. Kornilov may even have contacted her. I have also ordered a search in Israel and France for Mandelbaum's daughter. It was to be with her that he wished to leave the Soviet Union."

Gorbachev turned his head and looked through the windows at the bright morning. Moscow's avenues and streets were becoming visible as the sun rose higher. Its rays flashed momentarily on the windshield of a moving vehicle far across the city.

The full implications of Mandelbaum's kidnapping were not yet clear because few Moscow insiders knew about it. Gorbachev and the late American president, Henry Clay Carpenter, had agreed in principle to negotiate an end to testing space-based defense systems. If the negotiations were successful, SDI would never be deployed.

Gorbachev desperately needed to eliminate the enormous research costs of the Soviet Star Wars program. Carpenter had conceded that the deficit-burdened Americans were also feeling the strain.

In both Moscow and Washington, cold war traditionalists, hard-liners, and visceral anti-Americans or anticommunists bitterly opposed the negotiations to stop testing SDI systems. Both Gorbachev and Carpenter retorted that they would be bargaining from positions of strength. The theoretic work of Gregor Abramovich Mandelbaum had given the Soviet Union a significant lead in one part of SDI development. America's advanced computer technology had bestowed superiority on the United States in other aspects of the exotic weaponry.

Then, suddenly, Henry Clay Carpenter died. The new president, James Forrest Burke, was weak and vulnerable, according to Gorbachev's analysts of American affairs. And now Mandelbaum, the crucial military asset, was gone. Unless he could be found, a dilemma would become a catastrophe.

Gorbachev turned back to Galkin. "If the Americans find or win Mandelbaum will they force him to tell them everything about his theoretic work?"

"Yes," Galkin replied, "but if we had Professor Mandelbaum's daughter" — he hesitated out of delicacy — "perhaps he would refuse to cooperate with them."

Gorbachev looked back toward the windows. The early morning haze had burned away. Trucks and cars were crossing Red Square. Swarms of pedestrians, black as insects in the sun's glare on Moscow's pavements, had emerged into view.

The president moved his plate and folded his hands on the table. "Is there evidence that others in the KGB assisted Kornilov in the kidnapping of Mandelbaum?"

"So far, no," Galkin answered. "I am inclined to believe that his help came from persons outside the Soviet Union."

Gorbachev nodded. "I don't envy you this task. Not only must you find Mandelbaum in six days, but you must be —" He looked at Galkin with the inquiring expression of a teacher who has just posed an arithmetic problem.

"Discreet."

Gorbachev laughed, briefly and softly. "Correct." His smile

disappeared. "It would obviously be better if as few people as possible were aware of this auction and your efforts to get Mandelbaum back before it takes place. Too many already know about the carelessness of the KGB in permitting such a man as Kornilov to be — even temporarily — the *nyanki* of the most important scientist in the Soviet Union."

The threat to himself wasn't lost on Galkin. "You have my assurance that only the most trustworthy personnel in Moscow and abroad will be involved in the search," he said.

"By that you mean people loyal to you, not your chairman?"

"Yes, Comrade President."

Gorbachev compressed his mouth for a moment. "The Americans will obviously be looking for Mandelbaum," he said. "The Israelis will probably be helping them. If there is violence . . ." He raised his eyebrows.

"There is no need to be concerned about violence," Galkin said, "unless the Soviet and American search parties discover the place where Mandelbaum is hidden at exactly the same moment. That is unlikely."

Gorbachev stood up. Slowly, he sidled around the table and crossed the room to the windows. He stood, hands thrust into his trouser pockets, looking at the light and the city's sprawl. "I dined with Mandelbaum a few years ago," he said, as if he were speaking more to himself than Galkin. "In most respects he is a highly intelligent man. But he refused to acknowledge the impossibility of permitting him to go to Israel." Gorbachev was silent. Galkin wondered if he was thinking with sorrow or outrage about the Jewish physicist. Gorbachev turned his head. "Now, Galkin. You."

"What about me, Comrade President?"

"I wish to know your motives. You have not been reluctant to assist me in this Mandelbaum business. You were not, as they say, born yesterday. You know that my enemies will now become yours."

"My chairman, Comrade Spassky, will not be pleased," Galkin said.

Gorbachev laughed softly. "Among others who would like to see me fall on my backside. Sergei Mikhailovich Spassky will not be chairman of the KGB much longer." Gorbachev looked intently at Galkin. "Do you hope to take his place? I urge you to be candid."

For years the KGB chairmanship had obsessed Valerian Aleksandrovich Galkin. Ambition had motivated his switch from the operations work he loved to the KGB bureaucracy. In his dogged climb up through the hierarchy of the vast police and espionage organization, he had permitted himself no close friendships. Friends can learn one's weaknesses and secrets. While Galkin had slept with many women, he had never loved one. Love might have deflected him from the prize he sought.

He had become more realistic as he grew older. He shrank from the tensions, the endless conflicts and expenditure of energy, that would be his lot if he became chairman of the Committee for State Security.

He dreamed instead of quiet and rest, of spending whole days propped up in bed with his little dog sleeping at his side while he read profound books and listened to West German recordings on his gramophone, of leisurely walks along the river on autumn afternoons, of splendid dinners, and winters in Italy.

"No, Comrade President. I am too old."

"What is it you want, then?"

Galkin had not expected to discuss his reward if he solved the Mandelbaum crisis. He pushed aside his fatigue and chose his words with care. "An honorable and comfortable retirement."

Gorbachev sniffed. He smiled quickly. "You wish to live a civilized life."

"A quiet life."

"They are the same thing," Gorbachev replied. "If you achieve this life, I will envy you."

Galkin pushed back his chair and stood up with a slight grunt of effort. His fatigue returned like the symptom of an illness as he thought of all the stress and labor that awaited him during the next seven days — including the day just beginning.

FIVE

THE ROAR of a helicopter settling onto the White House pad penetrated the Oval Office and spurred the president's dread. The helicopter was carrying a man from Andrews Air Force Base. The man was bringing in a dangerous, probably insoluble, problem. The president's anxieties had made him indecisive and caustic.

The shadows were lengthening on the Rose Garden and South Lawn. The sun had started its descent toward the western rim of the world. President James Forrest Burke turned away from the windows. "I can't remember his name," he said.

His national security adviser was standing on the other side of the desk. "Mandelbaum," he answered.

"No," Burke said irritably. "The man they're landing out there. The spy."

"Yarrow," said General Cresteau, "Jake Yarrow. He's not —"

Burke made an impatient, dismissive gesture with his right hand. "I know he's not a spy. He's an analyst or something."

The sound of the helicopter's engine dropped to a low rumble. It abruptly stopped.

The president was thin, of medium height. His face was sallow. The corners of his mouth were crimped and his eyes were dark and intense. He looked older than his fifty-five years. His features were usually arranged in the dyspeptic expression of a man plagued by stomach trouble. He slept badly, and frequently dreamed of people spitting at him.

He pulled back his chair, sat down at the desk, and flipped again through the twelve-page cable that Yarrow had sent to Edgar Pollack from Copenhagen the previous evening. "Christ," he muttered. He looked up at Cresteau. "This fellow Kornipov or whatever his name is —"

"Kornilov."

"He's done what no man or event has been able to do since

Reagan went to Moscow in eighty-eight. He's started the cold war again."

Cresteau looked at his watch. "I'd better fill you in on what's been going on and what's likely to happen at the meeting with Yarrow and the others."

The president nodded. "Sit down."

Cresteau drew a chair up to the desk and took a two-page synopsis from the breast pocket of his gray suit.

Through the long day, as *Air Force Two* crossed the Atlantic, bringing Jake Yarrow back to the United States, the American intelligence establishment had been assembling the components of an emergency task force. Its daunting assignment would be to discover where, in the great maze of the world, Gregor Abramovich Mandelbaum's kidnappers had hidden him. Some Hellenophile CIA official gave the task force its name — Orion, for Greek mythology's huntsman who became a constellation of stars.

The question of who would run Orion was temporarily put aside; it would be decided at an early evening meeting in the president's office. Copies of Jake Yarrow's cable from Copenhagen, plus updated interagency files on Kornilov and Mandelbaum, were classified top secret and distributed to seventeen top officials. The names, résumés, and clearance levels of specialists and technicians who would be available to Orion's director were pulled from the personnel files of seven federal intelligence agencies.

Because of the need to keep Orion's operations as secret as possible, half a floor of a downtown office building was requisitioned from the Federal Communications Commission, swept for bugs, secured, and put under guard. By midnight it would be fully equipped and staffed.

A synopsis of what had been planned, decided, allocated, appointed, arranged, and analyzed during the day was delivered to General Cresteau's White House office at 5:10 P.M. Copies were distributed to the senior intelligence officials who had been summoned to a meeting in the Oval Office at 6:00 P.M.

"Who'll be here besides Ed Pollack and Yarrow?" the president asked.

❖　66　❖

"Howard Cunliffe from State," General Cresteau answered, "Phil Teague from Defense —"

An expression of distaste crossed Burke's face. "Is there any way we can keep that son of a bitch out?"

"No," Cresteau replied. "But General Dunn will be with him."

The president grunted.

"We've also included Mary Sharp from the FBI," Cresteau added. "If there's going to be any disagreement at this meeting, it will be over who runs the Orion task force. I'm told that Phil Teague wants it based at the Pentagon, with himself in charge."

"No, goddamnit!" Burke snapped. "We're in enough trouble without Teague turning this thing into a right-wing sideshow!"

"Most people think that someone from the agency should be the director of Orion's operations, reporting to Ed Pollack," Cresteau replied. "Ed's already said he wants to put Jake Yarrow in charge."

"Is Yarrow willing to do it?" the president asked.

"Ed talked to him by radio telephone," Cresteau said. "He's apparently enthusiastic."

"What do you think?"

"I'm for it."

"Then that's decided," Burke said.

"If Teague makes a fuss," Cresteau said, "you can tell him that this is a job for CIA Operations and the Soviet specialists, not weapons experts."

The buzzer sounded on the president's twenty-line telephone console. Cresteau reached across the desk and picked up the receiver. He listened.

Burke swung his chair halfway around toward the windows. The light from the sunset glowed like molten gold. The eastern sky had turned pale in the vanguard of the approaching evening.

"Give us a couple of minutes," Cresteau said. He hung up the telephone.

The president swiveled his chair back. Indoor dusk was gathering in the Oval Office.

"They're all outside waiting," Cresteau said. "Mrs. Burke's holding on line eight."

The president took a deep breath. He reached for the telephone. "Turn on a few lights, will you?"

He felt as if he were powerless and knew nothing.

Almost daily, James Forrest Burke cursed the inconstant fate that had made him president of the United States. His true political vocation was in the Senate, where he had served quietly and usefully for twenty-one years. Then, with a vague sense of foreboding, he accepted the Republican nomination for vice president. The power brokers of the party needed his moderation and innate decency to balance a ticket headed by Henry Clay Carpenter, a tempestuous conservative.

Burke's foreboding had been justified. On New Year's Day, less than a year after his inauguration, President Carpenter suffered a fatal coronary at the luncheon table. Later that bleak winter afternoon, a federal appeals court judge administered the presidential oath to James F. Burke in the living room of the vice president's mansion, overlooking Massachusetts Avenue.

To survive the secret revelations, the institutional warfare with Congress, harassment by the press, public derision, international crises, and an official ceremonial and social life that would have destroyed Louis XIV, a president must be driven by a vision, a cause, or insatiable egomania. James Forrest Burke was not driven. He was secretly haunted by an unshakable conviction that he was inadequate. The presidency's relentless demands for decision, its recent tendency to displease most of the people most of the time, and the dangers inherent in the misuse of its enormous power intimidated Burke. After only three months in office, his days of executive duty were wearing him down like the waves of a corrosive sea.

He was alternately depressed and infuriated by the bitterness of his opponents. The remaining loyalists of President Henry Clay Carpenter despised Burke because he was not an ideologue of the right. Liberals despised him because he had served one. At dinner parties in Georgetown, Cleveland Park, McLean, and Rockville, women remarked with a pretended sadness that was really derision, "He's such a *little* man."

The president's accursed belief in his own inability was blighting the political landscape around him. Because Burke agonized and dithered over policy decisions, Congress ignored him in planning legislation. His cabinet was split between his own appointees and Carpenter holdovers. The bureaucracy, sensing deadlock, idled and waited. Burke was aware of the federal torpor his self-doubt had created. The realization intensified his insecurity. He yearned to give substance to his wasted decency.

Yarrow had been in the Oval Office more than fifteen times, and it always vaguely depressed him. The high-ceilinged room was too large for one man to work in with any feeling of intimacy. Even in the early evening, warmed by lamplight, with eight people filling it, the office of the president of the United States was white, bland, and antiseptic.

Brigadier General Marcus Aurelius Dunn, the director of the Defense Intelligence Agency, sat down on a sofa beside Yarrow. "Are you as tuckered out as you look, friend?"

Although Yarrow was wearing his usual jaunty combination of tweed jacket, bow tie, gray slacks, and loafers, exhaustion showed in his eyes and the deepened creases on his face. He smiled. "I got out of bed in Denmark a little before you did in Washington this morning, Marcus," he answered.

Dunn, a lantern-jawed Texan, took a 1928 Elgin railroad watch from his trouser pocket. "It's five past six here," he said. "That makes the time on your mental clock a little after midnight."

"Plus four thousand miles of air travel and nine hours of what passes for thinking at my age," Yarrow replied.

General Dunn put the watch back into his pocket and looked around the Oval Office. President Burke stood at his desk talking on the telephone. Edgar Pollack and Howard Cunliffe, the rotund, smiling head of the State Department's Bureau of Intelligence and Research, chatted with Deputy Director Mary Sharp of the FBI. General Cresteau was listening to Phillip Teague, an aging preppy who had been appointed assistant secretary of defense for international security affairs by President Carpenter.

Dunn bent his tall frame toward Yarrow. He lowered his voice. "You may be in a fight before you get out of here this evening, Jake," he said.

Yarrow shook his head. "Not me, Marcus. Too tired. If anybody wants something bad enough to fight me, he can have it."

Dunn looked across the room again. "The great defender of the republic over there thinks he should run the pack of dogs that'll be looking for Mandelbaum."

Yarrow raised his head. "Who, Phil Teague?"

Dunn nodded.

"Why does he want to do that?"

"Because he's fixing to grab the Russian professor for the Pentagon if our side does find him. Teague wants to make sure the DIA and the weapons analysts are the folks who pump all the information out of Mandelbaum," Dunn answered.

Yarrow looked at Teague again. "Well," he said, "if Phil wants to interrogate Dr. Mandelbaum and then make him work for our side, I guess I will have to pick a fight after all." He turned back to Dunn. "How do you feel about it?"

The general squinted in disdain. "I couldn't care less who handles the fella as long as the Russians don't get him back," he said. "But I'm just a little old general. Pretty-boy Teague over there's an assistant secretary."

The president finished his telephone conversation, hung up, and came around his desk muttering greetings and shaking hands with Mary Sharp, a pretty woman in her mid-forties. Burke sat down beside the fireplace. The senior executives of American intelligence settled into chairs and sofas around him.

Outside, the sun's lingering light had turned coppery red.

"Well," Burke said. "Welcome back, Mr. Yarrow. I don't mind telling you, I wish you'd sent us more cheerful news last night."

Yarrow had settled his large body at one end of a sofa. His right elbow rested on the arm. His hands were clasped against his chest. "I imagine the Soviets feel even more frustrated than we do, sir," he answered. "Their only consolation is that they've got a one-day head start on us in the search for Dr. Mandelbaum."

"What will they do with him if they find him first or manage to buy him?"

Yarrow looked at the cold, dark fireplace for a moment. His eyes shifted back to the president. "Technically, under Soviet law, he could be charged with treason."

"The man was kidnapped, for God's sake!"

"Yes, sir," Yarrow answered. "But Professor Mandelbaum made the kidnapping possible by trying to leave the country illegally with Major Kornilov."

"That's known as communist logic," Phil Teague said. He was thirty-six years old. His tousled blond hair and youthful elegance belied the virulence of his ideological passions.

"I doubt that there's much chance of anything as drastic as a treason trial if the Soviets get Dr. Mandelbaum back," Yarrow said. "He's too valuable. I expect they'll force him to return to his research."

"Jake," said Howard Cunliffe, "in your cable you quoted Kornilov to the effect that the Soviets had no way of making Mandelbaum go back to work."

"They didn't, as long as they were trying to be agreeable," Yarrow answered. "Now that a state of open hostility exists between Dr. Mandelbaum and the Soviet leadership, there is one, very ugly persuasion they can use."

"Torture," Phil Teague said.

Yarrow ignored him. "Dr. Mandelbaum's daughter lives in Israel and France, sir," he said to the president. "If she were abducted, taken to the Soviet Union, and held hostage to her father's cooperation, he'd go back to his research institute."

"Has anybody warned her?" Burke asked.

"Yes, sir," Edgar Pollack said. "After we got Jake's cable from Copenhagen last night, we told Israeli intelligence what's happened. They said they'd arrange immediate protection for Dvorah Mandelbaum."

"And what will the Soviets do if *we* manage to find or buy her father?" the president asked.

"I expect that the old-line ideologues will accuse us of staging the kidnapping," Yarrow answered. "They'll try to use the loss of Dr. Mandelbaum as a device to force Gorbachev to cancel the SDI negotiations." Yarrow shrugged slightly. "There will be an almighty row in the Politburo, the SDI talks will finally be rescheduled, and you'll get an agreement rather quickly, sir. The Soviets can't afford the research."

"Or so they claim," Phillip Teague said.

The president glanced at him, then at Yarrow. "I hope you're right, Mr. Yarrow," he said.

The sun had gone below the horizon. Its dull afterglow spread across the metallic sky.

"Edgar," Cresteau said to Pollack, "the question that's on all our minds is whether, realistically, we have a chance of finding Mandelbaum in the next six days."

The sandy-haired director of Central Intelligence compressed his lips in thought for a moment. "Well, to be frank," he said, the Soviets probably have a better chance. The way to find where Mandelbaum's been hidden — or to win him in the auction, if it comes to that — is to get inside Kornilov's mind, to try to reconstruct how and why he planned this operation. The KGB has more information about Kornilov than we do. They have access to people who know him — his estranged wife, his colleagues and superiors, his father."

Pollack turned to the president. "That's one of the reasons the agency wants Jake Yarrow to take charge of the Orion task force. He's talked to Kornilov and at least has a sense of him. Also, Jake's got more experience in dealing with the Soviets generally and the KGB —"

"No." Phil Teague had straightened up in his chair. He looked angry.

To his admirers, the young assistant secretary of defense was an uncompromising patriot. His detractors thought he was slightly crazy. Both, to some degree, were right. Phillip Teague's love of his country was the exasperated love of a father for a willful child that refuses to accept parental views of what's good for it.

"No, Ed," he said again to Pollack. "Not on. Mandelbaum's doing weapons research. Defense is the department most directly involved —"

"Mr. Teague."

Teague turned to the president. "Sir?"

"I've already approved Ed's request," Burke said. "Mr. Yarrow will head up the Orion task force. This is a job for the CIA's Operations people and Soviet specialists, not the weapons experts."

Teague looked at him in silence. Then he said, "Am I correct in assuming that if the task force succeeds in finding Dr. Mandelbaum, he'll be turned over to the Defense Department?"

Burke glanced at General Cresteau, then back at Teague. "That hasn't been decided yet."

Yarrow had picked up on the president's sudden alarm. "You don't need to decide it, sir," he said.

Teague grimaced angrily. "The hell he doesn't!"

Cresteau had also sensed the president's alarm. He ignored Teague's outburst. "I presume, Jake, that you have your own ideas about what we should do with Dr. Mandelbaum if we manage to save or buy him."

Yarrow nodded. He inhaled deeply, thrust his legs forward, shoved his hands in his trouser pockets, and looked around the circle. "Have you all read the file on Dr. Mandelbaum? Mr. President?"

"Wally's briefed me."

"Good," Yarrow said. "Our information conforms with what Major Kornilov told me. Mandelbaum's reason for wanting to come to the west is his daughter. His motives for leaving the Soviet Union, in other words, are personal and have nothing to do with political disaffection." Yarrow looked at the president. "I think we should do everything we can to get him away from Kornilov and then turn him over to the Israelis."

"The *Israelis?* Of all the —"

"Be quiet, Mr. Teague," Burke snapped. His dark, exhausted eyes were fixed on Yarrow's face. "Your sentiments are noble, Mr. Yarrow. But I'll have a congress and public to answer to if all of this comes out. What does the United States get in return for its effort, manpower, and perhaps fifteen-million-dollar auction bid if we rescue Mandelbaum and then give him away?"

Yarrow drew in his legs and leaned forward, elbows resting on his knees, hands clasped. "Depriving the Soviet Union of Dr. Mandelbaum's work, his genius, would be a major victory for this country, sir. That would be more than sufficient recompense for our time and money." Yarrow paused. "I have a pretty good sense of Dr. Mandelbaum. He's not a member of the Communist party, but he is a loyal Soviet citizen. He says of himself that he's as much Russian as he is Jewish. I don't think we should force him to compromise himself in return for our efforts on his behalf."

President Burke took a deep breath. "I still think that's a rather —" He paused, trying to find a dignified word that expressed his doubt. "— *generous* point of view, Mr. Yarrow."

"It's known as quitting before you get ahead," Phil Teague said. "Jake, whose side —"

Burke glanced at him. "Mr. Yarrow hasn't responded to my thought, Mr. Teague."

Yarrow smiled. "I think it's a practical point of view, Mr. President. You're about to start negotiations with the Soviet Union which, if successful, would end the research and development of space defense systems on both sides. If the KGB found out — and they would — that Dr. Mandelbaum was in this country working on our SDI program, your credibility in the negotiations would be destroyed. The Soviets would assume that we brought Dr. Mandelbaum here because we intend to go on working in secret on the American Star Wars project."

"Mr. President."

Phil Teague spoke in a flat, controlled voice. His facial expression was calm. His fists clenched on the arms of his chair were the only visible expression of his outrage. "I hope to Christ we *will* go on with space defense research in secret, because that's what the Soviets are going to do," he said. "Gorbachev's just trying to con us into ending *our* program until his thugs can steal enough of our technology to catch up. That's precisely why we *have* to have Mandelbaum working for us — to stay ahead.

"This man, Dr. Gregor Abramovich Mandelbaum —" Teague abruptly stopped speaking. Mentally, he groped for a more forceful argument. "Mr. President, we're talking about one of the greatest research — Jake Yarrow's actually proposing, sir, that we decline to avail ourselves of a man whose genius, if put together with our superior technology, *could turn the dream of space defense against nuclear attack into reality.*"

"Now, wait a minute, Phil," General Dunn said. "Even our own scientific folks aren't sure they can make all the parts of this thing work —"

Teague flushed. "Shut up, Marcus!" he snapped. "There's a lot you don't know!"

The assistant secretary's sudden, savage reprimand of General Dunn momentarily embarrassed everyone in the room.

The darkness outside the windows was nearly total. Lights sparkled on the Mall and glowed up the sides of the towering Washington Monument. President Burke sat with his right elbow propped on the arm of his chair. His right thumb was beneath his chin. His lips were pressed against his crooked right finger. His eyes had shifted to Teague.

"Phil," said Howard Cunliffe of the State Department's Bureau of Intelligence and Research, "Jake's got a valid point. If we forcibly recruit Dr. Mandelbaum we could be jeopardizing the SDI talks. That treaty with the Soviets —"

"— which hasn't been negotiated, or ratified by Congress yet," Teague snapped. He looked around the room. "*I* know what we ought to do with Mandelbaum," he said, his voice still tight with anger. "And I believe my opinion's shared by a majority in Congress and every American who isn't taken in by *glasnost* and the rest of Gorbachev's candy bar communism." He turned to Yarrow. "Tell us more about your solution, Jake. We turn Mandelbaum over to the Israelis, right? Then he goes to work on *their* weapons programs, right?"

Still leaning forward, Yarrow ignored Teague's icy sarcasm. "The Israelis aren't working on space defense. Dr. Mandelbaum's particular field of expertise would be of no use to them." Yarrow looked back at the president. "If Dr. Mandelbaum volunteers information about the Soviet SDI system, fine," he said. "That would be a bonus. I'm still against having him do research for us — even if he volunteers that, too — unless the negotiations with Moscow break down. If he refuses to cooperate in any way, I think we should ask the Israelis to reunite him with his daughter and then find someplace in the world where both Mandelbaums could live safely and in peace."

Teague was either genuinely amused or pretending to be. "Someplace like, say, *Patagonia*, Jake? Or an unmapped topical island where the Soviets couldn't find them?" he asked. He was smiling.

Yarrow nodded. "And where we couldn't find them, either, Phil."

Teague turned to Burke. "Sir," he said, "this is absurd."

The president hadn't changed his posture. His eyes shifted to Yarrow. Jake leaned back in the sofa. "What would you do if Mandelbaum refused to work for us, Phil?" Yarrow asked.

Teague's smile persisted, thin and utterly devoid of mirth. "I'm a realist, Jake. So's Sergei Spassky, the chairman of the KGB."

"Does that mean you'd do what Spassky would do?" Yarrow asked. "Lock Dr. Mandelbaum naked in a freezing blackout cell? Shoot him full of the kind of will-destroying drugs they still use on especially annoying dissidents in Soviet mental hospitals?"

Teague's smile remained.

"Would you kidnap his daughter, Phil?" Yarrow asked lightly. "Hold her hostage until her father cooperated?"

"One of your agency's venerable men, James Jesus Angelton, locked a KGB defector in solitary confinement for three years," Teague answered. "I'm talking about war, Jake. We're still at war with communism."

Yarrow turned to the president. "I don't envy you the job of deciding between us, sir."

Burke raised his head like a daydreamer who has suddenly been brought back to reality. "This has just come up," he said. His voice sounded as if it were on the verge of breaking. "We haven't talked about what happens to Mandelbaum . . ."

"The president needs time," Cresteau said. "And the search for Mandelbaum can't wait. Jake, does this mean you won't take charge of the Orion task force unless —"

"No," Yarrow answered. He looked across the room at Teague. "I'll run the search for Dr. Mandelbaum, Wally. I want to save this man. We'll do our damnedest to find him."

"That's swell, Jake," Teague said sardonically. "The Department of Defense will be really grateful when you hand him over to us."

"It will be my pleasure," Yarrow answered. "As soon as the president gives me a written order."

*

The young CIA driver put Yarrow's suitcase on the porch. "Don't you want me to take it upstairs for you, sir?" he asked.

By the light of a street lamp on the corner, Yarrow was trying to separate his front door key from others on a ring. "No thanks. I'll manage," he said.

"I'll tell them to have a car pick you up at six."

Yarrow found the key. "All right. Thanks again. Good night."

"Night, sir."

The young man went down the porch steps and crossed the sidewalk. Rain had been falling when Yarrow, Mary Sharp, and Edgar Pollack left the White House together. It had stopped after a few minutes. Wet leaves plastered to the cement pavement gleamed in the lamplight.

As Yarrow grew older, the sounds, textures, and images of his Oklahoma childhood had reappeared vividly in his senses and memory — the September smell of burning leaves, the hiss of snow and ice needles against his bedroom windows in winter, summer evenings spent on the front porch in Tulsa listening to the nocturnal buzz of insects.

After his separation from Louise he looked for a house that would evoke the vanished American time and the distant American place where his life had begun. It had to be old, made of wood, surrounded by trees — and it had to have a porch.

The white turn-of-the-century house he finally chose was in Cleveland Park, two blocks north of the National Cathedral. One porch curved around the front and west side. Another, at the back, overlooked a sloping garden.

He unlocked the front door, picked up his suitcase, and went inside. He turned on a lamp and flipped through the mail on the hall table, looking for Louise's distinctive handwriting or Mexican postage. There was no letter from her.

Yarrow went upstairs, into his room, and switched on the reading light beside his bed. He set down his suitcase and opened two windows to the moist, spring evening. At his desk he started to press the telephone answering machine's replay button.

He stopped. He was afraid.

He turned on the desk lamp, took off his raincoat and tweed jacket, and sat down.

It was 8:32 P.M. in Washington, 2:32 A.M. in Copenhagen.

Perhaps exhaustion had started the depression that he felt seeping into him, supplanting his brief apprehension. Perhaps his hope that there would be a letter from Louise — or a telephone message — had become an expectation.

Yarrow pulled apart the knot of his bow tie and drew the tie out of his collar.

He looked at the answering machine on the desk. His depression was stronger, adding its psychic lethargy to his physical and mental fatigue. It occurred to him that in Mexico Louise might have gotten a different perspective on her life, she might have decided that her freedom was too precious to surrender.

He told himself to stop being a damned fool. He pressed the replay button on the answering machine.

The tape whirred in reverse for eight full seconds. It stopped, readjusted itself, and then the voices began.

Between bleeps, they invited him for dinner, to an all-Mozart concert at the Kennedy Center, they asked him to call, wondered where he was, cracked inside jokes, and suggested an evening at the movies.

Yarrow listened, waiting for the faint static that would precede a call from Mexico.

Instead, Edgar Pollack's voice spoke after the sixth bleep. His tone was terse, urgent.

"It's ten minutes to eight. I know you're tired, but I need to speak to you immediately. Call the private number at my office."

On the tape Pollack hung up. The machine made another bleep. It was followed by the drone of a dial tone. There were no further messages.

Through the open windows Yarrow heard a car pass, its tires swishing on the wet street. He forcibly put Louise out of his mind and dialed Edgar Pollack's private line at Langley.

"It's Jake," he said. "What's up, Edgar?"

"You remember I told the president that we'd been in contact with the Israelis about protecting Dvorah Mandelbaum?" Pollack asked.

"Yes?"

"I had a telephone call from Moshe Simmel in Jerusalem when I got back here this evening," Pollack said. "He thinks something's happened to her."

"Tell me precisely," Yarrow said.

"Dvorah was scheduled to return to Tel Aviv from France this morning," Pollack answered. "She was to start filming a series of television commercials tomorrow. Her aunt says she wasn't on the plane from Paris. El Al listed her as a no-show. Dvorah spent the last three weeks in her house at Montreuil-sur-Mer, in northern France. It isn't certain yet when she left there."

"Are they sure she *did* leave?"

"Simmel tells me that Mossad's been in communication with Paris all day," Pollack said. "The French DGSE has established that on March sixteenth she made a reservation on today's flight to Tel Aviv. The DGSE sent people out to Montreuil-sur-Mer. They found Miss Mandelbaum's house in a mess — broken glass, pictures torn off the walls, chairs smashed. Something violent happened in that place before she left it. She emptied her local bank account and her car's missing."

"That's it?" Yarrow asked.

"That's it so far," Pollack answered. "Dvorah Mandelbaum's vanished. Gone."

❖ SIX ❖

BIZAARE and sluttish, Ailya Ivanovna Kornilova sat on a bench in the basement of Lubyanka screeching her indignation.

"People will be told!" Kornilov's wife shrilled.

Galkin and his assistant, Genady I. Oblomov, stood in a windowless office watching her on a closed-circuit television monitor.

"You will personally hear from people!"

Her interrogator, a young corporal, was reading from a folder on the table before him. He made no reply.

"My husband, General Maxim Petrovich Kornilov of the First Chief Directorate, is away on important business! But only temporarily!"

Although Ailya Ivanovna was still young, her short, plump body was already solidifying into a pillar of unyielding fat. Her bleached hair resembled a mass of sticky cotton candy. She had turned her face into a petulant mask with smeared-on scarlet lipstick, blue liner around her tiny eyes, and pancake makeup. She was wearing a black miniskirt. There was a hole in one black net stocking.

"You will personally hear from my husband, the general, the moment he returns!" she shouted. "He is well known for dealing harshly with anyone who subjects me to indignities!"

The uniformed interrogator finally raised his head. "Your husband, comrade, is not a general, but a major. He has not served in the First Chief Directorate of the KGB for twenty years."

Ailya Ivanovna glared at him. Her mouth was crimped into a little arc of umbrage.

The corporal placed his pen on the table. "Major Kornilov has committed serious crimes in which you may have played a part. We wish to know when you last heard from him —"

"I am a respectable woman!" Ailya Ivanovna screamed. "It is an impertinence —"

"You have been convicted twice for acts of prostitution at the

❖ 80 ❖

National Hotel," the corporal replied quietly. "Your former lover, Anastas Hagopian, an Aeroflot worker, has filed charges against you for stealing four hundred and seventy-three rubles and a short-wave radio —"

"Hagopian is a liar! A pederast!"

"The short-wave radio was found in your husband's flat when you were arrested there with a Belgian electrical engineer this morning," her interrogator replied, "a man you picked up outside the National at eleven forty-five last night."

Ailya Ivanovna squeezed her eyes shut, clenched her fists, drummed her small feet on the floor, and squealed.

Galkin twisted the channel knob of the television monitor. Other reception chambers flashed on and off the screen. He wondered where they were all located in the warrens of the old prison. Most of Lubyanka had been turned into offices and storerooms to accommodate the overflow from the KGB's adjacent headquarters on Dzerzhinsky Square and other buildings around Moscow. The main prison for interrogations was now Lefortovo.

But when Galkin first joined the KGB, Lubyanka had been the most dreaded building in the Soviet Union. Like the czarist fortress-prison of Peter and Paul in Leningrad, it was a symbol of the official sadism that pervades both Russian and Soviet history. Lubyanka had been a crypt for the living, a center for confession whose torturers had to be kept half drunk to make their work bearable. On some nights during purges the condemned were shot at three-minute intervals, filling the corridor outside the execution cells with bitter smoke, making the cement floors slippery with blood, vomit, and urine. Galkin believed that he could still smell the disinfectant that was supposed to disguise the stenches of Lubyanka's horrors the way Stalinist proletarian rhetoric camouflaged mass brutalities inflicted on the Soviet proletariat.

Two women and an old man in a sunny room appeared on the screen.

"That's him," Oblomov said.

Galkin turned up the sound.

The old man was sitting in a metal chair. He was dressed in a worn jacket with three medals pinned to its left lapel. His tieless shirt was buttoned at the throat. His face came to a sharp point at the tip of his nose; he had blue eyes and a thin, toothless mouth. He hadn't been shaved for several days. He tossed a red ball in the air, caught it with both hands, and threw it again.

One of the women wore the uniform of the Second Chief Directorate, the other a white smock. "Tell Sergeant Solovyov about Maxie," the one in white said.

"Eighteen," answered Petr M. Kornilov, catching the ball and tossing it into the air over his head again.

"Has he written to you, telephoned you lately?" the sergeant asked.

"Nineteen," the old man said, catching and tossing.

"He'll stop in a moment," the woman in white said. "It's an exercise for the reflexes they make them do at the Institute of Gerontology."

When Kornilov had completed his twenty-fifth catch he lowered the ball to his lap and seemed to notice the two women for the first time. He smiled at the one in the smock.

"Sergeant Solovyov wants to know if you've had letters or a telephone call from Maxie," she said.

The old man's eyes widened. "A woman sergeant!" he exclaimed softly. "Imagine!"

"Petr," the woman in white said. "Try to remember when you last heard from your son, Maxie."

"I saw him on Friday," Petr M. Kornilov answered, raising his eyes to the sergeant. "He came to visit us."

His gaze shifted. He looked at the sun-filled window. "Maxie brought sausages from Moscow," he said, rolling the ball in his lap. "There was a red mark on his collar. His mother says it was lipstick. Maxie said it was ink, a special red ink they use to write out their examination papers in the legal faculty at the university." He looked back at the woman in the white smock. "My wife doesn't believe him. She says he carouses with whores . . ."

"His wife died in 1977," the woman in the white smock murmured to the sergeant.

". . . She threw the sausages away because she said Maxie probably infected them with filth from the whores." Old Petr Kornilov sighed. His eyes suddenly filled with tears. "I don't know why she had to do that. She even accuses *me* of engaging in dirty practices with other soldiers when I was at the western front. Her priest — she's one of the Old Believers, you know — her priest says everybody is aware —"

"Maxie," the woman in white said. "Your son, Maxim P. Kornilov, is a major in the KGB. Try to remember if he's telephoned you or sent a message in the last few weeks."

The old man looked back at the windows. On the television screen the morning sunlight glowed like a nimbus behind his head. "How would a priest know what soldiers suffered?" he asked in the voice of a querulous child.

Galkin switched off the television monitor. "If he remembers anything it will not be reliable," he said. "Keep him here. See to it he is well cared for."

Breathing heavily through his nostrils, Oblomov followed him out a narrow corridor of whitewashed stone. "If Major Netsin's men are persuaded that Kornilov hasn't been in contact with his wife, let her go," Galkin said. "And have her watched twenty-four hours a day."

"Providing we can find enough people to put under that number of beds." Oblomov chortled at his own joke. He was a fat man with a ruddy complexion and red hair. Genady Ivanovich Oblomov had been put in the world to serve someone important. He excelled in the professional assistant's gifts of efficiency, zeal, and subtle self-depreciation. He knew exactly how to calibrate the special intimacy of servant and master. He was a compulsive wisecracker in a milieu where humor was as rare as pity.

They reached the end of the corridor. A uniformed sentry saluted and opened a heavy door. The first deputy chairman and Oblomov stepped into a freight elevator. The door clanged shut behind them. Galkin could hear the metallic echo volleying back along the passage, as if Lubyanka were reassuring him that, in its stone soul, it was still a prison.

Immediately after leaving the president's penthouse in the Kremlin the previous morning, Valerian Aleksandrovich Galkin had gone to his own office at 2 Dzerzhinsky Square. He had summoned Oblomov and his senior "reliables" — three veteran KGB officers who were longtime collaborators of the first deputy chairman. He had picked their brains about Kornilov's crime, motives, and modus operandi until late in the afternoon. Word of Galkin's secretive new activity would quickly percolate through every directorate of the KGB. A cover story was invented to explain it. The three reliables then went away to assemble groups of specialists who would help run the search for Mandelbaum.

Galkin wrote a confidential report to President Gorbachev summarizing the theories and arrangements arrived at during the day-long conference in his office. It was after midnight when he arrived at his apartment. He had been too tense and preoccupied to switch off his mind. Accompanied by four Ninth Directorate bodyguards he walked his little dog, Yosip. The cool urban darkness did not soothe him. Neither did a glass of hot milk taken at 1:17 A.M. Neither did a sleeping capsule.

Oblomov had scurried about for most of the night, ordering files, dossiers, maps, satellite photographs, and overseeing the installation of temporary offices and communications and technical equipment on the fifth floor of Lubyanka's west wing. Then he picked up the arrest report on Ailya Ivanovna Kornilova and went to the canteen at 2 Dzerzhinsky Square. As the sky brightened into morning, Oblomov drank black coffee, ate seven cream buns, and guffawed at the arresting officers' description of finding Kornilov's wife and the Belgian engineer in the bathtub.

Now, riding up in the old prison's elevator, Valerian A. Galkin tried to throw off the exhaustion that was denying him full access to his mind. He had finally fallen asleep at 4:30 A.M. and arrived at Lubyanka three hours later. As on the previous morning, brilliant sunlight was burning off Moscow's dawn mist. The air was moist and fresh.

Only six working days remained before the auction of Gregor A. Mandelbaum by Kornilov and his accomplices.

Oblomov giggled. "When they found the woman and the Belgian humping like porpoises this morning —"

"I do not wish to know the details," Galkin said stiffly.

The fat man expressed his own fatigue with gleeful banter. "You'll *have* to look at some of the details brought in from Kornilov's apartment," he said. "Wait until you see his private collection of photographs! If they gave a Lenin Prize for dirty minds, Maxim Petrovich —"

"Enough!" Galkin snapped.

The elevator stopped.

Still grinning, Oblomov said, "I think you will find everything — and everyone — as you ordered it. The workmen will be gone within the hour."

A guard opened another heavy metal door. Galkin stepped into a hallway. Before he could visually assimilate his surroundings he was assaulted by the combined sounds of a woman shouting on the telephone, other telephones ringing, a high humming noise, the whizzing mutter of several telex machines, and heavy, rhythmic blows of a hammer.

They were standing in a curved hallway ten meters wide. There was a row of dim, grimy windows high on the whitewashed stone walls. The floor was littered with sawdust and flattened cardboard packing cases. To the right, beyond two armed guards, newly constructed partitions rose halfway to the ceiling. Galkin could see that the partitions had turned most of the corridor into three large rooms; the hammering was going on in one of them.

Galkin looked left. A newly erected wooden wall sealed off the rest of the corridor. A third sentry stood before it.

"What was this place?" Galkin asked.

"A storage loft," Oblomov answered. "I chose it because it has never been used for offices and, therefore, it has never been bugged by the vigilant cockroaches of the Second Chief Directorate who spy on their colleagues."

"When you insult me, you insult the first deputy chairman of our organization!" the woman shouted from behind the first partition. She was one of Galkin's three senior reliables. "I will give you inside information! The Fifth Chief Directorate recommends that you be transferred to other work — washing the underwear of dwarfs, Uzbeks, and incontinent lunatics! *You will have those missing documents on MAXIM PETROVITCH — not Vladimir Sergeivich — Kornilov in First Deputy Chairman Galkin's office within fifteen minutes!* Do you understand, you yak's anus?"

"A true heroine of Soviet labor." Oblomov grinned. "I

love her." He gestured down the corridor. "Your room is this way."

The smell of fresh varnish burned V. A. Galkin's throat and eyes.

On being told to prepare an office for a high official at the end of the fifth-floor corridor, Oblomov's workmen had spent the night putting up plywood walls, which were then varnished.

"Let us review our discussion of yesterday," Galkin said. He blinked hard, cleared his throat, and shifted his stocky body in his chair. "We agreed that Mandelbaum conspired with Kornilov to leave the Soviet Union illegally. But he was obviously *not* an accomplice in his own abduction once Paavo Waltari had guided them to Finland."

The workmen had painted every windowpane black as a security measure. From behind his desk, Galkin spoke in an artificial twilight to the three reliables and Oblomov. They were sitting at a conference table in the center of the room. A green-shaded lamp suspended just above the surface of the table cast a stratum of light across the chests of the KGB officials. Their faces were in shadow.

"When Mandelbaum left Paavo Waltari's farm, then, it was as a prisoner," Galkin said. "This means that he had to be transported by automobile, private aircraft, or small boat to the place where they have hidden him. Therefore, that place — and the area we must search — is within one day's journey from Paavo Waltari's farm by such means of transport. Kornilov called our Copenhagen embassy on the morning of April sixth. Any comments?"

No one replied in the acidic dusk. Galkin's eyes were beginning to water. He took out a pocket handkerchief. "Our problem is, which of these means of transport did they use to take Mandelbaum to the hiding place?"

"My people have found something that may answer that question, Valerian Aleksandrovich," a male voice said. A chair was pushed back from the table. A small man rose and crossed the back of the room. "Sonya?"

From the table a slide projector shot a beam of light across the room. A mottled gray picture appeared on a screen in a far corner. Within seconds it was brought into focus.

"This is an image of the Soviet-Finnish frontier taken by the satellite Cosmos 1704 at five twenty-nine on the morning of April fourth," said the man beside the screen. His finger pointed to its right edge. "This is Soviet territory. This is the border. Here" — the finger pointed to a dark patch — "is Paavo Waltari's farm on the Finnish side of the border. We assume that Kornilov's associates were waiting for him and Mandelbaum at the farm. The town of Ivalo" — his index finger moved across the projected aerial photograph to its center — "is here, forty-four kilometers to the west. Sonya, if you please."

The next black-and-white satellite picture which appeared on the screen was gritty and, on first viewing, barely decipherable. "The airport at Ivalo," said the man beside the screen, "enlarged. This" — he pointed to a shape on the runway at the slide's upper right-hand corner — "is an American-built Cessna 210. The angle of the shadow beneath it indicates that the airplane was taking off as the satellite photographed it just after sunrise on April fourth. Thank you, Sonya."

The projector was switched off. The screen went black.

"Now," said the man at the screen, "let us, please, open the windows. This place stinks like a chemical dump."

A uniformed officer rose from the table and walked to the windows. He pulled up the first with a muscular yank. Morning light fell on his flat, expressionless face and black hair. He was a Mongol. He moved to the next window, inserted blunt fingers into the clasps, and jerked it open. He was middle-aged but his abdomen was flat. He was tall by the standards of his race. His shoulder insignia identified him as a colonel-general of the KGB Border Guards Directorate. He opened a third window. Air as refreshing as a sudden rain in the desert swirled through the office's acrid atmosphere.

There were murmurs of relief.

"Thank you," Valerian Galkin said.

General Khorloin Tseden returned to the table. Academician Yuri F. Tsarapkin left the projection screen and also resumed his seat. He was a tiny man; his dark gray mustache, bristling hair, and small string bow tie made him look like a Mexican bandit. Tsarapkin was a member of the Soviet Academy of Sciences. He was also a senior official of the KGB's Directorate T, which specialized in the theft of advanced technology and technological secrets from the west. With an expert's vanity, Tsarapkin loved reciting facts and figures. He was regarded as a genius and a compulsively garrulous bore.

"The Cessna 210 can carry five people including the pilot," he said. "Its range, at maximum, is a thousand statute miles. It was photographed about five and a half hours after Kornilov, Mandelbaum, and Paavo Waltari came over the border."

There was a knock on the plywood door. Oblomov got up and crossed the room. A uniformed enlisted man handed in an envelope. Oblomov came back to the table and gave the envelope to Sonya Krebsky, the woman who had been shouting when Galkin arrived on the fifth floor. "From the first deputy chairman's office," Oblomov said.

Sonya Krebsky was a clinical psychologist in KGB counterintelligence. She was tall and broad-shouldered with a prominent jaw. She wore a blue sweater, trousers, and American running shoes. Her dyed blond hair was raffishly unkempt. She tore open the envelope, took out a stapled document, and flipped through its middle pages. She read, looked puzzled, and then turned back a number of pages. "Idiots!" she suddenly barked.

"What's happened?" Galkin asked.

She held out the document as if it were contaminated. "Your Directorate of Personnel first sends the file of the wrong Kornilov! Now they send the right one, but look — *look!*" She folded back the thick wad of paper and thrust it toward Galkin. "Page eighty-eight! The end of section three — Kornilov, M. P., service at the Copenhagen residency —" She turned a page. "One hundred and fifteen! On page one hundred and fifteen he is back in Moscow! Everything between page eighty-eight and one hundred fifteen, all the London information — *missing!*" She threw the dossier over her shoulder. It hit the wall behind her and landed on the floor in a sprawl of pages. "Galkin! Is it possible that your friend Mikhail Sergeivich Gorbachev could persuade those fools in personnel —"

Galkin scribbled a note on his desk pad. "I will get you Kornilov's complete file," he said in the quiet voice he had always used to calm her. Sonya Krebsky had been his last lover. Now in her late forties, she had become a passionate feminist. She refused to use her patronymic and shared her large flat in the Arbat district with a woman plumber.

"Thank you," she said sarcastically.

Galkin nodded at Tsarapkin. "This Finnish airport at —"

"Ivalo," Tsarapkin answered. "Commercial flights arrive and depart in the afternoon. Small planes like the Cessna are hired by parties of hunters and sport fishermen. But not at this season. The Cessna's departure at sunup that morning was definitely unusual."

"It was taking off in which general direction?" Sonya Krebsky asked.

"Southwest."

"Kornilov worked in Denmark and Britain," Oblomov said. "May we assume that this small airplane could have reached either during daylight hours on the fourth of April?"

Tsarapkin nodded. His eyes were bright in his small, leathery face. "Leaving Ivalo at five thirty that morning, the Cessna could have made a refueling stop at Uppsala in Sweden around nine thirty or ten, given favorable winds and weather conditions. From there, two and a half hours flying time to Copenhagen, a little over five hours to the English Midlands."

"If they filed flight plans and used commercial airports," Galkin asked, "how would they unload Mandelbaum, drugged or bound as a prisoner?"

"My guess," said Tsarapkin, "is that the Cessna made an unscheduled landing somewhere — in a pasture, on an abandoned airfield, perhaps — put Mandelbaum and one or two guards off the airplane, and then continued the flight to its registered destination. It would have disappeared from crowded radar screens for less than ten minutes. Later, with new registration numbers, it could have been flown back to the place where Mandelbaum was being held prisoner."

"I have something . . ." Sonya Krebsky was rummaging through a large canvas bag.

Morning noises floated in from the KGB compound all around them and the city beyond. Prokofiev's exhilarating Classical Symphony blared from a small radio speaker. Closer, on some adjacent window ledge, pigeons made throaty love sounds. An automobile horn blared far, far away in the radiant day.

Krebsky took a clear plastic envelope out of her canvas bag. There was a small green booklet inside. "A forged Polish diplomatic passport found this morning taped to the rear underside of the sink in Kornilov's apartment," she said. "It carries the name Jerzy Wadlewski. Using his official *Soviet* travel documents, as we know, Kornilov flew to France to see Dvorah Mandelbaum on the eighteenth of January. In this counterfeit passport there are stamps which show that he went to London late on the afternoon of the eighteenth. As Jerzy Wadlewski he arrived in Copenhagen on the evening of the nineteenth, returned to Paris on the morning of the twentieth. He took an Aeroflot flight back to Moscow at noon that day using his Soviet passport."

"Very clever," Oblomov said.

"Too clever, I think," she answered. "Hiding such an incriminating document in such an obvious place . . ." She tossed the plastic envelope on the table and looked at Galkin. "It is my guess that we were supposed to find this counterfeit passport. But the reason eludes me for the moment."

The first deputy chairman shifted his stocky body in his chair again. His right hand arranged and rearranged three pencils and a pen on the desk before him.

"You have brought us back to the most important question," he finally said, "one that became clear to me as I thought about our discussions of yesterday." Galkin raised his head and looked at Sonya Krebsky. "Is Kornilov shrewd, or is he a man of limited intelligence? If he is shrewd, then he *wants* us to find the forged Polish passport and satellite photographs of the aircraft leaving Ivalo. A shrewd Kornilov would plant such evidence in the hope that we would concentrate our search for Mandelbaum on Denmark and Britain — which means that Mandelbaum has been hidden somewhere else."

Galkin was perspiring, a symptom of his tension. He rose slowly and took off the double-breasted jacket of his English suit.

The action made him feel exposed. As he aged he had come to regard his body as ugly.

He crossed the room to the center window. "Or," he said, "we may be dealing with a man of limited intelligence." He looked down into a small courtyard. "I do not mean to suggest that Kornilov is stupid. He could be capable of conceiving a plan to kidnap and auction Mandelbaum but unimaginative in thinking out the details."

The fresh morning air was cooling the first deputy chairman. Outside, the pigeons departed with clattering wings. The radio was now playing martial music. Galkin turned around to his senior subordinates sitting at the conference table.

"This Kornilov of limited intelligence *would* hide a forged passport behind a kitchen sink last January because it had cost him money and could be useful another time," he said. "It might never occur to him that a Soviet satellite would photograph an aircraft taking off from northern Finland."

He returned to his desk and sat down slowly. "Such a man would hide Mandelbaum somewhere in Denmark or Britain — countries he knows, whose languages he remembers, where, possibly, he still has friends whom he visited in January using his forged Polish passport."

Galkin looked at General Tseden. "I have spent much of the night considering this critical question of which Kornilov we are dealing with. I have concluded that he is the man of limited intelligence — an ordinary man, if you prefer, not someone of exceptional intellectual powers. Everything we have discovered about him so far suggests such a conclusion."

The Mongol general nodded. He was head of training for the KGB's 350,000 border guards, and that chief directorate's principal disciplinarian. Tseden was feared and hated by his Russian subordinates. After twenty-five years in the Soviet Union, he still spoke Russian that was choppy and ungrammatical. "I have choose three men. We begin at smuggler's farm. We talk to him."

There was an encyclopedia of unimaginable brutalities in the phrase "talk to him."

"Perhaps," Sonya said, "there is someone who was on duty at the Ivalo airport on the morning of April fourth —"

"We talk to them," General Tseden said.

Oblomov shuddered. Khorloin Tseden's personality — if he had one at all — was unreadable. He had been recruited by the KGB from the Mongolian People's Republic, where he commanded border patrols in the Gobi Desert. Oblomov had heard sickening tales of what happened to Chinese bandits when the Mongol manhunters captured them.

Galkin had a concerned expression on his face. " 'We'? Are you planning to go with your men to Paavo Waltari's farm and Ivalo?"

"Yes."

"But if you were caught in Finland . . ."

"I am not to be caught." Tseden pushed back his chair and stood up.

Yuri F. Tsarapkin was stuffing papers into his briefcase.

"You will all report to me immediately if there are new developments," Galkin said. "General, reserve a short-wave radio sideband for your communications."

"It's been taken care of," Tsarapkin said. He smiled at Tseden with an expression of self-satisfaction.

The Mongol general conveyed his annoyance by staring blankly at Tsarapkin.

"Bring me the list of our reliables in Denmark and Britain," Galkin said to Oblomov. "Sonya, a moment more of your time."

Tsarapkin left, followed by General Tseden and Oblomov, who closed the door behind him.

Sonya Krebsky remained seated at the conference table, facing Galkin. He was momentarily embarrassed by his own sentimentality. To him, physical intimacy created a special bond between those who shared it. He knew that Sonya had had too many lovers of both sexes to entertain such romantic notions about any of them.

"Your opinion, please," Galkin said. "Have I made the right assumption about Kornilov?"

Her gray eyes contemplated him for a long moment. "I cannot be completely certain until I have analyzed all the data on him," she finally replied. "But, as you said, there are no indications of brilliance in what we know about him so far."

"What else?" Galkin asked.

"In my opinion you were wrong when you said that Kornilov may still have friends in Denmark and Britain," she said. "It is already obvious that this man's depression and profound feelings of inadequacy make him incapable of friendship with men. I expect that he has never experienced love for a woman, only sexual fantasies." She was silent again for a moment. "This presents us with another question." She took a light blue packet of French cigarettes from her canvas bag. "May I smoke?"

"Pazhalsta."

Sonya lit a cigarette, exhaled, and picked a bit of tobacco from the tip of her tongue. "It is obvious that Kornilov is not operating alone. He has people, a whole organization. Who does a friendless man go to for help in making such arrangements? Who can he trust?"

Galkin took a deep breath. He folded his hands on the desk top, turned his head, and looked through the open windows. The sun was in its midmorning ascent. The radio was playing a waltz.

"Someone who can travel abroad, meet people, make contacts and arrangements," he replied. He looked back at Sonya. "A man whose connection with Kornilov is not based on friendship but a mutual desire for money. Greed."

"A mutual desire strong enough to overcome sexual jealousy?" she said.

Galkin nodded. "Or perhaps Kornilov deliberately arranged his wife's infidelity with Anastas Hagopian to disguise the fact that the two men had pooled their resources to kidnap and auction Mandelbaum. It would not require great originality to think of such a protective strategy."

Sonya crushed out her cigarette in a heavy glass ashtray. "No, just the morals of a goat. Do we know where Hagopian is at present?"

Galkin picked up a yellow report sheet from his desk. "Oblomov brought me this an hour ago. Hagopian was chief steward on an Aeroflot flight to Copenhagen on April third. He failed to report for the return trip to Moscow the next day. We have begun the usual searches."

Sonya Krebsky nodded. "So. Substance for your theory. Could

Kornilov and Hagopian alone organize the Mandelbaum abduction?"

Galkin shook his head. "No. But Hagopian could recruit the necessary people in the west. Probably among the criminal classes in Denmark and Britain. Kornilov's clandestine trips to London and Copenhagen in January could have been for the purpose of meeting the candidate accomplices contacted by Hagopian."

Sonya Krebsky took a thick brown envelope out of her bag, stood up, and moved around the table. "My people are waiting for me in our elegant plywood room outside," she said. "Please do not forget that I need the London pages of Kornilov's dossier." She stopped beside Galkin's desk and looked down at him.

"I will remember," he said. He was embarrassed again. Being physically close to her agitated him. He was afraid that she would make some overture, a gesture that he was no longer capable of responding to.

She laid the brown envelope on the desk. "A little present, my dear. Something I thought might amuse you."

Galkin was puzzled. He looked up at her. "What is it?"

"Major Kornilov's collection of pornographic pictures. It was also found taped under the sink in his apartment this morning and delivered to me."

She suddenly smiled at him. Whether it was a seductive or mocking smile Galkin could not tell.

He had not heard bird song or any other country sounds. Nor, in the small room where he was being held, did Gregor Abramovich Mandelbaum hear the swelling and diminishing noises of a city by day and night.

All four walls of the room were made of concrete. There were no windows. Daylight entered through a small square of translucent glass in the ceiling. The door was made of heavy timbers bolted together vertically.

Gregor Mandelbaum had put the room's rough, wooden table beneath the skylight, stood on the table, and pressed his hands against the glass. It was thick, slightly flexible, and, he suspected, shatterproof. He could open the skylight a few inches but not enough to wriggle out through it.

Sometimes Mandelbaum picked up the sounds of trucks and automobiles passing the building in which he was imprisoned. Once he had heard a man singing drunkenly late at night and then shut up as a high voice remonstrated angrily in an undiscernible language. Frequently, during the afternoons, the physicist heard the shouts of young men engaged in a game, football perhaps. These sounds suggested that he was in a village or small town, that the building in which he was being held was near a school.

There had been five men waiting in Old Paavo's barn when he, Kornilov, and the smuggler arrived just before midnight on April third. To Mandelbaum's astonishment, one of the men knocked him down. Another pointed a military rifle at him while his arms and legs were bound. Then the man who had hit him slit the right sleeve of his coat and shirt up to the elbow and injected something into him with a hypodermic needle. Within a minute Mandelbaum had lost consciousness.

He had awakened on the concrete room's small cot with aching shoulders, wrists, knees, and ankles. He was ravenously hungry. These symptoms indicated that he had lain, bound and unconscious, for a very long time, a day or more perhaps. It became immediately obvious that his captors did not want him to know where he was.

Since then he had been fed in the morning and at dusk by a silent young man who wore dark trousers, a heavy shirt, and workman's boots. Shaving equipment was brought to him after breakfast by the young man, who watched and then took away the soap, towels, foam, and razor when Mandelbaum had finished.

When he had asked for books, pencils, paper, and permission to bathe, the young guard-servant ignored him; he was obviously under orders not to speak to the prisoner. This was evidently part of a security plan. Mandelbaum had no way of knowing whether his captors were Russian or whether Kornilov had recruited foreigners to help him. His only real discomfort was the staleness of his unwashed body.

As he rested and exercised his stiff joints, Gregor Mandelbaum considered everything that had happened. It was obvious now that Major Kornilov had been plotting to kidnap him since their first meeting on the eleventh of January, that his demand for one hundred thousand dollars was a ruse. This conclusion did not make the physicist angry, just profoundly sad; he had allowed himself to believe that Kornilov would get them safely out of the Soviet Union and that Dvorah would be waiting for him. Mandelbaum had written to her, telling her where he would cross the border into Finland and approximately when. He knew that putting such things on paper entailed great risk. But he had come to trust Kornilov and the secret postal drop the Yevsekzia officer had set up for exchanges of letters with Dvorah.

Now, in his concrete room, Mandelbaum wondered what desperation underlay Kornilov's gray, melancholy nature.

He had concluded something else; they were going to auction him. There was no other logical reason for kidnapping him.

He did not want to think about what the Soviets might do to him if they won, or what the Americans might demand of him. Both of these powerful countries knew that Gregor A. Mandelbaum had a daughter. Both were capable of taking Dvorah prisoner — as a hostage to ensure her father's cooperation, or to inflict the official wrath of the Soviet Union upon her.

The maximum danger to Dvorah would be after the auction was over. But if neither side won, she would be left in peace.

Thus, on the second day of his incarceration, Gregor Abramovich Mandelbaum decided that he would kill himself before his captors could sell him.

He looked around the concrete room at his tweed jacket, at the two blankets on his bed. He pulled out his shirttail and examined it. He calculated that, using his fingernails, he could unravel enough thread and tear off a sufficient number of cloth strips to weave a rope long and strong enough to bear his weight. He would break off a chair leg, tie the rope to one end, slip it through the skylight, and stand on the table with the other end of the rope knotted around his neck.

He would have to work fast. He felt great peace within himself. He was sure that God, who knew his thoughts, would forgive him.

REGIMENTS OF RAIN marched across the night, drenching Washington, drumming on the porch and roof of Yarrow's house, rumbling away to the east, to Chesapeake Bay and the dark Atlantic. Twice, summoned by thunder, he drifted up to semiconsciousness, listened, and then slipped away to sleep again.

He awoke to a day of low clouds and fitful rain. He shivered in the raw cold as he crossed the bedroom to close the windows. By 6:15 A.M. Yarrow had bathed, shaved, and dressed and was standing in the kitchen drinking coffee and reading the op-ed page of the *Washington Post*. Perry and Harry Dockerty were the enraged twins of political journalism. On the morning of April 9 their column was shrilling wrath at the chairman of the Joint Chiefs of Staff because he supported Soviet-American negotiations to end the testing of SDI systems.

At 6:25 A.M. the doorbell rang. Yarrow folded the newspaper as he walked out into the front hall and opened the door. A short, dark-haired young man from the Directorate of Operations was standing on the porch.

"Hello, Tiger," he said.

"Good morning, sir," Chadwick replied.

"To what or whom do I owe the pleasure of your company this morning?"

"They've assigned me to you for the duration," Tiger Chadwick answered.

"As what?"

"Bodyguard. Doubling as chauffeur was my own idea."

Elwood Potter Chadwick IV — aka Tiger Chadwick — had been born on Boston's Beacon Hill. Since 1824 every Chadwick had gone to Harvard. Tiger enrolled at the University of Michigan to annoy his father and grandfather. Law and business were considered appropriate academic pursuits for Chadwicks. Tiger had majored in Russian. Then, being a born snoop, naturally aggressive, and having nothing better to do, he joined the CIA and was assigned, after training, to Operations.

Yarrow looked puzzled. "Why in the world would I need a bodyguard?"

"I can go out for coffee and kill people who annoy you," Chadwick said.

"That's a thought," Yarrow replied, shrugging on his raincoat and following him down the porch steps. Tiger's cheerful pugnacity amused him.

Margery Ferrall, Yarrow's assistant for thirteen years, was in the back seat of a Chrysler limousine double-parked on Macomb Street. She was a plump, amiable woman who wore horn-rimmed glasses and also spoke fluent Russian. "Hi," she said as Tiger closed the door. "How's your jet lag?"

Yarrow settled himself on the seat. "Nonexistent so far," he said. "I trust you've been behaving yourself."

"Without even trying."

Tiger slid in behind the wheel and slammed the front door.

"What's up?" Yarrow asked.

"You've got clearance from Mr. Pollack to have Henry Muffin run all the task force's operations in Scandinavia," Margery said.

"Do we bypass the Helsinki station chief?"

"No, we tell him about Kornilov and Mandelbaum, tell him not to tell his ambassador, and then tell him to give Henry whatever he needs."

"I think I got all that," Yarrow said. "Repeat it to me at noon."

The limousine was hissing through the wet streets of Cleveland Park, passing Victorian and 1920s stucco houses set back from the sidewalks. Lights were being turned on. Men in bathrobes and pajamas retrieved newspapers from porches. Dogs, stupid with sleep, stood on lawns considering urination. A light wind swayed the trees, shaking momentary showers onto the car's roof, hood, and windshield.

Margery described the Orion task force. The staff was small. It was composed of Soviet analysts and other specialists plus a few technicians. A variety of experts in several disciplines from other U.S. intelligence organizations had been cleared and put on standby as consultants to Orion. There would be two twelve-hour shifts with a senior CIA Sovietologist in charge of each. The National Security Agency had taken charge of communications.

"We moved onto the fifth floor at M Street just after midnight," Margery said. "You can make any personnel changes you want. This is just a start-up crew appointed by the director."

"If Edgar Pollack picked them, they're the people I would have chosen," Yarrow said. "Have you been up all night?"

"Yes. You have a meeting at seven thirty. Henry Muffin will be looped in on a secure circuit from Copenhagen."

"I want you to go home," Yarrow said. "Somebody else can help me today."

"I'll go home when I'm tired," she replied.

Tiger had turned the Chrysler into Massachusetts Avenue. Washington is a city of early commuters. It was not yet seven but a heavy stream of traffic was already passing the British embassy compound.

"The director's coming in for lunch before he goes up to brief the Senate Intelligence Committee," Margery said.

Yarrow wondered if Louise would call before the day was over. He wondered if his office at Langley would let him know if she did. He forced himself to put her out of his mind and focus on the problem of where and how to search for Gregor Mandelbaum. Only six days remained before Kornilov's auction. Yarrow's solar plexus tightened.

"Who's been in charge so far at M Street?" he asked.

"Joe Humphrey."

"Good. I'd like him to go on running things overnight as long as we're in business."

Rain was falling again. Blue, black, and striped umbrellas bobbed across Dupont Circle and down gleaming sidewalks as the limousine turned into Connecticut Avenue.

Tiger stopped it at a red light. "Has anything hard on Mandelbaum turned up yet?" Yarrow asked.

Margery shook her head. "Nothing."

The conference room of the Orion task force looked like a combined military bunker and picture gallery. Enlarged satellite images and maps of the northwestern Soviet Union, Finland,

Denmark, and southern Britain covered one cream-colored wall. More than sixty photographs of Gregor Mandelbaum, his daughter, Dvorah, and Maxim Petrovich Kornilov had been taped to another. A massive blackboard divided into days and hours hung at the far end of the room. Its space for April 9 was already a third filled with summaries of telephone calls, radio communications, and meetings, scribbled thoughts, reported rumors, notations of events and assignments.

At 7:25 A.M., on his way to the head of the conference table, Yarrow paused to look at the pictures of Mandelbaum. After reading and rereading intelligence files on the Soviet physicist's life, work, and character, Yarrow had a distinct sense of the man. The seventeen photographs on the wall helped make him visually real. Yarrow admired Mandelbaum. The contempt he had felt for Kornilov on the beach in Denmark still festered in him. He ignored the photographic display devoted to the Yevsekzia officer.

As a professional model in Israel and France, Dvorah Mandelbaum had been photographed for more than a decade. Yarrow was struck by her dark, frail beauty.

He was about to sit down at the head of the table when he noticed an official Soviet portrait of Valerian A. Galkin fixed to the wall with thumbtacks. "What's that doing here?" he asked.

"It's our morning surprise," said Joe Humphrey, a slightly paunchy, dark-browed CIA Soviet analyst in his early fifties. "Galkin had a private breakfast meeting with Gorbachev yesterday, according to a message just passed to us by our best friend in Moscow. Dzerzhinsky Square's jumping with rumors that some sort of scandal's coming down and that Galkin's been assigned to damage control."

Yarrow shoved his hands into the pockets of his auburn tweed jacket as he contemplated the photograph of Galkin.

The two men had known of each other's existence for thirty years. They had sparred at long distance, met half a dozen times at summit and disarmament conferences. They once spent three days together in Lisbon negotiating an exchange of captured spies. Yarrow admired Galkin's professional abilities and personally disliked him. The feelings were mutual.

"Well," Yarrow finally said, turning away, "the scandal they're speculating about is undoubtedly the disappearance of Mandel-baum." He pulled back a chair and sat down at the head of the table. "Since Volya Galkin went to Denmark to talk to Kornilov, I've been assuming that he's running the Mandelbaum recovery squad in Moscow."

Lester Brundance, the senior operations officer, took the seat at Yarrow's left. He was a tall, impeccably dressed man who, at fifty-five, looked forty. He spoke in the vowel-flattened accent of Providence, Rhode Island. His habitual amiability overlay a character so tough that Brundance was liberated from the need to prove how tough he was. "Want me to ask about your jet lag?" he said to Yarrow with a grin.

Yarrow shook his head. "Margery already has."

The conference room was narrow and windowless. Banks of fluorescent bulbs on the ceiling filled it with bright, diffused light.

Joe Humphrey sat down at Yarrow's right. A stenographer had set up her dictation machine at the far end of the table.

There was a small microphone, a speaker, and a telephone on the table in front of Yarrow. "Is Henry Muffin with us?" he asked.

"I hear you, Jake," Muffin's voice answered from the speaker.

"Good morning," Yarrow said. "Give Dorothy my love and tell her I'll be writing to thank her when this thing's over."

"Right."

"Time is not our friend," Yarrow said. "Let's get started." He leaned forward and folded his hands on the table. "Henry, Joe tells me you've sent a man from Helsinki up to Lapland."

"To a town called Ivalo," Muffin's deep voice answered in the speaker. "If you've got a map . . ."

Brundance stood up and turned to the large map of Finland on the wall. "The Soviet-Finnish border," he said, touching a meandering line far above the Arctic Circle. He moved his finger. "This is Ivalo — about fifty kilometers or so to the west."

"Thank you," Yarrow said. "We see it, Henry."

"Kornilov told you that he and Mandelbaum came across the border on the third of April," Muffin said. "But he didn't say where. I believe he mentioned that when they left Moscow it was ostensibly to go fishing on the Tuloma estuary."

"He did," Yarrow said.

"If they set off for Finland from there after the middle of March," Muffin said, "then it's more than likely they went south-west, parallel to a highway, and crossed the border somewhere around Ivalo on April third. When I was station chief in Helsinki I had a pretty good asset there, an old smuggler named Paavo Waltari who sometimes escorts people across the Soviet forbidden zone if the price is right. I sent Pete Durward up this morning to see if Old Paavo knows anything."

"Presuming he does know something, will he talk?" Yarrow asked.

"Like I said," Muffin answered, "if the price is right."

"We found out last night that Dvorah Mandelbaum's missing," Yarrow said.

"So I read in the overnight traffic."

"In her letters to her father she wrote that she'd be waiting for him when he came out of the Soviet Union —"

"Durward has a picture of her," Muffin replied. "He'll ask around."

"Good," Yarrow said. "Anything else, Henry?"

"Not at the moment."

"Stay with us." He looked around the table. "Let's review our first assumption — that Mandelbaum's being held somewhere in Denmark or Britain."

"Kornilov may have confirmed that for us," Joe Humphrey said. He got up and turned to the photographs on the wall behind him. "We sent copies of every picture we've got of him to our colleagues in London and Copenhagen late yesterday afternoon. We had an interesting fax back from the Brits at about five this morning. We enlarged their most important picture."

He pointed to a grainy black-and-white photograph measuring eleven by fourteen inches. It showed Maxim P. Kornilov talking to a uniformed man seated on a stool behind a tall desk. There was a crowd of people in the background.

Humphrey's jowly face was gray with fatigue in the fluorescent lighting. "Jake, I believe Kornilov told you that he met Dvorah Mandelbaum at her house in France on the eighteenth of January?"

"Right. In the early afternoon, I think he said."

"Okay. French immigration records confirm that he arrived at Orly airport from Moscow on the morning of the eighteenth," Joe Humphrey said. "That evening a man carrying a Polish diplomatic passport went through British immigration at Dover. The name on the passport was Jerzy Wadlewski. The Brits secretly photograph every East Bloc diplomat who enters the country." Joe Humphrey turned around and looked again at the large, coarse photograph on the wall. "This is the shot they took of Jerzy Wadlewski at Dover on the evening of January eighteenth. They recognized him as Kornilov from the batch of photographs we sent to London. Presumably Maxim Petrovich bought the fake Polish passport in the Moscow underworld."

There were murmurs of surprise.

"Dvorah Mandelbaum's house is at Montreuil-sur-Mer, near the Atlantic coast," Humphrey said. "That's about thirty-five miles from Calais, where the ferries and Hovercraft leave for Dover. Kornilov had plenty of time to drive from Paris to Montreuil-sur-Mer that day, talk to Dvorah, and then go on to Calais and catch a night boat for Dover."

"What have you got from the Danes?" Brundance asked.

Humphrey took a sheet of legal paper from the table. "Jerzy Wadlewski went through Danish immigration at the Copenhagen airport on the evening of January nineteenth," he said. "He left for Paris the next morning." Humphrey looked at Yarrow. "Major Maxim P. Kornilov was a passenger on the noon Aeroflot flight from Paris to Moscow that same day, the twentieth."

Yarrow looked back at him for fifteen seconds. "The way this supposedly clandestine trip was carried out seems pretty amateurish for a man who once worked abroad for the KGB First Chief Directorate," he said. "My question is, were we *supposed* to find that picture and, alerted by it, check the dates Kornilov went to London and Copenhagen under an assumed name? Did Kornilov make that trip last January to persuade us now that Mandelbaum is hidden in either Britain or Denmark?"

"When did MI-5 start photographing East Bloc diplomats at immigration stations?" Brundance asked.

"Good question," Yarrow said.

"We don't know that, either," Humphrey answered.

"If the photographing started after 1971, after Kornilov was deported," Yarrow said, "he'd have no reason to think that we could connect his face to Jerzy Wadlewski's name."

Brundance picked up a telephone, punched three numbers, and murmured an order.

Humphrey stood up and moved around behind his chair, the long sheet of legal paper in his hand. "We got a couple of other items from London," he said. He gestured at an eight-by-ten photograph on the Kornilov section of the wall. "This was taken in October 1970 through the window of a Chinese restaurant on Fulham Road."

Yarrow took off his glasses and got up to see the picture.

It was a black-and-white scene that reminded him of one of Edward Hopper's paintings of night and human loneliness. Behind its glass window, the Chinese restaurant was empty except for a couple at a table in the center of the room. The man was unmistakably a younger Kornilov. He sat with his hands in his lap, looking at the limp paper decorations hanging from the ceiling. His narrow clerk's face was expressionless.

His companion was a woman in an overcoat sitting with her back to the camera. She had long, dark hair that fell over her shoulders like fabric. She was leaning slightly forward, as if she were eating. The breakdown of communication between Kornilov and the woman was palpable. "Her name is Ellen Worth," Humphrey said. "*Lady* Ellen Worth."

He pointed to another photograph that was taped to the wall. It showed a long-haired young woman with a full face and large, intense eyes. Her mouth had been caught in a sensuous half smile. "Here's what she looked like in 1967."

Again, he looked down at the sheet of paper in his right hand. "Daughter of a hereditary peer, joined the British Communist party while she was at Oxford in the sixties, briefly married in 1966, met Kornilov in March 1970." Humphrey looked at Yarrow again. "At least that's when the MI-5 people following Kornilov began to pick up on her. The relationship lasted until Kornilov and everybody else in the KGB residency were kicked out of Britain in the autumn of seventy-one."

Yarrow sat down again. "Do they know if Kornilov contacted her when he was there last January?"

"MI-5 and the police are trying to find her," Humphrey answered. "She seems to have dropped out of sight sometime after Christmas." He looked at his watch. "Okay. It's eight fifteen, Jake," he said. "One fifteen in London, two fifteen in Copenhagen, half a day gone, only five and a half days left to find Mandelbaum —"

Yarrow's right leg had become numb. He pushed his chair back, stood up, and began to knead his thigh. "Just a moment, Joe," he said. "Les, tell me briefly how you've organized the first stage of the search."

"Well," Brundance said, folding his arms, "MI-5 in Britain and Danish counterintelligence are drawing up lists of people who might have known Kornilov twenty-five years ago — prostitutes, old Communist party members. We're feeding London and Copenhagen everything useful that our readers pull out of American and Israeli files." He looked up at Humphrey. "I assume they're working on the criminal circuit, yes?"

Humphrey nodded. "Began last night."

"What's that?" Yarrow asked.

"Word's being passed around the London and Copenhagen underworlds that somebody's offering a lot of money for information on men being held prisoner, hostages," Brundance answered. "The same message is going out offering rewards for information about foreigners trying to recruit professional criminals — wheelmen, gunsels, tough guys, airplane pilots, you name it — in London or Copenhagen for a big-money kidnapping operation." He paused and looked across the table at Yarrow. "We're trying to decide whether to send out photographs of Mandelbaum and Kornilov to friendly services around the world, saying we're looking for one or both of these guys but not why. The trouble is, Mandelbaum's so well known that everybody would catch on in five minutes."

"Wait on that for a few hours," Yarrow said. He straightened up and leaned against the wall, hands clasped behind his back. "Obviously, he isn't working alone —"

Brundance nodded. "But we know absolutely nothing about his organization, how he put it together, whether its members are Russians or outsiders —"

"And we haven't time to find out," Yarrow said. "We simply have to start with an acknowledgment that the organization exists. I have a question about it, but I want you to talk first. Are you actively looking anywhere else?"

"In Finland," Brundance said. "But not as thoroughly as Denmark and Britain. Like Henry said, a man from the Helsinki station's gone up to the Ivalo area to look around."

Yarrow was silent for a moment. He raised his head and stared at the large, oblong map of Finland on the wall to his left. "I have two questions that need answers — or at least theories."

He looked back at Lester Brundance. "First, is Kornilov the man actually running this kidnapping operation or is he working for somebody else? And second, if he is in charge, is he shrewd enough to plan that trip in January in order to manipulate the way the Soviets and ourselves think in April? Or did he go to London and Copenhagen believing we'd never find out about it?"

"Theory only?" asked Henry Muffin's voice.

Yarrow leaned toward the microphone on the table. "Let's hear it," he said.

"The fact that it was Kornilov who met you on the beach in Liseleje — and the whole setup there — tells me he *is* the head man." Muffin said.

"Go on," Yarrow said.

"There was that black-haired guy with the rifle in the dunes behind him, along with another bodyguard," Muffin said. "They were there for one of two reasons — either to protect their chief, Kornilov, or to kill him if he tried to double-cross some other leader.

"Kornilov was wearing a radio transmitter, microphone, and earpiece," Muffin went on. "You told him you wouldn't talk to him until he unwired himself. He broke his microphone cord to oblige you. The guy with the rifle would have blown his head off when he heard the radio circuit go dead — *if* he and his pal were there to make sure Kornilov obeyed somebody else's orders."

"I've come to more or less the same tentative conclusion," Yarrow said. "Does anyone else —"

The telephone rang. Lester Brundance picked it up, listened, murmured "Thanks," and replaced the handset. "Margery's just talked to Eric Cope in London," he said. "MI-5 began photographing East Bloc diplomats at immigration stations in 1974."

"Three years after Kornilov left Britain," Joe Humphrey said. "You've got a hard fact, Jake. Kornilov didn't know he'd be photographed when he went to London on January eighteenth. It wasn't a manipulation of us, he was really there on business. Let's get off our asses."

Yarrow held up his hand. "Wait. Tell me something about the preliminary psychiatric analysis of Kornilov. I see on the board that one's been worked up overnight, yes?"

"Yes." Lester Brundance opened a folder on the table before him and leaned over to read a document. "A depressive, a man of low self-esteem," he said. "The psychiatric profilers think he's incapable of forming real friendships. His isolation from other people means he trusts no one. If he had any close friends he'd probably be willing to share authority in this caper with them — he's not obsessive about being in charge of things." Brundance raised his head. He turned his tanned, boyish face toward Yarrow. "But he hasn't any close friends."

"All right," Yarrow said. "Henry, do you have everything you need?"

"Yep," said Muffin in Denmark. "I've got three of our guys working the street and nine from the PET — that's the national police and counterintelligence here, in case anybody doesn't know. They can whistle up anything we want, from criminal contacts to the Royal Danish Navy. They've also put two people full-time on cross-filing for more Kornilov information from the late sixties."

"Go," Yarrow said. "Have your man in Lapland report to us directly, and we'll need to hear from your office every four hours at least."

"You got it."

Yarrow looked at Lester Brundance, "What about Britain?"

"We've briefed Mike Lodge, the London station chief," Brundance said. "He's also been ordered to keep his ambassador in the dark. He's using four of his own men. Eric Cope's assigned ten MI-5 types to us, plus organizational backup."

"Tell Mike and Eric to get going," Yarrow said to Brundance. "I'd like to see you in my office in fifteen minutes to talk about the worldwide distribution of photographs." He smiled at Joe Humphrey. "Good work. Go home. You're exhausted. There'll be an information update meeting here at nine thirty. Anybody have anything else?"

Humphrey shook his head. "What are your own thoughts, Jake?"

"They're numerous," Yarrow answered. "And mostly skeptical."

On his way out he stopped at the door. The stenographer was packing her equipment. "I want just one copy of these meetings transcribed," he said. "Typed, not done on a word processor. The copy, along with your tape, should be given to Miss Ferrall in my office."

She was an overweight, pale young woman with straw-colored hair. "Yes, sir."

Yarrow smiled. "Thanks for coming in so early."

Her round cheeks reddened. She returned his smile and was almost pretty.

The Orion task force had been installed in a suite with seven offices opening off a large, central room. The bland cream walls, rust-colored carpeting, and gray metal desks were designed for the sensibilities of toilers in the minor federal bureaucracy.

Yarrow went out into the main room. The sounds of the task force were muted. He heard high-speed Teletypes buzzing and chiming softly, voices speaking in English and Russian. He looked into a storage room that had been turned into a temporary communications and recording studio by technicians from the National Security Agency. He introduced himself to the two on morning duty. "Am I right in assuming that you'll be taping all the telephone conversations and radio transmissions we get and send?" he asked.

"Yes, sir," a sandy-haired young man answered. "They're doing backup recording of us out at Fort Meade just in case something breaks down here. Both are totally secure."

"Good," Yarrow said. "And your worldwide monitors know what sorts of radio transmissions are of special interest to us?"

"You can bet on it, Mr. Yarrow," said a young black woman with a set of earphones around her neck. "We'll also trace all your incoming calls. We can get a fix on where they're from within twenty seconds."

"Amazing," Yarrow said.

He went back to his own office. Through its open door he could see a rain-streaked window and the CBS News Washington bureau on the other side of M Street.

Margery was standing at her desk with a handful of telephone messages. "Louise called the office at Langley," she said. "She's coming back from Mexico tonight, changing planes at Houston. She'll be on a Continental flight that gets into Dulles at ten forty-four. It might be nice if we sent Tiger out to meet her."

Yarrow felt exhilaration rise within him. It was instantly followed by the strange anxiety he felt whenever he tried to think about Louise, himself, and the future.

"I'll go," he answered, "unless war breaks out."

She stood at the edge of the birch grove as the sun died behind the western hills. She was fighting to keep time in sequence and to focus her mind on the real images before her. Up in the barn the old man was bellowing in pain and fury.

Without her medicine, she'd felt her sense of time collapse and fragments of the past swarm up to mingle with the realities of the present. That afternoon she'd kept hearing the gray policeman telling her in Russian that her father would suffer if she didn't go back and live with him. As she crawled out of the cave and went down the wooded hillside, she'd been simultaneously reliving the weeks of hiding in her house, trying to fight off the pressure. She'd wandered in the woods but didn't see them because she was re-reading her father's letters that told her he was going to escape. There was pressure behind her eyes as if her head were going to explode.

At the top of the meadow the square door of the barn was filled with light. The four men who had come across from the Russian side at first twilight were hurting the old man in his barn. He roared again, he cursed, he screamed through his phlegm-clotted throat.

If the Soviets killed her father as he was trying to escape, it would be her fault because she refused to go back to Moscow. The chair told her that, and she had smashed it. She decided to stop taking her medicine because she wanted to withstand the pressure without its help. That's when past and present began to get all mixed up together. After she dumped her pills down the toilet of her house in Montreuil-sur-Mer, they began to torture the old Finn.

There were fiery streaks behind the hills in the west. The old man's tormentors were yelling at him. She had gone totally out of contact a week after she threw away the medicine. Everything that showed her reflection made her face look twisted. She had smashed everything that made her look twisted and grotesque, everything that told her it was her fault.

The old man howled, his sound penetrating through the cataract of noises and images in her mind, the fragments of the past that kept repeating themselves, over and over. If the old Finn who had left out food for her died, it would be her fault.

In the darkness she saw the frown of Madame Dessarin at the bank. "So much money, Mademoiselle, are you certain —"

"*Oui,*" she whispered, knowing that her beautiful face looked mad, that her eyes, wide and staring, looked mad. "*Oui, suis sur . . .*"

The old Finn kept fuel in a large can that stood in the tall grass beside the barn. She knew that because sometimes she had walked around his farm, even into the house, when he wasn't there.

He howled again and again in agony and outrage. She clamped her hands over her ears, but she still heard him. Everything in her house reminded her that it would be her fault if Papa died. She smashed pictures, furniture, kicked rugs into corners, broke windows, flooded the bathroom trying to drown the distorted, ugly vision of herself in the cabinet mirror.

The old man kept matches and cigarettes on a workbench just inside the back door of the barn. She had tried to burn down her house because it blamed her. The gray policeman from Moscow had put the blame on her like a hex, and the house quivered with the reverberation of his blaming for weeks after he left.

The old Finn screamed in a voice unredeemed by the nobility of outrage. She remembered that he had been kind to her, leaving food and blankets in a cage on a plank. If he died, it was not going to be her fault.

She dashed up the sloping meadow in the dark. She fell, got up, and ran again, fast. She had driven fast in the car to escape from the house and furniture, which kept blaming her. She drove and flew on airlines to the place where she had told Papa in her letters she would be waiting for him. She had left her medicine behind in the pipes of the toilet because she had to deal with everything on her own — reading the map, finding the place to go, booking the airline tickets.

The night was like the nights that came upon her at noon when her illness was at its worst. She needed light. She unscrewed the top of the fuel can and sloshed it, emptying it on the side of the barn. The roaring in her head was from the past and present, the accusing Russian policeman's voice in her house, the desperate cries of the Finn.

She opened the back door. In the barn's bright interior she saw the old man's half-bald head, the twirls of his thin gray and blond hair as they held him down on a table. One torturer was sawing off his thumb. Another, an Oriental whose face expressed neither anger nor compassion, was leaning over, questioning the old man. He writhed and twisted in the grip of his tormentors, a dreadful, gibbering growl coming from his throat.

She took the matches, backed out, and closed the door.

The sea at Pointe de Lornel on a summer morning. The sea at Natanya, north of Tel Aviv, on a summer morning. She went out at dawn and swam naked, luxuriating in the cool of the sea and the warmth of the rising sun.

A cool evening wind brushed over her, extinguishing the first match. She felt the heat as the side of the barn burst into flame the instant she threw the second match. The torturers inside shouted and cursed.

She picked up a small scythe from the workbench as she walked back into the burning barn through the rear door. Chunks of wood fell into the flames around her as she reached the table and cut the ropes that bound the old man.

With her arm supporting him, Paavo Waltari was able to stumble toward the barn's rear door. His left hand hung at his side, a fingerless, thumbless pad of bloody flesh.

In front of the barn, his arm raised to shield his face from the heat, General Khorloin Tseden squinted at the inferno. For an instant he saw the woman.

Her clothes — a brown-gray suede jacket and jeans — were torn. Her gray-streaked black hair was matted with mud and tangled. Dirt smudged her face. There were cuts and bruises on her cheeks, forehead, and hands.

Tseden turned away from the blistering heat for a moment. When he looked back, she was gone.

Dvorah Mandelbaum had dragged Old Paavo out of the barn, into the night.

❖ EIGHT ❖

AFTER DARK, the floodlit terminal at Dulles International Airport becomes a fantasy Japanese temple — which was what its architect intended. The airport, twenty-five miles west of Washington, is thus an alien structure on the lip of Virginia's Shenandoah Valley.

The temperate winds of an April night blew in romping gusts as Yarrow drove out the long access road to Dulles. His little Honda was rocked by one final buffeting as he turned it into the airport parking lots.

Yarrow locked his car, dropped his key into his jacket pocket, and walked toward the main terminal. Bright floodlights shone on the parking lot's damp asphalt and were reflected in wide puddles left over from the day's rain.

He crossed a sidewalk and stepped onto a rubber pad. Doors whished apart. Yarrow went into the terminal and up to the domestic arrivals level. He glanced at his watch. It was exactly 10:30 P.M. On the announcement board above the escalator, Continental Airlines flight 848 from Houston was posted for arrival at gate ten in fourteen minutes.

Yarrow bought a cup of coffee and leaned against a wall. The airport's night people — sleeping children, crying children, passengers arriving or waiting to depart, airline employees, ennui-numbed janitors pushing long brooms up and down the crowded concourse — were human ciphers around him.

He had spent the afternoon and early evening presiding at conferences and information update meetings, reading documents, and holding conversations. Reports, rumors, and exchanges of theory with the British and Danish police and counterintelligence services had poured in on the Orion task force's communications circuits. Late in the day a National Security Agency official arrived with a tape recording of five odd radio transmissions made at Fort Meade during the previous thirty-six hours. They were bursts of unconnected words in Russian and came from the general area of northern Scandinavia. The cryptologists of the NSA had been unable to discover a code pattern or to pinpoint the origin of the ten- and twelve-second broadcasts.

In Europe, only five days remained before the auction. The sixth day was ending in the American night.

Yarrow sipped lukewarm coffee and watched an airport policeman trying to give directions to a trembling, haste-pressured old man. Yarrow tried to avoid looking at a seated young couple entwined around each other, kissing noisily. He glanced across the concourse and saw his wife coming through smoked-glass doors, looking around hopefully.

Louise Cassidy Yarrow was fifty-four and startlingly beautiful — but not by the conventions of the late twentieth century. Her dark red hair, only slightly muted by touches of gray, was piled on top of her head in a large Victorian bun. Her face and long neck were dense with freckles. Her eyebrows were so light as to be almost invisible. She had cool, gray eyes. The first time Yarrow saw her, it had seemed to him that nature had copied her mouth from the mouth of a cherub in some airy scene of paradise by Giovanni Battista Tiepolo. The lines and creases her face had acquired were the imprints of character that distinguish womanly beauty from youthful prettiness.

She stopped, a small canvas bag in one hand, a large straw hat in the other, and scrutinized the faces of people passing her. Yarrow knew she was too nearsighted to see him on the other side of the hall. He put his half-empty coffee container in a trash bin and walked toward her, his heartbeats accelerating.

She was wearing a white blouse, calf-length gray skirt, and sandals.

Suddenly she saw him. She dropped her hat as she waved, her smile brightening her whole face.

Yarrow sidled around a group of arriving, embracing, exclaiming people, some still wearing shorts and T-shirts sporting slogans in Spanish.

He bent down to pick up Louise's hat. She stopped him by putting her long hand under his chin. "Hello, Yarrow."

"Hello." He kissed her cheek. He reached down and retrieved the hat from between the moving legs of a fat man, who stumbled.

"Get the hell outa the —"

Louise turned her smile on him. "He's with me, Eddie," she said. "He's the one I was telling you about."

"Aaaah," the heavy man said. "Hey, no hard feelings, ha?"

"Not a one," Yarrow answered.

"Boy," the fat man said, grinning, "you sure know how to pick 'em! Take care now, Weezie."

Louise waved again as the exuberant tide of greeters swept him away.

Yarrow looked at her in amusement. "Weezie?"

"That's what he got out of 'Louise,' " she said, sliding her hand through his arm. "It's un-American not to have a nickname, or didn't you know that, Jakie?"

"What did you tell him I was?" he asked as they stepped onto the escalator.

"A Cadillac dealer from Bethesda who picked me up at the bullfights."

"You didn't, really."

Still smiling she shook her head. "No. I said you were my husband." She was standing one step below him. She looked back up at him. "Don't answer, don't say anything about that yet," she said. "I have a — I've got something to —"

Yarrow put his hand on her shoulder.

For one moment she laid her own long hand over it. In the next she stepped off the escalator.

She didn't speak again until her bags were in his car and Yarrow was steering into a line at the parking lot tollgate. As he braked the Honda to a stop, Louise twisted her slender body around and put her hat on the back seat. "I thought of something today. Right after we were married we got our first stationery from Camalier and Buckley —"

Her face held its radiance in the glow of the dashboard lights. "I remember," Yarrow said. "The envelopes glued themselves shut in the heat."

"Didn't we try to steam them open?"

"Yes, and it didn't work," he said. He moved the car forward, paid at the tollbooth, and accelerated into the windy darkness. "What made you think of that?"

She was leaning back, hands clasped in her lap, her vision fixed on the highway and the night speckled with approaching headlights. "I don't know, really. It's funny what pops into the mind, isn't it?"

"I had a dream about your father the other night."

"Jaysus, Joseph, and Mary," she answered in mocking imitation of her late, egocentric father's Dublin accent. She took a deep breath. "Jake, it was wrong of me to write you that note and then lope off to Mexico."

"Wrong? Why?"

"Because I was completely absorbed in what I wanted to say to you." She turned to him and smiled. "All your life you've been badgered by people who want you to enlist in their causes — including me. Enough is enough."

Even though she was reproaching herself, the new confidence she had acquired was still firmly in place. It had grown as his own emotional conflict congealed. Yarrow deeply loved Louise and could not bear the thought of living his life without her near him, casting her spell around him. But he kept imagining himself as a famous artist's deteriorating old appendage.

"You're being too harsh," he said. "There wasn't anything wrong with writing a letter telling me" — he groped for noncommittal words — "what you told me, and then giving me a chance to think about it."

"No. It isn't a fair fight, Jake," she said. "I've got you at a disadvantage. I know what I want." She turned to him and smiled. "You don't — and I don't blame you one damned bit."

A red, white, and blue shield emblazoned with "495" and the legend "1 mile" appeared overhead in the glare of the headlights. The Honda flashed under it. The traffic was heavier, the landscape hilly as they approached Route 495, the beltway that encircles Washington. A long line of automobile taillights lay in a curving pattern on the road ahead like the irradiated vertebrae of a serpent.

"My letter to you was a final wavering, a last-minute blurt before I decided something," she said. "I was a little desperate and very scared."

"What were you scared of?"

"Justified recrimination," she answered. "You have every right to say, 'Listen, Cassidy, you walked out on me to find yourself — or whatever you called it. You put me through eight different kinds of hell —' "

Yarrow glanced at her. There was a questioning expression on her face. "Or didn't I?"

"Put me through hell?"

"Yes," she said.

Yarrow took a deep breath. He nodded.

"I wouldn't blame you if you said, 'And now that you've rooted around in your female mystique to your heart's content and made it as a painter — *now* you tell me you love me and have the gall to say you'd like to be my full-time wife again as if nothing had happened.' "

Cars came at them, headlights glaring, passed, and the night repossessed them. "You know I'd never say that."

"Yes," she answered, "I do know you'd never say such a thing to me. You're too gallant. Too kind." She paused. "So I've come back to — is 'absolve' the word I want? Do I absolve you from having to reply to that letter?"

"It's the right word," he said, "but the wrong sentiment."

He eased the car across several lanes to the right, glancing at the mirror, the road ahead, and the mirror again as he made for the Route 495 exit. Neither of them spoke until the Honda was in the center lane of the beltway, heading north at fifty-five miles an hour. The hazy glow of Washington was spread across the eastern sky.

Yarrow leaned back in his seat. He was tight with apprehension. "You said you have decided something. What is it?"

She didn't answer until they crossed the Potomac on a wide bridge. Yarrow slowed the Honda and, again, moved over to the right lane. He flipped on the right turn blinker.

"I wasn't just thinking about our first stationery on the way back from Mexico City today," Louise said. She deliberately paced her words as she tried to control her emotions. "I was rehearsing my apology and absolution, I was trying to imagine living on the Maine coast —"

"Louise, what in the name of God are you talking about?" he demanded.

"Leaving Washington," she said, her restraint suddenly breaking, her speech accelerating, "making a clean break. Harry Pentland died last spring, did you know? Mary wants someone on their place at North Brooklin. She offered to sell me that little guest house and the barn for a stu —"

"You're jabbering," he said.

"If I don't jabber I'll cry."

"You can't cry," Yarrow said. "I forgot to bring a handkerchief."

On the breaking edge of tears she laughed, a gesture of bravado in the tumult of her feelings that evoked the autumn afternoon in Massachusetts more than thirty years before, when he proposed to her.

They had been walking west along the Cambridge side of the Charles River. The waning sun's defiant blaze was in their eyes, the cold current slipped past them, and the November air numbed their ears and faces. "I can't believe you're surprised," Yarrow had said when she didn't answer.

Bundled up in a gray coat, a long knitted scarf twisted around her neck and thrown over her shoulder, Louise shook her head. She took his arm, made him stop and turn to her. A swatch of fiery red hair fell down over her forehead and right eye. "No, I'm not surprised. I love you," she had said. "I kept kidding myself I'd figure out a way to say something you have to be told . . . eventually . . . but I've always really known that I wouldn't be able to find the right words when you asked me to marry you . . ."

Her gray eyes were blurring in her cold-flushed face.

"Then don't try to find the right words," he said to her. "However you phrase it, the facts will still be the same."

She wiped her eyes with the end of her scarf.

"I told you about a man, David Schneider, six years ago . . ."

He nodded.

"I got pregnant, Yarrow. I had an abortion. It was pretty vile, but worse than that . . . I can't . . . it was such a botched goddamned —"

"You can't have children."

"No — I mean, yes, that's what you have to know. There was infection, I had to have a hysterectomy. Our doctor's a nice man. He didn't tell my father why it was necessary."

A cold wind was approaching from the southwest. It fluted the gray surface of the river, churned the leaves lying on the bank, and stung their faces. Yarrow felt no shock at what she had told him.

He took his hands out of his duffel coat pockets and embraced her. "It doesn't make any difference."

Her arms were gripping him. Her cheek was pressed against his, cold and wet with tears. "Do you promise?"

"I promise it makes no difference."

She was trembling. "Do you promise that if it *does* make a difference after you've thought about it, digested it, you'll tell me?"

"I promise," he said. "Maybe it's for the best. I have a secret too."

She held him tightly. "What?"

"I signed a contract with the Central Intelligence Agency on Wednesday," he said. "It me took until yesterday morning to get their permission to tell you."

"Will you be a Soviet specialist?"

"Yes. That's what they want me for. It's what I'm going to do with my life," he said. "That, and be your husband if you'll have me."

"Oh, Jesus . . . darling Jake, I'll have you and never stop loving you." To keep herself from weeping with relief, she had laughed.

Yarrow eased the car up the narrow driveway of her house on Forty-seventh Place and turned off the ignition. In town, on the western edge of Washington, the wind had dropped. For a moment he gripped the wheel so that Louise wouldn't see the trembling of his hands.

"Do you want to go to Maine, Louise?"

"I'd love to go if you went with me. But I don't want to live here, near you, yet not with you." She lowered her eyes and put her long hands over her face for a moment. She dropped her hands into her lap. "Christ," she said, "is there any way I can explain this to you without sounding like a completely selfish, mixed-up —"

"Yes," he said. "Just tell me the truth."

She looked at him. For a moment he saw panic in her eyes. "But the truth's *changed*. It was true when I said I had to get away from you, true when I wanted your friendship because I couldn't bear a total, final separation from you, true when I wrote —"

"My truth's just as complicated," he said. He opened the door. "I can't stop you from going to Maine," he said, "but I don't want you to go." He got out of the car and looked at her in the front seat. He tried not to sound aggressive. "Your decision can't be one-sided. It involves me — what you feel about me, what you think I feel about you, what I really feel. I think you owe us both a chance to talk about the assumptions you've made, about my doubts, which I don't understand myself —"

She had been looking up at him in the pale glow of the dashboard lights. "Three cheers," she said softly.

"For what?"

Louise smiled. "Jake Yarrow, after a lifetime of paying other people's debts, finally decides *he's* owed something."

"I don't know what that means," he said.

Louise opened the door on her side of the car. "It's one of the things we'll have to talk about," she said. She got out and looked at him across the roof of the car. "It may take a lot of talk and a lot of time, my dear."

"Suits me."

"And it may all come to nothing . . ."

"That would be better than not trying at all," he said.

She smiled in the dim cast of the porch light. "Let's go in," she said. "I'll make some coffee."

He carried her bags inside and set them down in the hall. "I'll have to make a telephone call," he said.

"You know where it is in the kitchen or, if you need privacy, there's one in the bedroom upstairs."

He went through the dining room, turned on the overhead light in the kitchen, and took a wall telephone off its cradle. He dialed a number at the Orion offices that fed incoming calls through a scrambler. A woman's voice he didn't recognize answered.

"This is Yarrow," he said. "Is Joe Humphrey available?"

"Hold on a sec, Mr. Yarrow."

The telephone in the task force communications room was punched onto hold. A scratchy recording of "The International" began to play. Although he was still tight with apprehension, Yarrow chortled.

The communist hymn stopped abruptly.

"Hi," Joe Humphrey's voice said. "We've been trying to find you."

"What's up?" Yarrow asked.

"The guy Henry sent to Ivalo — you know, up in Lapland —"

"Yes. His name's Durward."

"He's just come up on a circuit."

"To report what?" Yarrow asked.

"You'd better come in unless you're talking on a safe line, Jake. We've got a puzzle and a problem on our hands."

Yarrow looked at his watch. It was twenty-five minutes past midnight. He tried to think of an excuse not to go in. He couldn't. "All right," he said. "I'm on my way."

"Want a car sent for you?"

"No," Yarrow said. "I'll drive myself." He glanced up and saw Louise appear in the kitchen door. Instinctively, she backed away. He beckoned her into the room. "Any good news?" he asked.

"A lot of stuff coming in, but none of it seems to add up to much," Joe Humphrey said. "It's all just getting murkier and more complicated."

"I'll get there as soon as I can," Yarrow said. He hung up.

"I'm sorry," Louise said. "I wasn't trying to overhear."

"It's all right," Yarrow said. "I should have told you. I'm involved in something."

"We can talk when it's over," she said.

"No," he said. "Are you free for dinner tomorrow night?"

She hesitated for a moment. "Jake, it can wait. I'm not going anywhere until we do our damnedest to thrash out —"

"Can't you understand?" Yarrow demanded. "I'm a middle-aged man trying to prove he can still juggle two crises and one woman at the same time."

She was leaning against the sink, clasping its curved rim with both hands. She laughed.

"I don't know what time I'll be finished tomorrow night."

"It doesn't matter. I'll cook dinner whenever you're available." For a moment she looked at the green and white linoleum squares on the kitchen floor. Then her head came up. The radiance had returned to her face.

"If you wouldn't mind meeting at my house," he said, "I really should be near a secure phone line to the office."

"No, fine."

"I'll have Tiger Chadwick drop off a key tomorrow morning."

"The sophomore spy." She grinned. "Do you really have bratty little Tiger working for you?"

"I'm afraid so. I don't know what time I'll be —"

"You've already said that. It doesn't matter. I'll go through your desk and read all the love letters you've gotten in the last four years and be jealous as hell."

He sat in a windowless room under bright overhead light. There were a microphone and two speakers on the table before him. Joe Humphrey sat across from him with several sheets of notes in his hand. An NSA technician was at the end of the table behind a console and Ampex tape recorder.

"Do you want Peggy to play back our conversation with Durward, or will my summary do?" Humphrey asked.

"Just the summary for now," Yarrow said. He had been up for nineteen hours. Weariness had finally found him as he drove down Foxhall Road, through Georgetown, and up to M Street. He forced his mind into focus.

"Okay," Humphrey said. He looked down at his notes. "The day tower controller came on duty at the Ivalo airport at four o'clock this morning local time. His name is Lerinaan. He was getting set up when four men shot out the lock on the downstairs door, came up into the tower, and started punching him around."

Yarrow folded his hands over his stomach. "Did Durward get descriptions of them?"

"Yeah. He talked to Lerinaan in the Ivalo hospital before he called us. All four spoke Russian, one did the talking in Finnish with a Russian accent. One was Chinese, Lerinaan said." Humphrey looked up. "We took that to mean any Asian."

Yarrow nodded.

"The Chinese-looking guy asked most of the questions, with the Finn-speaker interpreting. They wanted to know about a Cessna 210 that had flown out of the Ivalo airport just after sunup on the morning of April fourth. Lerinaan remembered that airplane because it had landed without authorization sometime during the night when nobody was at the airport. No runway lights. It left illegally the next morning."

"What do you mean, illegally?" Yarrow asked.

"It refused to make radio contact with the tower," Humphrey said. "The first Lerinaan had known about it was the sound of its engine starting. He saw it taxiing onto the main runway, yelled his head off on the radio, but the Cessna took off without answering."

"Did he tell that to the Russians this morning?" Yarrow asked.

Humphrey looked down at his notes. "Not until they broke his nose and two of his fingers. Lerinaan told Durward that the airport tower logs are supposed to be confidential. He sounds like a tough cookie."

"What happened next?"

"The Russians ripped out the telephones, smashed up the radio equipment, and left. They shot out one tire on every car they saw in the airport parking lot.

"These four men may also have burned down Paavo Waltari's barn during the night," Humphrey said. "Waltari's the smuggler who was Henry's asset up —"

"I remember," Yarrow said. "What happened to his barn?"

"Somebody torched it," Humphrey said. "By the time Pete Durward got up here, hired a car, and drove down to the border, the

Ivalo fire brigade had saved the house and sifted through the ruins of the barn. Waltari's missing." He looked at Yarrow. "My guess is, the four Russians questioned him about whether Kornilov and Mandelbaum came across from the Soviet Union on that night, April third, then killed him so that we couldn't ask him the same questions."

"Is that what Durward thinks?"

Humphrey nodded. "After sunup he went back down to the border. He must've passed the Russians on their way to the Ivalo airport. He didn't find any trace of Waltari."

"Did he see anything else?"

"Just one of the KGB Border Guards watching him through binoculars."

Yarrow pursed his lips. Under the harsh light the wells of his eyes, the lines down either side of his nose, and his fleshy chin and throat were shaded and etched by shadows. "Well," he said, "we don't know enough yet to make any sense out of this." He looked at Humphrey. "You said you had a problem, Joe."

Humphrey pushed back his chair and stood up. "Let's go over to your office."

Yarrow followed him out of the little room. They crossed the main chamber. Two young men from the FBI were guarding the entrance to the suite.

Humphrey closed Yarrow's office door, crouched down, and dialed the lock on the safe. "You ought to stay in contact, Jake, or at least let us know where we can find you."

"You're right," Yarrow answered. "I'm sorry. I was meeting someone at Dulles. I'll wear a beeper."

Humphrey opened the safe, took out several sheets of print-covered computer paper, and put them on the desk. He sat down in a visitor's chair. "I thought part of this should be for your ears only.

"The printout's from the Moscow station. Our best friend's been in touch again. Volya Galkin's instructing his staff to keep the kidnapping of Mandelbaum secret. Just like we are."

Yarrow leaned forward and picked up the document.

"Our best friend tells us that Galkin's working out of a temporary fifth-floor suite in Lubyanka," Humphrey said. "He has three senior deputies — a woman named Sonya Krebsky, Y. F. Tsarapkin of the T Directorate, and a border guards colonel-general named Khorloin Tseden. Okay?"

Yarrow looked up from the communiqué Humphrey had taken from the safe. "So far so good. What's the problem, Joe?"

Humphrey looked out the window. The top floor of the CBS News bureau across the street was brightly lit. He could see people moving about. "I ordered up routine archive profiles of all three of them," he said. He looked back at Yarrow. "Langley had the files on Krebsky and Tsarapkin back to us within twenty minutes."

"Why not — what was his name?"

"Khorloin Tseden, colonel-general? Because he's border guards and, therefore, the file on him's at the DIA. So our computer room whistled up Defense and asked if they had Tseden." Humphrey's face flushed. "Yes, they knew all about Tseden, and no, we couldn't have anything on him."

Yarrow put the computer printout on his desk. "I don't understand."

"Any requests for material from the archives of the Defense Intelligence Agency must be submitted in writing and cleared by the assistant secretary."

"Did your computer room tell them it was for the Orion task force?"

Humphrey nodded. "Any requests for material from the archives of the Defense Intelligence Agency must be submitted in writing and cleared by the assistant secretary, who won't be available to even consider such requests until noon tomorrow."

Yarrow was silent for a moment. "That's outrageous," he said softly.

"Yes, sir. I used a slightly soiled version of just that word when I telephoned the night duty officer over there. He said not to yell at him, buddy, he was just doing what they told him, and if I had any complaints why didn't I take them up with the director of the DIA? So I did. I took the liberty of waking up General Dunn. I used your name."

"What did Marcus say?"

"He hadn't heard about the order. He said he'd try to get it reversed ASAP, sent you his apologies, and used a lot of Texas profanity on the assistant secretary in question."

"Phil Teague."

"None other than."

❖ NINE ❖

THE TELEPHONE CALL at 7:14 A.M. on April 10 propelled him out of sleep like a fired torpedo. By 7:30 he had shaved, showered, and was tucking a Wembley into his waistband just below the small of his back, when Dorothy came up from the kitchen with two cups of coffee.

Henry Muffin and his wife were about to deceive each other. He made himself appear calm. Reaching for his suit jacket, he smiled at her.

Dorothy's deception was to act as if she believed his. "I have a meeting, then a lunch date in town," she said. "If you don't need the station wagon . . ."

Muffin kissed her cheek. She was wearing a blue dressing gown. He stopped trying to make sense of what he had been told over the telephone. "Take it," he said. "The cops are sending a helicopter for me."

"I'm appropriately impressed," she said, smiling. She was filled with the dread that is the lot of everyone who loves a spy; Dorothy Muffin knew she couldn't be told what the telephone call had been about; her dread began when she saw him arming himself to deal with it.

Muffin opened a dresser drawer and took out a shawl. He put it around her shoulders. "Let's wait outside. It's a beautiful morning."

It was a hateful, frightening morning. "I could stay in town and drive you home," she said.

"Let's see how the day goes."

Pretending, they went downstairs together.

On the little embankment above the beach, Muffin breathed the aromas of kelp, shore, and salt. He looked at his watch. It was eleven minutes before eight. Only four days remained before the auction of Mandelbaum. Muffin's excitement was accompanied by a growing sense of frustration.

Dorothy had paused at one of the small dogwood trees she had imported from Massachusetts. As she plucked off withered blossoms, Muffin watched gulls wheeling over the bright water of The Sound. A pale blue haze cloaked Helsingborg, the Swedish port city on the opposite shore; its buildings gleamed in the sunlight as if they were made of beaten silver.

Carrying her coffee cup, Dorothy came down the lawn and put her free arm around him. He knew that she yearned for ordinary days, ordinary, unexciting weeks, months, and years. He had just turned fifty-four. He was beginning to feel the same yearning in himself.

"I spoke to Jake on a circuit yesterday," he said. "He sent you his love and said he'll write soon."

Dorothy smiled again and looked across the water. "What a dear, lonely man," she said.

Her complexion was dark, her eyes deeply set. She had a strong jaw. Her features were Negroid, not pseudo-Caucasian. She had become more beautiful as she grew older.

She heard the clatter of a helicopter and, an instant later, saw it drop out of the sun's nimbus, turn, and approach them just above the surface of the water. It looked like an egg on skis with half its shell transparent, the other half covered by a dun-colored metal skin; its blades blurred in the morning light.

The engine's stuttering roar engulfed them. Muffin took Dorothy's hand. The helicopter flung a wide spray of water as the pilot angled it sideways onto the narrow beach. It was emblazoned with large white letters, "PET" — standing for *Politiets Efterretning Tjeneste,* the Danish National Police. Dorothy's head touched Muffin's chest for a moment, a gesture of affection as old as her love for him.

He kissed her, stepped sideways down the bank, and climbed into the clear plastic bubble beside the pilot.

The world tilted beneath him as the helicopter lifted off, rolled sideways, accelerated across the water, and then rose suddenly into the sky. Muffin mentally reoriented himself so that he, not the surface of the earth, seemed askew. He buckled a seat belt over his shoulder and across his lap and looked back.

Dorothy was still standing at the end of the lawn, one hand holding her coffee cup, the other waving.

The helicopter made a complete circle and headed inland, crossing the tree-lined coastal road. Muffin could see the roofs of houses like his own, cars driving up toward Helsingør.

The pilot climbed to fifteen hundred feet as they flew over the E4, the main north-south highway. The traffic heading into Copenhagen was bumper to bumper as far as Muffin could see.

On the open countryside far ahead, villages were separated from one another by meadows, neat fields, and clusters of forest.

The 7:14 A.M. telephone call had been from Aksel Tausen, a captain of Danish counterintelligence. He headed the PET contingent working with the Americans on the search for Mandelbaum. At that hour Tausen knew only a few facts, but they were stunning: two men had been shot just after sunrise near Herslev, a tiny village on Roskilde Fjord. One was a deputy press attaché at the Soviet embassy in Copenhagen. The other victim was an elderly Dane named Bo Larsen; he was a man Maxim P. Kornilov and other Soviet embassy personnel had occasionally hired as a fishing guide twenty years before. Larsen's name and connection to Kornilov had surfaced the night before in a PET archive file on another 1960s-era KGB officer stationed in Denmark. There were two witnesses to the murders. The local police had been ordered to cordon off the area and disturb nothing until Tausen and Muffin got there.

At 8:32 A.M. the chopper began a controlled fall out of the sky. Off to the left Muffin saw the spire of Roskilde Cathedral, the burial place of Denmark's kings and queens. The market town around the great church's brick plaza was alive with cars and people in the April sunlight.

The pilot leveled off at three hundred feet above the ground. He was following a road that curved around a forest, past a stately, neo-Georgian mansion with a cobbled courtyard and stables. Directly ahead, a farmer was plowing. A swarm of sea gulls circled above the red tractor and dropped into the new furrows to gobble seed and freshly unearthed worms.

As the PET helicopter thundered across the field, scattering gulls, Muffin saw a cluster of low stone farm buildings, a boat yard with sailing yachts suspended in their cradles. Police cars lined the side of the road, which had been blocked off by a red-

and-white-striped barrier. An ambulance, a police van, and a dozen private cars were parked in the boat yard's lot, which was surrounded by young poplars and wild rose bushes. Men in uniform, men in civilian clothes, and a few uniformed women were standing about, some talking, a few looking up at the approaching helicopter. A stone wall separated the parking lot from another field, plowed and gray. Muffin saw a small blue tarpaulin lying across the furrows. There was an oblong shape beneath it. Two uniformed police officers and a tall blond man in a black raincoat stood beside the tarpaulin. As the chopper went down slowly, Muffin could see the twisting shoreline of Roskilde Fjord, boats swaying in the gentle morning swell, a one-story house with a porch near the edge of the water, a large tree in front of the house, a small dock with another blue tarpaulin spread on it, another inert lump beneath the tarpaulin, a solitary policeman on the dock, his hands clasped behind his back, gazing out over the water so that he wouldn't have to look at his neighbor, death, on the weathered planks beside him.

The helicopter settled onto the field with a slight bump. Muffin unbuckled his seat belt, nodded his thanks to the pilot, and opened the door. Dust was whirling around him; the two policemen stood on the edges of the tarpaulin and grabbed their caps. Muffin stooped over and hurried out of the rotor's radius. As he straightened up, the helicopter rose, banked, and clattered away across the landscape.

The blond man in the black raincoat held out his hand. "Good morning, Henry," he said in Danish.

With the helicopter gone, Muffin heard only the wind. "Hello, Aksel," he replied, shaking the police captain's hand. He looked down at the human outline beneath the blue cover. "Is that the Russian?"

"Yes, but I must tell you that he is a terrible sight."

"I appreciate the warning," Muffin said. "Let's have a look at him."

Captain Tausen nodded at one of the policemen, who bent over and pulled away a corner of the tarpaulin.

Muffin crouched and drew back the opposite corner.

The dead man lay on his back. He was in his mid-forties,

slightly built, bald, with a mustache. His gray face was twisted into a teeth-clenching grimace, eyes squeezed shut. He had died clutching handfuls of his blood-spattered blue shirt. Below his chin his soft upper throat was blown away. In the ragged crevass Muffin could see the stump of his severed windpipe and pieces of splintered vertebrae.

"Jesus," he said softly. He looked up at Tausen. "That had to be a very powerful weapon fired from only a short distance away."

Tausen nodded. "While Kelyev's head was turned."

"Wait," Muffin said, taking a notebook from his inside breast pocket. "Give me the name again."

"Boris Ivanovich Kelyev," Tausen said. "Don't bother to write it down, Henry. We'll have a copy of his markup sheet on your desk by the time you are back in Copenhagen." The counterintelligence captain squatted beside Muffin, a pencil in his hand. He was a slender man in his early forties. His square face was florid. His blond hair was cut short in a stiff brush. "Kelyev was walking across the field away from the parking place, toward the house over there, when he was shot," Tausen said. "He must have turned his head just before the bullet struck him. Look." He pointed with his pencil to the left side of the wound in the dead Russian's neck. "The flesh is badly torn here, the artery ends, the strands of muscle are forced inward. At the other side —"

"I see the difference," Muffin said. "Any idea of the caliber?"

"Not a dumdum, I think," Tausen said, standing. "Larsen, the other victim, over on the dock, was shot in the back with, we must presume, the same weapon. The bullet didn't expand in him but went out through his chest. In my opinion the rifleman used steel jackets."

Muffin rose to his feet. He looked across the field at the glassy waters of the fjord. The haze was burning off. He could see distant islands. He turned back to Tausen. "Has the Soviet embassy been told?"

Tausen nodded. "They were called as soon as Kelyev's ID was confirmed. Do you want to look at Larsen, Henry?"

"Not at the moment," Muffin said. "I presume he's been photographed."

"Yes. Nothing will be touched in the house until you see it. Bent Jorgensen has just finished taking the statements of the two witnesses. He's in the van over there."

"Let's hear what Bent has first," Muffin said.

Sinking slightly in the soft earth, they walked back to the parking lot. They passed two uniformed morgue attendants carrying a stretcher out onto the field.

"You mentioned that Kelyev's cover was deputy press secretary," Muffin said. "What else was he?"

"A rather strange intelligence officer of the KGB Copenhagen residency," Tausen replied. "He came here three months ago. We've been on him since ten days after his arrival."

"I never heard of him," Muffin said. "Was he trying to buy and run Danish agents?"

"Not diligently, no," Tausen answered. "The reason you didn't know about him is that he did almost nothing." The police captain took a handkerchief from his pocket and blew his nose. "Kelyev tried some rather clumsy recruiting among the journalists he saw in his cover job as deputy press secretary. None of them bit, of course. The KGB residency used him as a pickup man a few times, a courier occasionally. Frankly, we don't quite know what he was doing here."

They had reached the stone wall. Muffin stepped over it. "Maybe he was somebody's special man in Scandinavia," he said. "We know that Valerian Galkin's running the Soviet search for Mandelbaum."

"Ah," Tausen said. "That could explain why such a low-ranking officer was sent to question Larsen this morning. Possibly Kelyev belonged to Galkin."

Possibly."

A morning breeze was coming from the fjord. It rustled the foliage around the parking lot. Muffin followed Tausen to a large Ford police van. They climbed in the front seats.

A thin, middle-aged man was seated at a desk in the rear of the van. He had white hair and a narrow face and wore horn-rimmed glasses. He was writing in a notebook and didn't look up as Muffin and Tausen slammed the doors. "Good morning, Henry," he said in English with a slightly affected Oxbridge drawl, "won't be a moment."

"Take your time," Muffin said.

"Our witnesses are the quaint old couple in tweeds having a chat with Nils Sorenson."

Muffin twisted around so that he could see through the back window of the van. Two people who at first glance appeared to be aged twins were standing beside a blue Saab sedan talking to a plainclothes policeman.

Both were small, thin, gray, and bright-eyed. Both wore tweed caps, matching knickerbocker suits, checked shirts, and black ties. They had leather binoculars cases around their necks. After a moment Muffin saw a bun at the back of the woman's head and a white mustache on her husband's face.

"Right," Bent Jorgensen said, punctuating his last written sentence with a light jab of his pen. He looked up and smiled at Muffin. "How's Dorothy?"

"Never better," Muffin said.

After primary and secondary schooling in Denmark, Bent Jorgensen had finished his education at King's College, Cambridge. He decided on a career in counterintelligence, he once told Muffin, because it was more amusing than growing up. "Give her my love," he said.

He adjusted his glasses and flipped back through the pages of his notebook. "Now then," he said. "The witnessing couple's name is Pilegaard, they live in Roskilde and come here in the spring and fall to watch migrating water birds, ducks and things."

The Pilegaards had pulled into the parking lot that morning as the first, red sunlight was streaking the fields and still water of the fjord. Another car was already there. Its driver had forgotten to turn off the headlights. As Mr. Pilegaard climbed out of his Saab he saw Kelyev walking across the field toward the house. Someone started shouting. A tall man with a rifle stepped out onto the porch and shot Kelyev. The impact of the bullet spun the KGB officer around. He landed on his back in the field. Mrs. Pilegaard scrambled out of the Saab. She and her husband saw a second man, identified later as Bo Larsen, dash from the house. He was partway out on the dock when the rifleman fired at him. Larsen fell with a thud that was audible two hundred meters away in the parking lot. The sniper ran around to the far side of the house. A few seconds later Mr. and Mrs. Pilegaard heard an engine start. They saw a Land Rover drive away. The bird-watchers went back to the farm beside the boat yard and called the police.

Muffin was sitting with his arm across the back of the seat, looking at Jorgensen. "Did the Land Rover have a paint spill on its rear roof and hatch?"

Jorgensen raised his eyebrows in surprise. "As a matter of fact, yes. How did you know?"

"Tell you in a minute," Muffin answered. "Did the Pilegaards see or hear anyone else come out of the house?"

Jorgensen looked down at his notebook. He turned two pages. "Here it is. Mrs. Pilegaard says she only saw the sniper, and her husband says he heard a lot of men shouting before the Land Rover's engine started. There's a door on the far side of the house."

"Which Pilegaard do you believe?" Muffin asked.

"Madam," Jorgensen said. "The old gentleman's a bit over-wrought."

"Did they describe the shooter?"

"Yes," Jorgensen replied, "they agreed on that. He's tall, as I said. His most prominent feature is close-cropped black hair."

Muffin turned around and looked through the windshield. After a moment he turned to Tausen. "The rifle's probably a Warsaw Pact–issue, ten-shot Dragunov SVD," he said. "Scope-mounted, three-hundred-meter range. The day Yarrow met Kornilov on the beach at Liseleje, a 110 series Land Rover with a paint spill on it was parked nearby. Kornilov had a black-haired bodyguard carrying a Dragunov rifle. I'm surprised it didn't take Kelyev's head off."

"So! It means that Kornilov and Mandelbaum are still in Denmark."

"Let's have a look inside that house," Muffin said.

Yuri F. Tsarapkin, the tiny academician, paused in the door-less entrance to Sonya Krebsky's plywood room. She was standing at her desk holding a telephone receiver to her right ear. It was 2:46 P.M., Moscow time. Tsarapkin was wearing a little black raincoat and a soggy little cloth cap and carrying a large briefcase. There were droplets of water on his brows and mustache.

His dark, inquisitive eyes darted from Sonya to General Khorloin Tseden, who was standing, hands clasped behind his back, inhumanly trim in his uniform, looking up at one of the barred windows in the stone back wall.

The atmosphere in the temporary workrooms on the fifth floor of Lubyanka's west wing was ominously subdued. Telex printers pattered and whizzed, computer keyboards clattered. But the few people who spoke did so in low voices. They were engaged in collective cowering.

Tsarapkin came into the room and unbelted his raincoat. "What is it?" he asked.

General Tseden turned his head. "Man killed."

"What man?"

"Galkin's man. Copagah."

Tsarapkin took off his hat. He walked across to Sonya's desk and set down his briefcase. "What is he talking about?"

Sonya Krebsky was wearing her American jeans and running shoes. She had put on a white, wide-sleeved Georgian blouse and tied a red bandanna over her head. She looked overblown. She cupped her hand over the telephone mouthpiece. "Galkin had a reliable in Copenhagen — Hello?"

The person for whom she had been waiting had apparently come on the line. "Permit me to congratulate you!" Sonya said loudly and sardonically. "After only seven attempts, you sent the correct file to the first deputy chairman's office this afternoon!" She picked up a folder on the desk before her. "I am actually holding in my hand the missing dossier on the London years of Maxim Petrovich Kornilov!" She listened. "Very well. I offer you my apologies for distasteful insinuations about your career capabilities. When you return home this evening and let your mother out of her kennel, please give her my compliments." She slammed down the receiver.

Tsarapkin tittered despite his exasperation. He took off his raincoat. General Tseden had resumed his contemplation of the gray patch of sky visible through the small window.

"You were telling me —"

Sonya Krebsky sat down behind her desk. She opened the dossier. "Something important has turned up in Kornilov's London file," she said. "He had a lover who was a titled aristocrat *and* a member of the British party . . ." She looked down at the open folder. "Her name was Lady Ellen Worth. She may have been the person Kornilov visited when he was in Britain on his Polish passport last January."

"I must insist —"

Sonya raised her head and looked across the desk. Her heavy, oddly sensual features were set in an expression of severity. "Be quiet, Tsarapkin! I am giving you news! If *we* have Lady Ellen Worth in our files, so does the British MI-5. We must assume they have already given her name and Kornilov connection to the Americans. An hour ago we sent a signal to Galkin's London people ordering them to find this woman immediately, before —"

Tsarapkin felt like screaming. *"Copenhagen!"* he said. "Will someone who can speak the Russian language *inform me about this man who was killed in Copenhagen?"*

General Tseden turned his head. He stared icily at Tsarapkin through half-lidded Mongol eyes. He detested the little scientist, who was forever deriding Tseden's pronunciation of certain words and names and acting in a superior manner. Khorloin Tseden permitted himself fantasies about cutting off Tsarapkin's ears and slitting his tongue.

"Sit down," Sonya said.

As Tsarapkin drew back a chair and perched on its edge, she lit a cigarette. "Three months ago Galkin sent a new reliable to Copenhagen. He was a colonel named Boris Ivanovich Kelyev. The KGB resident in Denmark is a protégé of Spassky.

"Last night we sent Kelyev a signal on a back circuit ordering him to visit a certain Bo Larsen, whose name has turned up several times in Kornilov's Danish file. This morning Kelyev was found dead in a field near Larsen's house. Murdered."

"How?" Tsarapkin demanded. "By whom?"

"It is unclear. Information is still coming through the Copenhagen embassy. Volya has been extremely upset . . ."

Oblomov appeared in the doorway. His round face was more flushed than usual and gleamed with perspiration. He was wearing a rumpled gray suit. The pressure of his belly had widened gaps in his shirtfront between the buttons. "Galkin wishes to see all of you," the fat man said. For once there was no undertone of mirth in his manner. "Immediately."

Tsarapkin slipped off the chair. Oblomov was already waddling back down the curved stone corridor. Tseden, Sonya Krebsky, and Tsarapkin hurried after him. They passed the other plywood-partitioned rooms. Somber faces, thin KGB clerical faces made pale by fluorescent lighting, watched them.

Oblomov waved his hand impatiently at the Ninth Directorate sentry outside Galkin's office and opened the door himself.

Fitful episodes of rain had begun at dawn. A low ceiling of mottled cloud covered Moscow. The air was moist and cool between downpours.

The windows of the first deputy chairman's office were still open even though the reek of varnish had all but disappeared. Valerian A. Galkin sat at his desk, his tan overcoat draped like a cape over his shoulders. Papers, files, and dark, streaky wirephotos were spread out before him. His little dog, Yosip, dozed in a basket beneath the windows.

The uniformed sentry closed the door, shutting out himself and the rest of the world.

As Tsarapkin took his seat at the conference table with the others he smelled wet concrete and heard the distant, rainy-day whine of tires on asphalt. The pigeons muttered and crooned on some ledge nearby.

Galkin was staring through the windows. His agitation was expressed in the grim set of his mouth and a slight trembling of his excess throat flesh.

Oblomov had brought him the first telex message from Copenhagen at 11:40 A.M. The first deputy chairman had immediately gone into shock. He had spent several tense hours trying to discern the deeper meaning of the event.

He turned his head and nodded at Oblomov. "Show them," he said.

Oblomov took the wirephotos from the desk and laid them on the conference table, beneath the low light. Tsarapkin leaned forward to look.

The pictures were of a man's head, naked shoulders, and chest. His eyes were squeezed shut, his teeth clenched. There was a large, ragged gap where his throat had been. The man was obviously dead, lying on a morgue slab. The pictures, taken from three angles, were utterly horrible. Tsarapkin salivated and thought he might throw up. He glanced to his left. Sonya was looking at the photographs with a clinician's detachment, lips compressed, a cigarette smoldering in her right hand. The corners of General Tseden's mouth were curved down as he scrutinized the pictures.

"Kelyev," Galkin said.

Tsarapkin didn't want to look again. "Excuse me," he said. "While the death of your reliable, Colonel Kelyev, is regrettable —"

Suddenly, uncharacteristically, Galkin slammed both his palms on the desk in an eruption of fury. The dog awakened with a start and sat up in his basket.

"I have not called you here for expressions of condolence!" Galkin snapped. "I wish to discuss my analysis of this murder!" He took out a handkerchief and delicately blew his nose. Panic lingered in him like a fever. "I have concluded that there are three possible explanations. First, someone at KGB Copenhagen may have intercepted our signal to Kelyev last night and had him killed."

"Why?" Sonya asked.

"As a warning to me from Spassky's people in the Denmark residency," Galkin replied, stuffing the handkerchief back in his pocket. He rearranged several documents on the desk before him. "Such a warning would read: 'We discovered that Kelyev was your man. We know, therefore, that you are spying on the spies of the Soviet Union. We choose to believe that Gorbachev has given you freedom to act as you please. We have struck at Kelyev to put you against the wall. Your chairman and ours, Sergei Mikhailovich Spassky, will strike at you to put Gorbachev against the wall.' "

"Your second theory," Sonya Krebsky said.

"Kornilov and his associates were holding Mandelbaum in Larsen's house," Galkin said, "and Kelyev discovered them. One of Kornilov's men shot Kelyev. The embassy has been discussing the case with the Danish police. The latest dispatch from Copenhagen informs us that Larsen was also killed."

An intruding breeze lifted one end of a paper on Galkin's desk. He turned his fleshy face to the windows again. "Third," he said, "it is possible that the Americans killed Kelyev. Doubtless they were given Larsen's name and his Kornilov connection by the Danes. Perhaps an American intelligence officer encountered Kelyev at Larsen's house this morning and shot him to prevent him from getting to the fisherman first."

"And then killed Larsen after questioning him," Sonya said.

"Your first theory is inconceivable," Tsarapkin said. "I personally arranged your back circuit to Kelyev. It is absolutely secure," Tsarapkin said to Galkin. "It bypasses the residency and embassy completely. It is not possible that your order to your reliable last night was intercepted by KGB Copenhagen."

"Then what is your explanation for Kelyev's death?" Galkin asked.

"Your own most logical one — that Kelyev came upon the place where Mandelbaum was being held and one of Kornilov's men killed him."

Outside, the rain was falling in heavy curtains. It darkened the stone facades of Lubyanka, made ponds on the alleys and courtyards five floors below, and splashed heavily on the window ledges. Yosip hopped out of his basket and shook himself.

Galkin snapped his fingers. The dog pattered across the floor and sat down beside his chair. "Sonya?" Galkin said.

"I believe that Yuri Feodorovich is correct," Sonya Krebsky replied, "which means we now know something. As of this morning at least, Mandelbaum was being hidden in Denmark."

Or is that what the shrewd Kornilov wishes us to believe?" Tsarapkin asked.

"We have already deduced that Kornilov is intelligent but not shrewd," Galkin replied. "Therefore, we must assume that the appearance is the reality — that Mandelbaum was being held prisoner in Larsen's house."

He pulled his slipping raincoat back over his shoulders. "The Danish authorities — and therefore the Americans — also know that," he said. "The Danes will be watching every airfield and seaport." He reached down and rumpled his dog's ears. "Two possibilities occur to me. After killing Kelyev, Mandelbaum's captors took him to a new hiding place in Denmark; or, second, they flew him out of the country before surveillance of airfields could be organized. Oblomov?"

Genady I. Oblomov opened a folder on the table before him. "There is a private airport twelve kilometers from Herslev," he said, reading from notes. "It is near a village called Snoldelev. If the Kornilov gang kept their Cessna aircraft there, they could have taken off with Mandelbaum less than an hour after Kelyev was killed."

"Do you have satellite pictures of airfield?" General Tseden asked.

"No," Tsarapkin answered, his face flushing.

"Stupid," Tseden grunted.

The rain fell heavily, steadily, as if it would not stop until all moisture in the universe had been emptied upon the world.

"If they left this airport, they left Denmark," Sonya Krebsky said. "Kornilov has one other backup hiding place — London. There is one other person in his past with whom he was intimate. Lady Ellen Worth."

Galkin nodded. "What you say is logical. With the murder of Kelyev, Denmark is now on full alert — aroused, alarmed. Britain will be a safer place to hide Mandelbaum, London a larger city. It is imperative that we find the Worth woman."

"The search for her by your London reliables has already begun," Sonya Krebsky said. "With help from British party members — if any can be found under the age of ninety-five."

Galkin looked at Tseden. "I wish you to go to London and take charge of this search. The Americans will be looking for Ellen Worth, too, with the assistance of MI-5."

Tseden nodded.

"I will see you and Yuri Feodorovich at four o'clock," Galkin said to Sonya. "General, in communicating with us —"

"I will use ordinary telephone," Tseden said, rising to his feet. "Back circuit not safe."

Gregor Abramovich Mandelbaum sat at the table in his concrete room, the empty plate and cup of his evening meal before him.

The small square of daylight coming through the glass on the ceiling had traveled its God-ordained course down the west wall of the concrete room, made its way across one corner of the table, and up the opposite wall. Now, late in the afternoon, the square of sunlight was turning rose-colored and dimming. Soon it would disappear into the shadow of the ceiling. After a period of darkness, the skylight would fill with the dull glow of the moon and stars.

The rope and the strips of cloth that Mandelbaum had torn from his jacket lining and shirt were beneath his mattress. He wished that he smoked. Sitting at the table with a cigarette would make him look idle and bored when the silent young guard came in to take away the dinner dishes.

Once it was night and Mandelbaum could be sure no one would disturb him, he would resume his plaiting.

His finger joints ached, his nails were broken, and his fingertips were raw and tender. But he felt triumphant and was eager to go back to work.

He had attacked the jacket lining first, picking out the stitching that fastened it to the tweed, then tearing the silk lining into long strips. It was exacting work that he had to perform lying on his bed. If the young guard came in unexpectedly, Mandelbaum could roll on his back, pull the jacket over him with the lining beneath it, and stare at the ceiling.

Nights were the time for sitting at the table and tying the silk strands together, pulling each knot tightly. He tested the ties with vigorous jerks. Then he wove the strips together in threes, the way his wife had braided Dvorah's hair when she was a child. In two nights of plaiting he had made a strong rope almost a meter in length. He had calculated that he would need two meters to hang himself. He was satisfied that his rope would bear his weight.

That afternoon he had begun to shred and tear his shirt below the waistline. When that was used up, Mandelbaum would begin ripping his underwear into strips.

He had worked for several hours at a rear leg of his chair, twisting and yanking it. The wooden leg was now loose enough to be broken off when the time came. At his present rate of work, the rope would be finished in two more nights and days. Then he would thwart his kidnappers and the great nations that wanted him by dying — and Dvorah would be safe.

The lock mechanism of the door rattled. The door opened. The expressionless young man in civilian work clothes came in with a tray and began to gather up Mandelbaum's supper dishes.

"Please give my best wishes to Major Kornilov," the physicist said, smiling. "Tell him I hope he is well and pray that his unhappiness will end soon."

The guard made no sign that he understood.

❖ TEN ❖

POLITICS CAN BE, among other things, a neurotic search for love. Most lovers have a single beloved. The politician whose primary quest is for love looks to an entire town, constituency, state, or nation for the affection that affirms him. Because the politician's beloved has no single face, because the adored one's adoration swells and ebbs in opinion polls, his quest for love is tormenting, insatiable, and mad.

Although James Forrest Burke would have preferred four years in federal prison to another term as president, he was an instinctive political seeker of love and approval. At 4:58 on the morning of April 10, he despised himself for what he had done the night before. He was aware that millions of Americans would also despise him if they knew about it.

Unable to sleep despite two Dalmanes taken with warm milk, his burning ulcer unappeased by Tagamet, the president left the family quarters of the White House and took the elevator downstairs. He was wearing pajamas, slippers, and a blue wool bathrobe. A Secret Service agent appeared from a darkened hallway. Unspeaking and unacknowledged, she followed him outside, where the air was raw and the darkness was giving way to flinty half-light. Ten feet apart, with Burke in the lead, they walked along a columned promenade to the West Wing.

A second bodyguard, a young man, had been alerted by the first's walkie-talkie and was standing at the outside door of the Oval Office. "Good morning, Mr. President."

Burke nodded without smiling as the Secret Service agent opened the door for him.

"Would you like the kitchen to send up coffee, sir?"

"No," the president said. He went inside and shut the door. He crossed the dim office and sat down behind his desk. The desk lamp had remained lit through the night. James Forrest Burke wished he could relive the previous evening, do it differently. The wish became a momentary fantasy. He leaned forward, squinting his disdain. "Tell me that again," he said aloud in his raspiest Harry Truman voice.

In his imagination he replayed the proposal he had listened to in reality eight hours before.

"You've forgotten something, mister," he said flatly, with contempt. "This is America, not goddamned Nazi Germany or the Soviet Union. My name's Burke, not Stalin. We don't do things like that to people. I expect to find your resignation on my desk when I come in tomorrow at eight."

His voice echoed back at him from the bare walls and high ceiling of the Oval Office. Burke bowed his head, chagrined, and hoped the Secret Service man outside hadn't heard the president of the United States talking to himself, pretending to do what he had not done.

He massaged his temples with his right thumb and middle finger. He needed someone to agree with him, someone to say aloud that he had had no other choice. He needed his national security adviser in particular to exonerate him.

Burke wished he understood that chemistry that made men like Wallace Cresteau respected by everyone. The trim, bald ex-army officer seemed to possess the power to validate opinions and actions by agreeing with them.

The president picked up a pale green telephone.

"Good morning, Mr. President," said a woman's voice.

"Get me General Cresteau," Burke said.

"One moment, sir."

Holding the telephone against his chest, the president turned slowly in his chair. He looked at the desolate panorama outside the Oval Office windows. The South Lawn, the Ellipse, and the shape of the Washington Monument were emerging in the gray light. The city was misty and deserted.

"Mr. President?"

He raised the telephone to his right ear. "Yes?"

"General Cresteau's secure line is engaged —"

Burke glanced at a clock on the table behind his desk. "At ten past five in the goddamned morning?"

"Yes, sir. If you wish, I can break in and tell him —"

"No," the president said, "don't break in." He swiveled back to his desk and replaced the telephone. "Don't tell anybody," he said aloud to the empty room.

He switched off the lamp and went upstairs to bathe and dress.

Sally Edgerton brought two cartons of Cadbury's up from the basement and put them on the counter beside the cash register. As she caught her breath she looked through the window at Stratford Road, London, W8. It was 10:35 A.M. The day was overcast. Mrs. Domby came out of the block of flats opposite with her dog, Harry, which should have been put out of his misery he was that old. A lorry rumbled by. A gray Toyota was parked in front of the greengrocer's for the second day. The man sitting in it was pretending to read the *Daily Mail*. Becoming a regular in the road, he was.

Sally started putting the Cadbury's in the sweets rack. She decided the man in the Toyota must be a private detective watching one of the studios in the mews behind the iron gates. The people who lived down there. When Sally worked as a char in the studios, she never knew who she was going to find in whose bed of a morning. They could do with a bit of watching, that lot.

Yarrow sat on the edge of his bed in his pajamas, listening on the telephone to Edgar Pollack. "What made him do that?" he asked.

"I don't know any more than I've told you," the director of Central Intelligence replied. "Wally just called me and said that Phil Teague came in for a talk with the president last night. Burke's made up his mind — if we find or win Mandelbaum, the Defense Department gets him."

"For debriefing and work on the American SDI program as long as it lasts?" Yarrow asked.

"Yes," Pollack said.

"And Teague tried to have the Orion operation closed down?"

"That's what Wally said. So far Burke's refusing to do it."

"Doesn't make any sense," Yarrow said.

"Can you be in Wally's office by six thirty?"

Yarrow picked up his bedside clock. "Yes," he said. "I want to know what's going on."

"I'm coming in too," Pollack said. "Same reason."

Yarrow hung up, shaved, bathed, and dressed in a blue shirt, red bow tie, and cavalry twill trousers and a gray herringbone jacket.

As he drove through the deserted streets, sunlight broke over the tops of trees and the roofs of taller buildings and lay in bright paths across Connecticut Avenue and Dupont Circle. It seemed to Yarrow that his first dawn drive to the White House on the Kornilov case had been years before. It was, in fact, only four days earlier.

He was cleared at the Southwest Gate. He parked on West Executive Avenue and walked toward the basement entrance. The air was fresh and cool. The rococo, nineteenth-century Executive Office Building towered above him against a clear April sky; the shadow of the White House lay across its first two stories.

On the ground floor of the West Wing, General Wallace Cresteau worked four doors away from the president. The national security adviser's spacious corner office was flooded with morning sunlight. The furnishings were spare and elegant. A Fitz Hugh Lane painting of a square-rigged ship at anchor was the only work of art on the walls. Cresteau's desk was a refectory table on which Captain Basil Liddell Hart, the British military theoretician, had done much of his writing. At the far end of the room a silver and china coffee service for three stood on a low table flanked by armchairs and a sofa.

Edgar Pollack was seated in front of the desk as the secretary closed the door behind Yarrow. Cresteau stood up. "Good morning, Jake," he said.

"Good morning, Wally," Yarrow replied.

"Edgar tells me you know what's happened."

Yarrow nodded. "But not why."

Cresteau gestured toward the far end of the office. "Let's have orange juice and coffee. Would either of you like toast? Eggs?"

"Not me," Yarrow said. He was trying to suppress his irritation as he crossed the room followed by Cresteau and Pollack. Yarrow had been in government service for over thirty years and was used to losing policy arguments. But this loss was charged with personal vitriol.

As they settled themselves with their backs to the office, the sun was touching the silver coffee pot with eye-burning glints; it lay in a warm swath across the thick carpet.

Cresteau handed Yarrow a cup of coffee and gave another to Pollack.

"Thank you," Yarrow said. "Now. What's up, Wally?"

Cresteau finished his coffee and set the cup and saucer on the low table. "Phil called Ted Green yesterday at about four and said he had to see Burke before the day was over. Assistant secretaries of defense usually don't have private meetings with the president — but Phil's no ordinary assistant secretary of defense. He's the ambassador from the party's right wing. Everyone around here and at the Pentagon knows it.

"Ted called me," Cresteau said. "I told him I wanted to sit in on the meeting. Phil came in at nine fifteen last night."

"And what did he say?" Yarrow asked.

Cresteau took a deep breath. "He began with you, Jake. Phil told the president he didn't think you ought to be running the Orion task force. You're too old, on the verge of retiring, not mentally up to it, your heart's not in it."

"Did Phil say he should take over from me?" Yarrow asked.

"He left the impression he could be persuaded to become the new head of Orion. There was something else . . ." Cresteau hesitated.

"Don't worry about hurting my feelings," Yarrow said. "You and Edgar and I have been in too many policy arguments to take any of it personally."

"I'm afraid Phil meant his last point about you personally," Cresteau answered. "He suggested that you couldn't be trusted, that it wasn't inconceivable that Orion — if you were still running it — might find Mandelbaum and turn him over to the Israelis without authorization from the White House."

"That son of a bitch," Pollack said. "Of all the —"

"It's all right, Edgar," Yarrow said. "What was the president's response, Wally?"

"Roughly the same as Edgar's," Cresteau answered. "Phil saw that he'd overdone it. He backed off. He told Burke that he isn't going to oppose the SDI negotiations any longer."

"The hell he isn't," Pollack snapped.

"Phil's new line," said Cresteau, "is that he wants the administration to negotiate from a position of maximum strength. He said last night that we'd be in that position if the Soviets knew that Mandelbaum had told us everything about their space defense program — and that he's working on ours."

"Did the president fall for that?" Edgar Pollack asked incredulously.

Cresteau shook his head. "No," he answered. "He caved in when Phil started threatening."

"Threatening what?" Yarrow asked.

"The worst scandal since Iran-contra if the president turns Dr. Mandelbaum over to the Israelis," Cresteau answered. "Phil laid it all out for Burke. Perry and Harry Dockerty's column in the *Washington Post* would break the story that the leading Soviet military research scientist defected and President James Forrest Burke turned him over to Israel."

"A story leaked to those Dockerty bastards by the Honorable Phillip Teague," Pollack said sardonically.

General Cresteau nodded. "The news would be all over the front pages of every major paper," he said. "It would lead all the network newscasts. The president would have to hold a press conference. He'd be bullied into admitting that he'd refused to insist that Mandelbaum submit to debriefing by American defense officials." Cresteau laughed briefly. "Phil made your argument sound so absurd, Jake, that he almost had me convinced."

"Of what?" Pollack asked.

"That Burke's choice on Mandelbaum — if we get him — is stark and simple. He can come out of this as a peace-through-strength president. Or, if he does it Jake's way, he'll go down in history as the biggest damned fool to sit in the White House since Harding."

"And Phil has the power to make all these bad things happen," Yarrow said.

General Cresteau nodded. "So he convinced the president." He leaned forward and picked up the silver coffeepot. "Refill?"

Pollack and Yarrow shook their heads.

"From what I read in the newspapers a majority of the public supports the SDI negotiations," Pollack said. "I would have thought Burke could explain his decision on Mandelbaum by simply telling the truth. The man was kidnapped, we bought him, didn't want to return him to the Soviet Union or jeopardize the SDI talks by using him on a research program we're hoping to close down anyway. So — we did the humane thing."

"My thought exactly," Cresteau said.

Pollack leaned forward, resting his elbows on his upper thighs. "Wally, did you try that line of argument last night?"

"I tried," Cresteau said. "Burke was badly shaken. He knew that he was being threatened. It wasn't a time for rational discussions."

"He told you to shut up, didn't he?" Pollack said.

Cresteau shoved his hands in the trouser pockets of his olive serge suit. "Something like that. The blunt fact is, Edgar, I lost. Phil won. At least for the moment. Maybe if Burke calms down . . . I just don't know."

Yarrow's irritation was turning into deep anger. "Did Mr. Burke ask Phil how he planned to force Mandelbaum to work on the American weapons program?"

"No, but I did," Cresteau said.

"And what was the answer?"

Yarrow only half heard a small noise in the office behind him. He and Pollack were too intent on the conversation.

"Mandelbaum's daughter is mentally ill," the national security adviser answered, "or has emotional problems of some kind. Phil suggested that, if we found her — do I understand that you have an idea where she is, Jake?"

Yarrow nodded. "Pete Durward's heard rumors about a strange woman wandering the country around Ivalo," he said.

"You aren't going to like this much," Cresteau said. "Phil proposed that both Gregor and Dvorah Mandelbaum be brought here, to Washington. We would then deny Dvorah psychiatric treatment until her father tells us everything he knows about the Soviet SDI program and agrees to work on ours."

There was an expression of shock and disbelief in Edgar Pollack's light blue eyes.

"And what did the president have to say about that?" Yarrow asked.

"I agreed to it," answered a voice in the office behind them.

Startled, Yarrow, Cresteau, and Pollack turned, stared, and rose to their feet almost simultaneously.

President James Forrest Burke stood by the door holding a sheaf of papers in one hand. He was wearing a blue three-piece suit whose buttoned vest hung loosely at his midriff. He looked ill and worn out. "I signed off on Mr. Teague's plan, Mr. Yarrow," he said in a dry voice. His eyes shifted to his national security adviser. "I tried to call you a little after five this morning. Your line was tied up."

"I was inviting Mr. Pollack and Mr. Yarrow to come in for this meeting," Cresteau answered quietly. "The communications people have orders to interrupt any call I'm on if you want me."

"I told them not to." The president looked from Cresteau to Pollack, from Pollack to Yarrow. "You've come in to talk about what happened — what I decided last night."

"Yes, sir," Yarrow replied.

Brittle as a burned tree, Burke stood in the morning sunlight as silence filled the large office. "Teague wants to take over your operation — what's it called again, Mr. Yarrow?"

"The Orion task force," Yarrow said.

The president peered through the windows behind Cresteau's desk. The melt of April had turned the White House lawn a voluptuous green. Red and white azalea buds were uncurling into brave new blossoms. "He wants me to fire you, Mr. Yarrow." The president turned back to the office. "I'm not going to do it," he said. "Go on looking for Dr. Mandelbaum."

"Yes, sir," Yarrow said.

"And his daughter. We want that young woman —" Burke stopped himself in midsentence. His sallow face reddened. "Wally, I was calling you at five o'clock to apologize —"

He stopped himself again.

The papers in his hand were trembling as he stared the length of the office at the three men who seemed to epitomize a confidence and dignity that he knew he would never achieve.

"Goddamnit," he said, "I can't stand Phil Teague any more

than the rest of you. But I had to go along with him. There wasn't any other choice."

The fluorescent light in the conference room flattered none of them. Joe Humphrey, at the end of a night's work, was jowly and heavy with fatigue. In the flat, unfocused glare Lester Brundance's tie was too bright, his shirt's stripes too garish, his tan forehead gleaming. Edgar Pollack's blond-gray hair made him look incongruously younger, and unwell. Yarrow's face was a map of pale plateaus and lakes of shadow. He stood at the end of the table, the others gathered around him listening to Henry Muffin on the radio speaker. It was 7:40 A.M. Yarrow and Pollack had just arrived from the White House as the NSA technicians were switching the circuit from Copenhagen into the conference room.

"His name was Kelyev," Muffin's voice said, "Boris Ivanovich. He held the KGB rank of colonel, arrived Copenhagen sometime early in January. Embassy cover, deputy press secretary."

Yarrow raised his head and looked at Margery Ferrall. "Would you see what we have —"

She nodded, scribbled the name on a pad, and left the room.

Pollack bent down to address the microphone. "Good morning, Henry. This is Ed Pollack. Where was Colonel Kelyev's body found?"

"Hello, Ed," Muffin answered. "He was near the house of a man named Bo Larsen on the fjord of Roskilde. Kornilov used to hire Larsen to take him fishing twenty years ago. Larsen was also killed this morning. Aksel Tausen was going to send a couple of guys out to talk to him today."

Yarrow pulled back a chair, sat down, and listened as Muffin described the killings at sunrise that morning.

"What happened next?" Yarrow asked.

"Aksel, Bent Jorgensen, and I had a good look around Larsen's house before the fingerprint people and photographers moved in," Henry Muffin answered. "There was a lot of superficial evidence that a man had been held prisoner there for several days —"

"What do you mean superficial?" Yarrow asked.

"Probably planted evidence," Muffin answered through the speaker. "We found a pair of handcuffs attached to an iron bed frame, three sleeping bags on the front room floor, one in the bedroom where they found the handcuffs. There were piles of unwashed shirts and underwear in two closets, a length of rope knotted to a chair in the kitchen, lots of dirty dishes, a frying pan in the sink, shells of a dozen eggs lying around — as if five or six people had had breakfast. We found several paperback novels in Russian."

Yarrow was trying to take firm possession of his mind and make it think about subjects of his choosing. But it insisted on reliving his conversation with Louise on the way in from Dulles airport the previous evening. For the third time since he and Pollack had left the White House, Yarrow forcibly wrenched his attention back to the present. "Sounds a little too good to be true," he said.

"That's what we thought," Muffin replied, "especially since the water line to a spare bathroom was shut off. There was a packet of defrosted squid in the refrigerator plus two fresh flounder."

"The significance of the flounder and squid escapes me for the moment," Yarrow said.

"The flounder tell us that Larsen had been out fishing sometime in the past twelve hours, probably yesterday evening," Muffin answered, "using squid as bait. If Kornilov and company had taken over Larsen's house several days ago they wouldn't have let him go fishing. By the way, Jake, as the two witnesses describe the sniper he sounds like the same guy who was in the dunes at Liseleje on the day you met Kornilov."

Yarrow looked down the length of the table for a moment. "Do you and the PET people think the sniper was the only one of Kornilov's men at that house," he asked, "that he'd been there only a few hours?"

"Looks that way," Muffin said.

"And he was holding the fisherman prisoner while he waited."

"Right."

Yarrow pursed his lips and nodded.

"Henry —"

"Is that Les?" Muffin asked.

Lester Brundance sat down beside Yarrow and turned the microphone halfway toward himself. "Yes," he answered. "I have a thought. Kornilov — or whoever's doing his thinking for him — knew that we and Galkin's people would come across Larsen's name in our files. He knew that both the KGB and the CIA would send somebody to talk to Larsen. Does it seem to you that the first Russian or American to get there was *supposed* to be killed? To make it look as if he'd stumbled on the place they were hiding Mandelbaum?"

"Absolutely," Muffin replied. "Kelyev was just unlucky."

Yarrow was looking at Brundance. "If you're both right," he said, "I have another question for you: Why is it suddenly so important to Kornilov that we think Mandelbaum is in Denmark?"

Paunchy, unshaven, Joe Humphrey was leaning against the conference room wall. His hands were thrust deep in his trouser pockets. His right shoulder was planted on a photograph of Dvorah Mandelbaum. "Maybe it's because of Lady Ellen Worth," he said. "We haven't discussed her yet this morning. As of two hours ago, MI-5 and Mike Lodge's guys from our London station thought they'd traced her to a mews house in west London. They've got it staked out. Maybe Lady Ellen saw strangers watching her and made a panic call to Kornilov. It could be that he's trying to divert our attention from Britain." He looked at Yarrow. "Just a guess."

"It's a good guess," Yarrow said. "An interesting thought. What else is happening, Henry?"

"The witnesses also saw the same Land Rover we saw at Liseleje," Muffin answered, "the one with paint spilled on it. The PET's putting on a huge search for it — every cop and patrol car in this part of Denmark has a description, they're using helicopters, watching all the ferry ports."

"I presume they're looking for the sniper too," Yarrow said.

"Yes. The two old bird-watchers and I were questioned for a police artist's portrait of the guy."

Margery Ferrall opened the conference room door. She came down the left side of the table, squeezed past Humphrey, and handed Yarrow a slip of paper.

He read it and raised his head. "According to our files Colonel Kelyev was one of Volya Galkin's loyalists."

"What do we make of that?" Edgar Pollack asked.

"Nothing at the moment," Yarrow said. "There's too much else to do today."

"That radio transmitter they can't locate was talking again this morning," Humphrey said. "Three broadcasts, the longest eleven seconds."

"Has the NSA made any progress on figuring them out?" Yarrow asked.

Lester Brundance shook his head. "They don't think the speaker's using a code. It's just the daily *prizak* based on phrases Kornilov's people in the field have memorized."

"What does *prizak* mean?" Pollack asked.

"Orders," Yarrow answered, "directives for action."

Old Paavo heard the evening wind at the mouth of the cave as he drifted up to consciousness. He was huddled beneath blankets and a fox pelt from his own bed. His fury took precedence over all other sensations, even the dying of his arm.

He had lost consciousness as the madwoman dragged him into the cave, regained it briefly while she was wrapping clean, wet rags around the bloody stump of his hand. She did not speak to him, her eyes didn't acknowledge him. Paavo Waltari would have thought that she was unaware of his presence beside her had she not been ministering to him.

Thereafter, he slept. He didn't know how long. When he awoke, he smelled smoke, a sign that she was in the cave. He no longer felt pain in the piece of flesh that used to be his hand. His arm had gone numb. He had the idea that the rest of him would die the same way, inch by inch. Before he was completely dead he had to get even with the Russians for sending men to saw off his fingers and thumb.

He propped himself on his other, living arm. The fire's glow was on the rock wall of the cave's deepest end. The madwoman squatted beside it. She was cooking something.

"Hei!" Paavo croaked.

She ignored him. In silhouette he could not see the dirt smudges on her face or her torn clothes. She was beautiful. Her hair's tangle ended at the exquisite curve of her forehead, and he could see the slender nose, the delicate mouth with a slightly protrudent upper lip, the small, perfect chin.

He tried to call out to her again, to tell her he was awake and grateful to her for pulling him out of the barn.

Again, she paid no attention to him. Her hands were busy with her work. But her mind seemed to be in another country.

Paavo Waltari had spent over fifty years avenging the deaths of his brothers in Finland's 1939–1940 winter war with the Russians. He had smuggled drugs into the Soviet Union, killed border guards, and brought out people who wanted to escape from the country. How, he wondered, could he punish the Russian turds for maiming him, for ending his life as a man? He wasn't afraid of dying. It was time for him to die, anyway.

But he couldn't let go until he had taken from the Russians something they prized as much as a man prizes his fingers and thumb.

The madwoman stood up with a steaming bowl and spoon in her hand. She walked back to him. She set down the bowl beside him. She was illuminated by the firelight. Her frail beauty was even more vivid as it shone through the dirt and scratches on her face. Paavo didn't want her as a woman. He felt a different warmth toward her.

She stood looking at him, but not seeing him. Her eyes were wide, staring fearfully at something that existed for her alone. She didn't speak. She turned and walked up to the cave's entrance. She sat down with her back against the rock wall and listened to the wind singing in the dying of the day.

Six hours later the sun had slid below the wet earth, shrubbery, and streets of Cleveland Park. Yarrow emerged from a government limousine into dusk. He paused on the corner in front of his house for a moment and looked through a lattice of branches and twigs at the cathedral two blocks away. The central tower stood in the gray of evening, its four pinnacles still tipped with sunlight. This was the place, the season, and the hour that Jake Yarrow loved most. He stood, entranced by the spring twilight, trying to let its impact on his senses quiet the anger within him.

He had returned to M Street from the morning meeting at the

White House in a state of cold outrage — at Phillip Teague, at the president for allowing himself to be bullied by Teague, at Teague's plan to use Dvorah Mandelbaum's suffering to coerce her father. The pressures and events of the day had distracted Yarrow from his anger. But, suppressed beneath his courtly manner, it was still within him, an icy quagmire.

In the deepening dusk on Macomb Street, Tiger Chadwick came around the front of the limousine. "Here's your briefcase, sir."

Yarrow took the worn leather bag from him. "Thanks for delivering the keys to Mrs. Yarrow this morning. Did you see her?"

"Yeah. She looked great. Those paintings are awesome."

"They certainly are."

"You shouldn't have driven yourself downtown today."

"I know," Yarrow said.

"Shall I pick you up at six thirty tomorrow morning?"

"Yes," Yarrow answered, "that'll be fine."

"You're having an awesome dinner," Tiger said. "Mrs. Yarrow told me what she was going to do."

"You need another adjective besides 'awesome,'" Yarrow said.

He heard singing. The chill within him receded. He walked up the concrete path, mounted the steps, and crossed the porch. The front door was unlocked. When he opened it a Mozart soprano aria flowed over him in a cascade of silver sound. Lamps had been switched on in the living room. He looked up. Through the banisters that lined three sides of the second-floor landing, he saw a vase of fresh flowers on a hall table. He smelled roasting lemon-rosemary chicken. Louise had brought his house to life and filled it with sounds, aromas, and light.

"Hello!" he said loudly.

She emerged from the kitchen wearing one of his long striped aprons over blue jeans and a high-collared chambray shirt. She had tied back her hair with a blue bandanna. Her freckled face was flushed. She smiled. "Hi, Love." She wiped her hands on the apron and kissed his cheek. "You're supposed to call a man named Humphrey at your office."

"Okay," he said. They were still standing face to face. He looked puzzled.

"What's the matter?"

"I haven't stood this close to you for years," he said.

"How do you like it?"

"Not bad," he said. He looked at her forehead. "Have you grown, or have I shrunk? You're almost as tall as I am."

"I've always been almost as tall as you are." She took his briefcase. "Go call Mr. Humphrey."

He tossed his raincoat on a chair and climbed the staircase. Louise had moved the stereo speakers out into the upstairs hall so that the music would fill every room of the house.

In his bedroom he saw his father's bound manuscript lying on the chaise lounge. He was pleased that she had been reading there. He turned down the volume on the stereo and dialed his office.

"Joe Humphrey," he said when the young woman of the overnight staff answered.

"Hang on a sec, Mr. Yarrow. He's down in the computer room."

He was put on hold. The old, scratchy recording of "The International" had been replaced with a parody by one of the Soviet Union's raunchier rock groups. Yarrow smiled at the off-color lyrics.

Joe Humphrey came on the line. "Hi. Those negotiations you had Les working on all afternoon —"

"With the Finns."

"Yes," Humphrey said. "Langley had a call back from Helsinki just after you left the office. At first light tomorrow morning the Finnish Border Patrol will send thirty men, one helicopter, and four military vehicles into the area east of Ivalo to look for Dvorah Mandelbaum."

"Good," Yarrow said. "Where are they going to start?"

"At Paavo Waltari's farm. They'll move up and down the border from there, checking on villages and Lapp settlements where she's been seen."

"Call me if anything happens," Yarrow said. "I'll be here all night. You can even put radio transmissions on this phone. It's secure."

He hung up and took off his jacket and bow tie. In the

bathroom he washed his face. He put on a black V-necked sweater, switched off the stereo, and went downstairs.

He found Louise bending a blue plastic ice tray. It crackled. The cubes rattled into the sink. She scooped up a handful and plopped them into two highball glasses. "Still not drinking?" she asked.

"Not a drop of the hard stuff for four months," Yarrow answered. "This is the year of the stomach. Diminishing its size." He filled one glass with Evian water, another with scotch and soda. Louise was leaning against a counter. He handed the highball to her.

"Cheers," she said.

"Cheers."

She drank and lowered her glass. "You're upset," she said.

He nodded. "But not at you."

"I know. May your trouble fly over the sea."

"Did your father say that?"

She laughed softly. "He wouldn't have even *thought* it about someone else's trouble. I read it somewhere. Synge, maybe."

"How long before dinner?"

She pulled open the oven door and glanced inside. "Fifteen minutes."

"Want to sit on the porch?"

She pushed her tall, slender body away from the counter and smiled again. "I set the table for dinner out there."

"You'd make somebody a good wife."

"I keep telling you."

He followed her through the dark dining room and into the living room, where the French doors were open to the soft spring evening. On the porch Yarrow pulled around two fan-backed wicker chairs so that they faced the screen — and the floodlit cathedral partially visible through trees and houses. There was a faint aroma of lilac mingled with the comforting, musty odors of the porch.

Louise sat down, put her arms on the chair's arms, stretched out her long legs, rested her head against the back of the chair, and closed her eyes. "The moments of peace are few and far between, aren't they?"

"Yes. And unexpected. I saw Henry and Dorothy not so long ago. Your little painting of eternity hangs in their guest room."

Louise turned her face toward him. Her reopened eyes shone in the dim light. "My picture of eternity?"

He nodded. "It's of a man and woman standing in the waves at the edge of the sea. He's holding her hand and pointing toward a brightness somewhere beyond the frame. It's a picture of peace. Hope. Promise."

She smiled at him without speaking for ten seconds. Then she said, "What a lovely — thank you, Yarrow."

He looked at the cathedral. It was too early in the year for insect sounds.

"How are Henry and Dorothy?" she asked.

"Fine. I think Henry will retire rather than take a desk job at Langley. In fact, he told me he would."

Louise raised her glass. "I hope they come back to this country. I do miss them."

"Dorothy said she owed you a letter. She sent you her love. They both did."

Louise drank and lowered her glass to the wicker arm. "I was going through your father's manuscript this afternoon."

"So I saw."

"Was it all right to do that?"

"Of course."

"It's been years since I looked at it," Louise said. "I don't un-derstand the parts in Czech, of course, but in English he describes himself very vividly."

"If I may ask, why did you want to reread it?"

"Because you and I are trying to sort ourselves out," she an-swered quietly, "and we both had difficult fathers."

For a moment Yarrow was taken back to the theater of child-hood memory — reexperiencing his desperate wish to please a man who showed pleasure in nothing.

"I was rereading his manuscript to see what orders your father gave you when you were a kid."

Yarrow looked through the screen at tangled branches and shrubbery. He felt a spurt of unease, as if Louise had uttered a blasphemy. "Orders . . ." he said. He was silent for a moment. "He didn't give me orders. His values, sure."

Louise stood up. "I'd better look at that chicken."

"I don't think I understand," Yarrow said. "Explain it to me again."

Their plates were empty, knives and forks placed side by side. The two candles on the table were reflected as spearheads of flame on the bowls of their wineglasses. Outside the screened porch, moonlight spread across the sky.

Louise sat with her elbow on the table, her chin resting in the palm of her left hand. She pulled a knobby strip of wax spill from one of the candles and rolled it into a ball between her right thumb and forefinger.

"I never realized until I was reading the manuscript this afternoon that your grandparents were Czech nationalist activists," she said. "Or, maybe I'd forgotten it."

Yarrow nodded. "My grandfather was arrested quite a few times by the Austro-Hungarian authorities."

"Your father had a terrible adolescence — at least as he describes it," she said. "He was raised to hate the government he lived under, his parents taken away when he was in his midteens, living in the city streets of a country whose language he couldn't understand, fighting in the First World War." She paused, raised her eyes, and looked at him in the candlelight. "Jake, why do you think he wrote that manuscript?"

Yarrow grimaced slightly and shrugged.

"Was it for himself or for you?"

"I don't think I understand the question."

She looked down at the ball of wax in her palm. "I'm not trying to explain your life to you." She raised her head. "Please believe that."

He smiled. "I believe it."

"But something occurred to me as I was reading the manuscript. It's a thought I've had before." She paused. "Jake, was your father — how do I say it? — *instructing* you to right all the wrongs of his life? Rid the world of the monstrous men and ideas that were responsible for the terrible things that happened to him in his youth?"

The past, a cluttered attic, was briefly illuminated in Yarrow's mind as if by a lightning flash through a dusty window. He couldn't — or wouldn't — see his father's face. He remembered the silent dinners in the gloomy kitchen and his boyhood desperation to please Conrad Yarrow.

He looked at the dark tree branches again. Etchings of silver moonlight lay on them. Yarrow was still angry at Teague and the president. He suddenly felt as if Louise had discovered a secret that was, somehow, shameful. He told himself to stay open and not retreat into cold aloofness.

"I've known you for nearly thirty-one years," Louise said. "Do you realize that there are two parts of your life we've never talked about?"

He looked back at her. He shook his head. "No. What are they?"

"What home was like when you were a kid," she replied. "You've told me about the boys you played with, about sitting on the porch, about the times you ran away. But you've never taken me inside your parents' house."

"And the other thing I've never talked about?"

"Why you chose an intelligence career."

"That's fairly obvious, isn't it?" he asked. "I'm the son of a Central European refugee who taught me a lot about modern history and the origins of tyrannies." Yarrow looked at her long face and inquiring eyes in the candlelight.

She smiled.

"As a matter of fact," he said, "I didn't choose intelligence. It chose me. The army found out I'd been raised bilingually and sent me to Russian language school, then to Germany . . ."

"Did you like army intelligence?"

Images of rainy winter mornings in Berlin drifted past him, of broken stone monuments to several German pasts standing in reproach to the bleak impersonality of the Allied occupation; teams of analysts trying to assemble snippets of information into military truths with the dispassion of lobotomized mental patients putting together a jigsaw puzzle; Soviet sentries, faceless inside their steel helmets, guarding their country's war memorial near the Brandenburg Gate; cigarette smoke hanging like fog in American military offices; rain on the window glass; British army officers who acknowledged their allied colleagues with the faintly derisive courtesy of the schoolmasters who had instructed, flogged, and lusted for them; limousines with official flags fluttering, speeding and splashing through the streets; Soviet officers in immense overcoats saying, through Yarrow's translation, that whatever American officers wanted or demanded could not be done, that whatever the Soviet Union was bitching or bawling about that week was "well known"; sudden onslaughts of cold called "Hitler's revenge"; the thin, white corpse of a thirteen-year-old girl who had frozen to death while trying to sell herself in a side street off the Kurfurstendamm. "It was worth doing," he replied. "It pushed me toward the CIA."

"And I know how much you've loved your work there." She smiled. "Can you accept that I've loved the fact of your doing it?"

He nodded. "Of course. But I take it you think I've been motivated by subliminal instructions from my father."

She looked across the table in silence for a moment. Then she nodded.

The dusk-dimmed kitchen of his parents' house in Tulsa appeared in his memory again. For a split second he reexperienced Conrad Yarrow's silence; it spoke to him still, stirring a shapeless anxiety that lay deep within him.

"Jake," Louise said softly, touching his hand, "this isn't about why you've lived your life the way you have. It's about why I felt overpowered by your kindness, your selflessness, when I left four years ago, about understanding now what made you that way . . ."

"Aside from demanding that I make up for his sufferings, what else do you think my father instilled in me?" Yarrow asked.

"An overpowering sense of obligation," she said. "A sense so great that you became a compulsive doer for others, a man incapable of receiving —"

"Really?"

Her beautiful face in the candlelight nodded. "Yes," she murmured. "I'm sorry. I know how much it must hurt hearing that." She looked away a moment, then back at him. "We had a terribly — what? — *unreciprocal* life together, Jake, darling. If that's a fault, at least fifty percent of it belongs to me. I took and took. It became so easy."

"We were talking about me," he said.

"I thought up a phrase . . ."

"Tell me," he said.

She smiled. "The tyranny of the benefactor."

It stung like a whiplash across his heart. He returned her smile. "Not bad."

"Let's stop this part of the conversation," she said. "I hate it. Let's have some coffee."

He stood up. "I'll clear and —"

Louise stood up. "No. *I'll* clear and make coffee. You sit down, defy your instincts, and let me do something for you."

"I'm not very good at talking about myself," he said.

"I know," she said.

"Do you understand what I've just told you?"

She was leaning against a porch pillar, her empty coffee cup held in both hands, looking down at him. One candle had burned out. The moon had moved on.

Louise nodded. "Yes. You can't figure out what role you'd have in a new — if you and I got back together."

"And that I love you."

She nodded. "Yes. You love me." She took a deep breath. "Do you understand that I love you?"

"Yes."

"Believe it," she said. "I think you're barking up the wrong tree, Yarrow."

"Why?"

"Well . . ." She turned her head and looked up, through the black twigs and branches, at the sky, the stars. The remaining candle cast its anemic light on her neck. Shadow began above her curved jaw. Yarrow could not see her face above her cheekbone. "Did I ever tell you I spent some time with a psychiatrist after I left you?" she asked.

"No. Was it useful?"

She nodded. "I learned one thing — that the problem usually isn't the problem. It's the way you *think* about the problem." She pulled back her chair and sat down, putting the coffee cup in its saucer on the table. "I didn't love you — I don't love you — because you were my caretaker. I love the good, real man who shines through your self-denial and your compulsive generosity. But, much as I love you, Jake, I couldn't live with your self-denying stoicism again, I couldn't stand watching you being ground down a little more every year by the burden of slaying your father's dragons."

Yarrow felt an urgent requirement to deny what she was saying. "With all love and respect," he said, "I have to tell you that I don't buy it," he said. "I am what I choose to be. Not what my father ordered me to be."

Her gray eyes were looking directly into his eyes. For a moment she said nothing. Then she withdrew her hand and sat up straight in her chair. "Do you believe in the value of symbolic acts?"

"If they're relevant to the matter at issue, yes."

"I think that Conrad Yarrow possesses you. You say that he doesn't." A small, tired smile curved her Tiepolo mouth. "Prove it. Give me his manuscript. Let me walk out with it, knowing you'll never see it again."

A panic he did not understand whirled up from the darkness within him. "You dislike my father, don't you?"

Louise shook her head. "No. I never knew him. He's irrelevant, Jake, except as a phantom that still haunts you. He inspired you to do wonderful things, to become a wise man. But I'm trying to loosen his grip on you now that your professional life is coming to an end. I want to be your wife again. But I want you to be able to take from me as much as you give, ask as much as you respond. Conrad Yarrow won't let you do that. Until I reread his manuscript this afternoon I'd forgotten the power of his bitterness and self-pity . . ."

The remaining candle was guttering down. Louise pinched its

wick and the flame was gone. Her face was colorless in the star-light. "You've obeyed him, Jake, darling. You've done everything he asked of you. Now put him behind you."

"It's too late," Yarrow said. His voice chilled her. "Think of some other symbolic act."

He was looking directly across the table at her. His mouth was set in a straight line, his eyes were too deep in shadow to read.

"You're still trying to please him, aren't you?"

She had discovered the oldest truth about him. He knew that he would lose her if he refused to acknowledge it.

"Yes," he said.

His right hand lay on the table. Louise covered it with both her hands. "Jake," she said, softly, urgently, "for both our sakes, let me take that damned manuscript — or burn it yourself and be free of him . . ."

"No," he said.

THE SUN GLOWED just above the dunes to the east. The black-haired rifleman stood on the driveway of the house in Liseleje, the salty breeze of the Kattegat strait in his face. It was eight seconds before 7:00 A.M. He took the little short-wave radio from his jacket pocket, switched it on, made sure the dial light was set properly on the 20-meter band, and listened.

He heard static and faint music. The static blended with the fluttering sound of the wind under the porch eaves.

A male voice suddenly barked words and phrases through the speaker. It talked rapidly for fourteen seconds. It stopped. Once again the rifleman heard static and music so distant that it seemed to be left over from the night before.

He switched off the radio and went to his duffel bag, which was lying open on the grass. He spent the nights outdoors. Being inside the house alone at night would be too terrifying. He knew he would see the phantom of the fisherman standing in the moonlight by a window, grinning at him. Maybe he'd have seen the other one too, the one he shot in the field.

He felt safer sleeping outdoors, under the stars, hearing the sea.

Twenty minutes later he had changed into blue jeans, running shoes, a black nylon jacket, and a knitted cap. He went up onto the porch and got the case holding the disassembled Snayaperskaya Vintovka Dragunova semiautomatic rifle from a woodbox where he'd hidden it. He put five clips of steel-jacketed bullets in a cardboard box and shoved the box under his arm.

With his free hand he unlocked the garage, pulled open the door, and went inside. He put the rifle and box of ammunition on the floor of the Land Rover and inspected the black tape masking the paint spill on its left rear roof and hatch.

He unlocked a drawer in a workbench at the back of the garage and took out two automobile license plates. He knelt down, unscrewed the license from the front of the Land Rover, and put a new one in its place. He replaced the rear plate. He put both old license plates inside the vehicle.

It was 7:24 A.M. when the rifleman backed out onto the driveway and turned the Land Rover up onto the beach road. He got out and locked the garage. He was glad to be away from the house. Even in broad daylight it seemed ghostly to him. It was too silent in there. The specter of the fisherman might be sitting in the kitchen waiting for him. He preferred going without breakfast to walking in there.

He drove into the center of Liseleje and turned south with the morning traffic toward Route 16, which would take him across the country, into Copenhagen.

"It's four twenty-five in the goddamn morning!"

"I know," Yarrow said.

There was a look of exasperation on Joe Humphrey's darkbrowed, jowly face. "Are you coming in early or have you been out somewhere you didn't tell me about?"

They were standing in the communications room. The technician on duty was recording a voice at triple speed off a National Security Agency circuit from Fort Meade. With the speakers turned down the sound was, Yarrow thought, like an animated cartoon conversation of termites chattering among the consoles, dials, lamplights, cool lights, hot lights, circuits, tape decks, reels, and switchboards. "Coming in early," he said, without looking at Humphrey. "What's that?"

"The morning *prizak*," said the technician, a tall, pale young man. He stood in front of an Ampex tape recorder watching two large reels turning at fifteen inches per second.

The termite chattering ceased. The technician punched a button. The reels stopped. The tech jabbed another button. The reels whirled backward and stopped again. "It ran fourteen seconds this morning," the young man said. "Want to hear it at regular speed, sir?"

Yarrow shook his head. "Is Fort Meade making any progress locating the transmission point?"

The young man rethreaded the tape on the Ampex. He shook his head. "These Soviet guys are on the air and off too fast. All we know is that it's coming from northern Europe — way north."

"I need to talk to you, Jake," Joe Humphrey said.

Yarrow stopped for a cup of coffee in the kitchen and went into the duty office. He closed the door and settled himself in a soft leather chair. Humphrey leaned against the windowsill. "Our best friend made contact again in Moscow this morning."

Yarrow sipped at the scalding black coffee, hoping it would shock him out of his rusty lethargy. "Good. What did he say?"

"That Volya Galkin's really pissed off about his guy Kelyev getting the swat yesterday at Larsen's house," Humphrey answered. "Guess what?"

"I give up," Yarrow said. He looked out the window. It was still dark, the same darkness in which he and Louise had reached an impasse. Along with every other feeling he could identify within himself — numbing fatigue, despair, love that hurt like an amputated limb, regret — Yarrow's anger remained. It baffled him. He had broken out of its icy grip as Louise was leaving. They were standing at the open front door, the dark porch behind her. He was trying to say that he needed time to think, he needed to talk to her some more, when she put her hand around his wrist and raised her head —

"Well?" Humphrey asked.

Yarrow looked up at him. "I'm sorry," he said. "I was distracted for a moment. Tell me again."

"Galkin's sent the Mongol manhunter to London."

"General Tseden," Yarrow said. "What for?"

"To run the Soviet search for Ellen Worth."

Yarrow thrust out his lower lip and raised his eyebrows. "Volya must think she's pretty important. That means we'd better think so too."

Bits of stone. The idea. In the three years Sally Edgerton had worked at the minimarket nobody had complained about the dog food. Then bold as you please, Mrs. Domby comes in tugging mangy old Harry on his leash, claiming that there were bits of stone in his tinned food. Stone. Don't be daft, Sally had told her.

The woman had glared and said that she would never set foot again as long as she lived, even if it meant walking all the way to Knightsbridge for the shopping. She had yanked the leash and tried to stalk out the door but flung poor old Harry into a stack of loo paper instead.

Sally picked up the last roll — it was on the far side of the shop — put it back with the others, and straightened up. Her back didn't half ache. She looked through the windows at Stratford Road. A second detective had arrived in a blue van that morning. The first one was still in his gray Toyota parked across from the minimarket.

Sally had noticed the second detective when she opened up at eight o'clock. Hel-lo, she'd said to herself, what's this, then? He was an older chap, gray hair. His blue van wasn't half dirty and pranged up.

Drugs, Sally Edgerton told herself. They must be looking for drugs. With all the foreigners about — she'd already seen a Chinaman in the road that morning. The two men watching Stratford studios clearly weren't together. Maybe he was one of those drug peddlers they always talked about. Very odd. It wouldn't surprise Sally a bit if the police nicked the whole lot of them who lived down there — the film director, the doctor with his new girlfriend, her loopy ladyship. Come to think of it, *she* might be on drugs. She acted it, with her loud voice and airs and all.

Sally saw another roll of bog paper out on the pavement. Mrs. Domby had left the door open when she finally got Harry sorted out. Bits of stone indeed.

Silly old cow.

At twenty minutes past noon the traffic flow through central Copenhagen was heavy but steady. The rifleman drove past the Tivoli Gardens, past the art museum, and over the bridge. He passed the Scandinavia Hotel and turned a half right onto Amagar Brogade.

The sun was at its apex. The rifleman's plan satisfied him. It would keep them guessing for days if it came off properly.

He drove four blocks and turned right again. He was in a working-class neighborhood cluttered with shops, low apartment buildings, and old stone houses. He slowed the Land Rover and turned left into an alley, carefully easing his way between a brick wall and a row of trash cans. When the vehicle couldn't be seen from the street, he set its emergency brake, found the two old license plates, and got out. Working quickly, the tall, black-haired man changed the plates again, bolting the old ones back on. He stripped the black tape off the cream-colored paint spill on the roof and rear door. He got back in, took the rifle from its canvas case, and assembled it. He shoved in a ten-shot clip and laid the Dragunov just under the front seats.

Two minutes later the Land Rover was out of the alley, parked against the curb, and locked. The rifleman crossed the sidewalk, entered a building, and rode the lift up to the third floor. He found a window from which he could see the street.

Even in broad daylight he didn't like being alone indoors. There was a corridor leading down to the apartments. The sniper didn't dare look at it in case he saw someone he had killed standing there, smiling at him.

He checked the snub-nosed .38 revolver tucked in his belt just behind the buckle, zipped his jacket, and looked down at the street instead.

Louise had been holding onto him as tightly as if she were drowning and his wrist was rope. But the words she was speaking were a farewell. "I can't think of any more arguments, I can't make you see —"

"Louise," he had answered, "you're asking me to change —"

"Yes," she said. "Change for me — both of us. Give me your weakness as well as your strength! Admit that you're a prisoner — I admitted *I* was — to dogma, nuns, original sin — and you helped me free myself." In the dim light her eyes were pleading in accompaniment to her words. "Can't you see that I need to give — or my love for you means nothing?"

"You asked me to make a symbolic act," Yarrow answered. "The real issue is what's symbolized — you're asking me to change the way I think about myself, my life —"

"Does that frighten you, Jake? Changing? Reexamining?"

For a long moment he didn't answer. His father had always

stood like the phantom of Hamlet's father on the ramparts of Elsinore, demanding justice. Now Louise was telling him that the phantom itself was unjust, that his doubt was both sane and righteous. "I don't know what to say," he replied.

That was when she had let go of his wrist, turned away, walked halfway across the porch, and stopped.

"I've never pleaded with you," Yarrow had said.

"Don't."

After a moment she had gone down the steps and turned right on the sidewalk. Yarrow had stood watching as she unlocked her car, got in, and drove off into the night.

Now, in the full light of morning, he sat in his office trying to define what had happened. He didn't know if the standoff at his house the previous evening had been their last chance at reconciliation. He didn't know if it had been one painful encounter in a whole sequence they would have to endure before they finally achieved reunion or separated forever.

Yarrow desperately wanted to telephone her, to convince her — and himself — that there was still hope, possible compromise. But it was only twenty minutes past seven in the morning. Louise was a late sleeper and slow to come to full, functioning consciousness. He was also afraid that, if he called, she would tell him that she had decided to give up, that his father had won.

Someone knocked.

"Come in," he said.

Margery Ferrall opened the door. "They're waiting for you in the conference room," she said.

Yarrow nodded. "Right."

Margery scrutinized him for a long moment. He was in his shirtsleeves. His face was pale and puffy. He appeared to be preoccupied, almost dazed. "Jake," she said, "are you all right?"

He made himself smile. "Sure. Fine." He stood up and took a folder off his desk. "Who's with us this morning?"

"Les," she said, opening the door wider to let him out, "Joe, me, Mike by circuit from London — not Henry."

"I was hoping we'd have some news about how the search for Dvorah Mandelbaum's going in Finland," Yarrow said, crossing the main suite.

"Durward's standing by on a circuit from Helsinki," Margery said behind him.

Yarrow opened the conference room door. "Where's Henry?"

Joe Humphrey looked up from his seat at the table. "Henry's gone out," he said. "His office told us that Aksel Tausen called him about a half hour ago."

Old Paavo was cold. He felt the madwoman's hands on his shoulder, shaking him. She was speaking to him for the first time, a frantic whispering of words he didn't understand.

He opened his eyes and looked up at her. "Talk Russia," he said.

"Men!" she hissed. In the half-light her eyes were wide again beneath the mess of hair that hung over her face.

"What men?"

The madwoman helped him sit up. He pushed off his blankets. With her arm supporting him, they crawled up to the cave's entrance. He heard a roaring sound. Propping himself against the rock, breathing heavily, he looked out.

At the bottom of the hill a Finnish Border Patrol helicopter was settling onto the field below his farm. Finnish jeeps were parked on the dirt road nearby. Officers and men with dogs were swarming around everywhere. Paavo saw border patrol troops coming back on foot from the north.

It was midafternoon. Paavo saw a KGB Border Guard standing beside the Russian grove on the Soviet side, watching his Finnish counterparts maneuver their helicopters and jeeps and observing the returning patrol from the north. The KGB men in Tower 118 were also watching through glasses.

"Finns," Paavo said in his broken Russian. "These right down here Finn man. Border patrol."

The powdery dirt on the madwoman's face was streaked with tears. "They'll find me," she said as she crouched behind Paavo. "They'll take me away. I have to stay until Papa comes . . ."

Old Paavo suddenly understood the scenario of her insanity. She had come to Lapland possessed of the idea that her father — some Russian who was fool enough to try crossing the forbidden zone — was going to get out of the Soviet Union and take her away with him. Old Paavo still didn't know who she was. But at least he understood why she was wandering around the forests, swamps, and hills along the border.

The madwoman pointed off to the right. "There! There!"

Paavo put his cheek against the rock and peered at an angle down the side of the hill. Two Finnish patrolmen were coming up slowly, trudging, pausing, their eyes on the ground.

Old Paavo reached into his pocket and found his knife. He handed it to the madwoman. "Open!" he commanded.

She stared at him, hesitant and afraid.

"Open! Quick!"

She pried open the large blade and handed the knife back to him.

She gasped as he sliced off his bandages. The remnant of his hand was purplish black. There was pus and a protruding splinter of bone where his thumb had been. He drew the knife blade across his palm, feeling nothing. Blood spurted into his sleeve.

Clutching the rock wall with his other hand, Paavo pulled himself to his feet. Chills raced down his spine and thighs. Swearing and muttering, he squeezed himself through the entrance, into the bushes and vines.

He sat down in the shrubbery. He turned his head. In the cave's gloom he saw the madwoman's wide, demented eyes. "Go back!" he grunted softly. "Back! Wait for Papa!"

The ground dropped away steeply below him. The cold mud was soaking through his trousers, chilling his thin buttocks. Paavo pushed himself forward.

He half slid, half tumbled down through the wooded side of the hill. He hit trees, bruising his hard body. He felt as if he were falling out of time and light, rolling over and over, gathering up his childhood, images and memories, his dead brothers, his women and reindeer, as he went.

He crashed into a thicket and stopped. He got to his feet and staggered out of the trees. The two Finnish border patrolmen stared at him in horror. Paavo sat down on the ground and thrust out his bloody stump to show them evidence of his life and of his sacrifice for the madwoman who had saved him. Then he fainted.

Hands were lifting him, carrying him. He was in a vehicle,

tucked in, warm and being taken somewhere over roads of ruts and bumps.

He was safe. The question was asked in Finnish. "A woman. Young. A foreigner. Have you seen her?"

Paavo Waltari remembered what he had been doing. He had left the cave to lead them away from her. He resurrected her in his mind with his eyes closed so that only he could see her.

"There was such a woman," he said. "She was here a long time ago."

"Did you see her?"

"Twice, perhaps three times."

"Not lately?"

He didn't want to open his eyes and lose the memory of the beautiful, dirty child-woman. He shook his head. "Not for a long time," he said, pleased to be lying. "Maybe the Russian bastards got her. They cut off my fingers —"

"Yes, you've had a bad time. We're taking you to the hospital in Ivalo."

"Maybe their dogs got her," Old Paavo said. "Maybe she's dead now."

It wasn't that Muffin didn't understand. He understood exactly what was happening, and the realization frustrated him almost beyond endurance.

"They must have abandoned it," Aksel Tausen said. "They aren't stupid enough to think we wouldn't see it parked in the street."

Muffin was sitting in the front seat of Tausen's car, arms folded, chin down, which gave him a slightly belligerent expression as he stared through the windshield at the Land Rover. It was parked half a block away on the right-hand side of the street. They had been watching for an hour and fifteen minutes.

"They want us to find it," Muffin answered in Danish. "Our black-haired friend knows he can get our attention with that vehicle. He knows we'll have to consider several possibilities — that Mandelbaum's being held in the vicinity of the Land Rover, that he's somewhere else and the Land Rover's been brought here to distract us . . ." He shrugged.

Tausen looked through the glass. In the bright sunlight of early afternoon an old woman carrying a net shopping bag was the only moving being on the street. Supporting herself with a cane, she was poking along slowly toward the corner where Tausen's car was parked. Trucks, vans, and automobiles stood bumper to bumper along both curbs. Nine of them were unmarked PET vehicles. Bent Jorgensen sat two cars behind the Land Rover. Muffin had left his blue Volvo station wagon around the corner on Amagar Brogade.

The Danish police captain turned to him. "Distract us from what?"

Muffin shook his head. "I don't know," he said, "and neither does Yarrow. But distraction's what these appearances of the shooter and the Land Rover are about. My guess is that the killings at Herslev yesterday may have been as much to stop us from doing something as to keep us from talking to Bo Larsen."

"If killing is a part of the technique of distraction, we could have a dangerous situation here," Tausen said.

"We could," Muffin answered. "That's why I suggested you use a bomb squad if you decided to look through the Land Rover. It could be wired." He watched the old woman for a moment. "Aksel, what would it take to search every house, apartment, room, and basement on this street?"

The blond counterintelligence officer leaned forward, folded his arms over the top of the steering wheel, and squinted in the sunlight. "The best way would be to put a man behind every house and building to watch the rear exits, then blockade both ends of the street . . ." He looked at Muffin. "Two hundred and fifty people, an hour and —"

"Aksel!" Bent Jorgensen's voice burst through the radio speaker. "He's moving!"

Tausen snatched his microphone from its hook beneath the dashboard. Muffin grabbed the door handle and peered through the windshield.

The black-haired man, wearing jeans, a black nylon jacket, and running shoes, was walking across the sidewalk to his Land Rover. "I'll take him," Muffin said, opening the front door.

"Henry goes first!" Tausen barked into the microphone. "After he passes, Bent, you follow!"

The rifleman had walked into the street and was unlocking the Land Rover. As Tausen watched, he opened the door and climbed in.

Tausen turned to Muffin. "*Go!* Both of you — *be careful!*"

Muffin slipped out of the car. He walked swiftly to Amagar Brogade and got into his blue Volvo.

The rifleman saw the cop two cars back. He saw the black man go around the corner. It was working. They were doing just what he wanted them to do. Had he the gift of exhilaration or its vocabulary he would have laughed aloud in delight. He was relieved to be outdoors, out of the eerie building.

He started the Land Rover. Its engine roared. He put the gear in reverse, backed up, shifted again, twisted the wheel, and moved out into the street.

The sun was in his eyes. The rifleman pulled down the visor. The speedometer needle rose to fifteen kilometers an hour as he proceeded down the street. No faster. He would go no faster. Everything depended on the mixture of speeds.

He glanced at the rearview mirror. A blue Volvo station wagon was coming up behind him. Another car was pulling away from the curb behind the Volvo as the rifleman braked slightly and turned the Land Rover around a corner to the right.

The street before him was empty. He pressed down the accelerator. The Land Rover shot forward. The speedometer needle swept up to sixty. He slammed on the brakes after a half block and turned the next corner to the left. He looked in the mirror. The blue Volvo hadn't reached the first corner.

The rifleman went fifty feet and stopped. He flipped a catch below the dashboard of the land Rover. The rear hatch swung open. He picked up the Dragunov. There was already a bullet in the chamber. He twisted his body around and rested the rifle on the back of the seat.

The Volvo station wagon came around the second corner. Sunlight flashed on its windshield for an instant. It approached the

Land Rover, the driver slowing down, obviously puzzled. The second car turned the corner behind the Volvo.

The rifleman fired.

The Volvo's windshield imploded, blasting inward, shards and splinters of glass following the trajectory of the steel-jacketed bullet into the front seat, into the face of the driver.

The rifleman put the Dragunov back on the floor, released the handbrake, and drove off. Through the open rear door he heard a grinding, metallic crash, then the hollow thud of another collision.

As he swung the Land Rover around a third corner he glanced back. The blue Volvo station wagon had crashed into the side of a parked van. A thin jet of steam was hissing from the Volvo's crumpled hood. Its windshield frame was empty, gaping like a wound. The car that had been following it had rammed into the back of the Volvo. There was glass and water or gasoline all over the street.

FROM SINGAPORE to Kansas City, from darkness to
noon, bells jangled in newsrooms as the world's wire services transmitted the fact of Henry Muffin's death. Yards
of copy followed, written and rewritten based on the few details
released by Danish authorities, rehashing historic cold war murders, quoting baffled experts on their bafflement.

It had been late afternoon in Moscow when Genady I. Oblomov read the five-line item on a Tass machine. Alarmed, he ripped
off the bulletin and hurried down Lubyanka's fifth-floor corridor
to Valerian A. Galkin's office.

France Soir was the only Paris newspaper that published an
Associated Press photo of the body. The picture had been taken
through the open front door of the Volvo station wagon. In profile, Muffin's lips were slightly parted, his eyes open. The upper
half of his forehead was gone. Glass fragments and splinters covered his shoulders and chest.

In London two tabloids scheduled the gruesome photograph
for their morning editions. The BBC ran the story of the killing
in Copenhagen as the lead item on its nine o'clock television news.

Radio stations in New York filled the afternoon with updates
consisting of predictable and therefore meaningless reaction stories interspersed with telephoned reports from stringers in Copenhagen.

At 5:45 P.M. the managing editor of the *Washington Post*
threatened to fire a photo editor who argued too long for pub-
lishing the picture of Muffin's corpse.

Twilight came down on the Eastern Seaboard.

Coolly, crisply Canadian, Peter Jennings said good evening.

As the batteries of clocks and television monitors behind him
went out of focus, he launched into the American Broadcasting
Company's chronicle of the world. "We begin tonight with the
murder of an American diplomat in Copenhagen," he said.
"Henry Muffin —"

A six-year-old photograph of Muffin appeared in the upper right-hand corner of the television screen.

"— was shot and killed in his car this afternoon as he was driving through the Danish capital," Jennings said. "Mr. Muffin was assassinated one day after a Soviet diplomat was murdered in Denmark. The Danish parliament spent the evening in emergency session. Left-wing and conservative parties alike demanded a full investigation and diplomatic protests to Moscow and Washington by the coalition government of Prime Minister Nils Hansen . . ."

A TV screen glowed audaciously in a dusk-dimmed reception room on the seventh floor of the State Department. Four people — the Danish ambassador to the United States, General Cresteau, Edgar Pollack, and Jake Yarrow — stood together, watching.

"World News Tonight" switched to Copenhagen. Positioned in front of the floodlit parliament building, an ABC correspondent said, "It was common knowledge in this city's diplomatic community that Henry Muffin, officially a senior political officer of the U.S. embassy, was the CIA station chief for Denmark. The Soviet embassy's deputy press attaché, Boris I. Kelyev, a shooting victim near the cathedral city of Roskilde yesterday, is believed to have been a colonel in the KGB."

"There, Mr. Pollack, is your problem," said Tove Buhl, the Danish ambassador. She was a tall, full-bodied woman in her early fifties. Her blond hair was cut short, her face was wide and amiable. She wore a tweed suit and carried a cream-colored envelope in her right hand.

Edgar Pollack's rage showed in the straight set of his mouth and the tightness of his folded arms. He glanced sideways at her. "What problem?"

Ambassador Buhl nodded at the screen. "That journalist is one of fifty who arrived in Copenhagen today from all over Europe. The Mandelbaum secret has been kept well. I was informed about it only this afternoon in a briefing telegram from Danish counterintelligence. But now, suddenly, a great many newspeople will be trying to find out what lies behind these murders."

Peter Jennings was back on the screen. "There has been no

comment from Moscow," he said. "In Washington the Central Intelligence Agency has, as is its custom, declined to confirm or deny that Mr. Muffin was its chief operative in Denmark. We understand that the Danish ambassador went to the State Department forty-five minutes ago —"

"Mr. Yarrow."

Yarrow turned. A receptionist at a wide antique desk said, "A call for you, sir."

Yarrow crossed the large antechamber to a wing chair in a corner of the room. He picked up a telephone from a side table. "Jake Yarrow."

"It's Margery," his assistant said.

"Hi," Yarrow answered. "What's up?"

"Mike Lodge just called from London. Joe and Les are talking to him," Margery said. "Louise is on the line to your office at Langley. She's pretty upset. I think you ought to speak to her."

Yarrow looked at the shadowy group in the center of the antechamber. On the television screen purple cartoon raisins that looked like middle-aged Middle Eastern middlemen were dancing and singing their way through a commercial.

"Of course," Yarrow said.

"I'll have her transferred," Margery said. "Hold on."

Yarrow looked again across the reception room. The seventh-floor offices of the secretary of state — the most elegant official suite in Washington — command a view over parks, avenues, the Lincoln Memorial, the Potomac and its Virginia shore. The last scorching streaks of sunset lay across the western horizon. At ground level, lights glittered among the budding trees.

"Jake?" Louise's voice said.

"Hello," he answered, trying to sound as warm as his need for her compelled him to be and as reserved as his surroundings required. "I take it you know."

"I heard it on 'All Things Considered,' " she said, her voice skittering along the brink of tears. "I was driving back . . . now it's on every television news program. God, how awful. *Henry* . . ."

Yarrow imagined her standing in the kitchen of her little house on Forty-seventh Place, the telephone in one hand, tears gleaming on her cheeks. He suddenly yearned to be with her, to distract himself from his own grief by comforting her. "I know," he said. "I tried to get ahold of you this afternoon."

"Oh, Jake . . ."

"Look," he said, "I'm going to be tied up until about —"

"Is it all right if I call Dorothy?" Louise asked.

"Yes, sure," Yarrow said. "I talked to her a couple of hours ago. When I'm through this evening I want to see you."

She didn't answer for a moment. Then, "I can't even think about it now, Jake."

"Louise, that isn't why I want —"

Wordlessly, she began to weep.

Yarrow raised his head again. The television set had been switched off. Wallace Cresteau, Edgar Pollack, and the Danish ambassador were standing at the windows, their backs to him. The receptionist was engrossed in a telephone conversation of her own.

Yarrow had been stunned, then paralyzed by emotional turmoil after Lester Brundance brought him the news of Henry Muffin's death at noon. In his anguish he remembered his wife's plea that he drop his mask of self-confidence when there was no confidence in him and concede his sorrows and doubts to her.

On the telephone her sobbing had quieted. "Louise, last night you asked me —"

"Dear Jake . . ." She hesitated.

"Say it."

"I think we used up all our words last night," she replied. "I want to go to Copenhagen if Dorothy needs me."

He felt as if she had slapped him. "I think Dorothy will need you," he said, his voice suddenly cold and impersonal.

"Wait, wait, I meant —"

"Margery will be glad to help with airline reservations or whatever."

"Jake —"

Yarrow hung up and walked across the waiting room to where Pollack, General Cresteau, and Ambassador Buhl stood by the windows. The sunset had burned out. He saw the first stars.

*

"I think that now you have a serious problem, Tom," the Danish ambassador said.

Seen in lamplight, Secretary of State Thomas L. D. Ballard's mustache looked like a small, white patch on his red face. The secretary's hands were curled around his chair arms' wooden ends. He stared at nothing and nodded. "Yes," he said distractedly.

Ballard was a former legal counsel to the State Department and American ambassador to the European Organizations in Geneva. His older brother, Hugo, was secretary of defense — and totally cowed by Assistant Secretary Phillip Teague. The Ballard brothers were Wall Street lawyers, honorable men, but not equipped intellectually or by force of character for great office. President James Forrest Burke had chosen them because the Ballards were moderate Republicans and because he felt superior to them.

Thomas L. D. Ballard was wearing a red-striped shirt, green tie, and a rumpled gray suit. He was forty pounds overweight. He brought his attention back to the handsome woman sitting on the opposite side of a coffee table at one end of his office.

"First," she said, "I am instructed by the queen and my government to express their condolences to Mr. Muffin's family and his Central Intelligence Agency colleagues."

Seated on a sofa beside Yarrow, Edgar Pollack unfolded his arms. "Please thank Her Majesty and Prime Minister Hansen," he said.

Ambassador Buhl laid her envelope on the coffee table. "Now the serious business. This is a formal letter from the Danish foreign ministry, Tom," she said. "I have come this evening to express our outrage over this violence in our country. Many people believe it is Soviet-American political violence.

"The Folketing was in session until after midnight, Copenhagen time, tonight," Ambassador Buhl continued in her fluent, slightly chanted English. "The conservatives are demanding that we suspend diplomatic relations with the Soviet Union. The left-wing parties say that now Hansen must remove Denmark from NATO altogether . . ." In the subdued light, her expression had become grim. "Shooting deaths are shocking to us, Tom. The appearance of *politically motivated* shootings —"

"Oh," the secretary of state said. "I don't think it's . . . it wasn't political —" He took a linen handkerchief from his hip pocket and wiped his palms. "Mr. Yarrow here is in charge of our task force . . . the people looking for Professor Mandelbaum. I asked him and Mr. Pollack to join us to answer any questions you or your government may have . . . about the search, you know . . ."

"Yes." Ambassador Buhl turned toward Yarrow. "Is it your belief that Professor Mandelbaum is a prisoner somewhere in Denmark?"

Yarrow shook his head. "I doubt it, Madam Ambassador," he answered. "My associates and I think that Henry Muffin and Colonel Kelyev were killed to make it *appear* that they were getting too close to places where Dr. Mandelbaum was being held in Denmark."

"Do you mean they were murdered as diversions?"

"Yes."

"But why, Mr. Yarrow?"

"Because somewhere else, somebody, Soviet or American, may be getting too close to the place where Dr. Mandelbaum really is hidden," Yarrow answered. "We think that place is either in Finland or Britain."

Ambassador Buhl raised her head. "How outrageous," she said softly. "To kill two men as a diversionary tactic . . ."

Ballard turned his florid face to Cresteau. "Wally?"

"Ms. Buhl," Cresteau said. "The president takes your government's concerns very seriously. We all hope we can find, or win, Dr. Mandelbaum without any further violence."

"Edgar?"

Pollack shook his head. He had withdrawn back into his fury over Henry Muffin's death.

Tove Buhl stood up. "Thank you, gentlemen. I am sorry that I must come here on an errand of reprimand." She held out her hand to Secretary Ballard. "But now there is a political crisis in Denmark. Something else for which we can thank this Major Kornilov."

Yarrow gazed through the windows at the deepening twilight until the secretary of state had seen the Danish ambassador to the door. Ballard came lumbering back across the office and seemed to collapse into his chair. His shirt collar was too tight. His belt was too tight. Red veins on his cheeks looked like tiny worms trapped beneath the skin.

"It's all coming apart," he said, a quaver in his voice. "People are being killed . . . a mob of reporters milling around downstairs, demanding that we say something . . . Tomorrow the right-wingers will be yelling about suspending the SDI talks with the Soviets, the liberals will accuse the CIA of starting a private war with the KGB . . ."

Suddenly the secretary of state seemed to realize that he had begun to whine. "I'm sorry," he mumbled. "It's just that time's running out. How many days left?"

"Today's almost over," Yarrow said. "Three, Mr. Secretary."

Ballard nodded miserably. "There is still a chance it will all be all right, isn't there, Mr. Yarrow?" He managed a weak smile. "None of us want the Russians *or* Phil Teague to get their hands on Dr. Mandelbaum."

Like a man in remission who suddenly remembers that he's ill, Yarrow was stung again by the fact of Henry Muffin's death, by the fading hope of reconciliation with Louise. "Yes, sir," he answered, "there's still a chance." He glanced out the office windows. The Lincoln Memorial's interior glowed in the April darkness. Jets returning to National airport flew down the river at three-minute intervals, their wing lights flashing.

In the elevator going down to the State Department's basement garage, Yarrow stared at the floor for a moment. His hands were thrust into his trouser pockets, the flesh of his neck was squashed into several chins above his shirt collar and bow tie. He raised his head. "If you have no objection," he said to Edgar Pollack, "I'll be going to London tonight. The British have found a woman who used to be Kornilov's lover. I'd like to talk to her myself. Nothing else is working very well at the moment. We're getting reams of information from criminals, senile ex-communists, KGB defectors. We've expanded the American and local search teams in London and Copenhagen — and all of it's led us nowhere."

"Go," Pollack said. "When will you be back?"

"Tomorrow afternoon. Les Brundance will take over while I'm gone."

"I was interested in what you told Tove Buhl about Kelyev and Henry's murders being diversions," Cresteau said.

Yarrow nodded. "That's half the equation — killing a man to make it look as if we're getting close to Mandelbaum. The name of the game now is to find out, if we can, where they're trying to steer us — or the Soviets — away *from*."

The elevator decelerated. It stopped with a soft bump. The doors slid apart.

Four men, including Tiger Chadwick, were standing behind three government limousines in the garage, which smelled faintly of old oil. One of them, seeing Cresteau, Pollack, and Yarrow emerging from the elevator, spoke into a walkie-talkie. There was an answering burst of static and talk.

"I've ordered Tiger to move into your house, Jake," Pollack said. "If you're going abroad, I want him to go with you."

"Oh, I don't think that's really —"

"As of this evening we regard the Mandelbaum case as dangerous," the director of Central Intelligence said. "And I don't feel like arguing about it."

"Jake, I'll tell General Fitzmaurice that you may be needing air force overseas transportation later tonight," Cresteau said. "There will be a telephone number you can call at any hour."

Yarrow nodded. "That's kind of you, Wally. How's the president taking Henry's death?"

"How do you think he's taking it?" General Cresteau replied.

"Sorry I asked," Yarrow said.

As Tiger drove him through the evening streets of Washington, Yarrow's new beeper began chirping frenetically in the pocket of his tweed jacket. He called Margery Ferrall on the government limousine's telephone. She told him the news about Paavo Waltari and said there was new information about Lady Ellen Worth.

Lester Brundance, in his shirtsleeves, tie unknotted, was waiting in the brightly lit fifth-floor hall at 2025 M Street when Yarrow, followed by Tiger, came off the elevator.

"You should have gone home hours ago," Yarrow said.

"Not with Henry dead, Old Paavo turning up alive, and Lady Ellen breaking cover," Brundance answered.

"Where was she?" Yarrow asked as they went in to the Orion task force offices.

"Joe will tell you all about it."

As Yarrow crossed the suite, two secretaries outside the communications room stared at him as if the loss of his friend had disfigured him.

Brundance opened the conference room door and stood aside to let Yarrow enter first.

Joe Humphrey, dark-browed, his blue shirtsleeves rolled up to the middle of his forearms, was standing at the side of the table before the microphone and speakers. He expressed his grief over Henry Muffin's death with extra voltages of exasperation. "She's sitting in an apartment in Fulham," he said to Yarrow. "The goddamned Brits can't talk her into moving to safer custody and won't force her."

Margery Ferrall had followed Yarrow into the conference room. "See if you can get Sir Eric Cope on the telephone," Yarrow said to her. "Apologize for waking him in the middle of the night."

When she had gone, he pulled off his raincoat and took his seat at the head of the table. "All right," he said. "Tell me what's happening — in sequence."

Humphrey sat down. Brundance and Tiger Chadwick leaned against the wall.

"The Finnish Border Patrol found Paavo Waltari," Humphrey answered. "Pete Durward has flown back up to Ivalo from Helsinki. Waltari's in bad shape, been tortured, apparently. They're going to amputate his arm tomorrow."

"Did he say anything about Dvorah Mandelbaum?"

Humphrey opened a folder and peered at a document inside it. "Burned barn," he muttered, "blood poisoning . . . Dvorah . . ." He looked up. "He told the border patrol officer that he's seen her, but not recently."

"Anything else on Waltari?"

Humphrey shook his head. Beneath the fluorescent glare from the ceiling he looked pale and soiled.

"All right," Yarrow said. "Tell me about Lady Ellen Worth."

"An MI-5 plant inside the British Communist party heard that she's been shacked up with a guy on Stratford Road, Kensington, since January," Humphrey said. "The Brits put watchers on the place to verify her location in a mews house off the main street. About noon today, London time, Ellen Worth came out carrying two suitcases and looking scared. She took a taxi to an address on the Wandsworth Bridge Road in Fulham."

Humphrey leaned forward and looked at his notes again. "The watcher on duty followed her. MI-5 says one of her Communist party buddies lives in a small apartment above a shop there. The Worth dame refuses to leave. MI-5 surrounded the building and then called us."

Margery opened the conference room door. "Lady Cope on line three," she said.

Yarrow punched a blinking button and picked up the telephone. "Sarah, it's Jake Yarrow. I'm sorry —"

"You do know there's a five-hour time difference between London and Washington, don't you, Jake?"

"Yes. I wouldn't have disturbed you if —"

"It's two forty-five in the morning here," Lady Cope said. "We dined at the Perrys' and didn't get in until —"

"I'm sorry, Sarah," Yarrow said, "but someone's life may be at stake."

"God, I'm bored with you people calling Eric at all hours —" There were muffled noises in London as she put her hand over the telephone speaker. A moment later Yarrow heard a cheerful male greeting. "Jake! How are you?"

"Fine, Eric. Sorry to wake you —"

"Don't give it a thought," said the head of MI-5, British counterintelligence. "I expect you're calling about the Wandsworth Bridge Road standoff."

"That's it," Yarrow answered. "I —"

"Hold on half a tick."

Yarrow said nothing for ten seconds.

"Right," Cope said. "She's on her way downstairs to shove the dog out for a pee. Shoot."

"Something made Lady Ellen move this afternoon," Yarrow said. "Any idea what it was?"

"We've had people watching her friend's mews house in the Stratford Road," Sir Eric replied. "I imagine she knew we were there. Then a second watcher turned up this morning in a small blue van and took pictures of her coming out of a mini super-market on the corner. She saw him, seemed to panic, dashed down the mews, packed, and left an hour later — God knows why."

"Who's the second watcher?" Yarrow asked.

"A short, heavy chap, sixtyish. Identified from photographs our stakeout took of him as one Kenneth Rightie, thug."

"Political?" Yarrow asked.

"Criminal," Sir Eric answered. "The smut trade, dirty pictures, books. He's gone inside twice for kiddie porn films."

"Interesting," Yarrow said. "That could tie him to Kornilov."

"Your Russian likes a bit of filth, does he?"

"So we gather," Yarrow said. "Did Rightie follow Lady Ellen to Wandsworth Bridge Road?"

"Yes. Took note of where she was and then left. We put a tail on him. He went to a block of flats in Camden Town and parked the van. About nine thirty this evening he came out, drove down through central London, Chelsea, and Fulham, got on the Hammersmith flyover — and then our tail lost him, damnit."

"Refresh my Fulham geography," Yarrow said.

"The Hammersmith flyover leads on to the M4 which takes you to Heathrow airport — among other places," Sir Eric answered.

"Do you happen to know if there were any flights from Copenhagen this evening?" Yarrow asked.

"We've been keeping track of such things since Mr. Muffin was killed in Denmark and we've found Kornilov's ex–lady friend here in London," Sir Eric answered. "Yes. A BA flight from Denmark came in at seven twenty."

"So, if Kornilov's sniper was on it, your man Rightie didn't meet him?" Yarrow asked.

"Because Rightie went to Heathrow at nine thirty?" Cope asked. "You'd make a hopeless operations man, Jake. If I had a badger arriving on a scheduled air flight, I'd assume I was being followed. I'd get word to the badger to disembark, take himself away to some inconspicuous place around or near the airport. Then I'd go fetch him a few hours later."

"Of course," Yarrow said. "Eric, could you get ahold of a blue van like Rightie's if we needed it?"

"Piece of cake," Sir Eric replied. "But why would Kornilov want Lady Ellen killed?"

"Just guessing," Yarrow answered. "She may know something that would lead us to him. Perhaps they sent the rifleman to England to help guard Mandelbaum until the auction. Or, he may not be there at all."

"Caution requires us to assume that he is and that he's after our troublesome lady in Wandsworth Bridge Road."

"I called to ask about her situation," Yarrow said. "Is there any way you can get her to move to a safer place?"

"Sorry, old boy, not possible. We've talked to her by telephone. She insists on staying with her friend in the flat above the shop. She's committed no crime, and unless we get a court order —"

"No," Yarrow said, "don't do that."

"If I were you, I'd get started quickly trying to persuade the woman to cooperate," Sir Eric Cope said. "I'm told she's difficult and somewhat eccentric. Has Mike Lodge got a bod in the London CIA station who could have a go at her?"

"No," Yarrow said. "Her questioner has to be familiar with every file we've got on Kornilov. Someone from Washington, in other words."

"Yes, I can see that," Sir Eric said.

"I thought I'd come over myself tonight," Yarrow said.

"Good," Cope said. "Fast as you can, Jake. What with the possibility that this sniper's somewhere about, the situation is very unstable, and I don't mind admitting we're not completely in control."

"Shall do," Yarrow said.

"We're all shocked about Mr. Muffin," Cope said. "I never met him, but I understand you and he were friends — and that he was among the best."

"He was," Yarrow answered. "I haven't quite taken it in yet.

Thanks again, Eric. If I don't see you tomorrow, it will be soon, I hope. How's young Eric getting along at Oxford?"

"Dropped out," the head of MI-5 answered. "He's living in an ashram in the Punjab, lucky devil. I understand they never bathe and the ladies —"

"You and I were born thirty years too soon," Yarrow said.

He replaced the telephone and got to his feet. He gathered up his raincoat and went down the side of the table.

Lester Brundance took his jacket from a chair back and shrugged it on. "Jake, you know how sorry we all are about Henry."

Yarrow nodded. "Yes. I know. Me too. Tiger and I will leave for London immediately. Back tomorrow afternoon, I should think. I told Edgar Pollack you'd take over."

Margery Ferrall handed Yarrow a slip of paper as they came out of the conference room. "The duty office at Andrews," she said. "They have an aircraft staffed, fueled, and ready for you." She appeared to be close to tears.

"Thank you," Yarrow said. "I wonder if they're mourning for Colonel Kelyev in the west wing of Lubyanka."

Joe Humphrey came out of the conference room. "As if they were real people?" he said sardonically.

Yarrow took a deep breath. He started to say something but changed his mind.

Tiger parked the limousine across the street and one hundred feet away from Yarrow's house. He switched off the headlights and looked through the windshield. "Don't get out yet, sir," he said. "I think we've got a visitor."

Yarrow peered over Tiger's shoulder. A young man in a parka stood beneath the streetlight on the corner. He was of medium height and his posture conveyed the impression that he'd been waiting for some time.

He stared down Macomb Street. Then he turned, walked beyond the perimeter of light, turned again, and walked back in. He stopped, and thrust his hands into his parka pockets.

"That man wants to be seen," Tiger said, "and he wants to be sure somebody *knows* he wants to be seen."

"Seems that way, doesn't it?" Yarrow answered softly.

They looked down the street in silence. The man looked back at the black limousine.

"Now watch," Tiger murmured. "He's sure we're us. He's beginning to wonder why we don't get out. He's thinking about how he can appear even more harmless. Know what he's going to do next?"

"No."

"Take his hands out of his pockets, so we won't think he's got a gun."

The man under the street lamp took his hands from his pockets.

"Bingo," Tiger said.

Yarrow opened the rear door and got out.

Tiger opened the front door. "Hold it, sir —"

With Tiger beside him, Yarrow walked diagonally across the street.

He heard the sound of Wisconsin Avenue traffic a block away. A squirrel scampered up the sidewalk and veered off into the darkness. Someone in some nearby house was singing.

The young man stood with his hands at his sides, motionless, watching Yarrow approach.

Tiger moved out in front. They passed Yarrow's house and stopped ten feet from the corner. "My name is Jacob Yarrow," Yarrow said in Russian.

"Anastas Hagopian," the young man replied. "I have a message from Major Kornilov." He spoke in English.

"How do we know you're Kornilov's man?" Tiger asked.

"When Mr. Yarrow met Major Kornilov on the beach at Liseleje he drank two cups of coffee," Hagopian answered. "The first was with brandy, the second without."

"He's right," Yarrow said to Tiger. "Only Kornilov could know there was no brandy in the second cup of coffee."

"*Kharasho*," Tiger said. "What's the message?"

"You will submit your bid for Professor Mandelbaum on the afternoon of April thirteen at two P.M."

"To whom?" Tiger asked, watching the Armenian intently.

"Me. Your messenger will address me as 'Harry.' "

"Where?"

"On R Street in the first block west of Connecticut Avenue." Hagopian looked at Yarrow. "You will receive a telephone call in your office at midnight that night with instructions about where the results of the auction will be announced." In Russian Hagopian said, "Do not try any stupid tricks, Mr. Yarrow —"

"How come you couldn't say that in English?" Tiger asked in Russian. "Is the slang too difficult for you?"

"I doubt it," Hagopian replied in English, giving a lilt of hauteur to his voice. "What slang do you assume I cannot speak or understand, little man?"

"Maybe, like, fuck off," Tiger said in English.

Hagopian looked at Yarrow. "When you submit your bid on the thirteenth, don't send it with your pet ape here." He sauntered off into the darkness, down Thirty-sixth Street toward the cathedral.

THIRTEEN ❖

L ONDON'S OUTSKIRTS sprawl for miles across south-
eastern England, the rubbish spill of an old imperial capital.
On the morning of April 12 a cloud cover hung low over
the terraces of yellowish gray houses, factories, aluminum ware-
houses, high-rise offices, and dwelling blocks. The dual carriage-
way in from Heathrow airport was shining wet and crowded with
cars and trucks. The Jaguar entered Cromwell Road between
rows of drab little hotels. Their flickering neon signs beckoned
with the charmless enticement of an old harlot's wink.

"MI-5 parked a blue van like Rightie's just opposite the apartment," said Mike Lodge, chief of the CIA's London station. He
was a tall, angular man with enormous eyebrows. He sat in the
front seat of the Jaguar beside the driver. His body was half
twisted around so that he could talk to Yarrow and Tiger behind
him. "If either Ellen Worth or her friend look out the window
they've got to see it."

"Good," Yarrow said.

"We're all operating on the assumption that the bastard who
hit Henry was on that BA flight from Copenhagen last night,"
Lodge said. He looked through the car's side windows as if
Kornilov's sniper might be among the people on the sidewalk —
an old woman, a cycling boy, a postman, and two Arabs in rain-
coats and kaffiyehs. The Jaguar was entering Earl's Court Road,
an exotic clutter of Middle Eastern groceries, restaurants, shops,
and cinemas.

"What's Tseden up to?" Yarrow asked.

"He visited the Communist party offices on St. John's Street
when he arrived," Lodge said. "Then, yesterday morning he and
one of the local KGB types went over to Stratford Road where
Lady Ellen was holed up," Lodge said.

"Did Tseden follow Lady Ellen to the place she is now?"
Yarrow asked.

"Don't know," Lodge answered. "The MI-5 stakeout was too

busy trying to keep up with her and watch Rightie to notice what the opposition was doing."

Tiger Chadwick looked tired. Shortly after their military jet left Andrews Air Force Base outside Washington, Yarrow had fallen asleep. Tiger had stayed awake through the short night concocting violent revenge fantasies starring himself and Henry Muffin's murderer.

"When do I make the telephone call?" Yarrow asked.

"In a few minutes," Mike Lodge said. "The Worth woman's a little batty, Mr. Yarrow. Better make your main point fast."

"Do my best," Yarrow said.

The Jaguar slowed and turned left off New King's Road. The driver went around another corner and parked on Studdridge Street.

They were in a Fulham neighborhood of Victorian row houses built of brick with white window and door trim. Blossoming mock orange and ornamental cherry trees stood in front gardens. A young woman in a blue cardigan and tweed skirt was impatiently holding open the door of her station wagon for a small boy in a school uniform and a yapping Welsh terrier.

Three short blocks ahead, Studdridge ended at Wandsworth Bridge Road, a traffic-choked artery lined with shops. A short, bearded man in a soiled raincoat got out of a car, crossed the street, and slid into the back of the Jaguar.

"Hello, Gawain," Yarrow said.

Gawain Prior of MI-5 grinned through his beard. "Hello, my old darling. Ready for the dotty Bolshie ladies and all that?"

"Ready as I'll ever be," Yarrow answered. "This is Tiger Chadwick."

Prior scrunched up his shoulders and managed to shake hands with Tiger. "Nice to see you. Good morning, Michael."

"Morning, Gawain," Mike Lodge said. "Everything still in place?"

"Far as we know."

"Okay." Lodge took a telephone from its cradle beneath the Jaguar's dashboard. He punched up a number and handed the phone across the seat back to Yarrow.

As Yarrow put the receiver to his ear, the call was already being answered. "My name is Yarrow," he said. "Lady Ellen's life is in danger. I've come to help her."

There was a protracted silence. Then a woman's voice said — or asked — "American?"

"Yes," Yarrow said. He wondered if he was speaking to Lady Ellen or her friend. "Maxim Kornilov is in the west again."

" 'Ow would you know that, then?"

"Because I've talked to him," Yarrow replied. "A man working for Kornilov killed a friend of mine in Denmark yesterday . . ."

Mike Lodge held up a copy of the *Daily Express*. The photograph of Henry Muffin's body filled three-quarters of the front page.

"It's in this morning's *Daily Express*," Yarrow said.

"I saw."

"The gunman who did that may have arrived in Britain last night," Yarrow said. "We don't know who he's after —"

"The American killed over in Denmark was CIA."

"So am I," Yarrow said. "I've just come in from Washington this morning. I'm on Studdridge Street around the corner from your flat. I want to talk to Lady Ellen —"

"Comrade Worth . . ." The woman pronounced it "combraid." She left her sentence unfinished.

"British intelligence and the CIA are not her enemies," Yarrow said. "We are the enemies of Maxim Kornilov, who has had three people killed already. One of them was a Soviet KGB officer."

"She's in the loo," the woman said, dropping her voice to a rattling whisper. "She int 'arf scared out of her wits, that blue van comin' back an' all —"

"I'm going to walk over to where you are," Yarrow said. "I'm a heavy man, sixty-four years old. I'm wearing a brown tweed jacket and a bow tie. A young man will be with me. He's a professional bodyguard."

"I don't know if she'll —"

"We'll be there in approximately five minutes," Yarrow said. "Tell Lady Ellen not to go out, and to stay away from windows."

He handed the telephone to Lodge, who replaced it beneath the dashboard. "Gawain will take you from here," Lodge said. "I'll wait."

The ceiling of cloud was breaking up. The street onto which Yarrow, Tiger, and Gawain Prior emerged was in shadow. Ahead, pale sunlight fell on Wandsworth Bridge Road.

Prior and Tiger walked toward it together — two short men, one middle-aged, the other young and unmistakably American in his Brooks Brothers raincoat, gray slacks, and brown loafers. Following them, Yarrow wondered again why Lady Ellen had chosen drab Maxim Kornilov as her lover more than two decades before.

She had been beautiful and probably as passionate sexually as she was in her political convictions. According to her MI-5 dossier, she had joined the British Communist party during her student years at Lady Margaret Hall, Oxford. As a Marxist aristocrat she had, for a while, enjoyed a degree of celebrity in London's left-wing salons and at Soviet-sponsored international youth and peace conferences.

Gawain Prior looked back at Yarrow. "Stop a moment," he said.

They had reached the busy avenue. There was a bakery on the left, a greengrocer's open shop across Studdridge Street. The traffic on Wandsworth Bridge Road was momentarily gridlocked. Small, dull shops were interspersed with boutiques and trendy little restaurants. All the buildings were two stories high. Cars and small trucks were parked bumper to bumper at both curbs. "There's a few of our merry lads," Prior said, gesturing at three workmen who appeared to be patching a flat roof across the road.

"How many do you have staked out in cars?" Tiger asked.

"Seven," Prior replied. "Six more are walking about. Weapons have been issued. There's your blue van, Jake."

It was parked in front of the building where the roofers were working.

"The flat's four doors down," Prior said. "The owner's name is Lucy Tunney."

"What's behind her building?" Tiger asked. "On the side facing away from all this?"

"Private houses along Bowerdean Street. All swept this morning around eight," Prior said. He grinned. "Dads were getting ready for the capitalist rat race, mums feeding baby. The Metropolitan Police have Bowerdean under surveillance."

"Sounds good to me," Yarrow said. "I think we've given Lady Ellen enough time to think."

"The best of British luck," Prior said. "You'll need it."

Tiger and Yarrow turned the corner onto Wandsworth Bridge Road. They passed the bakery, a dry cleaner's, a tobacco and sweet shop. Tiger stopped at a brown door. There was a metal-lined mail slot but no bell.

He twisted the handle. The door swung open. Yarrow saw a steep staircase inside with a window at the top.

Tiger pushed aside his raincoat and took a Wembley automatic from a back holster and shoved it in the waistband of his trousers.

He started up toward the landing. Yarrow went in, closing the door behind him.

As he began to climb the stairs he smelled frying bacon. Somewhere far away a radio was playing rock music.

Tiger had reached the top.

"Let them see me first," Yarrow said softly. "I described myself."

At the top of the stairs, Yarrow paused to catch his breath. Then he knocked twice.

He heard a scurrying sound. A chain rattled and the door opened three inches. A thin, red-faced woman with white hair looked out at him.

"My name is Jake Yarrow, Miss Tunney," Yarrow said. "I'm the American who telephoned."

The door closed. The chain rattled again. The door swung open. Lucy Tunney wore an apron over a pair of slacks, work boots, and an incongruously frilly blouse. "I told 'er," she half whispered to Yarrow. "She's griteful you've come. Imagine! Oh, she int 'arf scared! But controlled. 'Ave to give 'er that. Very controlled —"

"Do stop *muttering*, Lucy!" said a loud voice.

"In the parlor," Lucy Tunney said.

Tiger squeezed into the apartment past Yarrow and went down the passage. He stopped at the door of a room overlooking the street. There was a window on the other side of the hall.

"I was expecting an *older* man!" boomed the hollow, patrician voice.

"He's right behind me, ma'am," Tiger said. "I'm supposed to check out everything first."

"Oh! The bodyguard!"

"Yes, ma'am."

Yarrow came into the apartment. Lucy Tunney slammed and locked the door, refixing the chain. She clumped along the passage and disappeared into a kitchen.

Yarrow went down the hall. He glanced out the window on his left. He saw the back of a brick house, a small, fenced garden, a stone terrace, a clothesline draped with diapers and a baby's shirts. One upstairs window of the house was partially open.

He looked through the door to his right. Tiger was in the middle of a tiny living room made spotty pink by rose-petal wallpaper. Lady Ellen Worth stood before a sofa in a long overcoat. She was holding a glass of sherry. The sounds of voices, heavy engines idling, and shoes scuffling on the pavement drifted up from Wandsworth Bridge Road.

For a moment Yarrow stared at Ellen Worth. According to her file she was forty-seven years old. She had not changed her manner of dress or her hairstyle to accommodate her age. She was a caricature of her young womanhood.

Her straight, shoulder-length hair was dark brown. She wore a beige overcoat. Her eyes were ringed with shadow the color of bruises; her cheeks and the flesh beneath her chin had become puffy. Her mouth, once captured by the camera in a sensual half smile, was now curved down at the corners, as if drawn by gravity.

"Mister —?"

"Jake Yarrow, Lady Ellen."

"Ah! The Northampton Yarrows! Ned, Betty —"

"I'm an American," Yarrow said. "My father was born in Czechoslovakia and changed his —"

"I was at school with Betty," Lady Ellen said. "But of course now . . ." She gestured slightly with the hand that held the sherry glass. "You see my circumstances."

She spoke in the exaggerated drawl of the English upper middle classes. Her version of the accent was made bizarre by its booming volume. "Comrade Lucy gave me your message," she said.

"You are a good and noble man to come so quickly! When we saw the blue van in the road and realized that that terrible person had found us —"

"Tiger," Yarrow said. "Perhaps you'd wait in the kitchen with Miss Tunney —"

"*No!*" Lady Ellen stepped forward so suddenly that sherry spilled down the front of her coat. She put her arm around Tiger's shoulders. "No! He has been sent as my bodyguard! Perhaps you aren't aware, Mr. Yarrow, but *another* man hired by Maxie has already killed three people, one a Soviet comrade! This bodyguard must be with me at all times!"

Tiger disengaged himself and pulled off his raincoat. "It's okay," he said, smiling at her. "I'll stay and protect you if you tell Mr. Yarrow what he wants to know."

"Oh! I can see that you are an honorable —"

"Only if you tell Mr. Yarrow about Maxie."

Lady Ellen gazed vacantly at Yarrow. A clock ticked somewhere in the room. "Sherry, Mr. Yarrow?" she asked.

"Thank you," he said.

He sat down on the sofa as she crossed the room to a pseudo-Jacobean wooden cupboard. Tiger leaned against the wall.

Lady Ellen filled two tiny glasses.

She recrossed the room, passing momentarily through a shaft of sunlight. The living room door was open. It faced the window in the hall.

"He was here last winter," Lady Ellen said, handing a sherry glass to Yarrow.

"Kornilov? Maxie?"

Lady Ellen returned to the center of the room. She sipped from her glass. Her eyes were fixed on one among the countless wallpaper rose petals. "He hasn't changed," she said vaguely, as if distracted by a passing thought. "He looked old when I knew him years ago." She sipped again. "So, you see, he hasn't changed . . ."

"Was he alone when he came to see you?"

Ellen Worth emerged from her reveries. "No, Mr. Yarrow, he wasn't alone. Maxie isn't — you must take note that I no longer refer to him as Comrade Maxie, not after what he's done. He isn't personally violent — the man who brought him to me in the blue van *is*." She suddenly looked at Tiger. "A terrible man!" she cried. "He said he'd kill me if I told!"

"Told what?" Tiger asked.

"I was frightened after they had gone," she said. "Stephen Hampton —" She turned toward Yarrow. "You know him, of course."

Yarrow shook his head.

"Mother's doctor. Stephen has wanted to do it to me for ages. Some younger men prefer women of experience, you know. I went directly to his house —"

"On Stratford Road," Yarrow said.

"In the mews. I felt safe there. Only the comrades knew where I was."

"You went to Stephen's in January?" Yarrow asked.

"It was winter."

"And you felt safe there until you saw the blue van in Stratford Road?" Yarrow asked.

"I came immediately to Comrade Lucy." She drained her glass of sherry. "Now I feel safe again with my bodyguard."

Yarrow sipped at his own glass. "What attracted you to Maxie all those years ago?" he asked.

Lady Ellen cocked her head. Her gray eyes contemplated him as if memory had fled from her again. "Maxie?" she asked. The sudden softness of her voice startled him. "Maxie was only our *decoy* . . ."

"I don't understand."

The clock ticked five times. "We knew they were watching us," she answered, still speaking in a muted voice. "The comrades are always under surveillance, Mr. Yarrow. We're threats, you see. We are the specter that haunts Europe . . ."

" 'All the powers of old Europe have entered into a holy alliance to exorcise this specter,' " Yarrow replied, quoting the next lines from the opening of Karl Marx's *Communist Manifesto*. " 'Pope and Czar, Metternich and Guizot . . .' "

Lady Ellen smiled at him, fleetingly but expressing her pleasure in him. "Oh! I can see that you are a true comrade, Mr. Yarrow!" she boomed. Miraculously, she had retained her train of thought.

"Since Georgi and I were being watched, Maxie became our decoy! He would come to my flat in the Pheasantry —"

"What was the rest of Georgi's name?" Yarrow asked, suddenly excited but forcing himself to appear calm.

"Maxie would come early in the evening bringing the followers with him. Oh, Mr. Yarrow! I watched them from upstairs! I could see them behind the windscreen of their motor in the King's Road!" She turned toward the sherry cupboard. "If Maxie and I went out for a bite to eat or to a film, they were right behind us."

She moved through the sunlight and opened the cupboard doors. "Then Maxie would leave, taking the followers away with him, and Georgi was free to come to me! It was delicious!" She turned her head and smiled at Yarrow again. She poured another glass of sherry and replaced the bottle in the cupboard. She turned toward the window overlooking Wandsworth Bridge Road. "We were true lovers."

"Lady Ellen," Tiger said. "I don't think you should —"

"Maxie knew he was our decoy," she said. "He was willing to do it because Georgi was his only friend. But he wanted to —"

Almost simultaneous with the distant crack of a rifle shot and the shattering of glass, Lady Ellen's body slammed forward against the window. An amber glob of sherry was flung into the sunlight, broke apart in droplets, and showered onto her flying hair as she crumpled, her hands clawing down the sides of the window frame. Yarrow heard Tiger yelling at him.

Lady Ellen was on her knees below the window, bent over upon herself as if in prayer. A bloodstain widened on the beige coat that stretched across her back.

Then she sagged to one side and tumbled in a dead sprawl across the floor, like a supplicant exhausted by her devotions.

At 6:05 that morning the Russian sniper had driven onto Bowerdean Street. He was not wearing his black wig. He parked the stolen Ford, switched off the engine, and waited.

At 7:44 A.M. five uniformed London police officers, four men and a woman, had arrived in two cars. They rang the doorbells of all the houses on the south side of the block, went into each, and searched.

By 8:11 A.M. four of them had driven away in one police car. The fifth policeman had parked the other. He sat for ten minutes watching the street, then got out and walked around the corner to Studdridge Street. Leaving for coffee — or whatever he was after — saved his life. The Russian was about to walk to his car and kill him with a small-bore pistol shot in the back of the head and then prop his body upright in the front seat.

Instead, the sniper picked up his rifle, which was wrapped in brown paper, got out of the Ford, and walked over to number 39 Bowerdean. It was a semidetached house with a parking space on its left. He rang the bell. A smiling man dressed in shirt, tie, and the trousers of a business suit opened the door. The sniper saw a woman carrying a baby down the stairs behind him.

Thirty seconds later the front door of number 39 was closed. Within two minutes the sniper was upstairs, sitting in the back bedroom, unwrapping the rifle, and looking across the garden at the building where Ellen Worth had taken refuge.

He'd lain on the bed, sighting through the rifle's scope and tight with fear. The ghost of someone he'd killed *was* in the house. The sniper had heard it moaning somewhere nearby — and scratching, as if the hideous thing was trying to claw through the lid of its coffin. But he was determined to kill the woman, however terrified he was, however long he had to wait.

He had kept his right eye fixed to the scope. He squinted across the Bowerdean Street house's back garden, through a window of the apartment where Ellen Worth was hiding, through an open living room door, across the living room to a second window overlooking Wandsworth Bridge Road. Sweat covered the sniper's forehead, trickling down around the eye fixed to the eyepiece. He itched in a dozen places, but he kept watching. He whimpered but did not let his body jerk in terror when, at the beginning of the third hour, the ghost wailed — a long, mournful sound from another world.

Rightie had given him a Belgian-made semiautomatic rifle and pictures of the Worth woman. The sniper's trigger finger hadn't moved a millimeter when other people passed the hall window or went into the living room — an old woman, a young man, an older man. The image of Ellen Worth was imprinted on his mind.

He would shoot, once and perfectly, when she and she alone paused long enough in the light between the hall and living room windows.

She passed through once — too quickly.

She returned to the middle of the living room — too quickly.

She walked through his sights a third time — too quickly.

She reappeared and turned toward the window overlooking Wandsworth Bridge Road.

He fired.

The window overlooking the back garden exploded. Ellen Worth sagged, held on a moment, and then disappeared from view.

Clutching the rifle, the sniper rolled off the bed. He was in a panic to get out of the house. The police would be there within three minutes. The phantom was already somewhere on the upper floor.

The sniper bolted out of the bedroom and moved quickly down the stairs to the landing. He leaped over the body of the wife, which was sprawled on the first flight, her blond hair touching the floor of the hall. The baby lay motionless, facedown, in a corner.

The sniper leaned his rifle against the wall by the front door. The next move was to open the door, keeping back in the hall, take five seconds to study the police car, aim, and shoot the policeman inside it. The sniper had already killed one man sitting behind a windshield. He could kill another.

He reached for the doorknob.

A voice behind him said something in English he didn't understand.

The sniper knocked the rifle across the hall as he spun around.

A young man wearing an American-style raincoat was standing in the kitchen, legs spread, straddling the head of the husband, who lay on his back, eyes open. The young man was holding an aluminum kettle by its handle. Behind him, the kitchen's sliding glass doors were wide open. So was the broken window on the back of the building forty feet away. The young man had dropped ten feet into the garden and run across to the kitchen as the sniper came downstairs.

"The next time you kill a family at breakfast time, turn off the electric teapot," Tiger Chadwick said in Russian.

The sniper yanked the pistol from his jacket pocket. Tiger tossed the kettle at him underhand. "Catch!" he yelled.

The sniper's hand jerked up to protect his face. The scorching metal seared his palm and struck him on the cheek. He fired reflexively. The pistol bullet tore into the ceiling, showering plaster down on the dead man lying with his head and shoulders in the kitchen, his torso and legs in the hall.

Siren erupted, howling, warbling, as the first police cars arrived in the street outside.

There was no time to fire again. Gripping his pistol, the sniper scrambled over the body of the woman in her dressing gown. Ignoring the pain in his hand, he sprinted up the second flight and ran down the hall, past the bedroom where he had lain patiently half the morning waiting to kill Ellen Worth.

There were three doors at the end of the hall. They were closed. One of the rooms behind them would have a window overlooking the parking space below. That window would be the safest escape route out of the house.

The sniper was afraid of closed doors, of the spirits that might be lurking behind them. But he was more afraid of the young man downstairs, who would be coming after him in a few seconds.

He grabbed the handle of the door on the left. He flung it open and saw a baby's room. The curtains were still drawn. He saw a crib. He saw a changing table.

Unmistakable in that semidarkness, the ghost of one of his victims stood in the middle of the room baring its fangs at him.

The sniper screamed, dropped his pistol, and sprinted back down the hall. He tripped at the top of the stairs. The banister sagged as he lurched against it. The sniper flailed his arms as the wood splintered and broke.

Falling, he screamed a second time, in terror at what he had just seen, in the realization that he was about to die.

Skin split, bones snapped, breath and life belched out of him as his muscular body crashed and broke on the hall floor.

Tiger Chadwick lowered his Wembley. He stepped around the

corpse of the husband lying half in the kitchen, over the bleeding body of the sniper, and stared up at the second floor.

A dog, a large golden retriever, looked down through the gap in the broken banister. Its tail swished slowly back and forth. Its mouth was open as it panted, its teeth showing.

❖ FOURTEEN ❖

```
SMERDYAKOV, GEORGI GEORGIVICH _ expelled from
United Kingdom, October 1971. Transferred to
KGB Second Chief Directorate, data analyst,
Sverdlovsk command, 1971-1984; deputy direc-
tor for data analysis, Second Chief Director-
ate, Sverdlovsk command, 1984. L.K.R. colonel.

PONAMAROV, GEORGI MAXIMOVICH _ expelled from
United Kingdom, October 1971. Transferred to
KGB Eighth Chief Directorate, Moscow headquar-
ters, systems review officer, 1971-1979;
Eighth Chief Directorate, deputy to chief of
telecommunications section, 1979. L.K.R.
major.

MIROSLAV, GEORGI PETROVICH _ expelled from
United Kingdom, October 1971. Subsequent KGB
career unknown. L.K.R. lieutenant.
```

"Goddamnit," Lester Brundance muttered as he read the three-line summary file on Georgi P. Miroslav, whose Last Known Rank had been lieutenant and whose post-1971 history was lost to the CIA's archival memory.

Brundance was sitting in the permanent dusk of the Orion task force computer room. The pretty young woman beside him seemed impervious to the sense of urgency that had seized everyone else that morning.

"The computer says that the British kicked out ninety KGBs in 1971," she said. "It'll take us —"

"We're only interested in men named Georgi," Brundance said.

She put her hands back on the keyboard. Her name was Nancy. Her black hair was tousled. "How come?" she asked.

"In London this morning Yarrow found out something about

a man named Georgi," he said. "He called Margery just before his jet took off."

It was 9:47 A.M. EDT, April 12. Brundance was feeling pressure.

"Is Tiger Chadwick flying back with him?" she asked.

"Yes."

Nancy gazed up at the computer screen with eyes like puddles of dreams. "That Tiger's kind of cute," she said as the next summary scrolled up onto the screen. "He patted my butt in the elevator."

```
ZAISTROSTIEV, GEORGI ANDREIVICH — expelled
from United Kingdom, October 1971, Transferred
to KGB Technical Operations, Ukrainian staff
headquarters, Kiev, 1972-1984; regional com-
mand, Kharkov, 1984. L.K.R. major.
```

The sense of endings, of failure, that possessed Genady I. Oblomov momentarily distracted him from the macabre spectacle he and the others had been summoned to observe.

There were only three days left to find Mandelbaum. The working group on the fifth floor, west wing, of Lubyanka still had no idea where the physicist was being held prisoner.

That evening the first deputy chairman of the KGB, Valerian Aleksandrovich Galkin, would fly to Berlin. The next morning, April 13, Galkin would go on to Washington. Results of the auction would be made known on the fourteenth. Oblomov was sure the Americans would win.

He was summoned out of his melancholy reveries by sounds so gruesome that, for a moment, Oblomov forgot they were fake. He felt a chilling in his bowels.

They were watching a closed-circuit television recording of a Lubyanka interrogation cell. Its occupant was Kornilov's wife, Ailya Ivanovna. She was listening with an expression of horror on her face. Out of her sight but not her hearing, a woman in a nearby cell was shrieking, pleading with someone not to insert the electric wires again, swearing she'd tell anything, *do* anything, if her tormentor would only desist.

Her cries diminished to a threnody of whimpers. Oblomov heard the deep murmur of a questioning male voice.

There was a moment of silence.

The unseen woman plaintively answered. Instantly she cried out in alarm. She howled in dread. There was another shattering scream.

"Enough," Galkin said.

Sonya Krebsky stood up and twisted a knob on the television monitor. The sound immediately went dead. On the grainy black-and-white screen, Ailya Ivanovna Kornilova looked like a silent film's parody of a plump, cosmetics-caked trollop with a beehive hairdo. She was wearing a dark miniskirt, a buttoned blouse that could barely contain her enormous breasts, and dead-white stockings.

"The woman pretending to be tortured in the next cell is an actress?" Yuri F. Tsarapkin asked. He was seated beside Oblomov in the monitoring office on the second level of Lubyanka's basement. Oblomov was perspiring. Tsarapkin's dark-browed, mustachioed little face was gray.

"She is a typist in my office," Sonya Krebsky answered, pushing another button. The screen went blank. She turned to Galkin. "At approximately ten forty last night, the laundry room of the Hotel National received a telephone call from Maxim Petrovich Kornilov."

"He was calling from outside the Soviet Union," Yuri Tsarapkin said. "The resonances and wavelengths of the static have been analyzed —"

"Later," Galkin said. He nodded at Sonya. "Please."

"Kornilov asked a woman on duty in the laundry room to summon his wife," she said. "When he called again at eleven thirty, she was there. Their conversation —"

"The transcript of their conversation was on my desk this morning," Galkin said. "I have read it. Tell me what happened afterward."

"The Kornilova woman was arrested in the laundry room when she had finished speaking to her husband," Sonya answered. "She was brought here and interrogated. She refused to cooperate, and made threats. So we sent the typist and Corporal Delchev to put on their show in the cell next to hers."

"The recording you have just shown us was not amusing," Galkin said. "I assume you have one of Delchev's interrogation?"

Sonya removed the spent cassette from the video machine and inserted another. She pressed a start button, twisted the volume control dial, went back to her chair, and lit a cigarette.

Black lines rolled down the television screen, and then the picture stabilized.

Ailya Ivanovna was cowering against the cell's steel wall. Apprehension stared from her wet, pudgy face. She was perspiring. She had been crying. Her nose was running.

Metal clattered on metal as someone unlocked the door. It swung open. The same tall corporal who had questioned Kornilov's wife a few days before came in and placed a folder on the table. He turned to close the cell door behind him and lock it.

"You will be seated," he said, drawing back the chair on his side of the table.

Ailya Ivanovna didn't move. Mascara had blurred into black circles around her eyes, giving her face a bizarre, masked appearance.

The corporal seated himself. "If you do not sit down," he said, "I will arrange to have you questioned in the next cell — strapped down."

Kornilov's wife lunged for the chair on the other side of the table, yanked it back, and plopped herself onto it. "I am sitting," she gasped. "You see that I am sitting as you ask . . ."

The corporal ignored her. He had opened his folder and was studying a paper. When he spoke he did not look up. "Where was your husband, Maxim Petrovich Kornilov, calling from?"

"I don't know, it has never happened since we, he —" Ailya Ivanovna swallowed hard. "I don't know," she whispered.

The corporal raised his head. "I think you are lying. Why would your husband telephone you at the laundry room of the Hotel National unless you and he had made an arrangement?"

"He was trying to find me through a friend, Ludmilla Alexeiyevna! He doesn't know where I live! I am not —" Ailya's soft, thick throat contracted as she swallowed a second time.

Again, the corporal looked down at the folder on the table before him. His handsome face was expressionless.

"— I am not lying," Ailya Ivanovna said in a small, quavering voice.

"When he spoke to you, Major Kornilov said that soon he would be very rich," the corporal said.

"Yes. He often says — said such things. He always had schemes for getting rich."

"And you did not believe him this time?"

Ailya Ivanovna's face — white, smudged with eye shadow, and terrified — gazed across the table. "No . . . not believe him . . ."

Oblomov could almost feel Galkin's intensity as he watched the recorded scene.

"He asked you if you would like to join him in the west," the corporal said.

"Yes . . ."

"And you called him a silly old fart. Was that a code phrase?"

The plump young woman squirmed in her chair. She tried to pull together the front of her blouse, which had popped a button during her hysterics over the torture sounds.

"Answer me!"

Alarmed, she let her mouth drop open. "No!" she cried. "No, no codes!" She lapsed into fearful misery again. She looked down at her hands nervously fumbling with her blouse buttons. "It is my opinion of him."

The corporal leaned forward and folded his hands on the table. "Major Kornilov said that he might arrange matters so that you would have to come to the west whether you wished to or not. What did he mean by that?"

"I don't know what he meant," Ailya Ivanovna whispered.

"If you are lying, comrade —"

"*I don't know anything!*" Kornilov's wife screamed. "*I don't know where he is! I don't even know why he called me!*"

*

MINDEVICH, GEORGI ALEKSANDROVICH — expelled
from United Kingdom, October 1971. Transferred
to KGB Second Chief Directorate, Perm Oblast
command, 1971-1986; chief of archives, Second
Chief Directorate, Minsk regional command,
1986. L.K.R. captain.

VEZHNESKY, GEORGI TEODOROVICH — expelled from
United Kingdom, October 1971. Subsequent KGB
career unknown. L.K.R. lieutenant.

"What are we looking for aside from the name Georgi?" Nancy asked.

"I don't know," Brundance answered.

The computer room door opened. Daylight speared through the dusk. Brundance twisted around. He saw Margery's plump silhouette. "Jake just called again from the air force jet," she said.

"Take a break," Brundance told Nancy.

He got up and walked out, crossed the suite, and went into the duty office overlooking M Street. He closed the door. Margery was behind the desk. "He's been asking for chronologies," she said, "specific dates and times of broadcasts from that transmitter in northern Europe, the precise hour at which we did things —"

"Where?" Brundance asked.

Margery picked up a legal notepad half covered with her neat handwriting in black ink. "In Finland, mostly."

"Have you been able to tell him what he wants to know?"

She nodded. "The young women here keep beautiful records."

Lester Brundance looked through the windows at the dish antenna on the CBS bureau across the street. He was wearing a white shirt, wide suspenders, a polka-dotted tie, dark gray trousers, and black shoes polished to a high gleam. The pressure was increasing on them all as the last forty-eight hours before the auction of Mandelbaum evaporated.

Margery tore a sheet off another legal pad and handed it to him. "Jake would like you or Joe to contact General Dunn — as discreetly as possible. This is what he wants."

Brundance looked at the lined yellow paper. "I'll be god-damned," he said softly.

```
ABLOGINSK, GEORGI ANDREIVICH — expelled from
United Kingdom, October 1971. Transferred to
GRU Eleventh Directorate, small arms cata-
loguer, 1971-1984; chief, catalogue division,
small arms, 1984-1987. Died in air crash, Sa-
markand, November 4, 1987. L.K.R. colonel.
```

The square of light lay on the end of the table in Gregor A. Mandelbaum's concrete room. That meant it was early afternoon, a quiet time in the village. Mandelbaum flexed the fingers of his right hand. The swelling of the middle one had lessened a little, although its upper half was still purple. He had driven a splinter beneath the nail as he was loosening the wooden chair leg. The swelling and pain had cost him a day's work on tearing his undervest into strips and weaving them into his rope.

He was about to resume ripping when he heard Russian-speaking voices raised in argument several rooms away. One of the speakers was Major Kornilov. Mandelbaum didn't recognize the other voice.

He lay on his bed, the half-demolished undervest in his hands, listening intently. Apparently a message had just been received. Kornilov was obviously alarmed.

"Yarrow was with her for at least fifteen minutes!" he said, his normally low voice brazen and afraid. "She could have told him —"

"Don't be a fool!" barked the other.

"You are the fool," Kornilov shouted. "She knew your name!"

The voice of the other became soothing. Mandelbaum could only pick up a few words — ". . . a few hours left . . . a simple telephone call . . . Yarrow."

There was silence. Then Kornilov spoke normally. He seemed to have been reassured, even pleased.

Mandelbaum heard boots or heavy shoes walking across a wooden floor. A door opened and slammed shut. After a few moments, he heard a car engine start in the street outside.

In his concrete and timber cell Mandelbaum wondered who
Yarrow was.

```
TZENTOVK, GEORGI MIKHAILOVICH _ expelled from
United Kingdom, October 1971, Transferred to
KGB Ninth Directorate, scheduling officer,
1971-1990, Died, AIDS, December 18, 1990,
L,K,R, major,

KAZMANOV, GEORGI NIKOFOROVICH _ expelled from
United Kingdom, October 1971, Subsequent KGB
career unknown, L,K,R, lieutenant,
```

Standing in the hallway outside Tsarapkin's plywood office,
V. A. Galkin said, "Why is the line in the hotel laundry room
tapped?"

"Because the clients of prostitutes, many of them foreigners
staying at the hotel, leave messages on that telephone," the little
scientist-technologist replied. He was dwarfed by his desk. He had
trimmed his mustache a few days before. Standing beside Galkin,
Genady I. Oblomov decided that Tsarapkin now looked more like
Charlie Chaplin than a Mexican bandit.

"And why was Kornilov's second call not traced? His first gave
adequate notice that he would telephone again."

"The second was made from a radio telephone," Tsarapkin
said. "By the time the proper tracking equipment was activated,
his conversation with his wife was over." He blinked. "Our tech-
nologists are not infallible."

Galkin moved down the hall. "Send Sonya to me," he said to
Oblomov. "We do not wish to be disturbed."

Oblomov nodded. It was a measure of his pessimistic mood
that he didn't bother to formulate a smutty thought about old
Valerian Galkin and the notorious dyke, Sonya Krebsky, trying to
reignite their ancient passion for each other.

When Sonya came in, Galkin was standing in his shirtsleeves at
the window, hands clasped behind his back. The dog, Yosip, gave
two wags of his tail as she closed the office door.

"You have read Tseden's report from London on the Worth woman?" she asked.

Galkin's hairless head turned to her. His mouth was fixed in a contemplative pout. He looked tired. "Yes."

"Do you believe that Yarrow was one of the two men who went to her flat just before she died?"

Galkin shrugged slightly and turned back to the windows. "Tseden thought he recognized Yarrow from photographs. Yes, he could have been there this morning. It has occurred to me that he is probably in charge of the American search for Mandelbaum."

The first deputy chairman irritated Sonya. He was being inaccessible. He had assumed just such a distant manner when their liaison was ending twenty years before. "Have you drafted the offer to Kornilov?" she asked.

Galkin returned to his desk. Only a faint smell of varnish remained in the room.

Galkin drew back his chair and sat down. "Not yet," he said.

Sonya was leaning against the conference table. She was wearing a deep blue shirt, paratooper's trousers, and running shoes.

"You seem to be as gloomy as the rest of them," he said.

"There is nothing to be joyous about," she said. "We have failed. The consequences to you, Volya —"

"The search for Mandelbaum has failed," Galkin replied. "The auction is ours to win."

She frowned. "*Ours* to win?" she asked incredulously. "You are dreaming! Kornilov has done this thing because he *despises* the Soviet Union! The Soviet KGB refused to reward or appreciate him, his slut of a Soviet wife abandoned him . . ." She raised her right hand, made a gesture of futility and dropped her arm to her side. "Despite this obvious reality, you tell me that Kornilov will sell Mandelbaum to the Sov —"

"No," Galkin replied. "*I* do not tell you this. Kornilov tells it to you. His message is clear to anyone with sufficient subtlety of mind to understand him; he will return Professor Mandelbaum to the Soviet Union if we offer him something the Americans cannot."

Sonya stared at him. "What message from Kornilov? Received when?"

Outdoor sounds, spring sounds, came through the windows with the fresh air. Sonya heard an airplane high in the white sky, the slight squeak of brakes as a vehicle parked in the alley five floors below, the busy cheeping of sparrows.

"You were a typist-stenographer for our organization when I first knew you," Galkin said. "Do you still have a stenographer's abilities?"

"Yes. Of course."

Galkin opened a drawer, took out a notepad, unclipped a pen from his shirt pocket, and held them out to her. "Thank you. As few people as possible should know the contents of our offer to Kornilov."

She circled the conference table and sat down facing him.

He swiveled his chair slightly, placed both small hands on its wooden arms, and looked through the windows. For a moment the Russian sky's light dimmed as a film of cloud passed beneath the sun.

"To Major Maxim Petrovich Kornilov," Galkin said quietly. He paused. "I send you the greetings due a worthy adversary. Your call to a Moscow telephone number, which you knew would be monitored by our Eighth Chief Directorate, was a brilliant stroke. Your wife is baffled by the meaning of what you said to her — as well she might be, since your message was not directed to her, but to me. I have read a transcript of your words and understand perfectly."

He turned his head and looked at Sonya. Her face was partly obscured by the light that hung above the table. The stenographer's pad was on the green surface.

"Am I speaking too quickly for you?" he asked.

"No."

Galkin turned back to the windows. The clouds had passed.

"I am authorized by President and General Secretary Mikhail Sergeivich Gorbachev, by the Presidium of the Supreme Soviet, and the Central Committee of the Communist party of the Soviet Union, to make you the following offer for the return of the scientist Gregor Abramovich Mandelbaum. I will personally be in Washington —"

"Volya."

Galkin turned back to her.

Sonya had set down the pen. Her square face framed by short, blond hair was fully visible below the light. "Send Tsarapkin to Washington," she said. "Or Tseden. Even Oblomov."

Galkin made himself smile. "I am touched by your concern —"

"Then do what I ask of you. Too many people have died, the latest only this morning. She was alone in a room with Yarrow and another CIA —"

Galkin shook his head. "Yarrow is many things," he said. "A poseur, arrogant, a man who regards himself as morally superior. But he does not kill. I believe — and Tseden believes — that the Worth woman was murdered by Kornilov's assassin."

Sonya took a cigarette from her shirt pocket, a wooden match from the same pocket. She snapped the match into flame with her thumbnail. She lit the cigarette and exhaled a thin stream of smoke. "Send someone else to Washington, Valerian Aleksandrovich, or at least take me with you if you care for me."

The words startled him. It had been years since any woman had appealed to him for affection. He waited for the sudden thrill that stirs the male heart when such appeals are received. He wished to feel it. He felt nothing.

"I have lived alone for too many years," he said.

"Volya . . ."

He swung his chair around so that it faced the windows again. "As well as fifteen million dollars," he said, "the Soviet Union will, in return for Gregor Abramovich Mandelbaum, give you what you asked for in your telephone call . . ."

SEMINOFSKY, GEORGI ADRIANOVICH — expelled from United Kingdom, October 1971. Transferred to KGB Administration Directorate, English language data clerk, 1971-1977; transferred to Registry and Archive Department, deputy director, English language section, 1977-1991; director, 1991. L.K.R. major.

Holding the telephone in his right hand, Lester Brundance stood at the windows of the Orion duty office. Five floors below, M Street and the sidewalks were filled with lunch-hour traffic. Bicycle messengers swooped and sprinted their way around cars and pedestrians with dangerous grace. The April noon was bright and blustery.

"You're sure it was Kornilov?" Edgar Pollack asked. He was speaking from his office on the seventh floor of the CIA building in Langley, Virginia.

"We have to assume it was," Brundance replied.

"What language was he using?"

"Russian," Lester Brundance said. "The call was automatically tripped from Yarrow's private line in your building to this office —"

"How would Kornilov know Yarrow's private number?" the director of Central Intelligence asked.

"Jake gave it to him when they met in Denmark."

"All right. I need to hear the whole sequence. Wally Cresteau's going to want it word for word. You're being recorded."

Brundance saw a blond woman in a tailored brown suit emerge from a stretch limousine in front of the CBS bureau across the street. A bald man was waiting for her on the sidewalk. He was smiling uneasily. Two young men carrying two briefcases each got out of the limo behind the woman.

"Lester Brundance, deputy director, Orion task force," Brundance said. "Nine minutes past noon, April twelfth. A telephone call from Maxim P. Kornilov — probably originating in Scandinavia, although NSA monitoring didn't have time to fix the precise location — was automatically forwarded from Yarrow's office at Langley to the Orion task force on M Street.

"Margery Ferrall, Yarrow's assistant, got the call," Brundance said. He turned around and glanced at a handwritten log lying on the desk behind him. "That was eighteen minutes ago. Kornilov said he had a message for Yarrow —"

"This Ms. Ferrall speaks Russian, I take it," Pollack said.

"Yes, sir."

"What was the message?"

Brundance took a deep breath. "Unless the American search for

Mandelbaum stops immediately," he replied, "Mandelbaum will be handed over to the Soviet Union at midnight tonight Greenwich Mean Time in return for cash and another inducement that Galkin already knows about.

"Kornilov said he wants a response — yes or no, on ending the American search for Mandelbaum — by two this afternoon our time."

"Who are you supposed to call?"

"He gave Margery a Washington number that will have an answering machine attached."

"The location is irrelevant, I suppose," Pollack said. "Kornilov's local man, Hagopian, can telephone the machine and rerecord our answer."

"Yes, sir. What do you think it will be?"

"I think the president will promise Kornilov to call off the search for Mandelbaum," Edgar Pollack said. "And I think he'll insist that we keep our word."

```
TSEBLOV, GEORGI PAVELOVICH _ expelled from
United Kingdom, October 1971. Transferred to
KGB Finance Department, disbursement clerk,
1971-1975; auditor, First Chief Directorate
accounts, 1975-1988; deputy chief auditor,
First Chief Directorate accounts, 1988. L.K.R.
major.
```

At 4:31 P.M. the U.S. Air Force transport bringing Yarrow and Tiger Chadwick back from London touched down at Andrews Air Force Base on the Maryland outskirts of Washington. It taxied to a far corner of the military field, passing a limousine parked on the edge of a runway. Air force ground crewmen waited with noise-deadening headphones clamped over their ears. One signaled the aircraft with Day-Glo batons; the VC-137 turned slowly, its engines screaming, and stopped on command. The crewman with batons looked, to Brundance, like an animal trainer putting some lumbering beast through its paces.

The jet noise became a diminishing whine and then stopped. Another ground crewman put blocks against the front wheels. A third backed a mobile stairway up to the plane's passenger door and braked it in place.

The black limousine moved forward, the afternoon sun glinting on its polished chrome, windshield, and roof.

As the forward door of the transport plane opened, Lester Brundance and Joe Humphrey got out of the limousine and went up the steel stairs two at a time. Brundance was carrying a brief-case.

Inside, a white-coated steward and Tiger Chadwick were waiting in the entrance passage. "He's been locked up in the rear cabin all the way across," Tiger said.

Humphrey followed Brundance through the beige-walled forward cabin. Brundance knocked on a door in the bulkhead and then pushed it open.

The rear cabin was furnished with a desk, soft chairs, a sofa, coat closet, and bathroom. Yarrow sat in his shirtsleeves at the desk. An empty coffee cup, a pad, and three sheets of paper covered with notes were on the desk.

Yarrow's heavy face was pale and fatigued. He lowered his head and looked through the windows at the sun-baked military airfield. "Why are we stopping out here?" he asked.

"The American ambassador to Panama is arriving at the main terminal," Brundance said. "He's been recalled because of the riots. The place is jumping with reporters. The director didn't want to run the risk you'd be spotted."

"I doubt if there's much danger of that," Yarrow said. "I'm not as famous as the ambassador to Panama." He stood up, pulling his jacket from the back of the beige chair. "All right, gentlemen, where are we?"

"You know about Kornilov's call to Marge?" Brundance asked.

Shrugging on his jacket, Yarrow nodded.

"The answer to your question is that we *are* nowhere and going nowhere," Joe Humphrey said angrily. "There was a White House meeting a little before two o'clock. That asshole of a president has closed us down. The search for Mandelbaum is over.

The FBI sealed off the Orion offices until ten thirty tomorrow night, when we'll be allowed back in to wait for Kornilov's last telephone call."

"What about the list of KGB officers named Georgi who were expelled from Britain?" Yarrow asked.

Brundance put the briefcase on the desk. "In here."

"Good," Yarrow said. "The other matters I asked you to arrange?"

"General Dunn is waiting for you at the Pentagon," Brundance said. "He suggests you come out on the Metro. It'll be less conspicuous. The director will be at your house at seven forty-five. He and General Cresteau have an appointment with the president at nine. Can you manage all that?"

Yarrow nodded again as he picked up the briefcase. "I believe so, yes. Thanks."

"Jake, what the hell's going on?" Joe Humphrey demanded. "The Worth woman gets killed in London, you come flying back here firing orders ahead of you like an attack helicopter — get me lists of guys named Georgi, chronologies of what happened on this day or that —"

Yarrow moved toward the cabin door. "I may know something that could change the president's mind," he said. "If I do, you'll hear about it when we meet with Edgar Pollack at seven forty-five. Now, I'd like a ride home so I can change my shirt before I go out to see Marcus."

FIFTEEN

B Y 6:10 P.M. the sun was burning down the western sky. Perfumed islands of lilac hung in the air.

Tiger Chadwick stopped Yarrow's Honda on the corner of Q Street and Connecticut Avenue, Northwest. Margery Ferrall, wearing a blue seersucker suit, was in the back seat. "Galkin arrives at Dulles early tomorrow afternoon," she said. "Do you want to meet him or have him met?"

"I don't think so," Yarrow answered. "We'd better let the Soviet embassy look after him. Did Louise get a flight to Copenhagen?"

"She's on an SAS overnight that leaves New York in about twenty minutes," Margery said.

Yarrow half turned and smiled at her. "I expect you arranged that," he said. "I'm grateful."

"Jake," she said, "you're so tired you look like a ghost's ghost. It's rush hour. Why not let Les or Joe go out to the Pentagon for you?"

"No," Yarrow said, "this is something I have to do myself. I should be back home by seven thirty or so."

He eased himself out of the car, closed the door, and walked across to the Dupont Circle Metro station. Carrying the briefcase Lester Brundance had given him, Yarrow rode down on the long escalator, bought a ticket, and waited four minutes. A standing-room-only train emerged from the tunnel, braked, slowed, and stopped. Yarrow squirmed his way on.

Normally he enjoyed watching faces and listening to snippets of conversation on the subway. But early on the evening of April 12, he was dulled by fatigue and depressed.

Before she was killed, Ellen Worth had told him something that changed his most fundamental assumption about Maxim Kornilov. The eight-and-a-half-hour flight back to Washington had given Yarrow time to rethink everything that had happened. His principal conclusion, he was certain, was about to be confirmed at the Defense Intelligence Agency. But he felt no elation. He was exhausted, still stunned by Henry Muffin's death, and depressed over the breakdown of understanding between himself and Louise.

The subway moved away from the illuminated platform and into darkness. The results were going to be known sometime within the next fifty-four hours. Whoever won, Gregor Mandelbaum would lose; he would either be forcibly returned to the Soviet Union or pressured by the Burke administration into betraying the Soviet Union. There would be no reunion with his daughter — if, indeed, she was even alive.

Yarrow got off at Metro Center, walked through the crowds to the Orange Line, and boarded a less-crowded train for the Pentagon. He found a seat by a window and rested his arms on the upright briefcase in his lap. The lights in the car were bright. He looked at his reflection in the window glass backed by the black subway tunnel.

He saw again what had happened to him as he aged; he had begun to resemble his father. Yarrow was now consciously aware of a truth that had lingered for years in the shadowed back hallways of his mind; he didn't want to look like his father or be like his father. Believing in Conrad Yarrow's values, Jake had refused to admit to himself that he despised the man's character. Louise had tried to free him from the conflict when she demanded that he throw away Conrad's manuscript. She had been trying to make Jake see that the ideals he had inherited from his father were now his own because he had enacted them in his life's work.

He wished that she were sitting beside him so that he could tell her she had been right. But she was gone, flying east into darkness.

He tried to imagine his life without her being close enough to at least touch its perimeters.

The thought was unendurable, and so he stopped thinking it.

Instead, he made up his mind what he was going to do if President James Forrest Burke refused to change his mind. Yarrow was surprised at the calm with which he accepted his own decision. He opened the briefcase, took out Lester Brundance's list of KGB officers named Georgi, and read it carefully several times.

* * *

Even before the subway train came to a stop at the Pentagon, Yarrow saw the tall figure of General Marcus Aurelius Dunn on the platform reading a newspaper. The director of the Defense Intelligence Agency was wearing a gray suit; the overhead light gleamed on his bald head and cast shadows in the recesses of his craggy face. Yarrow guessed that the newspaper was the *Houston Chronicle*. As he emerged from the train he saw that he was right.

He crossed the platform. "Hello, Marcus," he said. "What's the news from Texas?"

Dunn folded the paper, grasped Yarrow's hand, and grinned. "Too much oil, not enough money," he said. "How the hell are you, boy? Every time I see you, you've just gotten off an airplane that's brought you in from God knows where."

"I'm all right," Yarrow said as the train rumbled away softly and they walked toward an escalator. "It's you I'm worried about."

General Dunn stopped, pulled a visitor's identification pass from his pocket, and clipped it onto Yarrow's lapel. "Me? Why're you worried about me?"

"I understand you were at the White House meeting this afternoon when the president ordered the search for Mandelbaum called off."

They stepped onto the escalator. Dunn folded his arms. "That's right."

"What you've agreed to do for me could be interpreted as carrying on the search," Yarrow said. "I'm not even officially involved anymore since the Orion task force and I were put out of business this afternoon."

Dunn nodded. "Ole Phil Teague could hardly keeping from pissing his pants, he was that tickled."

"Phil will have your hide if he knows you've been helping me."

Marcus Dunn squinted up at the lights at the top of the escalator. "Well, first off, the president said nobody's supposed to go poking around *Europe* looking for Mandelbaum. You'n me're going to be playing with a computer in Washington, D.C. Second, you're my buddy and I'm on your side, not Phil's." He looked down at Yarrow and grinned. "Third, if Goldilocks Teague does fire me, you'n me'll go catfishing with worms like we did before you turned into a gentleman and they made me a general."

Yarrow shook his head. "Not me. I never went catfishing with worms."

"Then you were the only kid in Oklahoma who didn't," Dunn said. "Time you tried it."

Ten minutes later they were in a windowless room furnished with four desks facing a long table that was littered with an array of computer equipment and an outsized screen. The walls were painted light green.

General Dunn closed the door and leaned against it. "You going to tell me why you need to see what we've got for you?"

"I'd just as soon not," Yarrow said, pulling back a chair and sitting down at one of the desks. "I'm operating on the principle that what my friends don't know can't hurt them."

"Well, I appreciate the sentiment," Marcus Aurelius Dunn said. He crossed the room to the desk beside the one at which Yarrow sat. He picked up a telephone. "Brower? We're ready. Get yourself in here."

"This," said Emily Brower, "is an enhanced satellite image of your area, Mr. Yarrow." Her face was faintly illuminated by the light of the screen.

"Every twenty-eight days the bird makes a pass over the northern Soviet-Finnish border we see here," she continued. She was a civilian "blipper" — an aerial reconnaissance analyst — for the Defense Intelligence Agency. Her name was etched on an ID plate pinned to her blouse.

The room was in semidarkness. Yarrow and General Dunn were seated at two desks. Emily Brower stood at the computer keyboard making images appear on the screen. She was slightly overweight, dark-haired, and pretty.

"Now we're going to move in on . . . ."

Her fingers made the keyboard clatter. On the screen a picture of vast green and brown territory was replaced by a smaller, more detailed segment. Yarrow saw low buildings scattered along a highway, a secondary road branching to the right, passing through more forest, crossing some sort of checkpoint, and disappearing off the edge of the screen.

". . . Ivalo," Emily Brower said. "That's the town on Finnish national Route 4 you were asking about, Mr. Yarrow." She pointed to the branch highway. "Route 968 runs down to, and across, the border into the USSR . . ." Her finger traced the path of the road. ". . . here. It's three hundred kilometers from Ivalo in Finland to Murmansk on the Tuloma estuary in the Soviet Union."

Yarrow watched intently. "What's that cluster of buildings down at the bottom right?" he asked.

"Don't know," she said. "Let's have a look."

Again, she bent over the keyboard, and typed a command.

Instantly, a slightly blurred close-up of the buildings and surrounding forest filled the screen. "It's not perfect because it was taken from five hundred and eighty-five miles up on —"

"I presume that's in the Soviet Union, not Finland."

"Correct," Emily Brower said. "About a half a kilometer from the border. Here's a KGB watchtower. This is a patrol road . . ."

Yarrow's heartbeats accelerated. He saw a long, one-story headquarters building, four barracks, a large garage, mess hall, parade ground, military trucks and jeeps parked in neat rows, men walking.

"This image was registered at about noon two days ago," Emily Brower said. "I don't know what —"

"It's a KGB Border Guards installation," Marcus Aurelius Dunn said. "Got a SCIF on it?"

"I think so, sir. Hold on a moment."

Yarrow looked at Dunn. "What's a SCIF?"

"A data insert," the general said. "It's programmed to match this picture. It tells us what the DIA knows about the place."

The keyboard clattered again.

A block of yellow print was instantly superimposed on the lower left-hand quarter of the screen.

Yarrow leaned forward and read the text. "There you are," he said softly.

The room was silent save for the soft humming of the computer as Yarrow intently reread the block of yellow print.

"What're you seeing?" Dunn asked.

"What I hoped I'd see," Yarrow answered. "Is there any way of getting a print of that picture, a photo reproduction?"

"Sure," Emily Brower said. "With the SCIF?"

"Please," Yarrow said.

The young woman looked inquiringly at General Dunn.

"He's got the clearance," Dunn said.

"Give us ten minutes, Mr. Yarrow," Emily Brower said.

Yarrow called his house from a public telephone in the Pentagon Metro station and rode the Orange Line back to Metro Center. He walked to the Red Line and boarded a train. Rush hour was over. He got off at Van Ness Street, took the escalator up to the surface, and stood watching the headlights of outbound traffic pass him on Connecticut Avenue.

The evening gray was deepening. The dying fire of sunset lay in streaks across the western sky. It seemed to Yarrow that many months and several seasons of the year had passed since he stood at the seventh-floor windows of the State Department watching another twilight with Wallace Cresteau, Edgar Pollack, and Tove Buhl, the Danish ambassador. It had, chronologically, been only twenty-four hours before. After a transatlantic round trip, in the rush of events and consequences, Yarrow had lost all sense of time. Like a child demanding attention, time — the hours he had just spent and all the years he had lived — was impressing itself upon him. Weariness clotted in him.

A set of headlights flashed once in the line of approaching traffic. Yarrow walked to the curb as his Honda pulled over. "They got steaks," Tiger said as he slid into the front seat.

The darkness was almost complete and the porch lights were on at Yarrow's house on Macomb Street. He saw Edgar Pollack's black limousine parked at the curb. The driver and bodyguard leaning against it straightened up in a gesture of deference as they saw Yarrow get out of the Honda.

He smelled the lilacs briefly as he crossed the sidewalk. Mounting the front steps with Tiger behind him, he smelled hickory smoke. He saw Margery Ferrall in an apron pass the living room windows, then the oval glass pane on the front door, and go down the passage toward the kitchen. Lester Brundance, jacket off, was sitting in the living room talking to Edgar Pollack. For a moment Yarrow beguiled himself with the illusion that he was a man coming home to a family.

He opened the front door. "Where's Joe?" he asked.

Joe Humphrey appeared in the rear porch doorway at the end of the passage. He, too, was wearing an apron. "Still on night duty," he said. "Getting the barbecue lit."

"Come in," Yarrow said. "I've got something to show you."

"It had better be good," Edgar Pollack said, standing up as Yarrow entered the living room. He held out his hand. "Hello, Jake," he said, unsmiling. "I understand you're completely worn out."

"Oh, it isn't quite as dire as that," Yarrow said. He smiled at Brundance. "Is everybody taken care of? Edgar, have you been offered a drink?"

"I've passed," Pollack said. "I'm going to need all my wits about me later in the evening. I'm afraid I've got bad news for you, Jake — for all of us."

"Tell me," Yarrow said.

"Wally's just called," the director of Central Intelligence said. "Burke's asked Phil Teague to sit in on our meeting at nine tonight."

Yarrow looked at him in silence for a moment. "Well," he said, "it can't be helped. I don't suppose it matters much in the end. The president would have consulted Phil anyway before deciding what to do about the proposal you're going to make. I wish I could be there with you."

"Burke won't see you, Jake," Pollack said. "You have ideas on policy that threaten him and, because he secretly shares your sentiments, you're a reproach to him. He calls you 'that goddamn Boy Scout.' "

Yarrow nodded. He looked around. Margery and Joe Humphrey were standing in the hall doorway. Tiger was behind them. "What about you, Jake?" Margery asked. "A glass of wine?"

Yarrow shook his head. "I expect Edgar wants to get down to the White House to talk strategy with Wally Cresteau before they see the president," he said, setting the briefcase on a coffee table standing before the sofa. "I think we'd better make ourselves comfortable and get this over with."

He sat down on the sofa. Pollack was opposite him. Brundance and Margery on either side of him. Joe Humphrey leaned against the mantel. Tiger Chadwick took a chair behind the sofa.

The doors were open to the evening. Yarrow heard cars on Macomb Street in the cool darkness, leaf-whispers as night breezes passed.

He folded his hands. "You know that Lady Ellen Worth was shot this morning while Tiger and I were talking to her. It was dreadful — obviously." He looked around the room. "I have been in the Central Intelligence Agency for thirty-one years. I've never seen anyone killed. I hope I never do again."

He took a deep breath. "Before she died, Lady Ellen told us something very important. It changed my view of Kornilov. From that fresh perspective, I've tried to rethink this entire situation." He looked around the room. "I now believe I know where Dr. Mandelbaum is being held — and how to get him out."

"Where is he?" Joe Humphrey said.

Yarrow glanced at him. "Hold your horses, Joe." He looked back at Pollack. "I've read almost every American, British, Danish, and Israeli file on Maxim Petrovich Kornilov. They all portray him as a sociopath, a loner, a man incapable of friendship, even of making lasting human contact." Yarrow leaned back in the sofa. "That's always bothered me for one reason." He looked at Pollack. "As we've often told each other, this kidnaping and ransom of Dr. Mandelbaum is the work of an organization. You've all known my question: To whom does a friendless man turn for help in arranging such a complex operation?"

"What about Hagopian?" Pollack asked.

"I doubt if he's much more than a messenger and a fixer," Yarrow answered. "He was useful at the beginning because he could move in and out of the Soviet Union in his Aeroflot job. No, Hagopian's not the answer. The answer to this mystery is that one of our key assumptions about Kornilov was wrong; he *isn't* totally friendless."

A wraith of hickory smoke drifted in from the back porch.

Somewhere in the surrounding neighborhood of old houses and shaded streets, a window was open and a woman was laughing.

"Lady Ellen told us that, in his London years, Kornilov was close to, and trusted by, a fellow KGB officer whose first name was Georgi," Yarrow said. "This man, in fact, was Lady Ellen's real lover. Kornilov acted as their decoy — I believe the contemporary word is 'beard.' He pretended to be Lady Ellen's gentleman friend — we've seen photographs of them together — and lured MI-5's trackers away from her and Georgi. She was killed before we could get her to tell us the rest of his name."

"That's bad luck," Pollack said.

"I'll come back to the name in a minute," Yarrow said. "The important thing was the new premise Lady Ellen's information gave us — Kornilov *had* a friend, one inside the KGB, a man who owed him an old debt. If we accepted what she told us as true, it changed everything.

"Previously, our search for Mandelbaum has concentrated on two countries where Kornilov had known people — Denmark and Britain." Yarrow looked from Humphrey to Pollack. "The one place we never thought Mandelbaum might be hidden was the Soviet Union, because we assumed that, among his own people, in his own organization, Kornilov was regarded with contempt when he was noticed at all."

A wave of fatigue swept over Yarrow, momentarily disrupting his train of thought, like a gust of wind scattering leaves. He paused and forcibly dispelled the confusion.

"I asked Margery to give me chronological summaries of everything that happened in the twenty-four-hour periods preceding the murders of Colonel Kelyev and Henry Muffin," he said. "The day before Kelyev was shot, one of our people, Pete Durward from the Helsinki station, was at Paavo Waltari's farm, east of Ivalo in Finnish Lapland. He wandered down to the border and saw a man dressed in a KGB Border Guards uniform watching him through binoculars. Before Henry was killed, the Finnish Border Patrol had thirty men, jeeps, and helicopters swarming all over the same area searching for Dvorah Mandelbaum."

"You're saying that Kelyev and Henry were killed to distract us from that particular section of the border," Pollack said.

Yarrow nodded. "Appearances by unfamiliar people or any un-usual activity there seems to alarm someone on the Soviet side."

"Jake," Joe Humphrey said, "why couldn't that have been a coincidence which happened twice?"

Yarrow heaved his upper body forward with a slight grunt. "It could have been," he said, drawing the briefcase toward him. He unsnapped the brass clasps and opened the lid of the briefcase. "Let's see if we can't eliminate any possibility of coincidence."

He took out an eight-by-ten photographic print and laid it on the table. "Tiger," he said, "in the drawer of that table behind you there's a magnifying glass. Would you get it for me, please?"

Yarrow took the list of KGB officers named Georgi from the briefcase, turned to its second page, and laid it beside the print. "Now, Edgar," he said. "Come have a look."

Brundance stood up and moved aside to make room for Edgar Pollack on the sofa. He sat down and took the magnifying glass from Tiger.

"That's a satellite image of a KGB Border Guards regimental headquarters about half a kilometer away from Paavo Waltari's farm, just inside the Soviet Union," Yarrow said. "The image was made two days ago. The writing in the square on the lower left quarter tells what U.S. intelligence knows about the place. Read it, Edgar."

Pollack bent over the print and adjusted the magnifying glass. "Headquarters, Eighth Regiment, KGB Border Guards, Mur-mansk Oblast," he read aloud. "Commanding officer: Georgi Teodorovich Vezhnesky, rank, colonel —"

"I'll be goddamned," Lester Brundance murmured.

"Housing: Headquarters Company, Eighth Regiment," Pollack read. "Twenty-two officers, two hundred and forty-three en-listed —" In a delayed reaction he looked up. "What is it, Les?"

"He recognizes Colonel Georgi Vezhnesky's name," Yarrow said. He took the computer printout list from the table. "In Oc-tober 1971, ninety KGB officers, including Kornilov, were de-ported from Britain. After my conversation with Lady Ellen this morning, Les went through our files on those ninety men and pulled out what we have on the ones named Georgi." He handed the list to Pollack.

The director looked at the second page. "Vezhnesky, Georgi Teodorovich," he said. Expelled from United Kingdom, October 1971. Subsequent KGB career unknown. L.K.R. —" He looked up at Brundance.

"Last known rank."

Pollack laid the list on the coffee table. "Well," he said softly, "I think that does eliminate any possibility of coincidence, Jake." He looked sideways at Yarrow. "You've got me convinced — at least that this Colonel Vezhnesky's the guy who teamed up with his friend Kornilov and planned and carried out the kidnapping." He picked up the satellite image print of the Eighth Border Guards regimental headquarters compound. "Their jumpiness anytime someone comes near that border may prove they're holding Mandelbaum in this place. Your evidence could even convince the president. But his next question's going to be, What are we supposed to do, send two airborne divisions across the Soviet border and grab Mandelbaum?"

"That wouldn't be necessary," Yarrow answered. The blurring fatigue was approaching him again. "All it would take would be one Russian-speaking man or woman —"

Pollack stood up. "If that man or woman's supposed to be an American intelligence officer, forget it," he said. "If Burke believes your hypothesis, he'll be desperate to find some way not to act on it. Phil Teague will argue that a CIA officer walking into Colonel Vezhnesky's establishment would pose as great a risk to Mandelbaum's life as a military invasion." He looked down at Yarrow. "I think the president's going to decide to go with the auction."

Yarrow got to his feet. "Try this, Edgar. When Kornilov talked to Margery today he wanted us to stop the search for Mandelbaum immediately. He said if we didn't, he'd turn Mandelbaum over to the Soviets for fifteen million dollars and *an added inducement Galkin already knows about.*" Yarrow looked at Margery Ferrall. "Isn't that the way he put it?"

She nodded. "He did say 'added inducement.' "

"That could be moonshine," Yarrow said to Pollack, "a lie invented to pressure us. Or, it could mean that Kornilov's already told the Soviets what he wants for Mandelbaum — aside from money. If so, the auction's already over, Edgar — and Volya Galkin has won."

Pollack nodded. "Either's possible. I want to take this list and print in with me to show the president."

"The print was provided by Marcus Dunn," Yarrow said. "If Phil finds out that he helped me this evening —"

"I'll see to it that Phil won't lay a hand on Marcus," Pollack said. "Get some rest, Jake. Why don't I call you in the morning?"

"No," Yarrow said. "Tonight, please."

After Pollack had gone, Joe Humphrey asked Yarrow how he would like his steak.

Before he could answer, Margery said, "He's too tired for anything but a hot bath and bed."

"I want to wait up for Edgar's call," Yarrow said. "Medium rare, Joe. If I have time before dinner I'd like to go wash my face and hands."

Upstairs, he switched on the lamp in his bedroom and closed the door behind him. Slowly, he pulled off his jacket and laid it on the bed, slipped out of his loafers, and untied his bow tie. He opened two windows. A moth batted against a screen. Voices rehearsing Brahms's *German Requiem* drifted through the open doors of the cathedral two blocks away, swelling to familiarity and then, like fragments of memory, becoming indistinct.

Yarrow went into the bathroom and washed at the basin. He dried his hands and face on a soft towel, lulled by the lavender aroma of soap.

With only one lamp burning, his bedroom was tranquil, inviting him to rest. He was empty of thoughts. He lay down on his large double bed. It was only for a moment, he told himself. He closed his eyes as the voice of Johannes Brahms sang phrases and interrupted choruses to him. He would listen only for a moment, he told himself.

A hand gripped his shoulder, shaking him slightly.

Yarrow opened his eyes. He saw Joe Humphrey's large silhouette against the lamplight. He started to sit up. "Take it easy," Humphrey said. "Here."

Yarrow swung his feet over onto the floor. He was numb with

sleep. He smelled coffee. Humphrey slid a cup and saucer into his hand. "Got it, Jake?"

"Yes. Thank you. I must have —"

"Pollack's on the phone," Joe Humphrey said. "I told him you'd been out of it for three hours."

"Good Lord," Yarrow murmured. He sipped at the coffee. It was pungent and hot. He set the cup on the beside table, got up, and crossed the room.

He switched on the desk lamp and picked up the telephone. "Sorry to keep you waiting, Edgar —"

"I suggested to Joe that they let you sleep," Pollack said. "He reminded me that you wanted to know immediately what happened."

"I do," Yarrow said.

"You won't be surprised," Pollack said. "The president isn't buying. He got angry and asked what kind of an intelligence officer would propose a high-risk kidnapping operation inside Soviet territory because of what he claimed he was told by some British communist who's now conveniently dead . . . You can imagine the rest."

"Yes," Yarrow said, pulling back his desk chair and sitting down. "Yes. I can. He was saying that to please Phil."

"And meaning it because he's frightened of Phil and of making a mistake and anything else you'd care to mention," Pollack replied.

"I feel sorry for him," Yarrow said. "What happens now?"

"You'll represent the United States in the auction — not because Burke wants you, but because Kornilov does. As I understand it, Kornilov will call you after midnight tomorrow to tell you where to meet Galkin and Hagopian."

"That's the plan."

"I gave Wally your written recommendations for the American bid," Pollack said. "I understand that the final offer will be drafted tomorrow morning by a group that doesn't include you but does include Phil. Go back to bed, Jake," the director of Central Intelligence said. "If you aren't doing anything at midday tomorrow, come out for lunch."

"That would be nice," Yarrow said. "Good night."

He replaced the telephone on its cradle.

"Bad news?" asked Joe Humphrey behind him.

Yarrow nodded. "Yes, but I was expecting it to turn out this way."

"Margery and Les have gone home," Humphrey said. "Tiger will stay with you tonight."

Yarrow turned around. "That's really not necessary, Joe. I'll be —"

Humphrey put a small amber container on the bedside table. "Dalmane," he said. "You're probably too strung out to get back to sleep without help. Good night, Jake."

Yarrow undressed, showered, put on fresh pajamas, and took one of the sleeping pills Joe Humphrey had left him.

He was pulling back the bedcovers when the telephone rang. Wearily, Yarrow crossed the room and picked it up.

"Nice try, Jake," Phil Teague's voice said. "Better luck next time — if you get a next time."

"Thank you, Phil," Yarrow answered. "Good night."

He hung up the phone and stood for a moment at the open windows.

Brahms's requiem for Germany was over. The moth was still hurtling itself against the screen, maddened by unattainable light.

❖ SIXTEEN ❖

AN AMERICAN EMBASSY LIMOUSINE was waiting for Louise at Kastrup airport on the morning of April 13. The drive north across Copenhagen's sprawl seemed endless.

It was late morning when the chauffeur turned into the Muffin driveway from the coastal road. The waters of The Sound were at full tide, washing against the bank at the bottom of the garden. Louise saw marine guards standing on the lawn and driveway. Inside, an embassy secretary told her that Mrs. Muffin had declined to see a doctor; the ambassador and his wife, Danish and American friends, had paid condolence calls the previous evening; the secretary said that Mrs. Muffin had talked by telephone to her sister in Lansing, Michigan, and to Mr. Muffin's brother in Chicago as well as to the Yarrows. Mrs. Muffin had wanted no breakfast; she had stayed in her room all morning.

The embassy limousine took the secretary back to Copenhagen.

Louise made a pot of black coffee, found a tray, cups, and saucers, and went up to Dorothy's room. The two women embraced and then sat opposite each other, Louise on the curved window seat, Dorothy on a wooden chair. Dorothy was wearing the soft, autumnal tweeds favored by middle-aged Scandinavian women.

"You look exhausted," she said.

Louise shook her head.

"Dear friend, sleep a few hours."

"No, it's all right," Louise answered, not wanting to be a cause for concern, wanting to comfort this woman she loved, and knowing that there was no comfort nor refuge from the immutable fact of her husband's death.

Dorothy folded her long, brown hands in her lap and looked at the windows. "Jake must be hurting terribly," she said.

"Jake?" Louise asked, startled.

"He was the only man in the world who understood Henry," Dorothy said.

"You understand — understood him," Louise replied, shaken by the finality as she changed tenses.

"In one way, yes. But you and I aren't spies. We're wives, outsiders." Dorothy looked back at Louise. "Some men are spies for the wrong reasons, some for good reasons. And some are in that work because they must make payments."

"Payments," Louise said, immediately understanding and not wanting to. "What payment could Henry possible have —"

"I'll tell you," Dorothy said. "We can know now." She rose and went to the windows. She looked out on the grounds, the blue-gray water, and Sweden's distant shore. "Henry's father deserted from the army in 1942," she said. "Jake knew that. He understood what Henry felt — and somehow made it possible for him to put it into words. When a white man runs away, he's a deserter for any one of a thousand reasons. When a black man runs away, he's doing just what you'd expect of a cowardly nigger."

Louise looked at Dorothy's profile etched in the morning light. There were no tears left in her. "Henry was in the CIA as payment," Dorothy Muffin said, "to prove something, to make amends. Jake knew why Henry was in their trade."

Louise was stunned. "Sweetheart, this isn't what we should be talking about —"

Dorothy looked down at her. "It's all I'm able to talk about. I need to think — and talk — now about what was wonderful."

Louise felt grief rising in her throat. She turned her head and looked at the view across The Sound.

"I don't know when Henry told Jake about his life," Dorothy said softly. "I can't imagine either of them in that conversation. But they had it." She smiled. Her smile was a kindness, including her friend in the precincts of her own grief. "Henry could never admit his secret to me."

Louise was bewildered. "Then how did you find out about it?" she asked.

Dorothy turned back at the windows. "Do you remember when Henry was hurt twice in one year?"

Louise nodded. "Nineteen eighty-one," she said.

"The second time he was shot. They had to fly him back to Walter Reed for surgery," Dorothy said. "Do you remember that?"

"Yes. Of course. You stayed with us. When Henry got out of the hospital he came home to us —"

"He nearly didn't come home to me," Dorothy said. "It — I loved him. I begged him to leave the agency. He wouldn't. I thought I couldn't go on loving him and waiting for someone to kill him. I thought he was hanging on because there were so few blacks in the CIA in those days. One night while we were staying with you, I couldn't sleep. Jake found me in the kitchen. I talked to him about leaving Henry, getting away from him so that I could try to stop loving him." Dorothy pressed her palms together. She looked down at the floor. "Jake must have struggled hard with his loyalties. It must have been very difficult for him to tell me what Henry had told him." She took a deep breath. "But he did. He told me something Henry couldn't confess to me because it was about pride and shame. That was all right. All I needed to know was that Henry understood himself, that he had a good reason for staying in such work."

Looking up at her, Louise nodded.

"We had our best years after that," Dorothy said. She raised her head. "Look," she said.

Louise turned and looked down through the window. She saw perennial beds lying in graceful, serpentine curves between the lawn and the strips of forest that bordered the property. A flat of seedlings, a trowel, and a wide straw hat lay on the grass beside one of the beds of brown earth.

"Day lilies will grow in this climate," Dorothy said. "I was planting a bed of them when Joe Carley's call came."

"I'm sorry," Louise said, "I don't know who that is."

"The ambassador," Dorothy said. "A good man."

She returned to her chair. "Now I want you to sleep awhile," she said.

After Louise unpacked in the guest room she took a bath. She lay in the tub trying to reconstruct what she and Yarrow had said to each other the night they dined on his porch. She remembered trying to program herself as she drove away, trying to be furious, trying to construct an indignation so immense and unforgiving that she could stop loving him.

She wrapped herself in a terry cloth robe and slept for several hours. She awakened at 1:30 P.M., put on jeans and one of Jake's old shirts, and tied a blue bandanna over her hair. She went downstairs to the kitchen. A marine guard was sitting at the table with a glass of milk and a plate of cookies. He had dark brown crew-cut hair, dull eyes, and a jaw that looked muscular from years of chewing gum. He stood up quickly, as if she had discovered him in some wickedness.

"Do you know what time it is in the United States?" she asked. "On the Eastern Seaboard?"

The young man looked up at a wall clock. "Yes, ma'am. It's nearly two in Copenhagen," he said. "That would make it nearly eight in the morning back home."

"I don't know how to make overseas calls from here," Louise said. "Would you help me?"

"Yes, ma'am. What number did you want to call?"

"It's Washington, area code 202," she said. She took a pencil from a jar on the counter, wrote the number on an envelope, and handed it to him.

He put the slip of paper on the counter and dialed a long series of numbers. He stood erect, listening. Then he handed her the phone. "It's ringing, ma'am. I'll be outside if it's the wrong number or anything."

She smiled at him. "Thank you."

The back door closed softly. She leaned against the counter, holding the telephone to her ear, hoping Yarrow would answer, not his machine.

The meadow on which Jake Yarrow was standing was vast, western, and flooded with sunlight. It grew brighter and brighter. There was a clapboard house nearby. A black man was standing in the open door, facing Yarrow and pushing the doorbell, seeking admission even though he was already inside.

A room of the house. The sunlight filled the windows, nearly blinding Yarrow. He couldn't see a way out of the room so that he could answer the door. In the dream he knew that Henry Muffin was ringing the doorbell and if he weren't let in soon he would go away and never come back. "Wait!" he shouted, trying to shield his eyes against the light.

"Wait!" he shouted, waking himself up, squinting against the morning sunlight that streamed through his bedroom windows. He knew instantly that he'd been dreaming. He knew that he had left behind everything that his unconscious mind had manufactured for the dream. The bell shrilled a third time.

He got out of bed, crossed to his desk, and picked up the telephone. "Jake Yarrow," he said.

"Jake, it's Louise."

"Oh," he answered, trying to shake off a shroud of weariness and the dregs of sleep. "You shouldn't be — I wanted to call *you* today, I was going to when I —"

"I'm at Dorothy's. I woke you up, didn't I?"

"It doesn't matter," Yarrow said. "I was going to call you this morning —"

"You told me a few days ago you were involved in something. Is it still going on?"

Words wouldn't crystallize in the taffy of his mind. "Yes. It's — yes." He looked at the reading stand, at his father's manuscript lying on it, the binding soiled with age. It was important to him that what he wanted to say to her be said gracefully. But the right phrases still eluded him. "I've got to wake up before we have this conversation," he said, sitting down on his desk chair.

"Let me call you back in a few hours," she said. He heard uncertainty in her voice.

"Wait," he said. "How's Dorothy?"

"Brave. Suffering. What you'd expect. She's holding it all in, worried about everyone else. You sound muggy."

"It doesn't matter. My head will clear in a —"

"No. Listen to me, listen. Either go back to sleep and I'll call again in a few hours —"

"Louise, it's all right."

"— or make yourself a cup of coffee, have a glass of juice, and I'll call you in twenty minutes," she said.

"Let me call you."

"Don't be — stop being so benevolent," she said. "Do you re-member we talked about that?"

"All right," he said. "Call me in twenty minutes."

He brushed his teeth, combed his hair, put on a dressing gown, and went downstairs. He still felt exhausted. Tiger was sitting at the kitchen table eating waffles and reading the sports section of the *Washington Post*. "I hope it's okay," he said. "I toasted some frozen waffles and made coffee."

"If your waistline can stand it, I can," Yarrow said, taking a container filled with apple juice from the refrigerator. He filled a glass and set it on a tray. He poured a cup of coffee and put it beside the apple juice.

"Margery said she'd be here by nine," Tiger said.

"Fine."

For a tenth of a second Tiger hesitated. Yarrow had retreated into himself. Tiger had seen him this way before, not cold, just profoundly distracted. "Last day," he said. "We deliver the bid today, hear the result tomorrow. What else?"

"Nothing, until we go to the office tonight to wait for Korni-lov's call," Yarrow said. "Would you like to take the day off?" He tucked the main news sections of the newspaper under his arm and picked up the tray.

Tiger stood up as if he were about to make a speech. "No, sir," he said. "I'd like to go the distance with you."

Standing in the kitchen door, holding his breakfast tray, Yarrow nodded. "All right. We'll stay together through the auction to-night. If the phone rings, let me answer it, will you?"

"Yes, sir."

Yarrow went back upstairs to his bedroom. He put the tray on the desk and looked at the front page of the *Post*. He couldn't engage his mind in the lead stories.

He was trying to think about Louise's impending call. She and the rest of his life, their lives, were the matters most important to him. But he urgently needed to work out the final details of what he was going to do in the next two or three days.

The yellow pages directory was open on his desk. He was writ-ing a number on a pad when the telephone rang.

He picked it up. "Hello," he said.

"Jake —"

"Hello, Louise. Are you all right?"

"Yes, I'm fine. I'm as well as I suppose anyone would be under the circumstances."

"What about arrangements for Henry's funeral?" he asked.

"Dorothy hasn't — we haven't talked about it yet," she said. "That's not what I'm calling about."

He waited.

"I've only been here a few hours," she said. "It's a sunny afternoon. The water, you know, out on The Sound, is flat, the light on the Swedish side — none of it gives pleasure, Jake. I'm in a house with a woman who's had everything taken away from her."

"I can imagine the feeling."

"Henry's death fills everything," Louise said, "cancels everything, negates everything." She paused. "Jake — I've left you, come back to you, left again because you wouldn't confess your soul's secrets —"

"Don't be so hard on yourself."

"Jake, darling," she said. "I'm trying to stick to facts. I've been like a yo-yo because I couldn't —" She took a deep breath, a device, Yarrow knew, for making herself slow down. "We're different people in different circumstances. Three nights ago, having dinner on the porch, trying to get you to concede something you may or may not feel about your father —"

"Louise —"

"No, listen to me, listen." Now he heard the rising note of fear. Across four thousand miles she had reached out to him, felt his weariness and preoccupation, and assumed they were barriers against her. "Three nights ago I — we — had a lot of options before us — split, agree to settle for what we had, love each other, not love each other, keep on trying. This afternoon I'm standing in the house, the kitchen, of a woman who hasn't got any options except to love a dead man." She stopped speaking for a moment. The static on the line sounded like the wash of oceans. "Now. Say something."

"What I have to say will take longer than a minute," Yarrow

answered. "I wish we had a day, somewhere away from telephones and the rest of life. I'm not as good at words as I thought . . ."

Again Louise inhaled deeply, trying to be calm. "Then I'll have to be," she said. "In these circumstances, everything assumes a new — what? Proportion? Dimension? Do you understand what I —"

"Yes, of course," he said.

"I love you. You're alive. Everything I've always loved is still in you. Nothing else matters. If you're willing to meet, to try again in the hope of — Christ, I don't want to say 'reconciliation,' that's priest or lawyer talk . . . Jake, are you trying to find the right words to tell me that it's over, that we're over?"

"No," he said. "For God's sake no. I've just been trying to find the short version to tell you that I can't conceive of my life without you, that I wish I'd behaved differently the other evening." He looked at the bright morning. "I've lost the gift of brevity," he said. "I need time to tell you everything that I've come to realize. Look, will you be able to leave Dorothy tomorrow? For two days?"

"Yes, I think so. Why?"

"The matter I'm involved in is coming to an end," Yarrow said. "I have to take a trip. I want you to take it with me. I can't tell you what it's all about yet."

"Of course," she answered. The fear was gone, the encroaching panic had receded. "Where shall I meet you?"

He told her where and when, and then they hung up.

At 10:30 A.M. Yarrow was dressed in a yellow shirt, red patterned butterfly bow tie, lightweight, rust-brown jacket, tan cavalry twill trousers, and loafers. The exhaustion had left him for the moment as his adrenaline stirred and started its daily propulsion of his life and mind. He telephoned Edgar Pollack's secretary and said he'd be in the director's office for lunch at 12:30 P.M. He drove to the brokerage firm on M Street that for decades had invested and managed his inheritance from his father. He ordered a cashier's check for $32,405.79 and sent it by messenger to an office in Arlington. He drove to Langley and had lunch with Edgar Pollack. Yarrow told his old friend what he was going to do if the United States lost the auction. To his surprise, Pollack questioned and made several suggestions but did not argue. At 3:00 P.M. Yarrow was back home. He went upstairs, laid his jacket on the bed, and seated himself at his desk to compose two documents.

At 1:05 P.M. Valerian A. Galkin and his dog, Yosip, arrived at Dulles airport on a chartered Aeroflot passenger jet. He was met by the Soviet ambassador to the United States, the KGB *Rezident,* and four other senior embassy officials.

Fifty-five minutes later, Anastas Hagopian, browsing in a Dupont Circle bookshop, was approached by a young man with an addressed, stamped envelope. "Did you just drop this?" he asked.

Hagopian took the envelope, glanced at it, and smiled. "Yes. Thank you. A letter to my brother in California."

He left the bookshop, crossed Connecticut Avenue, and walked west on R Street. Halfway up the block he heard someone saying, "Hey, Harry!"

Hagopian bent down and looked into the open window of a red Toyota Tercel station wagon. "What a pleasant surprise! How are you?"

"Good," said Joe Humphrey. "Get in, I'll give you a lift."

Hagopian got into the station wagon. "You will take me to the Farragut North tube station," he snapped.

As Humphrey pulled away from the curb he said, "We don't call it the 'tube' in this country, you dumb bastard. 'Subway' is the word. The envelope's in the glove compartment."

"I don't understand," Hagopian said.

Humphrey maneuvered the station wagon around Sheridan Circle. "Open that trapdoor in front of you, stupid," he said in Russian.

Hagopian took an envelope from the glove compartment and put it in the inside pocket of his parka. "I instructed Yarrow not to send a messenger with body odor," he said in Russian. "You will tell him I am displeased."

"I don't know where you went to charm school," Joe Humphrey replied in English as he turned down Connecticut Avenue. "But you'd better write and get your money back."

" 'Charm school'?" Hagopian replied. In Russian he asked, "What does it mean, 'charm school'?"

"Academy of *kultury,*" Humphrey said, pulling over to the curb. "This is where you get off, sucker. Give our love and a kick in the ass to Kornilov."

Hagopian opened the door. He turned on his professional airline steward's smile. "I am sorry," he answered in Russian. "Major Kornilov does not share your particular perversion, so it does no good to send him your love. You will get no tickles or wet kisses from him. Farewell." He got out and slammed the Toyota's door.

Having thus picked up the Soviet and American bids for Gregor Abramovich Mandelbaum, Hagopian crossed the avenue, got on an escalator at Farragut North, and disappeared into the Washington subway system.

At the end of the cool Washington afternoon, lines of traffic were moving across the bridges and on the main arteries north and west into the expiring sun, the bars on M Street were jammed, flocks of starlings wheeled in formation against the pale sky, and beggars displayed hand-lettered posters proclaiming their desperation.

James Forrest Burke sat at his desk in the Oval Office, looking across the room at his national security adviser, General Wallace Cresteau, who was reading a memorandum from the American ambassador to Panama proposing diplomatic and economic retaliation for damage to U.S. property in the Canal Zone during the latest riots. The president was inwardly shouting, pleading with Cresteau to tell him it would end well, that the United States would win the auction, that the press would remain ignorant of the Kornilov-Mandelbaum affair until the auction was over, that history would reckon that President James Forrest Burke had done the right thing when he ordered an end to the search for Gregor A. Mandelbaum.

His desperate need for reassurance and his anxiety remained unexpressed. "What time's Pollack coming in?" he asked.

Cresteau lowered the memorandum. "Around midnight," he

said. "We'll probably have a late dinner while we wait to hear from Yarrow. There's no need for you to stay up, sir."

"I'll be up," Burke answered, wishing they'd invite him to have dinner with them. "I won't be able to sleep until I know who won the goddamned auction."

Writing usually came easily to Yarrow. But on the afternoon of April 13 his mind was turgid; it moved sluggishly as he tried to turn feelings into precisely stated arguments. The second document he had to compose involved only description and summaries of laws that Margery had been researching for him all day. He decided to postpone writing it until evening.

He looked at the little clock on his desk. It was 6:17 P.M.

He took off his shoes, stretched out on the chaise lounge, and immediately fell asleep.

At 7:00 P.M. Lester Brundance came upstairs, opened the door, and looked in. He switched on a bedside lamp so that Yarrow wouldn't wake up in the dark, closed the door, and went downstairs.

At 9:15 P.M. Margery put a tray on his desk and turned on another lamp.

Yarrow opened his eyes. He felt instantly awake, fresh, and uncontaminated by exhaustion.

"Kornilov's supposed to call in two hours and forty-five minutes," she said. "How are you?"

Yarrow sat up. "Ready for him," he said. He smiled at her. "And anybody else who's not on our side."

SEVENTEEN

KORNILOV CALLED from a Swedish town on the Gulf of Bothnia. He was brief, ordering Yarrow to meet Galkin and Hagopian at the National Cathedral at 1:15 A.M. After he hung up, Yarrow called the FBI. Then he and Tiger Chadwick left the Orion task force offices for the last time. The desk tops were bare of papers, books, and personal objects. The doors were closed. The suite's lifeless order reminded Yarrow of a furnished house whose occupants have moved to another town.

The cathedral church of St. Peter and St. Paul — more commonly called the Washington National Cathedral — stands on a fifty-seven-acre rise, Mount St. Alban, in northwest Washington. Like the medieval European bastions of worship and episcopal power on which it is modeled, the National Cathedral presides over a clutter of smaller buildings that are its architectural children. There are three preparatory schools on the grounds, a college of preachers, shops, a commercial greenhouse, residences for the bishop and a canon, the parish church of St. Alban's, lawns, gardens, playing fields, a landscaped forest, statuary, parking lots, and paved streets.

By day the great central tower dominates the skyline above Wisconsin Avenue and Cleveland Park. At night floodlights turn the cathedral into a Gothic fantasy of flying buttresses, gargoyles, saints, clerestories, and stone window patterning as intricate as lace.

At 12:50 A.M. street lamps radiated halos of blue-white light along the National Cathedral's streets and shone as solitary beacons in the deeper gloom of the grounds. To the southeast, the capital city was a glittering bed of tiny lights that cast a dull rose luster against the sky.

Tiger parked the Honda on Garfield Street at the foot of Mount St. Alban. Yarrow got out and stood for a moment watching shapes move on the cathedral grounds. FBI agents were crossing roads and playing fields, stationing themselves in the lower woods. Within a few minutes thirty-five or forty of them would be in place around the cathedral close — standing at windows, watching from the forest's edge, on streets and lawns, upper buttresses, rooftops, and unlit places, all of them armed, all of them photo-briefed to recognize the first deputy chairman of the KGB, Yarrow, Anastas Hagopian, and Tiger Chadwick.

Yarrow shoved his right hand into his jacket pocket and turned into the grounds on a street named Pilgrim Road. The air was cool. Tiger walked beside him. He was dressed in running shoes and a knit sweater whose hem bulged over a Wembley stuck in the waistband of his jeans. A young woman with a rifle in the crook of her arm stood at the head of a Japanese-style bridge arching into the woods to their left. Yarrow saw armed men on the football fields. They passed a concrete building. From there the road curved upward through an avenue of trees. Above the foliage Yarrow saw the floodlit cathedral thrusting into the blue-black sky. Valerian Galkin was standing on the road, a raincoat draped over his shoulders, his naked skull capped with a dull reflection of lamplight. His little dog sat beside him.

Reflexively, Tiger moved forward. Yarrow put a hand on his arm. "Stay back," he said. "I want to talk to him." He stopped for a moment to let the tempo of his heartbeats decelerate and his breathing return to normal. Then he walked the last hundred feet and held out his hand. "Hello, Volya."

"Greetings, Yarrow." Galkin shook hands.

Yarrow bent down and rumpled the little dog's oversized ears. "Welcome to America, Yosip," he said.

The dog wagged his tail twice.

A young man appeared on the parapet above them. "Mr. Hagopian is in the gazebo, Mr. Yarrow," he said. "In the bishop's garden, just to the right of the parking lot."

Yarrow nodded. "Thank you." He turned to Galkin. "Did you understand?"

Galkin leaned over and snapped the leash onto his dog's collar. He drew his raincoat closer around his shoulders. "I understood," he said.

Together they walked up the road into the brighter light with Tiger ten feet behind them. Amplified walkie-talkie chatter filled the night air. Yarrow and Galkin stopped in the parking lot that served the cathedral and the St. Alban's School for Boys. To their right, the pristine shrubbery of the bishop's garden surrounded a low gazebo. FBI guards were visible on the roadway above them. A limousine with diplomatic plates was parked at the top of the lot, its lights on and motor running. Two men leaned against it, arms folded, talking.

"Yours?" Yarrow asked.

"Yes. Come, Yarrow. Let us get this business over with."

"In a moment." Yarrow folded his arms. "Why don't we both give up, Volya?"

"Give up?"

Yarrow nodded. "Why don't we step aside and let the Israelis have Mandelbaum? They'll hide him where neither of us will ever find him."

Galkin stared at him for a moment. "And let the Israelis use him in their own weapons program? Don't be absurd, Yarrow!"

"The Israelis aren't building space defense systems," Yarrow replied. "Professor Mandelbaum's particular area of expertise would be useless to them. What about it, Volya? Shall we let them have him?"

"Why would the Soviet Union do such a thing?" Galkin asked. "Why would the United States?"

"It would be a kindness to the man," Yarrow said.

Galkin's heavy face looked down Pilgrim Road. "I have no instructions from my government to be kind, Yarrow," he said. "Neither have you."

Tiger came up to them and led them through the waist-high hedges of the bishop's garden. They circled the gazebo, seeing Hagopian's silhouette against the night sky, between the pillars.

At the entrance's low stone steps, Tiger leaped lightly up into the gazebo. He looked at Hagopian, glanced around the interior, and then returned to the doorway. He took Galkin's arm as the portly KGB first deputy chairman, carrying his dog, heaved himself in. Yarrow followed.

The cathedral floodlights above them and the dimmer glow of the street lamps below illuminated Hagopian's mocking features.

He was wearing his usual parka. He held a long, multibattery flashlight in one hand, an envelope in the other.

"Good evening, gentlemens," he said in English. He laughed briefly, nervously. "Major Kornilov also sends you greetings, in better grammar —"

"It is late," Yarrow said in Russian. "My colleague, First Deputy Chairman Galkin, has flown from Berlin —"

"Colleague?" Hagopian exclaimed in Russian, his voice light and taunting. "Major Kornilov and his associates have persuaded you to become *colleagues*," Hagopian said sardonically to Galkin. "It should be worth an Order of Lenin!"

For a moment, Galkin gazed scornfully at him. Then he sat down on one of the benches that lined the gazebo's interior. He drew his raincoat about himself. Yosip settled at his feet. Somewhere in the nearby gloom, a radio barked. An FBI voice answered quietly.

Hagopian looked at Yarrow. "Just a little joke," he said. "On such occasions —"

Tiger moved close to him. "If you don't start talking business in five seconds," he said in Russian, "I'll tear off your arm and shove it up your ass."

Hagopian opened his mouth, started to reply, saw the angry intention in Tiger's eyes, and closed his mouth. He fumbled with his flashlight and dropped the envelope. Tiger picked it up and handed it back as Hagopian switched on the electric torch.

The finale, the announcement they had all waited for with such intensity, came in a brief mumble from Kornilov's Armenian messenger. "Major Kornilov dictated his response to the American and Soviet bids." Hagopian turned to Galkin. "His letter is addressed to you, First Deputy Chairman," he said. "The Soviet Union has won the auction. Mandelbaum will be returned to you in exchange for fifteen million dollars and the delivery of Major Kornilov's wife to the west." Hagopian handed the envelope to Galkin. "In this letter you will find instructions as to where and how the money and Ailya Ivanovna Kornilova are to be exchanged for Mandelbaum. The transaction will take three days to complete."

Yarrow felt nothing, neither surprise, despair, nor a deflation of any expectation.

He turned to Galkin. "Congratulations, Volya," he said in Russian. "Treat him kindly. He's not an enemy of the Soviet —"

Galkin stood up. It was apparent in the way that he snatched the letter from Hagopian that he was angry. "There is no end!" he grunted. "Three more days!"

"If you'd lost you could have taken a holiday," Yarrow said. "Perhaps for the rest of your life." He held out his hand.

In the half-light Galkin looked like an old priest withered by self-deprivation and stricken by the failure of his god. "Spare me your jokes, Yarrow!" he muttered, ignoring the hand offered him.

"Tiger," Yarrow said, "perhaps you'd see First Deputy Chairman Galkin to his car, the black limousine."

"It is not necessary!" Galkin said, scooping up his dog. He crossed the gazebo and grasped the door frame as he groped with his right foot for the stone step below.

Tiger Chadwick moved quickly. He took Yosip from beneath the old KGB bureaucrat's right arm and steadied him until Galkin was standing on the step. Tiger handed him the dog.

Galkin looked up at him. "What is your name?"

"Chadwick, sir," Tiger replied.

"Where have you learned Russian?"

"At a university, sir."

"Persist in your studies," Galkin answered. "Someday you may speak as well as Yarrow." He looked up at the cathedral's central tower striving toward the stars. He stepped down to the ground, tucked his dog under his arm and walked away slowly on the path between the hedges.

In the gazebo, Yarrow turned to Hagopian. "Maxim Petrovich Kornilov and his associates aren't going to be popular in Washington when news of this gets around," he said in Russian. "If I were you, young man, I'd leave this country quickly. Later today, if possible."

Hagopian stared at him, emptied of his vulgar flippancy. He nodded.

When Yarrow and Tiger emerged from the garden onto the parking lot, the young woman with the rifle was standing beside a car. She had long hair and was dressed in jeans and a jacket that reached to her waist. She held a telephone in her free hand. "Mr. Yarrow?"

"I'm Jake Yarrow."

She held out the phone. "The White House, sir."

Yarrow took the handset from her. "Yes?"

"It's Wally, Jake. What happened?"

"The Soviets won," Yarrow said quietly. "Kornilov wanted his wife . . ."

"Sorry to hear it," Cresteau said. "The president will be, too."

"Well . . ." Yarrow said. He paused. Clusters of armed men were walking down Pilgrim Road toward the streetlight at the curve. Shadowy figures were coming from the cathedral, emerging from the dark forest, and crossing in front of the lights of St. Alban's School. The FBI was calling its bodyguards home.

"All may not be lost," Yarrow said. "Emphasis on the *may*, Wally." He looked at the young woman, who had moved back out of earshot. "Do you think the president would agree to see me alone now?"

"He may be just shaken enough," Cresteau said. "Get down here as fast as you can. Come to my office. I'll do my best with Burke."

He was carrying Lester Brundance's briefcase when a Secret Service agent brought him up from the basement entrance to the national security adviser's office. An unnatural hush filled the White House. Yarrow walked beside his guide toward the ground-floor section where the president and his senior aides worked. They passed another Secret Service agent standing, arms folded, near the empty press office suite. The pale buff walls, white door and window trim, the thick light-ocher carpeting, all illuminated by lamps set on low tables, were intended to create an atmosphere of dignified restraint.

A dark-haired young woman stood in the corridor outside General Cresteau's office. She wore a pale blue suit, white blouse, and a single strand of pearls. She looked as fresh as the coming sunrise. "Good morning, Mr. Yarrow," she said.

He smiled. "I'm sorry to have been the cause of keeping you up so late."

She laughed softly. "It's a little past both our bedtimes. I think we'd better blame the president."

"You take it up with him," Yarrow said, smiling. "I'd rather not."

She laughed again and opened the office door. "You're expected, sir."

Wallace Cresteau's office, like the hallway leading to it, was permeated with the hush of suspended power.

In the instant before the secretary closed the door behind him, Yarrow looked at the high ceiling, moldings, and carved mantel. He wondered if Theodore Roosevelt, the political visionary who had a six-year-old boy's enthrallment with cowboys and war, had ever attended a meeting in this room. Or Woodrow Wilson, neurotic and obsessed by love? Or Warren G. Harding, doomed forever to be the dunce of American chief executives?

President James Forrest Burke stood alone between the mantelpiece and the long table that served as General Cresteau's desk. The president was wearing a gray suit that hung like excess skin on his stooped frame. He had his usual executive prop — a sheaf of papers — in his right hand. The lamplight rendered his face the color of soapstone. Yarrow felt his tension as the office door clicked shut behind him. "Good morning, sir," he said. He put the briefcase on the floor at one end of the sofa. "I expect you know what happened," he said.

The president looked back at him in silence, as if he were trying to decide whether to disguise his dismay behind a squall of rage or simply to endure it. "Wally told me the Russians won Mandelbaum," he said. "But I don't know why."

"Because they could give Kornilov something we couldn't," Yarrow answered. "His wife."

"How did they know he wanted her?" The question was tinged with accusation.

Yarrow looked straight at Burke's eyes across the office. "I imagine Kornilov directly or indirectly told them so before the auction."

The president raised the papers in his right hand and slammed them lightly onto Cresteau's worktable. "Goddamnit," he said. "We give you people task forces, budgets, all the help you ask for, and we *still* lose —"

"It isn't over yet," Yarrow said, looking directly into Burke's eyes. "I think we've discovered the location of Dr. Mandelbaum's prison."

"So I heard," the president said sardonically. "On Russian territory, for Christ's sake!"

"We have worked out a way to rescue him without risking either his life or an incident with the Soviets," Yarrow continued. "I understand that Edgar Pollack tried to tell you about that plan last night. You refused to listen. Will you now?"

"No," Burke said. "I don't want to be an accomplice to any more goddamn stunts. Too many people have been killed. Mandelbaum's lost. It's over. Closed chapter. We're goddamned lucky the newspapers haven't had time to find out what was behind those killings in Denmark! You can bet your ass that bastard Teague won't leak the story. He looks bad now." Burke paused. "We all look bad."

Yarrow seated himself on the arm of the sofa and shoved his hands in his trouser pockets. "If it isn't an impertinence to ask, Mr. President, why are you so afraid of Phil Teague? What does he threaten you with?"

Burke looked through the window behind Cresteau's desk. It was 2:10 A.M. The April darkness was accentuated by lights on the Washington Monument, by street lamps bordering the Ellipse and lining the avenue that curved around the South Lawn of the White House.

The president turned his drawn face back to Yarrow. "Any president who says he doesn't give a damn about what posterity thinks is a liar. I'm trying to get out of here with a halfway decent reputation." He was silent for ten seconds. "Phil Teague is one of the right-wing SOBs in our party who want to see me fall flat on my face. They want to be able to say, 'See what happens when you have a wishy-washy moderate as president? See what a wimp Burke is? Oh, if Carpenter had only lived!'"

Burke took a handkerchief from his hip pocket and blew his nose. "The rest of the plan is — keep on making me look bad so that they can nominate somebody *like* Carpenter at the next convention. Teague's a true believer. That's why I'm scared of him, Mr. Yarrow."

"And that's probably why Phil kept interfering with the Orion task force," Yarrow said. "I expect he was afraid we'd find Dr. Mandelbaum, which would have turned you into a hero. Sir, if we did manage this rescue —"

Burke shook his head, pulled a chair to himself, and sat down. "No, absolutely not. Don't even ask. Your rescue party could get killed like Carter's commandos in the Iranian desert —"

"Mr. President —"

"— or get caught, and the hard-liners would force Gorbachev to put them on trial in Moscow, a gang of American thugs who tried to kidnap a Soviet scientist. I'm not willing to let a risk like that be taken, not on my watch, Mr. Yarrow."

"I'm sorry you feel that way, sir."

Burke shook his head again. "You're a well-intentioned man. It pains me to say no to you, to earn your hostility. I'm tired, Mr. Yarrow, and I don't want to hear any more. We've lost Mandelbaum and we just have to accept the goddamn fact." He paused. He almost smiled. "Before we close the case, I'd like to know something."

Yarrow looked at his eyes. "What is it?"

"During all of this Edgar Pollack's been telling me things that are passed on by somebody in Moscow you call your best friend. Just human curiosity, Mr. Yarrow. Who's the CIA's best friend in Moscow?"

Yarrow smiled. 'Only Edgar Pollack can tell you that, sir. I don't have the authority."

The momentary expression of amiability vanished from Burke's face. He nodded. "All right, Mr. Yarrow."

"One more matter, sir," Yarrow said, withdrawing his hands from his trouser pockets. He leaned over, took an envelope from the briefcase at his feet, and handed it to Burke. "This is a copy of my resignation from the Central Intelligence Agency," he said. "I gave Edgar the original today.

"I've chartered a Lear jet and hope to take off from Dulles airport before dawn. That will put me in northern Finland by nightfall. As a private citizen I'm going to cross the Soviet border tomorrow, the fifteenth, and see if I can't get Dr. Mandelbaum out of the place where they're holding him. If I'm successful, he'll be in the hands of the Israelis long before he's due to be turned over to Galkin. The Soviets will blame Kornilov, and the KGB will track him to the ends of the earth."

Burke looked at the envelope in his hands, then back at Yarrow. When he spoke his voice had dropped to a near-whisper. "You're going over that border? Alone?"

Yarrow nodded. "Unless you stop me, Mr. President."

"I think you're a goddamned crazy man! Has it ever occurred to you that you might get caught?"

"Yes, sir," he answered. "If I am, you'll be able to tell President Gorbachev — truthfully — that I'm no longer a serving intelligence officer of the United States. You can add that I may be mentally unbalanced. I've deliberately made that letter of resignation discursive, incoherent in places, and, I'm afraid, abusive toward you because of your handling of the Mandelbaum affair. Give a copy to the Soviet ambassador. It will reinforce the impression that my ramble across the Soviet-Finnish border was the act of a crackpot."

"You are a crackpot!" Burke's voice was rising. "A certifiable —"

Yarrow took another envelope from the briefcase. "Here's a map, a satellite image, and a written description of the place where I think Kornilov and Colonel Georgi T. Vezhnesky are holding Dr. Mandelbaum. I've included the name of the aircraft charter company I'm using, the two airports where we'll land for refueling, and the telex and telephone numbers of the tourist hotel in Ivalo where my wife and I will be staying before I go to the border. I've also outlined several laws I'll be violating in case you want to stop me here or en route to Finland. I'm sure the Finnish authorities would prevent me from crossing into the Soviet Union if you let them know I was going to try."

Again, President Burke looked at the envelopes in his hands. A shingle of dark hair fell across his forehead. "You son of a bitch," he said softly, "you're forcing me to make that choice, aren't you?"

"I'm afraid so, sir," Yarrow answered.

The president raised his head. "Why, Mr. Yarrow? Why are you doing this to me?"

"Because I'm acting on information I acquired as an intelligence officer of this country," Yarrow answered. "I owe you an opportunity to stop me if you decide that what I'm about to do is contrary to the national interest." Yarrow folded his arms and looked into Burke's eyes. "Also, I'm telling you my plans because you and I are the only people who can decide whether I try to free Dr. Mandelbaum or whether we let the Soviets have him. I've made my choice."

"Obviously."

"Perhaps you should sleep on yours, sir," Yarrow said. "My flight to northern Finland will take nine to ten hours. I'll be spending at least eight hours more at the Ivalo tourist hotel before I drive down to the border."

"You're obsessed with this man Mandelbaum," Burke said in the low, accusatory tone of the defeated. "Why? Do you know him? Is he a friend of yours?"

"I've never met him," Yarrow said.

"But it is something personal, isn't it?"

Yarrow looked down at the briefcase. "I wonder if I could leave that with Wally's secretary."

"I'll have somebody take care of it," Burke said.

"It belongs to a man named Lester Brundance in the CIA's Directorate of Intelligence, Office of —"

"We can find him," Burke said. "Goddamnit! I'm not trying to pry into your business!"

"Someday I may be able to tell you about the personal part of all this," Yarrow said. "I've only just begun to understand it myself."

Burke snatched his papers off Cresteau's desk, dropping one of Yarrow's envelopes to the floor. He bent down to retrieve it. "Go catch your goddamned airplane!" He straightened up. The exertion had brought a flush of color to his face. "That doesn't mean I go along with this crazy thing you're about to try! I may have you arrested at Dulles to protect you from yourself! Or I *may* sleep on it! Don't be surprised if there's a Finnish policeman sitting on your bed when you wake up tomorrow morning!"

❖ EIGHTEEN ❖

THE LEFT SIDE of Yarrow's Finnish bed depressed as someone sat down on it.

He rolled over and opened his eyes. A bright blade of morning light came through the slit between the drawn curtains. It lay on half of Louise's densely freckled face, shining in her gray eyes, glowing on her red hair, which flowed over a thin dressing gown covering her right shoulder; the light lay across her upper chest, where the freckles thinned to a scatter.

She had been part of what Yarrow had anticipated during the previous day — from sunrise over the Canadian Maritimes to the high gleam of afternoon five hours later as his charter plane left Edinburgh after a refueling stop, to the first intimation of dusk when the Lear 36 changed course over Uppsala, banked, and made a point north-northeast toward the top of Finland. The Gulf of Bothnia turned gray while the late sun's fire flooded the passenger cabin; the waters twenty-four thousand feet below became black and indistinguishable from the Finnish coast as the jet crossed it. Twilight invaded the cabin, bringing a dozing Jake Yarrow fully awake, reigniting the anticipation in him, an excitement he hadn't felt since his childhood, when the world was new.

And finally there was Louise, standing in the little Ivalo airport terminal, waving even when he was too close to be waved at, kissing him lightly, holding onto his hand as they walked out into the deeper twilight, to the car she had rented, admonishing him for his obvious weariness as she drove, taking his passport from his jacket pocket and dropping it on the reception desk of the modern hotel, picking up the room key, making him shower and go straight to bed, shushing him when he tried to talk, turning off the lamp, her clothing rustling in the darkness, slipping under the covers beside him, their naked bodies touching for the first time in years, kissing him when he tried again to speak, and putting her long arms around him. He had fallen away as images of the day repeated themselves before his closed eyes. He had entered the shadowed hallway of memory. Sleep possessed him, carrying him to the profoundest depths of the psyche, the grotto from which no dream can be recovered. He came awake ten hours later, anticipation rising in him once again.

He pushed down the duvet and reached for her. "Moment, moment," she murmured, moving an overly filled cup to the bedside table, spilling steaming coffee into the white saucer.

She bent over him, her long hair framing both their faces, his hands pushing the dressing gown down her arms. She brought the faint remnant of cologne blended with the dry, fresh smell of her body to him, touching his eyes with her lips, kissing the side of his nose, his mouth, her lips parting. Old, known love rituals drew him from the limitations imposed by his years, exciting him as they had when he was young and thrilled by the novelty of her.

Far to the west, in the American night, James Forrest Burke was awake, agonizing, not sleeping on it as he said he would. The moral dilemma of what to do about Yarrow, about Mandelbaum, about the threat to himself, had wrecked the unhappy president's repose.

In the Finnish morning, in the blade of light, Louise's discarded dressing gown had become entangled in the duvet. She lay upon Yarrow, her long legs apart, her head back, deeply set eyes closed as he kissed her neck, shoulders, and breasts. Older passion rises slowly, older lovers proceed slowly, using strategies of arousal perfected over years. If they avail themselves of the wisdom unattainable in the frenzied lust of youth, their first objective is to give, not take, gratification.

She raised her hips so that he could enter her easily, the homecoming. Her lips brushed Yarrow's as her inner muscles caressed him. Her tongue barely touched his tongue, her hips revolved in contrapuntal movement to his gentle thrustings. Yarrow kissed her deeply, feeling the breath quicken from her nostrils, watching her closed eyes as the movements of her pelvis and torso accelerated, as she clasped and unclasped him within her, and her fingers dug into his shoulders. He rejoiced in her approach to exaltation, he surrendered himself to her caress and writhings, feeling the unstoppable rush gathering within him. She tore her mouth free and gasped, "Oh . . . I — Wait . . . wait for me!" She fastened on him, gripped him with legs, hands, mouth, drove her body against him, and cried out into his throat three times as he came with her, the rapture convulsing his heavy body, erupting, spewing into her. Then deflating. They drifted down from ecstasy together. Louise's hands left his shoulders, she put her palms on his cheeks, her legs released him, and she opened her eyes.

"Yarrow, darling Yarrow."

"I love you," he said, kissing her throat. "I need you."

She showered first. While he showered she remade coffee on a little machine set into a wall niche. Yarrow dried himself and came back to the bedroom. He went to the window and pulled the curtain aside.

The morning sky was cloudless, the landscape flat and made yellowish brown by stalks of dead grasses. A little river with birch saplings on its banks wound past the hotel grounds, bending off toward the west a quarter of a mile away. Strips and patches of snow remained in places where logs, banks, or ditches shielded the earth from the sun. Yarrow opened the window. The air that came in, flowing around his damp upper body, carried the balmy temperance of midspring.

He closed the window, drew the curtains together, and returned to the bed. Louise lay naked on her back, her auburn hair radiating like a careless nimbus from her head, coils of it lying over two pillows, strands beneath her shoulders.

Yarrow took off the towel he'd wrapped around his waist and lay down beside her. He leaned over and kissed her. Louise's fingers touched his face.

He took the cup of coffee from the table on his side of the bed and handed it to her. Louise rolled over and propped herself on her elbows, cradling the cup in her hands.

She drank and passed it to him. "Sweetheart, if you have to give your full attention to whatever you're involved in, we can talk later."

He smiled at her. "It ends today," he said, "one way or another."

Louise looked down at her pillow beneath her hands. Suddenly, she was afraid. For a moment her mind was filled by the words of reassurance that Shakespeare put in the mouth of King Henry V on the morning of the Battle of Agincourt, the speech that began, "He that outlives this day and comes safe home . . ." Louise thought of Dorothy, of men who were in the work to make payments, and those, like Henry Muffin, who did not come safe home. She lifted her head and looked at Yarrow. "Can you tell me what today's about?"

"Some of it," he answered. He sipped from the cup, set it down, and turned to her. "I've resigned from the agency."

She stared back, expressionless. She pushed a bolt of red hair away from her face. "Why?"

He turned on his side and looked at the vertical band of light. "All my life I've dealt in ideas and theories, abstractions," he said. "Intelligence analysts help create policies that may change millions of lives. But I've never used what I've been trained to do to affect *one* life." He paused. "It's been a career of detachment." He looked back at Louise. He smiled again. "You were right. My father demanded that I make up for everything that happened to him and his parents. Today, if I can, I'm going to give a man's life back to him. Then my obligation will be over."

"Jake, darling, can't you just reject your father? He's dead, he was —"

"Everything you said he was," Yarrow answered. "But I've lived too long with this debt he laid on me. I can only get rid of it by paying." He looked back at the light. "And he was right about something he wrote — even if he was right for his own self-pitying reasons. No movement to save the world is worth a damn if it tramples individual lives." He looked back at Louise. "I resigned from the United States government in an argument over what we ought to do about this one man."

Her bare shoulders hunched forward, hands clasped on the pillow before her, Louise looked back at him. "Who is he?"

"His name is Mandelbaum," Yarrow answered. He took his watch from the bedside table. "It's seven forty-five. Let's get dressed, have breakfast, and I'll tell you about him in the car."

"Where are we going?"

"To the Soviet border," he said. "You stop there. I cross."

Louise's fear congealed. She thought again of Dorothy, of understanding men's debts and pretending not to be afraid.

Finland's national highway 4 goes north through Ivalo, a town made up of one-story wood and cinder-block buildings standing on either side of the road. There are small houses of plank, plywood, and logs built among thin evergreens, saplings, and brush, a bank, a hospital, a general store that sells toys, food, clothing, and tools. At the end of the town Route 968 crosses Route 4. A sign tells the traveler that Murmansk, the Soviet port city, lies three hundred kilometers to the northeast.

As Yarrow and Louise left the hotel, clouds were sliding over the bleak, beautiful countryside, dimming the sun and polluting the sky's perfect blue. Yarrow put a package, a briefcase, and Louise's kit bag, folding stool, and sketch pad in the back seat.

He drove up to the Murmansk sign and turned the little rental car east. After a distance of a mile or less, the macadam highway turned into an all-weather gravel road. At a curve on high ground they left the last dwellings of Ivalo behind them. Ahead, far in the distance, the clots of cloud cover were moving like a fleet of ships across a landscape of low, elongated hills toned light and dark gray, splotched with green and brown.

Yarrow stopped the car. "That's the Soviet Union," he said.

For a full minute, Louise looked through the windshield in silence. "How odd that I'm surprised it looks so normal, ordinary." She looked at him. "Are you afraid to go over there?"

Yarrow nodded. The car moved forward, tires crunching on the gravel as he began to tell her about Mandelbaum, leaving out secrets.

They were driving through raw, stony country of stunted pines and brush. They passed cold swamps where gnarled limbs of dead trees protruded from the black water. Here and there a section of woods had been logged out, leaving acres of stumps standing on the denuded, sloping land.

He told Louise that Gregor A. Mandelbaum was a Soviet Jew, a man of great value — he didn't explain what it was — to both east and west. He told her that Mandelbaum had been kidnapped by two recreant KGB officers and put up for auction, that the United States and the Soviet Union had been scouring the world for him.

As Yarrow talked he felt again the mixture of anticipation and apprehension from the day before. No American, no Finnish official had approached them at the hotel. But if Washington had passed word of him to Helsinki during the night, the Finnish government would have put him under surveillance. He would be arrested only if he tried to cross into the Soviet Union.

He told Louise about Dvorah Mandelbaum. A capricious wind threw a whirl of dust and old snow from a sunless birch grove at a twist of the road. Yarrow slowed the car. Ahead, to the right, a hill was pale against a sky the color of alabaster; the silhouettes of small pines lined its ridge like spikes on the back of a dinosaur. "We think she's living somewhere out here," Yarrow said. "A woman answering Dvorah's description has been seen in the forest and around Lapp villages."

"*Living* out here!" Louise murmured. "What for?"

"Waiting for her father to come across," Yarrow said. "She seems to have had a mental or emotional breakdown."

Louise looked through the windows. "The poor lamb — how has she survived?"

Yarrow shrugged. He put on the brakes and stopped. "Look."

Gray shapes were moving out of the woods to the right. A buck reindeer crossed the road slowly, twenty feet from the car. It sauntered with its chin jutting pugnaciously in the air, immense antlers almost lying on its back. The buck's legs were incongruously short beneath its powerful body, as if nature had made it from the leftover parts of other animals. Reindeer cows wandered across the road and up onto a brushy hillside.

"There's a bell around the male's neck," Louise said, rummaging in her kit bag for her camera.

"I expect this herd belongs to someone we're going to see," Yarrow said.

He took a map from the glove compartment and unfolded it. He found Ivalo and worked out their location on the road as Louise photographed the reindeer through the windshield. "Here we are," he said.

Her camera in her lap, she leaned over and looked at the map.

Yarrow pointed. "This little road leading off to the right along the border. That's where we're going."

Louise touched her cheek to his for a moment. "Who owns the reindeer?"

"A Finn named Paavo Waltari," Yarrow said. "He used to be a rather prominent smuggler in these parts."

She sat up straight on her own side of the car. Her hair was pinned in its bun on the top of her head. She was wearing a lavender blouse, long skirt, and walking shoes. A gray sweater lay across her shoulders with its sleeves knotted loosely on her breast. "Want to know what I like about you, Yarrow?" she asked.

"At my age I can use all the compliments that are going," he said.

"At your age you're terrific," she said. "What I like about you best at the moment is that you aren't telling me not to worry."

He smiled, shifted the car into first, and they moved forward again. "Don't be surprised if the Finnish Border Patrol's waiting for us at Waltari's place," he said.

A half mile further on, he saw dirt tracks leading off to the right between the red-bark pines and little birches. Yarrow turned the car in. Moving at ten miles an hour, it jolted across boulders half immersed in the earth, bumped over roots, splashed through wet potholes, and finally emerged into a cleared area. Meadow grasses had grown up higher than the stumps. Ahead, on the edge of the forest, Yarrow saw a brown, two-story log-and-timber house with a rusted tin roof, the half-collapsed ruins of several sheds, and an old pickup truck. Three cows grazed in the meadow that sloped down to the east. There was a long wooded hill opposite. Standing on the highest end of the ridge, dominating it, was a pale blue watchtower emblazoned with a red star. Below the tower were a grove of pines and a cleared field.

The sun broke through the clouds as Yarrow drove past the charred ruins of a barn. He stopped in front of the house. Chickens fled squawking into the tall grass. Yarrow switched off the ignition and climbed out of the car.

He was struck, first, by the distant silence. The chickens had instantly forgotten their panic and were clucking and crooning between the house and burned barn. But from the vast landscape there was no sound. No wind blew. No faraway voices spoke, no radio chattered pop culture's nervy racket across Soviet and Finnish Lapland.

Louise got out of the other side of the car. Simultaneously, a weathered wood door swung into the shadows of the house. Yarrow saw a stocky old woman in a knit cap, sweater, blue dress, and boots in the doorway. Her bright eyes looked at him, uncertain but unafraid. When she spoke, her unintelligible words ended in a question mark.

"Mr. Waltari?" Yarrow said in English.

She frowned, silently mouthing "Waltari" as he had pronounced it.

"Paavo Waltari?" Yarrow asked, giving the name a Russian lilt. Her face brightened. She was toothless. "Hei! *Paa*-vo!"

Yarrow saw someone in the shadows behind her. Half of the figure seemed to be draped in a dark material. "You Russia man?" asked a harsh, dry voice in Russian.

"No," Yarrow answered, "American."

The old woman was pushed to one side as Paavo Waltari shuffled to the door, into the weak sunlight. The woman squirmed against the frame, scolding and swatting at him.

Waltari was a sinewy man who appeared to be over seventy. His flat, bony face had been burned red by the winter cold. Remnants of grain-colored hair covered his skull. Old Paavo wore carpet slippers, dark trousers held up by suspenders, and a faded striped shirt buttoned at the throat. A military overcoat covered his left shoulder and side. No arm filled its flat surfaces and folds. He gripped a shotgun in his right hand with his forefinger curled into the trigger well.

He barked an order in Finnish at the complaining woman beside him. She retreated and watched over his shoulders.

"Sister from Rovaniemi," Waltari said in his broken Russian. "Stupid woman. She come take care for me since —" He shrugged his left shoulder.

"My name is Yarrow." He turned to Louise. "This is my wife. Henry Muffin was my friend."

Paavo Waltari's mouth moved as if he were chewing. He frowned. "Muffin. Black man. Used to come from Helsinki. We did business."

Yarrow nodded. "He's dead."

"Why?"

"One of Colonel Vezhnesky's men shot him."

Waltari squinted again. "What you want here, *Gospodin* Yarrow?"

Yarrow gestured with his head toward the Russian grove and the KGB watchtower. "I want to go over there," he said.

"You want to go in *Russia*?"

Yarrow nodded. He opened the back door of his car, took out the briefcase, and laid it on the hood. He drew an eleven-by-fourteen photograph of Gregor A. Mandelbaum from an envelope. He showed it to Paavo Waltari.

"This is a man who is very important to the Russians," Yarrow said. "Colonel Vezhnesky is holding him prisoner. I want to take him away from Vezhnesky and out of Russia."

Waltari looked at the picture for a long time. It was the same man he had picked up on the Russian side of highway 968 at night less than two weeks before. Old Paavo had guided this one and a gray-haired, thin man with glasses to Finland, nearly getting caught by a border guard who was pissing in the bushes by Tower 118. Paavo had paid the guard seventy American dollars. When he got the pair to his farm there had been four men in the barn. They wore Finnish workingmen's clothes, but they spoke Russian. They knocked down the man in the photograph and stuck a needle in him. They took him away in a truck. Old Paavo never wondered what it all meant. He had been paid by Vezhnesky. He didn't give a shit what Russians did to each other.

"That man gone now," he said. "They take him far away."

"That's what Colonel Vezhnesky wanted you to believe," Yarrow said. "He wanted to be sure you'd say that if you were asked — or even forced to talk. They paid someone to illegally fly an airplane out of Ivalo to make it look as if they were taking the man far away. But they didn't. He's back in Russia, in Vezhnesky's headquarters."

Old Paavo stared at Yarrow. He was getting angry. Because of

Vezhnesky he'd had his fingers and thumb sawed off and lost his arm.

"Has he said anything about Dvorah?" Louise asked.

In Russian, Yarrow asked Old Paavo about a woman who had been living in the vicinity. "You told the Finnish Border Patrol the Russians might have gotten her," he said. "Do you know anything more? This man in the photograph is her father."

Again Old Paavo was silent. He remembered he was going to make the Russians pay — for his lost arm, his dead brothers, his obsessive life. He calculated the debts he owed, especially to the madwoman who had saved him from the burning barn, who helped him to the cave and took care of him. "She crazy woman. Here, this house, this morning," he said to Yarrow. "My sister feed her. Wash her. She run away because she afraid you Finn Border Patrol."

Yarrow translated for Louise. "Where is she now?" she asked.

Paavo waved his right arm at the hills, the sky, the forest. "Hide. Watch. Wait for Papa. Crazy." Old Paavo leaned the shotgun against the house again, squatted, and picked up a stick. "Where you want to go in Russia?"

"To the road that leads to Colonel Vezhnesky's place."

"*Kharasho.*" Paavo drew a square in the dust. "Here. This house," he said.

Yarrow handed Louise the photograph of Gregor Mandelbaum and crouched beside the old smuggler.

Old Paavo traced a winding line. "Path behind house, in woods, down to" — he drew a small circle — "big stone." He drew a tripod. "Tower — here. Go this way from stone, not on path, and Russia men in tower won't see, you don't step in mine . . ."

Five minutes later Yarrow rose to his feet, snapped the briefcase shut, kissed Louise, shook hands with Old Paavo, and walked through the tall grass to the back of the house. He saw the path going into the forest just beyond the rusty corpse of an old automobile and a strutting rooster pecking morsels from the earth.

Old Paavo stood in front of his house watching Yarrow's wife. She was handsome. Paavo had always liked red hair. He had always liked women who wore clothes that made them look like women in films and magazines. Yarrow's wife was all those things. But she was still a woman, which meant, to Paavo Waltari, that she was probably either stupid or crazy.

After Yarrow left to cross the border, claiming he was going to rescue the man Vezhnesky was holding prisoner, his wife studied the photograph of the man. Then she took a big pad of drawing paper, a kit bag, and a folding canvas stool from the car and walked out near the trees. She put the kit bag on the ground, sat down on her canvas stool, laid the pad on her lap, and began to draw.

Paavo watched her for a while. He picked up his shotgun and walked over to look at her picture. She wasn't drawing the meadow, the Russian grove, the KGB tower, or anything else in plain sight before her. She was drawing the head of a man.

That confirmed it. She was a crazy woman. He walked back to his house.

By 11:45 A.M. the sun had triumphed. It had scorched a wide hole in the milky cloud cover and was in full glare against a swatch of blue. The day was growing warmer.

Carrying the briefcase, Yarrow labored up a steep bank. He was sweating and out of breath.

He clambered over a rain-softened ridge of dirt and walked to a log at the side of the road ten feet away. He sat down. His breathing and heartbeat came back to normal. He looked at the pattern of sunlight falling on a cushion of dead pine needles on a bank across the road.

An approaching vehicle announced itself with a loud engine roar as the driver geared down for the curve.

An oversized jeep came around the corner too fast. Yarrow saw three uniformed KGB Border Guards. The driver slammed too hard on the brakes. The jeep skidded and lurched to a stop diagonally across the road. For a split second the three helmeted guards stared in astonishment at the spectacle of a portly, middle-aged man wearing a tweed jacket, bow tie, and gray slacks in the middle of the forest.

One of the soldiers, a sergeant sitting in the rear seat, pointed a frame-stock automatic pistol at Yarrow. "You will raise your hands!" he barked, swinging one leg over the side of the jeep.

Yarrow stood up and walked across the road. "It is not necessary," he said coldly, brusquely. "I have been waiting for you. I have come to see Colonel Georgi T. Vezhnesky." Yarrow pushed at the sergeant's leg. "You will make a space for me."

The sergeant lowered his weapon and slid across the seat. Yarrow heaved himself into the jeep. "Go," he said.

The driver looked back at the sergeant. He slid the jeep's gear into reverse, backed up five feet, shifted again, and moved the vehicle forward.

A half mile down the road they went around another wide curve. The forest ended on the left side. Yarrow saw a meadow of rough grasses that had been leveled and equipped with two soccer goals. He recognized the buildings and parade ground of the Eighth Border Guards' regimental headquarters, which he had seen in Emily Brower's satellite image.

Men with their collars unbuttoned, some with military caps cocked at slovenly angles, their hair no more than short stubble, stood in clusters on the parade ground or walked toward the mess hall beside the motor pool garage. Two border guards were tussling with a soccer ball, laughing, tripping each other, the ball rolling between their stumbling, kicking legs.

The jeep passed the front of the headquarters building, slowed, turned left, drove a hundred yards, and parked beside a truck.

As Yarrow climbed out of the jeep the babble and horseplay on the parade ground subsided and then stopped altogether. In the new silence KGB border guards stared at the civilian whose clothing was obviously not Soviet or Eastern European. Chin elevated in the manner of a fussy Russian bureaucrat, Yarrow strode toward the front of the building, his leather briefcase clutched under his arm, followed by the three armed troopers, who appeared to be trying to keep up with him rather than controlling him.

Yarrow rounded the corner, mounted three wooden steps, and started across the porch toward a door.

"You, stop!" barked the sergeant behind him.

Yarrow stopped.

The sergeant stepped in front of him. He was a short, wiry man with a cruel mouth. "Name," he snapped.

"Jake Yarrow."

The sergeant turned, opened the door, and went inside. The two border guard privates pointed their weapons at Yarrow's back.

Men were coming over from the parade ground and gathering in clusters at the side of the porch and the bottom of the steps. They watched in silence, some with peasant incomprehension on their faces.

Yarrow heard a voice murmur in astonishment on the other side of the door. A chair scraped back. Heavy footsteps crossed a wooden floor. A tall, gray-haired man with an acne-scarred face appeared in the doorway. He wore equestrian boots and the uniform of a colonel in the KGB Border Guards. His eyebrows were raised, his mouth was half open, registering astonishment. The sergeant stood behind him.

"Good morning, Colonel Vezhnesky," Yarrow said.

"You are — *who?*" the officer asked.

"Jake Yarrow," Yarrow replied, speaking as loudly and clearly as he could. He raised the briefcase as if to show it to Georgi Teodorovich Vezhnesky. "I have brought the money."

Old Paavo watched as if it were one of the Lapps' spook tales come true. First he had spotted the madwoman half hidden beside a tree, watching Yarrow's wife draw. Then she moved out into the open field, her eyes intent on the face that the American lady was sketching on the big pad of paper.

As Paavo watched, Dvorah Mandelbaum moved slowly to Louise's side, frowning in concentration. She lowered herself to her haunches, took the pencil from the American woman's hand, and corrected two lines on the head of the man in the portrait. She handed back the pencil. Louise resumed her own drawing, occasionally looking down at Dvorah as if seeking her approval.

The madwoman was too low on the ground to see the sketch pad properly. Paavo Waltari muttered in exasperation, put down his shotgun, and went inside. He came out carrying an old wooden chair, walked across to the trees, and put it down behind Dvorah. "Sit," he rasped in Russian.

The madwoman raised herself and slid onto the chair.

Paavo looked over Louise's shoulder. The face on the paper was the face of the man in Yarrow's photograph, the same man Paavo had brought across the border. He recognized the mustache, the sad eyes, the pensive mouth, the hair combed straight back.

Yarrow's wife laid the sketch pad in the madwoman's lap and handed her the pencil. As Dvorah bent over the pad, Louise rummaged in her kit bag and brought out a comb and a small pair of scissors. Dvorah lightly traced over lines that made a picture of her father. Sitting beside her, Louise pulled twigs and briers from her black hair, clipped and combed.

Vezhnesky's office reminded Yarrow of an old summerhouse. It smelled of dust and dry rot. Its wooden walls were unpainted and splintered. The bright sunshine visible through low windows served only to accentuate the shadowy hush within. The colonel's desk faced the outside door. To its left there was an interior door, opening, probably, into a corridor that led to Vezhnesky's living quarters and other rooms. Yarrow wondered if that's where they were holding Mandelbaum.

He was sitting in a chair in the middle of the office, the briefcase in his lap. He had said little since Vezhnesky had brought him inside, trying to formulate questions. "What money are you talking about? Nobody here is expecting money!"

"Call Major Kornilov," Yarrow said quietly. "I'll explain everything to you both."

"Kornilov? There is no one here —"

"There isn't much time, Colonel," Yarrow said. "You will have a major problem if I don't go back across the border in" — he glanced at his wristwatch — "twenty-seven minutes."

The colonel made a telephone call, turning away from Yarrow and speaking in a swift, tumbling whisper.

He hung up and settled himself in the chair behind his desk. There was a portrait of Lenin on the wall behind him, another of Gorbachev.

"You have taken a serious risk," Vezhnesky said.

Yarrow nodded slightly.

"Serious consequences . . ." Suddenly the colonel seemed to realize that words spoken by him would not change the mystery of Yarrow's sudden appearance.

The door beside Vezhnesky's desk opened. Maxim P. Kornilov, in the uniform of a KGB Border Guards major, stood in the entrance.

The colonel got to his feet.

Kornilov came into the room and pressed the door shut behind him. Yarrow had forgotten how gray and gaunt he was. In uniform, Kornilov was almost a comic figure, a clerk dressed up as an officer. His mouth was partly open. His eyes, large behind his thick glasses, gazed at Yarrow in astonishment. His face was the color of old paper.

"Hello, Maxim Petrovich," Yarrow said.

Kornilov looked at Vezhnesky. The colonel shook his head.

Yarrow glanced at his wristwatch. "I told Colonel Vezhnesky that my friends are waiting for me and Professor Mandelbaum on the other side of the border," he said. "If we do not cross —"

Kornilov broke out of his stupefaction. "Mandelbaum is not here!" he said loudly, a pink flush appearing on his cheeks. "He is in another country! You have lost the auction for him, Yarrow! It is too late to come offering bribes!"

"I've brought no money, Maxim Petrovich," Yarrow said. "I have come to offer you something of infinitely greater value." He looked at his watch. "In twenty-three minutes friends of mine on the other side expect to see me and Professor Mandelbaum coming across the border."

Kornilov's voice rose to a semiscream. "You? *Mandelbaum? And you've brought no money?*"

Yarrow nodded. "Let's imagine a scenario of what can happen if I'm not bluffing, gentlemen. At Severomorsk, north of Murmansk, there is a paratroop division assigned to the Border Guard Chief Directorate and, therefore, on constant alert." Yarrow looked at the ceiling as if he were making silent calculations.

He lowered his head. "Now, if Dr. Mandelbaum and I do not cross the border into Finland in twenty-two minutes, some of my friends will call Ivalo by radio. Other friends of mine there will telephone General Khorloin Tseden in his temporary office on the fifth floor of Lubyanka's west wing in Moscow. Tseden will send a Zhukov priority alert to the one hundred nineteenth, three hundred and twenty-sixth, and eleventh brigades of the Severomorsk division. Four minutes to scramble, eight minutes flying time . . ." Once again, Yarrow pulled back his sleeve and looked at his watch. "The sky will be filled with parachutes before one o'clock, Maxim Petrovich."

"There is no paratroop division at Severomorsk!" Kornilov shrilled.

"Be quiet," Vezhnesky snapped. He had recovered from his shock. "The division is there. It includes those brigades."

"Thank you, Colonel," Yarrow said. He smiled. "You and Major Kornilov could, of course, make a run for it." He opened the briefcase. "Your first problem would be getting off this post alive. How many of your men did you employ to help you with the kidnapping of Professor Mandelbaum?"

"Eight," Vezhnesky replied.

"Why are you telling him these things?" Kornilov shrieked.

"Be quiet," Vezhnesky said again. He was controlled. He appeared to have accepted that it was over and to be cooperating in the hope of finding a way out. "Go on," he said to Yarrow.

"One of your men, the sniper, is dead," Yarrow said. "Several are doubtless on their way west through Finland to pick up the money and Mrs. Kornilova in two days. How many remain on this post now?"

"Five," Vezhnesky replied, "perhaps six."

Yarrow looked at his watch. "Nineteen minutes left." He raised his head.

The brief blush of color had left Kornilov's cheeks. He sat down in a chair beside Vezhnesky's desk and stared at Yarrow.

"Gossip travels fast in military camps," Yarrow said. "It is likely that at least some of the men you promised shares in the Mandelbaum profits know that a foreigner arrived here twenty minutes ago claiming he had brought money. If you and Major Kornilov were to leave now —"

"We would be shot," Vezhnesky said in a quiet voice.

"Yes," Yarrow said. He withdrew a manila folder from his briefcase and opened it. "Even if you did manage to get away from this post, Colonel, you could not cross into Finland on the highway." He glanced at Kornilov. "I take it you've been doing that frequently in the last ten days, Maxim Petrovich." Yarrow laid two large photographs, one of Vezhnesky, one of Kornilov, on Vezhnesky's desk. "The Finnish immigration officers at the highway border checkpoint have copies of these pictures of you. You have both been charged by the British authorities in the murder of Lady Ellen Worth."

Vezhnesky looked at the photographs in silence. Kornilov glanced at them and looked away. He sighed as if he were trapped in some immense tedium and gazed through the windows.

"You mentioned that you had something more valuable than money to offer us, *Gospodin* Yarrow," Vezhnesky said.

Yarrow nodded. "Your lives," he answered. "Give me Professor Mandelbaum. Order the sergeant to drive us to the place where I was picked up on the road. Call the tower and tell the men on duty there that we are to be permitted to cross the border." He looked at his wristwatch. "If we get back in time, there will be no call to Tseden, no parachutes. You have sixteen minutes left."

"*What will we do?*" Kornilov suddenly wailed. "*What,* Georgi Teodorovich?"

"We will cross to Finland tonight the way Yarrow is taking Mandelbaum," Vezhnesky answered.

"Ah," Kornilov said, as if he had heard nothing of significance. He turned his myopic gaze back to the windows.

"Come," Vezhnesky said.

He opened the door behind Kornilov. Yarrow followed him down a narrow passage illuminated only by small skylights set in ceiling wells. There was a heavy timbered door at the far end. A young man in civilian clothes was seated on a stool beside it.

"The money has come," Vezhnesky said to him. "We will divide the shares tonight. This man is taking the prisoner."

The young man grinned, got to his feet, and unlocked the door before them. He pushed it open.

Yarrow looked into a small, dim room with concrete walls. The man he felt he knew so well was standing beside a broken chair. Gregor Abramovich Mandelbaum had a stick of wood in one hand, a looped cord in the other. There was surprise, but not fear, in his eyes as he looked at his visitors.

"Good afternoon, sir," Yarrow said. " My name is Jake Yarrow. I've come to take you to Finland."

Paavo, who had been watching the border for half a lifetime, saw them first. The two men, following a KGB Border Guards sergeant, emerged from the Russian grove below the tower and went diagonally down the meadow on the Soviet side. Old Paavo knew that Yarrow and Vezhnesky's prisoner were being led around an electronic minefield ten meters long.

Paavo turned to a blond young American who had arrived with two other men at the farm twenty minutes before. The American spoke Finnish. "Yarrow's coming," Paavo said.

Doors slammed on the American's big, black station wagon. His two companions got out and looked down the meadow. Paavo's cows had grazed their way over to the birch trees in the course of the morning. The meadow was empty.

Pete Durward, of the Helsinki CIA station, called to Louise Yarrow, who was standing, watching, ignoring Dvorah at her side. "Waltari thinks he saw them!"

Louise shaded her eyes with her hand. "Where?"

"Where were they?" Durward asked in Finnish.

Suddenly Old Paavo was filled with preemptive disgust. It was going to be sickening when Yarrow and the other man appeared, walking up the meadow. The women were going to scream and cry. The men would run down the field, shouting to hurry Yarrow along. Vezhnesky's prisoner had to be gone before the Finnish Border Patrol helicopter made its regular early afternoon pass over the farm. Paavo's sister would hear the racket and come out of the house. "They're crossing at the dry streambed," he snarled at Durward. "You get them out of here fast, hah? I don't need no trouble with the Finn patrol. Hah?"

He turned around, shrugged the military overcoat higher on his left shoulder, walked slowly, bent, to the house. He lowered himself stiffly onto the front steps. He wished he hadn't stopped smoking. His missing arm was starting to hurt. "You got cigarettes?" he barked at nobody in particular.

Nobody answered because it was all happening just the way Paavo had told himself it would. The madwoman broke her silence with a long, warbling cry of astonishment as she saw her father and Yarrow coming up onto the meadow from the streambed.

She dashed down the slope toward them, her black hair streaming out behind her. The two Israelis who had come with Durward followed her at a half run. They wore dark suits, no neckties, and scowled. Durward was walking fast down the meadow. The American woman had gone to her car and was taking a package from the back seat. Old Paavo couldn't tell if she was laughing or crying. His sister came to the door behind him and asked what was going on. He shouted at her to mind her own business. She shouted back at him. The whole spectacle made Paavo Waltari sick.

Yarrow and the man he had rescued had stopped halfway up the meadow because the madwoman was embracing her father. Durward and the two men in dark suits were talking urgently to Yarrow. Old Paavo knew what they were telling him; the Finns send back most people who come across illegally from the Soviet Union. If the Finnish Border Patrol caught them, if the Russians wanted Vezhnesky's prisoner as much as Yarrow said they did . . .

When the sun had gone over its midday apex, the farmhouse and the tree-bordered edge of the meadow lay in dappled shadow. Yarrow and Durward followed Mandelbaum, Dvorah, and the two Mossad operatives into the shade. "My orders are to get them to Sweden as fast as I can," Durward said. "Two other agency guys from Helsinki are waiting in a van about twelve kilometers west of Ivalo. I think we can make Sweden by nightfall. Once we're there, the Israelis will take charge of the Mandelbaums. They'll ask him if our defense people can debrief him."

"Your orders from whom?" Yarrow asked.

"The president, sir, relayed by the director and General Cresteau at three o'clock this morning. The Mossad guys and I flew up to Ivalo by charter."

Holding the flat package from the car in one hand, Louise put her free arm through Yarrow's right arm and kissed him. "I actually prayed for you," she said, smiling, her face wet with tears. "How about that?"

"I hope you didn't commit either of us to expensive pilgrimages or hair shirts," he said.

She laughed. "No, I —"

"Excuse me for interrupting, Mrs. Yarrow," Durward said. "But we really have to get out of here, and the director ordered me to relay another message to Mr. Yarrow. Mr. Pollack wants you to call him, sir. He said to tell you that the president did a lot of swearing and tore up a letter you gave him. Does that make sense to you?"

Yarrow nodded. "I understand what it means, Mr. Durward."

"If you'd like to use the embassy's communications —"

"No," Yarrow replied, "but thank you. I'll call Mr. Pollack from Copenhagen. We'll be staying there for a while with Mrs. Muffin."

"Yes, sir," Durward said. "It was an honor to work with Mr. Muffin, sir —" He glanced around anxiously. Dvorah had left the two Israelis and was standing at the steps of the house, in front of Paavo Waltari.

Old Paavo had heard that crazy people sometimes know things that no sane person could ever know. This madwoman who now gazed down at him, her eyes clear, her beautiful face clean for the first time since he'd been aware of her, knew that someday her father really would come across from Russia.

She smiled at him. "In paradise you will have two hands," she said.

Mandelbaum stood in sunlight and patches of shadow, as if God had camouflaged him to make him safe as he entered a new country. "Why have you done it, Mr. Yarrow?" he asked. "For a man you never knew, to risk so much . . ."

Yarrow took the package from Louise and handed it to him.

"The answer is in another man's life," he said. "This is his manuscript. It's written in Czech and English, Dr. Mandelbaum, but I hope that someday you'll be able to read it."

Mandelbaum looked curiously at the parcel in his hands. "Who was he?"

"My father."

"But, surely then, his writings should remain with you."

"Please," Yarrow said. "I want you to keep it. I don't need to have it anymore."

Mandelbaum got in the back seat of the station wagon beside Dvorah. Just before he followed them, Durward shook hands with Yarrow. "If you don't mind, sir, wait here for an hour or so. We don't want to look like a convoy on the road to Ivalo."

Old Paavo was getting tired. His missing arm throbbed. He wished Yarrow and his wife would go away. But they didn't. The red-haired woman in the lavender blouse went back to her canvas stool and started drawing again. Yarrow sat beside her on the wooden chair, a pensive expression in his blue eyes, his lower lip thrust out slightly as he looked across at the Russian grove, the tower, and the long hills of the Soviet Union beyond — pale, dark, green, and gray in the afternoon light. It seemed to Old Paavo that Yarrow was listening, as if he thought the silent country could tell him a secret.

Finally the Yarrows said good-bye to him — Mrs. Yarrow kissed Old Paavo's cheek. Her touch and her perfumed aura would have stirred him to excitement a few months before. But he was too old for such arousal now. He had found that out when he discovered he loved the madwoman in a different way.

After the Yarrows had driven their car into the forest on the rutted dirt road, Old Paavo stood up, went into his house, and closed the door. It was a dark house that smelled of snuff and dried apples. Paavo heard his sister clattering around in the kitchen.

He walked slowly to his bedroom, holding onto the backs of chairs, steadying himself by putting his hand on the wall. He shrugged off his overcoat and lay down on his bed. He slept and dreamed of smoking cigarettes. The afternoon burned out in the west and dusk spread over the desolate hills and forests.

He woke up smelling roast chicken. His sister was standing in the lamplight beside his bed. Paavo told her he wasn't hungry.

She went back to the kitchen and he dozed, letting the world slip away from him.

Gunfire, sudden and sustained, brought him fully awake a second time. He pushed off the blanket that covered him, blinked a moment in the light of the lamp, and went to the window. The moon was high. It turned the sky and the land silver, gray, and black. On the Soviet side, the border guards were shooting. Paavo Waltari saw stuttering flashes from automatic weapons, the white spit of rifle fire above the Russian grove.

The bedroom door behind Paavo burst open. He turned. His sister stood in the lamplight wearing a nightgown that looked like a sack. Her eyes were wide. Her mouth was open with a terrified question in it.

Paavo told her somebody was trying to escape from Russia and the KGB bastards were killing them.

She asked why they kept on shooting.

He told her they liked to watch the bodies twitch and break. He told her to go back to bed, that they would quit soon.

He turned off the lamp, lay down on his own bed, and listened until the gunfire became sporadic and stopped. Old Paavo knew now that he would not die as the people who had just tried to cross the border had died. But it didn't matter anymore.

He closed his eyes and slept. He dreamed of a warm river in which he and his brothers swam with many women. There were no Russians in his dream and he had two hands.